PRAISE FOR W.E.B. GRIFFIN'S ALL-TIME CLASSIC SERIES

BROTHERHOOD OF WAR

A sweeping military epic of the United States Army that became a New York Times *bestselling phenomenon.*

"A MAJOR WORK . . . MAGNIFICENT . . . POWER-FUL . . . If books about warriors and the women who love them were given medals for authenticity, insight, and honesty, *Brotherhood of War* would be covered with them."
> **—William Bradford Huie, author of**
> ***The Klansman* and *The Execution of Private Slovik***

"*Brotherhood of War* gets into the hearts and minds of those who by choice or circumstance are called upon to fight our nation's wars."
> **—William R. Corson, Lt. Col. (Ret.) U.S.M.C.,**
> **author of *The Betrayal* and *The Armies of Ignorance***

"Captures the rhythms of army life and speech, its rewards and deprivations . . . A WELL-WRITTEN, ABSORBING ACCOUNT." **—*Publishers Weekly***

"REFLECTS THE FLAVOR OF WHAT IT'S LIKE TO BE A PROFESSIONAL SOLDIER."
> **—Frederick Downs, author of *The Killing Zone***

"LARGE, EXCITING, FAST-MOVING."
> **—Shirley Ann Grau, author of *The Keepers of the House***

"A MASTER STORYTELLER who makes sure each book stands on its own." **—*Newport News Daily Press***

"GRIFFIN HAS BEEN CALLED THE LOUIS L'AMOUR OF MILITARY FICTION, AND WITH GOOD REASON."
> **—*Chattanooga Times Free Press***

THE GENERALS

BROTHERHOOD

OF

WAR

BOOK

VI

BY W.E.B. GRIFFIN

J

JOVE BOOKS, NEW YORK

THE BERKLEY PUBLISHING GROUP
Published by the Penguin Group
Penguin Group (USA) Inc.
375 Hudson Street, New York, New York 10014, USA
Penguin Group (Canada), 90 Eglinton Avenue East, Suite 700, Toronto, Ontario M4P 2Y3, Canada
(a division of Pearson Penguin Canada Inc.)
Penguin Books Ltd., 80 Strand, London WC2R 0RL, England
Penguin Books Ireland, 25 St. Stephen's Green, Dublin 2, Ireland (a division of Penguin Books Ltd.)
Penguin Group (Australia), 250 Camberwell Road, Camberwell, Victoria 3124, Australia
(a division of Pearson Australia Group Pty. Ltd.)
Penguin Books India Pvt. Ltd., 11 Community Centre, Panchsheel Park, New Delhi—110 017, India
Penguin Group (NZ), Cnr. Airborne and Rosedale Roads, Albany, Auckland 1310, New Zealand
(a division of Pearson New Zealand Ltd.)
Penguin Books (South Africa) (Pty.) Ltd., 24 Sturdee Avenue, Rosebank, Johannesburg 2196,
South Africa

Penguin Books Ltd., Registered Offices: 80 Strand, London WC2R 0RL, England

This is a work of fiction. Names, characters, places, and incidents either are the product of the author's imagination or are used fictitiously, and any resemblance to actual persons, living or dead, business establishments, events, or locales is entirely coincidental. The publisher does not have any control over and does not assume any responsibility for author or third-party websites or their content.

For Uncle Charley and The Bull. RIP October 1979.
And for Donn. Who would have ever believed four stars?
And for Sp4 J.S.B. II
Btry "A" 2/59 ADA
1st Armored Division
Who Just Joined The Brotherhood

THE GENERALS

A Jove Book / published by arrangement with the author

PRINTING HISTORY
Jove edition / February 1986

Copyright © 1986 by W.E.B. Griffin.
The Generals was written on a Lanier "Super No Problem" word processor maintained by Gene Vajgert.

ISBN: 0-515-08455-7

JOVE®
Jove Books are published by The Berkley Publishing Group,
a division of Penguin Group (USA) Inc.,
375 Hudson Street, New York, New York 10014.
JOVE and the "J" design are trademarks belonging to Penguin Group (USA) Inc.

PRINTED IN THE UNITED STATES OF AMERICA

44 43 42 41 40 39 38 37

PART ONE

PRIORITY

0215 ZULU 15 OCT 62
FROM HQ MAC VIETNAM

TO JOINT CHIEFS OF STAFF WASH DC
INFO: C-IN-C PACIFIC HONOLULU HAWAII
    US EMBASSY SAIGON
SUBJECT: DAILY REPORT OF INCIDENTS INVOLVING LOSS OF
US MIL PERSONNEL FOR PERIOD 0001 ZULU–2400 ZULU 14
OCT 62

    1. TWO (2) US ARMY ENLISTED PERSONNEL HOSPITAL-
IZED SAIGON 1350 ZULU RESULT VEHICULAR ACCIDENT BE-
TWEEN US ARMY THREE-QUARTER-TON TRUCK AND
INDIGENOUS PASSENGER AUTOMOBILE.

    2. TWO (2) USAF ENLISTED PERSONNEL HOSPITALIZED
SAIGON 1410 ZULU SUFFERING EXTREME GASTROINTES-
TINAL DISTRESS BELIEVED CAUSED BY IMBIBING INDIGE-
NOUS IMPURE ALCOHOLIC BEVERAGES.

    3. ONE (1) US ARMY CAPTAIN, ONE (1) US ARMY LIEU-
TENANT, THREE (3) US ARMY ENLISTED PERSONNEL KILLED;
ONE (1) US ARMY ENLISTED MAN MISSING IN ACTION; TWO

(2) US ARMY ENLISTED PERSONNEL HOSPITALIZED RESULT WOUNDS SUFFERED DURING PERIOD 1430 TO 1615 ZULU DURING UNSUCCESSFUL VIETCONG ATTEMPT OVERRUN SPECIAL FORCES CAMP VICINITY NUI BA DEN.

4. ONE (1) USAF MAJOR HOSPITALIZED 1625 ZULU RESULT INJURIES SUFFERED IN CRASH LANDING T-28 AIRCRAFT DA NANG.

5. ONE (1) US ARMY MAJOR, ONE (1) USN LIEUTENANT (MC), ONE (1) USMC CAPTAIN, TWO (2) US ARMY LIEUTENANTS HOSPITALIZED 2030 ZULU SAIGON MINOR RESULT BURNS SUFFERED WHEN LIQUID PETROLEUM GAS COOKING STOVE BACHELOR OFFICERS QUARTERS #3 EXPLODED.

6. ONE (1) US ARMY ENLISTED MAN HOSPITALIZED 2205 ZULU DA NANG RESULT BLOW TO HEAD FROM BLUNT INSTRUMENT SUFFERED WHILE GUARDING US ARMY CLASS V DUMP DURING SUCCESSFUL ROBBERY.

7. SUMMARY:

KIA	MIA	TO BE EVACUATED	TO BE HOSPITALIZED IN COUNTRY
2 O	0 O	3 O	4 O
0 WO	0 WO	0 WO	0 WO
3 EM	1 EM	1 EM	6 EM

BY COMMAND OF GENERAL HARKINS:
JAMES C. WILINNS
BRIG GEN, USMC

I

The incident referred to in paragraph 3 of the Daily Report of Incidents Involving Loss of U.S. Military Personnel for the period 0001 to 2400 14 October 1962 took place at what was officially known as Camp 7.

Camp 7 was, however, known to its American garrison as Dien Bien Phu II, and there was a neatly painted sign to that effect. Even more informally, it was known as "Foo Two."

The American garrison consisted of nine soldiers: a captain, a lieutenant, two master sergeants, three sergeants first class, and two staff sergeants. There were also 160 Army of the Republic of Vietnam (ARVN) officers and men under the command of an ARVN captain. The ARVN troops were in many cases accompanied by their dependents, of whom there were 236, ranging in age from babes in arms (some of whom had been delivered by Sergeant First Class Dugan) to grandfathers and grandmothers. Most of these, though they looked to be about ninety, were in fact in their late forties or early fifties.

The American garrison was officially "A" Team #16 of the

First Special Forces Group. Two members of the Team were Afro-American: Lieutenant A. L. Wills, the Exec, and SFC Dugan, the Medic. The Old Man—who was twenty-six—Captain William French and everyone else save Master Sergeant Petrofski, the Operations Sergeant, were White, Anglo-Saxon Protestants. Petrofski had been brought to the United States as a teenager from Russia.

Once a month, in compliance with Army Regulations, Lieutenant Wills (who in addition to his other duties was Minority Affairs Officer) interviewed SFC Dugan to inquire if he had in any way been subjected to unfair treatment because of his race and/or color. Wills's report was afterward endorsed by the commanding officer and sent up through channels.

When the big attack came, Lieutenant Wills was in the command post, bent over a Royal portable typewriter, very carefully composing a letter to higher headquarters advancing the argument that practitioners of the Russian Orthodox faith were obviously a minority group within the U.S. Army, and that therefore, under the applicable Army Regulations, the Army was obliged to make provision for Master Sergeant Petrofski to have access to the spiritual guidance of ordained Russian Orthodox clergy. The enlisted man in question, Lieutenant Wills wrote (at the suggestion of Staff Sergeant Geoffrey Craig), was showing visible signs of lowered morale as a result of being without spiritual guidance. Under the tenets of his faith, Master Sergeant Petrofski was unable to seek such guidance from available Protestant or Roman Catholic chaplains.

Lieutenant Wills believed that Staff Sergeant Craig was an uncommonly clever fellow. Even though Craig was the youngest man on the team, he had been the unanimous choice of everyone to replace SFC Caseby as Assistant Operations Sergeant on Caseby's completion of tour. And Wills's concern for Master Sergeant Petrofski's spiritual welfare—a stroke of pure goddamned genius—had been Craig's idea.

There was no question in Wills's mind that when the letter was sent through channels, action would be taken. As Craig had pointed out, they would have two choices. They could either find some Russian Orthodox priest willing to come out to the boonies where there was a good chance of getting his ass blown off, or they could send Master Sergeant Petrofski on some reasonable schedule to the Russian Orthodox church in Saigon.

Even if he actually had to make an appearance at the Russian Orthodox church, that would give him anywhere from twenty to forty-eight hours in Saigon. In Saigon a Chinese copy of the Russian Moisin-Nagant rifle was worth a hundred dollars or a case of whiskey to the Chairborne Troopers. Kalashnikov assault rifle (in shorter supply and therefore in greater demand) was worth two hundred fifty, maybe three hundred in excellent condition. A Vietcong flag was worth at least a bottle of whiskey. Petrofski was a great big sonofabitch, and could carry maybe a half dozen of each wrapped in Vietcong flags in a couple of duffle bags.

The weapons bunker held nearly thirty Moisin-Nagants and eighteen Kalashnikovs. There weren't many Vietcong flags, but the ARVN dependents could make up a couple dozen over night. The very least Petrofski could be expected to bring back from his spiritual pilgrimage to Saigon would be a couple of cases of good Scotch and bourbon whiskey and maybe even a couple of grand. With a little bit of luck—by, say, bribing an Army Aviator—he could do much better than that: A new stereo system would be nice (theirs was on the fritz), and maybe a small refrigerator. The one they had was small, old, and showing signs of decrepitude.

Some months after Staff Sergeant Craig had joined the team, Lieutenant Wills had found the moment to ask him if there was anything to the stories going around that he was related to Lieutenant Colonel Craig W. Lowell.

"We're first cousins once removed," Craig had replied. "Or second cousins. I never got that straight. He and my father are cousins."

Lieutenant Wills had found that fascinating. Lieutenant Colonel Craig W. Lowell had quite a reputation within the

Green Berets. For instance, Lowell had been an asshole buddy of Brigadier General Paul T. Hanrahan, the ranking Green Beret, going back to some John Wayne escapade Lowell had been involved in with the general when Lowell was a young lieutenant in Greece. For another instance, when Lowell visited the general at the Special Warfare Center at Bragg, he usually arrived at the controls of his own personal quarter-million-dollar airplane. The word was—and the airplane seemed to prove it—that Lowell had more money than God.

"You rich, too?" Wills had asked.

"About as rich as he is," Staff Sergeant Craig had replied, matter-of-factly, "but we rich people don't say 'rich.' We say 'comfortable.'"

"Then what the hell are you doing in the Army?"

"Why, Lieutenant, I thought you knew," Staff Sergeant Craig said dryly, "my friends and neighbors selected me to keep the world safe for democracy."

"And then you volunteered for Forces?"

"Not exactly," Craig said.

"What does that mean?"

"It means that I was in the stockade at Fort Jackson facing a general court and five to fifteen at Leavenworth when Cousin Colonel offered an alternative."

"What the hell did you do?"

"I punched out my basic training platoon sergeant," Craig said. "The charge was 'assault upon a noncommissioned officer in the execution of his office.' I broke the sonofabitch's jaw."

"That was dumb," Lieutenant Wills had said, without thinking.

"That thought has run through my mind once or twice," Staff Sergeant Craig admitted. "On one hand, five to fifteen in Leavenworth is a long time. On the other, the last I heard, they weren't shooting at people in Kansas."

Afterward, Lieutenant Wills had wondered if asking Craig about himself had been smart. What he had back in the States had nothing to do with what was going on at Foo Two, but he was made a little uncomfortable knowing that a member of the team was so close to the brass. It might have been better not to know that.

The dull growl of the hand-cranked siren actually started a moment or two before the first mortar round came in.

"Oh, shit!" Lieutenant Wills said. In another couple of minutes, the letter would have been finished.

"What the hell!" Staff Sergeant Craig said, as he picked up his M-14 and started out of the command post.

Daytime attacks on Dien Bien Phu II were rare. They were too costly for the Vietcong. It was much easier in the daytime to locate Charley's mortar positions than it was at night. And Foo Two's ARVN mortar men were pretty good with mortars themselves. Charley could therefore expect incoming immediately after he had fired his third round. So it was much safer for Charley to sit out in the boonies in the dark, lob a couple of rounds in, and then get the hell out of there before getting himself blown away.

And Charley had also learned that if—because of mines, concertina wire with tin cans attached, and Claymores placed here and there—it was difficult to approach Foo Two at night, it was even more expensive to try during daylight, when there were 150 people shooting with everything from old M-1 .30 carbines to M-60 7.62-mm machine guns on tripods.

These considerations had been respectfully, and in some detail, pointed out to both the commanding officer of the 39th Infantry Regiment of the People's Liberation Army and to his political advisor by the commanding officer of Number 9 Company, who would lead the final assault on Foo Two.

The political advisor had explained to him that the war of liberation against the puppet regime in Saigon could not succeed until the people recognized the inevitability of victory. Though Captain Van Hung Au did not quite understand what that meant, he certainly didn't think he was in any position to question the judgment of a lieutenant colonel who had come all the way from Hanoi to offer his experience and guidance to the 39th Regiment.

And then there were several practical reasons why the base on Nui Ba Den had to be eliminated, the political advisor continued. Some of these were military in nature: The puppet soldiers, under American leadership, had reduced below a level that could be accepted the flow of arms and other supplies down the valley.

They were, furthermore, interfering with liberation efforts in their immediate area. It had become difficult, for instance, for the People's Democratic Government to collect the taxes necessary to support the war of liberation. In more than a dozen incidents, tax collectors had been betrayed. Thus, when they had entered villages to collect pigs, chickens, rice, and vegetables, and to find "volunteer" porters to carry supplies down the valley, they had been met by Green Beret and puppet troops.

This tended to breed disrespect for the People's Democratic Government. The situation, furthermore, was going to get worse, unless stopped. Because of the success of the base on Nui Ba Den, Intelligence had learned that the American Green Berets intended to establish bases at other points where they could disrupt the flow of supplies south, and breed greater disrespect for the People's Democratic Government.

It was consequently decided at the highest echelons that the base on Nui Ba Den had to be eliminated.

The commanding officer of the 39th Regiment had then explained the tactical situation.

First of all, as Chairman Mao had so often pointed out, it was the greatest wisdom to attack the enemy when and where he did not believe an attack would occur. Second, the Americans and their puppet soldiers on the mountaintop believed themselves impregnable to an assault by anything less than a regiment. There was no reason for them to believe that a regiment was anywhere near.

Consequently it was intended to attack the base on Nui Ba Den in regimental strength in daylight.

Since Intelligence had reported that approximately once every ninety minutes radio contact was made between the Green Berets and their headquarters, the plan called for the attack to begin immediately after the American radio operator signed off. Initial mortar fire would then be directed at the American communications bunker, and would continue until the bunker and/or its antennae were destroyed. Once this was done, there would be a period of at least ninety minutes during which the Americans' superiors would think that all was well at Nui Ba Den.

The next phase of the attack, lasting fifteen minutes, would be a heavy mortar and rocket attack on the base. Since the puppet soldiers were accustomed to return fire without much regard to their ammunition supply, they would fire what ammunition they had almost with abandon, confident that the attack would be like the others they had experienced. The defenders of Nui Ba Den would therefore expend their ammunition in futile counterfire against a force which, with the exception of the troops exposing themselves momentarily to fire their mortars and rocket launchers, would be safely below ground.

Phase Three of the attack would be the first assault wave. Nine companies of infantry were available for the assault, including Captain Van Hung Au's Number 9 company. These would attack three companies at a time. While it was to be hoped that the first wave would succeed in breaching the first and second perimeter lines, that seemed unlikely to happen.

What could be expected was that Nui Ba Den's defenders, still unaware of the size of the force attacking them, would expend what was left of their ammunition.

Five minutes after Assault Wave One began its assault, there would be another five-minute mortar and rocket barrage on the enemy positions. Immediately thereafter Assault Wave Two would begin its assault.

Finally, there would be one more rocket and mortar barrage, followed by Assault Wave Three. Assault Wave Three would be commanded by Captain Van Hung Au. It was politically necessary that he survive the battle, so that the local people, who knew him, would identify him with the victory.

There would be no prisoners—unless any of the Americans

were found alive. If that was the case, these were to be given first priority for medical attention. After all the Americans had been photographed, their wounded were to be taken away. (Publication of such photographs in the United States and elsewhere tended to diminish enthusiasm for the war.) Second priority was the removal of small arms and ammunition. Third priority was the removal of People's Liberation Army dead. It was politically necessary not to leave large numbers of dead People's Liberation Army soldiers on the site. Fourth priority was the removal of wounded.

The weapons, ammunition, and other liberated supplies would be cached in tunnels to be built for that purpose, together with the heavier weapons (mortars, rocket launchers, and ammunition) brought in for the assault. They would be moved after the anticipated sweep of the area had been accomplished by puppet troops.

The dead would be buried in tunnels, and the tunnel mouths sealed.

Insofar as possible, the wounded would be moved. But it would be regrettably necessary to eliminate the wounded who could not be moved or who seemed likely to expire. They would be buried in tunnels.

The assault force would then disperse.

Priority in the evacuation from the battle site was to be given to the photographers and, if there were any, American prisoners.

Captain Van Hung Au would be informed when his role in the assault was over, whereupon he would disperse his men and await further orders.

(Two)

Foo Two SOP (Standing Operating Procedure) in the event of an attack prescribed the duty stations of the officers and men of the "A" Team. The commanding officer, the operations sergeant, and the commo sergeant were to go to the CP (Command Post). The exec and the deputy operations sergeant were to go to Bunker Hill. The medic was to go to the Dispensary, a sandbag bunker identified with a Red Cross and a neatly lettered sign reading "Obstetrics and Gynecology." The others of the "A" team were charged with seeing that the ARVN troops did what they were supposed to be doing.

Dien Bien Phu II made reference to the heavily fortified French positions at Dien Bien Phu, which had been overrun by Ho Chi Minh's forces some years before the Americans had become involved in Vietnam. The implication was that Dien Bien Phu II, like Dien Bien Phu, was surrounded by enemies and about to get blown away. This wasn't a precise analogy, for Dien Bien Phu had been in a valley, and Foo Two was on the top of a mountain. Still, Foo Two was in the middle of nowhere, surrounded by hostile Vietnamese. And it was clear to every member of the "A" Team that, presuming Charley was willing to pay the price, Foo Two was just as vulnerable as the original.

"Bunker Hill" did not, except as a play on words, refer to the hill in Boston. Foo Two's Bunker Hill was a bunker built on the top of the hill.

The hilltop consisted of three granite pinnacles, each about ten feet tall, each separated from the others by a few feet. Bunker Hill used these three pinnacles as its foundation. The paths between them had been roofed over with timber, and the roof protected by layers of sandbags. Surrounding this structure was a four-foot-high wall of sandbags. Within the wall of sandbags were four M-60 machine gun positions, each roofed over with timbers and sandbags. Their fields of fire covered the entire compound and most of the approaches to the compound. There were also several sandbag-protected rifleman's firing positions. The heavy armament of Bunker Hill was mortars, of which there were four. Three were 60-mm M-19s, which could throw shells just over a mile. The one 81-mm M-29, Bunker Hill's heavy artillery, could throw its shells almost two miles. Two of the 60s were emplaced so as to cover the approaches to Foo Two where the terrain interrupted the machine guns' beaten zone of fire. The other 60 and the 81 were emplaced to bring the most logical approach to Foo Two under fire.

The passageways between the stone pinnacles were stacked with ammunition, as was the "room" formed in their center. Bunker Hill was both Foo Two's first and last line of defense. It was from Bunker Hill that the first rounds in defense would be fired; and if Foo Two was overrun, it would be the last place the enemy could reach.

It was for that reason that the exec and the assistant ops sergeant were assigned to Bunker Hill by the Foo Two SOP. The exec had telephone and Handie-Talkie communication with other defense positions, backing up the Old Man in the CP. The assistant ops sergeant was in charge of the ARVN riflemen, machine gunners, and mortarmen; and the ops sergeant, down below, was in charge of the troops manning Foo Two's defense perimeter.

Since at that moment there seemed to be one hell of a lot of incoming, Staff Sergeant Craig resisted his natural instinct to take cover (Christ, it won't last more than a minute or two at the rate they're firing) in one of the foxholes; instead, he ran like hell toward Bunker Hill, and then scrambled up its sides. The round-the-clock team of ARVNs on duty had already brought two of the 60-mm's into action, and as he jumped over the sandbag wall he heard the much deeper crump of the 81-mm.

Breathing heavily from the exertion, Staff Sergeant Craig ducked into one of the covered rifleman's positions and dug in his pocket for earplugs. The first time Charley had pulled this kind of shit, he'd found himself next to an M-60 machine gun, and the noise had made his ears sing for ten days. Master Sergeant Petrofski, taking pity on him, had given him a spare set of his earplugs. Later he showed him an ad in *The American Rifleman* from which he could order some for himself.

When he had the plugs (rubber and aluminum devices that permitted normal hearing until a ball-and-piston arrangement closed as sharp sound waves struck it) in his ears, he looked down at the compound.

"Oh, shit!" he said.

Lieutenant Wills, who could have been no more than sixty seconds after him out of the CP when the siren went off, was quite obviously dead, lying in a spreading pool of blood twenty-five yards from the CP. He had taken a near-direct hit from one of Charley's mortars.

There wasn't much left of the CP. It had taken Christ only knew how many rounds—enough to displace a lot of sandbags and to tear open most of those that were left. The roof and one wall were gone. And as he watched, two more rounds came in, so close that they nearly went off together.

The only place the mortars seemed to be landing was on the CP.

What the hell was going on?

What was going on was very simple. Charley was determined to take out the CP. Charley *had* taken out the CP, which meant that he had taken out the Old Man and Master Sergeant Petrofski as well.

That meant several other things—more things than it was comfortable to consider.

First of all, under the Foo Two SOP, it meant that command of Foo Two passed to Bunker Hill. But since the exec, who was to assume command in case the Old Man got blown away, was also dead, command passed to Master Sergeant Petrofski, the ops sergeant.

No one had really believed it would ever be necessary to go any further down the chain of command, but the Foo Two SOP listed it anyway—right down to #9, the assistant armorer.

Staff Sergeant Craig put his Handie-Talkie to his lips.

"Foo Three, Foo Four," he said, and listened, and then repeated it. There was no answer.

Foo Two radio call signs followed the chain of command. Foo One was the Old Man; Foo Two the exec; Foo Three the ops sergeant, and Foo Four the assistant ops sergeant.

The chain of command had descended to him.

"Foo Five, Four," he said to the Handie-Talkie. Five was the commo sergeant.

"Go."

"You all right?"

"Antennas are down. The generator's gone, too, so it's a moot point."

"When did they last check in?"

"About sixty seconds before all this shit started."

Goddamn! With the antennas down, they couldn't yell for help. Until the net tried to check in—and that wouldn't be for an hour and a half—nobody would have any idea that Foo Two was under attack.

"How soon can you get on the air?"

"Forget it," Foo Five said. "Where's Wills?"

"Dead."

"Shit!"

"Six, Four."

There was no answer.

"Seven? Anybody?"

"Nine, I'm here," the assistant armorer reported in.

"You all right?"

"Yeah, I'm fine. Wills and the Old Man are both dead?"

"They don't answer."

"This is Seven. I just took a look. I can't see anything. It looks like they're dumping everything on the CP."

"What about Eight? Eight? You there?"

"He's in that M-60 position, I think maybe his radio's busted. There's people over there."

"Let me know if you see anything," Craig said. He leaned against the sandbags.

And then he had one more uncomfortable thought: Just as soon as Charley was convinced that the CP and the communications had been taken out, he would divert his attention to Bunker Hill. And if he took out Bunker Hill, that would be the end of it.

There was almost a continuous roar of Bunker Hill's mortars. The ARVNs were well trained. They could maintain a steady fire of ten or more rounds per minute from each of the mortars, and if they could have unpacked the ammo from its wooden crates any faster, they would have fired faster.

As Lieutenant Wills had once solemnly pointed out, there was enough 60-mm and 81-mm ammo in the passages of Bunker Hill to fight a war.

Craig jumped to his feet and ran to the ARVN officer in charge. He tried English, and that didn't work, and then he tried gestures until the ARVN lieutenant understood him. His face showed that he thought Craig was either crazy or a coward, or both.

Why should they move the mortars under the protection of the timbers and sandbags of Bunker Hill when they were doing damned well what they had been trained to do, fire Bunker Hill's mortars in counterfire?

Craig held up his index finger, and pointed with his hand to the command post, nearly concealed in a cloud of dust and smoke and still taking a round every five or ten seconds. Then he extended a second finger, and indicated Bunker Hill.

The CP had been first, they were next.

The ARVN lieutenant got the message. He started in one direction around the wall of sandbags, ordering the mortar crews to take their weapons and the machine guns and themselves into the protection of Bunker Hill's passageways. Staff Sergeant Craig went in the other direction, making his point where he could with gestures, and in the case of the last mortar crew, with the muzzle of his M-14. For a chilling moment, he thought it was entirely likely that the sergeant in charge of this crew, who looked at him with loathing, was going to reply to his orders to stop firing by turning his carbine on him. He had a family below in a sandbag bunker that he felt compelled to protect.

But he gave in and ordered his crew and the mortar inside, then sent two of them to fetch the M-60 on its tripod and the half dozen cans of ammo beside it.

The first Charley mortar round landed on Bunker Hill as these ARVN soldiers squeezed by Craig into the passageway. The second followed a split second later. He was so stunned by the force of these explosions that his eyes went out of focus, and his ears rang, despite the earplugs. Something stung his lip, and he thought he had been dinged by a stone fragment.

He staggered farther inside the passageway, gesturing impatiently to two ARVN soldiers to block the entrance with whatever they could. Then he made his way to the "room" at the center of Bunker Hill.

The mortar barrage was intense now, rounds falling without pause. The force of the shock waves moved, it seemed, even through the solid granite pinnacles. A nearly steady fog of sand particles trickled between the timbers supporting the sandbag roof, and visibility, never good, was now really bad.

The pair of two-hundred-watt bulbs that normally burned around the clock in the room in the center of Bunker Hill were of course out. They had died when Charley got the generator bunker. But there was one Coleman lantern hissing and burning brilliantly on the table, and two ARVN soldiers were squatting on the floor, trying to pump another one into life.

There was something warm and wet on Craig's chin. He put his hand to it to wipe it off, and his fingers came away sticky and red. He looked down at them, and then at his shirt. There was blood on his fingers, and a teardrop-shaped patch of blood, glistening in the light from the Coleman lantern, on his shirt.

As he was examining this in surprise and shock (he felt light-headed, and wondered if he was going to throw up or crap his pants), the ARVN lieutenant came to him, pulled him none too gently to the folding chair beside the table with the Coleman on it, and pushed him into it.

He examined the wound carefully, his face so close that Craig could smell the garlic and whatever-the-hell-else on his breath, and then gave sharp singsong orders. A first aid kit (a Foo Two kit, not the official GI model: a 7.62-mm steel ammo can, packed with what the Old Man thought should be in a first aid kit) appeared on the table, and the ARVN lieutenant pushed Craig's head so far back that he had to close his eyes to keep from being blinded by the sand trickling through the spaces between the timbers.

"OK, Number One," the ARVN officer said finally, and Craig sat up and opened his eyes.

The ARVN officer made his thumb and index finger into a "C" to indicate the size of the wound, and then drew on his own face the location. It went from the center of the lip four inches into the cheek. Craig put his fingers carefully to his face. There were two bandages over most of his mouth, one on top of the other, held in place by adhesive tape looped several times around the base of his skull. If he tried to move his head, there was a sharp pain. There was also a dull, tooth-achelike pain extending from his mouth up to his forehead.

Stone fragment, my ass!

He wondered if he would have a scarred face.

He nodded his thanks to the ARVN officer, and then tried French: "*Beaucoup* ammo," he said. "*Tout les* ammo."

The ARVN officer raised his eyebrows questioningly, and Craig repeated what he had said, this time adding gestures. He wanted mortar ammo from the crates lining the passage un-packed, so that it would be more readily available when the barrage lifted, and they could go outside and start shooting back.

There was no longer any question in his mind what Charley was up to. Charley wanted to take Foo Two, not just lob a couple of rounds in to make people nervous.

He walked through one of the passages again, until he thought he was far enough so the Handie-Talkie would work.

"Four, anybody out there?"

"Where the fuck have you been?"

"I think they're going to start coming up the hill when the barrage lifts," Craig said.

"Figured that out all by yourself, did you?" Nine replied.

"In the meantime, make goddamned sure they don't get the M-60s," Craig said. "We're going to need them."

"You still got any mortars?" Seven asked.

"And lots of ammo," Craig replied.

"Maybe you're not as dumb as you look, Four."

"Check in, will you, guys?"

Seven and Nine checked in. There were no other replies.

Craig went farther inside Bunker Hill.

(Three)
U.S. Army OV-1A Aircraft Tail Number 92524
Heading: 040° True
Altitude: 10,500 Feet
Indicated Airspeed: 270 Knots
(Plateau Montagnards, Republic of South Vietnam)
1525 Zulu, 14 October 1962

The Grumman OV-1A "Mohawk" is a two-place aircraft. The pilot and the other crew member (most often, but not always, another pilot) sit side by side. The fuselage tapers from the noticeably bulbous nose, at the tip of which the cockpit sits, to the rear, where there is a triple vertical stabilizer tail structure. Excellent visibility is provided through large Plexiglas windows. The bulbous forward portion of the Mohawk has been likened to the tip of the male member, with eyes.

The aircraft is powered by two turboprop engines, mounted on the upper surface of the wings. Beneath the wings are hard points, from which auxiliary fuel tanks, weapons pods, and the like may be suspended. On some models, long side-looking radar antennae were mounted beneath the fuselage. The fuselage from the trailing end of the wings to the tail structure is equipped with doors. Behind the doors are shelves on which communications and sensory devices of one sort or another are mounted. These are called black boxes, and the Mohawk was designed to accommodate a great number of black boxes.

Army Aerial Observation had moved into the electronics age. The black boxes in a Mohawk, for example, could find by infrared and other sensory techniques, a tank, a truck, a motorcycle, a campfire, twenty soldiers; locate them precisely within a few feet, distinguish the truck from the tank or the motorcycle; and instantaneously transmit this data to equipment on the ground, which would then instantly print out a map of the area under surveillance, with neat symbols indicating the precise location of trucks, tanks, soldiers, campfires, and the like.

There were two pilots in Tail Number 524. They sat on Martin-Baker ejection seats, wearing international distress orange flight suits and helmets with slide-down, gold-covered face masks that completely concealed their faces.

The only visible difference between the pilot and the copilot of 524 was that the pilot was considerably larger than the copilot, and that his orange rompers bore the insignia of a major and a senior aviator, while the copilot was identified by his insignia as a basic aviator and a chief warrant officer (W-2).

524 was on automatic pilot. Both the pilot and the copilot sat with their feet on the deck (off the rudder pedals) and with their arms folded across their abdomens.

"Watch it a minute, will you?" the pilot said over the intercom. Then he searched through the multiple zippered pockets of his orange flight suit until he found what he was looking for, a folded piece of paper on which was written "Kilimanjaro 115.56."

He then turned in his seat, pushed his face visor inside the helmet, and leaned to his right toward the communications panel between the seats, next to the trim-tab mechanism. His face could now be seen. It was finely featured and very black. He was, he had often thought, the genetic result of sexual congress sometime in the late eighteenth century between some comely central African tribal maiden and an Arabian slave dealer who had dallied with the merchandise as it was being shipped to the New World.

His name was Philip Sheridan Parker IV. His father was Colonel Philip Sheridan Parker III, USA Retired, who had commanded a tank destroyer regiment across Africa and Europe in World War II. His late grandfather, Colonel Philip S. Parker, Jr., USA Retired, had commanded a regiment of Infantry assigned to the French Army (as opposed to the AEF) in World War I. His late great-grandfather, Master Sergeant Philip Sheridan Parker, had charged up San Juan and Kettle hills in Cuba with Colonel Teddy Roosevelt. Master Sergeant Parker's father, First Sergeant Moses Parker, had served with the 10th United States Cavalry (Colored) under Colonel (later Major General) Philip Sheridan, for whom he had named his firstborn. Parkers wearing the crossed sabers of Cavalry (in Major Parker's case, superimposed on a tank, for he had been commissioned into the Regular Army as a second lieutenant of Armor) had participated in fifty-three campaigns and/or officially recognized battles of the U.S. Army. Major Parker had participated in three campaigns of the Korean War, and was currently engaged in the fifty-fourth Parker campaign.

He dialed 115.56 on the AN/ARC-44 radio, and then put his hand on the Mohawk stick and triggered the radio transmit function.

"Kilimanjaro, Kilimanjaro, Army Five Two Four."

The copilot, his face still shielded by his face visor, turned to look at him curiously. "Who's Kilimanjaro?" he asked.

When there was no reply from Kilimanjaro, Major Parker repeated the call twice again. And when that didn't work, he put his hand on the second AN/ARC-44's controls, to the rear of the first set.

"A friend of mine has a nephew down there eating snakes," he said. "He asked me to say hello."

He repeated his call to Kilimanjaro three times. There was no response.

He folded his arms on his chest for a minute, thoughtfully, and then said, "You don't suppose we're up here without a radio, do you?"

The copilot pushed his face mask up inside his helmet and consulted the chart he had on a clipboard on his lap. Then he adjusted the first ARC-44 and pushed the radio transmit button on his stick.

"Grizzly, Grizzly, Army Five Two Four, how do you read? Over."

"Army Five Two Four, Grizzly reads you five by five."

"Thank you, Grizzly, Five Two Four reads you loud and clear. Out."

"Give me the chart," Major Parker said. The copilot handed it to him.

Major Parker studied the chart. It was an Aerial Navigation Chart, not a map, but Kilimanjaro on Nui Ba Den was listed on it as an auxiliary source of data for radio navigation.

"I've got it, Charley," Major Parker said, and reached up and turned off the autopilot.

"You want me to report what you're doing?" the copilot asked.

"Let's take a look first," Major Parker said. "It's only a couple of minutes."

He went back on the air three minutes later.

"Grizzly, Grizzly, Army Five Two Four."

"Go ahead, Five Two Four."

"Five Two Four is at coordinates Mike Seven Charley, Baker Three Baker. Kilimanjaro is under heavy ground attack and does not respond to radio calls. I say again, Kilimanjaro is under heavy ground attack and does not, repeat not, respond to my call."

"Five Two Four, hold your position and stand by."

Major Parker circled Foo Two for about five minutes at four thousand feet, which was presumed to be outside the range of Charley small arms and machine gun fire.

"Army aircraft in vicinity Mike Seven Charley, Baker Three Baker, this is Navy Two Two Seven."

"Go ahead Navy Two Two Seven, this is Army Five Two Four."

"I'm at two zero thousand, five minutes west your position. I'm a flight of four F-4 aircraft. What have you got for us?"

"There's a Green Beret camp on the top of the mountain under attack by what looks like a regiment. I can't raise them on the radio."

"OK, where do you want it?"

"You better make a pass, it's a pretty small camp."

"OK, I got you on the tube. Where are they in relation to you?"

"Half a mile north."

"OK. Making descent at this time. You guys wait for the word."

The first F-4 appeared not quite three minutes later, moving so fast that Parker didn't see him until he was almost over the smoke-shrouded camp. He then pulled up in a steep climbing turn.

"Get on my tail, we're going in on the deck with napalm," the Navy flight commander ordered.

The next time Parker saw aircraft, they were below him, flying in a V down the valley. They passed over the camp, and then a moment later, the approaches to Dien Bien Phu II erupted in great orange bursts, followed immediately by clouds of dense smoke.

They made four napalm passes before they communicated again.

"Army Five Two Four, we're out of ordnance, but there's help on the way. They will contact you on this frequency."

"Thank you," Major Parker said politely.

Three minutes after that, the copilot touched his shoulder, and pointed.

A flight of six Douglas A-1 Skyraiders—very large single-engine propeller aircraft with the capacity to carry an awesome amount of ordnance—were approaching from the north.

Parker wondered if the cure wasn't liable to kill the patient.

"Aircraft approaching Mike Seven Charley, Baker Three Baker, this is Army Five Two Four."

"We have you in sight, Five Two Four, go ahead."

"Charley has not, repeat not, overrun the target area," Parker said. "Avoid the encampment."

"Roger, Five Two Four. Where is Charley?"

"Everywhere but on the top of the hill."

"Roger. Understand everywhere but the top of the hill."

"Affirmative."

Major Parker then flew in circles to the south of Dien Bien Phu II, privately fuming at the brass assholes who forbade the arming of Mohawks under any but special conditions. The rocket and weapons pods on his Mohawk had been removed. Because his mission today was a medium-altitude electronic surveillance, he was at the controls of an unarmed and useless airplane: The goddamned brass were splitting hairs about which of the armed forces was permitted to shoot who and when.

He flew for about thirty minutes until a flight of helicopters appeared, obviously bound for Kilimanjaro. When they got closer, he was surprised to see that they were Bell HU-1Bs, the new Hueys. That meant the Utility Tactical Transport Helicopter Company, the first of its kind, was operational. This was, he thought, probably their first mission.

And then, because there was nothing left that he could do for Kilimanjaro, he headed toward Da Nang to refuel.

(Four)
Dien Bien Phu II
1620 Zulu, 14 October 1962

There were nine HU-1Bs in the relief flight; and Major Parker had guessed right, this was their first operation. The Huey was the first helicopter designed and built specifically for military operation. The nomenclature stood for Helicopter, Utility, Model 1, Version B. It was powered by a turbine engine, and it was a great improvement—especially in engine life— over the Army's previous cargo helicopters, the Sikorsky H-19 and H-34, and the Piasecki H-21 Flying Banana, all of which had gasoline piston engines.

The Hueys flew in three V's of three aircraft, the following V's a hundred yards behind and two hundred feet above the preceding V. There was only one helipad, a circular area a few feet wider than the helicopter arc, marked with an "H," but there was room for three Hueys to land within the inner barbed wire of Foo Two, and the first V came in for a landing simultaneously. The first chopper landed far from the H-pad, because it was going to be on the ground for a while, and didn't want to block other flights any more than it had to.

The first chopper to land carried the commanding officer of the First Special Forces Group, a tall, erect, very handsome bull colonel. Had he been sent over by Central Casting, a producer shooting a military film would have rejected him for being too young, too handsome, and too articulate to be a Green Beret colonel.

Blissfully unaware of the incongruity, he jumped out of the helicopter with a World War I Model 1897 Winchester 12-gauge trench gun in one hand and a leather attaché case in the other. These accoutrements were less strange than they at first appeared. There was paperwork to be accomplished here, and it simply made sense to bring the attaché case holding the paper; the case served as an efficient portable desk. And there had been no improvement since World War I in a shotgun firing 00-buck shot as an up-close people killer.

The first chopper also disgorged two physicians and four medics. The doctors wore the caduceus of the Army Medical Corps on their collar points, but not the Red Cross brassard of the noncombatant. Given the option of wearing the brassard and placing their faith in the willingness of the Vietcong to adhere to the provisions of the Geneva convention, or not wearing it and going armed, they had opted to be armed, one of them with an issue .45-caliber pistol, the other with a Ruger Super Blackhawk single-action .44 Magnum revolver.

The medics immediately started looking for wounded. The other two Hueys unloaded Green Berets, some of whom started moving through the carnage, and others to unload supplies— food, ammunition, stretchers, and a collapsible radio antenna— from the helicopters. When the supplies had been unloaded, two Berets started erecting the antenna, and the others picked up stretchers and went looking for the medics.

Colonel C. David Mennen took a quick professional look around the carnage and quickly concluded Foo Two had taken a clobbering. There was very little left of what had once been the command post, and Staff Sergeant Craig, a bloody bandage covering his mouth, was almost frenziedly digging in its rubble. At least, he thought, he would not that night have to write a letter beginning, "Dear Craig, I thought you would like to know what I have learned about how your cousin died."

It was tough writing those letters to strangers, infinitely tougher when they had to be written to friends, and soldier friends, who would be unimpressed with the phrases about "inspiring his fellow soldiers" and "in the highest traditions of the service."

The kid looked shook, and the wound looked nasty, but he was alive, and if he also looked a little hysterical, so what.

Colonel Mennen walked through the rubble and carnage, searching for whoever had taken charge. He found bodies covered with shelter halves and blankets, but no Americans. Then he walked to the Huey in which he had arrived. It had been turned into sort of an emergency aid station, with one of the doctors and two of the medics providing immediate attention to the most seriously wounded, the majority of whom were the dependents of the ARVN troops.

"What about our wounded?" he asked.

"Two," the doctor replied, looking up from his repair of the ugly compound fracture of a small boy's leg. "One took some small-caliber fire in the chest; it missed the vitals, or he wouldn't be alive. The other one took some superficial flesh wounds, but I think there's internal damage. They're both on their way out of here."

"That's all?"

"Four known dead, and almost certainly the CO died in the CP."

Colonel Mennen did the arithmetic. Four KIA plus one probable KIA was five, two evacuated was seven. Staff Sergeant Craig was eight.

"We're missing one," he said.

"The kid with the bloody mouth told me Charley made off with the operations sergeant."

"Goddamn!" Colonel Mennen said. If there was anything worse than getting killed or wounded, it was winding up a prisoner of Charley. When they weren't amusing themselves tormenting prisoners in their cages, they were marching them around showing them off to Vietnamese peasants.

"How is he?"

He was privately shamed with his awareness that his concern for Staff Sergeant Craig was less based on his welfare than on his availability.

"According to the commo guy, the one who took the small arms fire, he was a regular John Wayne. The others got blown away almost as soon as it started, which left him in charge.

All but one of the ARVN officers got blown away, too, so he ran the show. According to the commo guy, he saved everybody's ass with his mortars. They were inside the wire twice, he said."

"I was asking about his condition," Colonel Mennen said.

"I haven't looked at him," the doctor said, and gestured toward the small boy on the helicopter's seat. "Not as bad as these people. He's walking around."

Colonel Mennen nodded and walked away from the helicopter and climbed Bunker Hill. That had taken a real clobbering. A *real* clobbering. There were mortar fragments all over. You didn't see many fragments unless there had been a hell of a lot of fire. The ground, in places, was literally covered with fired 7.62-mm cases from the M-60s. There were several bodies not yet covered, because no one had been up here yet. And the ground was littered with ammo cases, so many that the defenders of Bunker Hill had been forced to throw them over the sandbag wall to have room to move around.

He entered the covered passageways. There was uncased mortar ammunition, some stacked neatly, and some loosely strewn on the ground. He made his way to the interior. A Coleman lantern was still hissing. There were two bodies on the floor, their faces covered with field jackets.

He carefully turned off the Coleman lantern and made his way in darkness back outside. He looked down at the carnage, spotted the place where Charley had come over the wire. You could walk on the bodies, he thought. It was going to be a hell of a job just cleaning them up.

The unmarked landing pads were now busy, flying in ARVN and American replacements, and flying out first the wounded and then the dead. Vietcong casualties were being evacuated as their medical condition gave them priority, in the judgment of the doctors. ARVN and American dead would be placed in rubberized body bags for later evacuation. Dead Vietcong would be taken down the hill and buried in a mass grave. Colonel Mennen realized he would have to airlift in a burial detail; there were too many bodies to expect the replacements to bury them.

The smell of burned human flesh was both permeating and nauseating, but it was the napalm, more than anything else, which had saved Foo Two from falling. Courage and coolness was one thing, odds of nine to one another. No matter how good the kid had been with his mortars, no matter how many thousands of rounds he had fired from his machine guns, Charley would have taken this place without the Air Force's rockets and napalm.

Colonel Mennen spotted Staff Sergeant Craig. He was standing by what had been the CP, a look of horror on his face, watching Green Berets free the crushed body of the detachment commander.

Mennen climbed down from Bunker Hill and walked over to him. Craig looked but did not salute.

"How are you, son?" Mennen said. "You did one hell of a job here."

"Charley took Petrofski," Craig said. "I saw it, but I couldn't stop it. I thought about blowing him away, too."

Green Berets knew fear. As a general rule of thumb, Colonel Mennen believed they could control it better than lesser mortals, but they were, almost to a man, terrified of becoming a Vietcong prisoner. There were often pacts between them, one Beret solemnly promising to take out a pal when the alternative was the pal becoming Charley's prisoner.

"I'm glad you didn't," Mennen said. "Petrofski is a resourceful fellow. Was he hit?"

"Sure he was hit," Craig said.

"Why don't you go to the chopper and have your face looked at?" Colonel Mennen asked, softly.

"When they evac the wounded, they're going to take me out, Colonel," Craig said. "That can wait."

"I would be ever so grateful, Sergeant," Colonel Mennen said, gently mocking, smiling, "if you could find it in your soul to give me just a smidgen of that cheerful, willing obedience to which we all aspire."

"Yes, sir," Craig said, smiling at him with the corner of his mouth visible under the blood-soaked bandage.

When, in Mennen's experienced judgment, the doctor had had enough time to be able to offer a sound opinion concerning the seriousness of Staff Sergeant Craig's wound, Colonel Mennen walked over to the chopper. Staff Sergeant Craig was on his back on the narrow rear seat of the Huey. The surgeon was kneeling over him, taking sutures in his lip.

"How is he?" Colonel Mennen asked.

"I don't even think there will be a scar," the surgeon replied. "It was just jagged enough to knit neatly. I'm about finished."

Mennen stood watching, arms folded, as the medic, with the surgeon watching him, applied a bandage and then fixed it in place with adhesive tape. Then he tapped Craig's shoulder and the young sergeant sat up.

"Another inch to the right, and you would have a perfectly satisfactory Prussian dueling scar," Colonel Mennen said.

"I hope this doesn't mean I don't get out of here," Craig said. His lip had been anesthetized, and that made his speech slurred. He sounds like a cretin, Colonel Mennen thought. But this lad was demonstrably not a moron.

"I wanted to talk to you about that," Mennen said. He saw surprise, and then bitter, resigned disappointment in Craig's eyes. "Will you excuse us, gentlemen? I would have a word with this young chap."

After the surgeon and the medic had stooped and then jumped out of the chopper, Mennen went inside and sat beside Craig.

"Why do I feel I'm not going to like what's coming next?" Craig said.

"What's coming next are effusive words of praise," Mennen said. "You done good, kid."

Craig smiled.

"I'm going to recommend you for the DSC," Colonel Mennen said. "You don't quite deserve the DSC, and you won't get it. But once the noble warriors of the typewriters have played their little game, I feel sure you will get the Silver Star, which you have honestly earned. I am sure, further, that our Vietnamese allies will be similarly impressed with your distinguished service, and you can expect one or more of their better little ornaments. And then, of course, the Purple Heart. With the Purple Heart and twenty dollars you can become a member in good standing of the Military Order of the Purple Heart, which I'm sure will thrill you no end."

"And now the other shoe, Colonel?"

"You are not especially awed with colonels, are you, Craig? I suppose that comes with having one in the family."

Staff Sergeant Craig's eyebrows went up.

"I am acquainted with Colonel Lowell," Colonel Mennen said.

"I was not trying to be a wise-ass, Colonel," Craig said. "I just want to get the hell out of here."

"I didn't mean to suggest you were," Mennen said. "As a matter of fact, I took it as a good sign, another indication that you have the ability to keep things in perspective. What I have in mind, Craig, is giving you a gold bar for your collar."

Craig looked at him. He was in some kind of shock, Mennen saw, but he was thinking clearly.

"I don't think so, Colonel," Craig said, spittle flying from his nerve-deadened lips. "Thank you, but no thank you."

"Pray grant me the courtesy of explaining my dilemma," Mennen said, dryly. "It would have been more than losing an 'A' Team and an ARVN company had Foo Two fallen," Mennen said. "That would have been academic to you, but it is something with which I must concern myself. I have been ordered to hold this charming geological feature against the forces of darkness and evil, and I intend to. We are, in a word, a sharp stick up Charley's ass here. I have little doubt that as soon as he can remarshal his assets, he'll have another go at it.

"I doubt if he will try that immediately, but I doubted that he would try it at all, so one must accept the possibility. That raises the question of staffing Foo Two. At the moment, I am a bit short of combat-experienced officers. I have a sufficiency of noncoms. I have one man, only, with combat experience here. In any event, you have just been screwed, Sergeant, by what are known as the exigencies of the service, from a ride out of here on these nice new choppers. I simply can't afford not to have someone with experience here if somebody is available. You are."

Craig thought that over.

"I understand, sir," he said. It came out "undershtand" and "shir."

"I have not finished, how could you *possibly* understand?" Mennen asked in exaggerated resignation.

"Colonel, I just got one hell of a headache. Is there something in here I could take?" He touched one of the Red Cross—marked equipment boxes.

"There probably is," Colonel Mennen said, "but I suspect this will be equally effective." He took a silver flask from his hip pocket and handed it to Craig. "Courvoisier," he said.

"Thank you," Craig said, and took a deep swallow. It made him cough, and then he took another.

"As I was saying, I have what at one time would have been called a 'command' problem, but we don't do that anymore, as you know. This is the new Army, and this is a personnel assets management problem."

Craig chuckled.

"My problem may be explained very simply. These are the facts. You will stay here, for the reasons I've explained. I intend to reinforce this place with experienced noncoms. They will all be senior in age and grade to you. There must be an officer in charge. I have no combat-experienced junior officers at the moment whom I can send here. It is not wise to send inexperienced officers to command experienced noncoms. They tend to consider them with a certain degree of scorn and derision.

"It was at this point in my thought process that I thought how nice it would be if Staff Sergeant Craig were a second lieutenant. The noncoms would regard him far more kindly than they would an officer yet to hear shots fired at him. And Craig, I thought, would be bright enough to heed much of the old sergeants' advice."

Craig started to speak. Mennen held his hand up to stop him.

"According to Army Regulations," Mennen said. "In these circumstances, I have the authority to commission you. I want to."

"If I took a commission, it would mean more time in the Army," Craig said.

"I believe the initial appointment is for four years," Colonel Mennen said, "but officers, you know, can resign. Such applications for resignation are approved by the appropriate general officer commanding. In this case, since you will return to Bragg when you leave here, that would mean General Hanrahan. I am sure that General Hanrahan would approve your resignation, once I had explained the circumstances to him."

"What circumstances?"

"That you didn't want it in the first place, and had only taken it because I told you I desperately needed you as a second john."

"He'd let me go?"

"Yes, I am sure he would."

"Then all I have to do is put on a bar until I go home, at the original time?"

"Correct."

"Why not?" Craig said, after a moment.

"You have warmed the cockles of this old soldier's heart with your emotional response to the honor being paid you," Colonel Mennen said. "I can hear muted trumpets playing the charge, the roll of drums—"

"I don't have anything against the Army," Craig said. "I just want to get out."

"If I were as rich as you are, Craig, I would feel exactly the same way," Mennen said. "Unfortunately, I have mouths to feed, and I think I would be a lousy stockbroker."

"I got married just before I came over here," Craig said.

Colonel Mennen looked at him and nodded.

"We'll do this as informally as possible," he said. "But I don't think we should skip the oath. Would you raise your right hand, please, and repeat after me. . . ."

Geoffrey Craig swore that he would defend the Constitution

of the United States against all enemies, foreign and domestic; that he would faithfully execute the duties of the office upon which he was about to enter; and that he would obey the orders of the officers appointed above him by competent authority; and that he was taking the oath with no mental reservations whatsoever.

He wondered about the last, but said nothing.

Colonel Mennen had come with a set of second lieutenant's bars and a pair of Infantry crossed rifles. He pinned the gold bar to the flash on Geoff's green beret.

Then he opened his attaché case and took from it several stacks of paper. He closed the attaché case and put in on Craig's lap.

"The first thing you sign is the Acceptance of Commission form," Colonel Mennen said. "And then the Acknowledgement of Call to Active Duty."

Craig signed the printed forms.

The third item was on printed First Special Forces Group stationery. Below the printed letterhead had been typed "'A' Team #16" and the date. Below that was typed "The undersigned herewith assumes command."

"Write 'Geoffrey Craig,'" Colonel Mennen said, "and under that, 'Second Lieutenant, Infantry, Commanding.'"

I'll be a sonofabitch, Lieutenant Craig thought, as he complied with his orders, *if that doesn't have a rather nice ring to it.*

"And now, Lieutenant, as a friendly suggestion from one officer and gentleman to another, may I suggest you change your shirt before I take you out and introduce you to your new command?"

II

(One)
Sioux Falls Municipal Airport
Sioux Falls, South Dakota
2115 Hours, 19 October 1962

John H. Denn, a tall, fair-skinned man of thirty-five who was a vice president for Corporate Relations of the Continental Illinois Bank, had arrived in Sioux Falls shortly before noon aboard one of CONTBANK's twin-engine Beech Queenaire corporate aircraft.

For five years now, John H. Denn had been taking friends and customers of the Continental Illinois Bank pheasant shooting in South Dakota. Normally, CONTBANK provided portal-to-portal service, transporting the bank's guests from Chicago, or wherever, to Sioux Falls, and then flying them home when they were finished. The party he was waiting for was traveling in its own aircraft, and while that wasn't unheard of, it was unusual. Denn had the feeling that this party was going to be unusual in other ways, and possibly even difficult.

The party's invitation to the Farm had come from the sixteenth floor, that is, from someone close to the very top of the Continental Illinois Bank. It had not come as a recommendation from the big boys, to be weighed by Corporate Relations against other recommendations concerning the potential guests who

would be of greater or lesser value to the bank. It had come
as a directive, in the form of a brief memo.

INTERNAL MEMORANDUM

From: J. B. Summersfield
To: J. H. Denn
      Corporate Relations

Please reserve the South Dakota Farm during the
period Oct. 19 to Oct. 26 for the exclusive use of a party
of five or six from Craig, Powell, Kenyon and Dawes,
New York. Guest list will follow when available.

Craig, Powell, Kenyon and Dawes were the New York–
based international investment bankers. There was a long-
standing relationship between them and Continental Illinois.
CONTBANK tried to take good care of its business partners,
and that included entertaining them.

There was an extraordinary amount of personal relations in
upper-echelon banking. This had at first really surprised John
H. Denn as he had begun to work his way up in the hierarchy
of CONTBANK. He had naively believed as a young man,
fresh from Northwestern (AB) and then Pennsylvania (MBA,
the Wharton School of Business), that after he had done his
ritual internship service in the trenches as a teller and moved
into the executive offices, the personal element would disappear. Business would be transacted based upon the pure facts
and upon a rational analysis of the business circumstances. The
personal element would play, at best, a minor part.

He had realized quickly that he was wrong; that bankers
were no different from car salesman; that a deal had a better
chance of going through when the participants were on a first-
name basis and when each side thought of the other side as
friends. More importantly, he had quickly learned that many
deals that met every criteria for a mutually beneficial profit
could and did fail because someone had taken a dislike to
somebody else.

Denn had been even more surprised to realize that he was quite good as a back-slapper and hand-shaker. He was called "corporate relations" in banking; but of course it was public relations. He had become an account executive, and then an assistant vice president and then a vice president much sooner than he had expected he would. And he was well aware that his rapid promotion had as much to do with his "corporate relations" skills as with his knowledge of banking.

He had earned the reputation at CONTBANK as the man to send on difficult or unusual assignments when potential customers were likely to be difficult. He could, he thought wryly, calm the natives when they were restless. People thought they saw in him someone like themselves, who understood the problem; and they would therefore listen to his suggestions.

And then there were situations like the case in hand, where his mission was simply on behalf of the bank *as* the bank to repay services or courtesies rendered, or to cause others to feel obliged to the bank—or at least to think kindly of it.

Shooting pheasant with customers had never been mentioned at the Wharton School of Business Administration, but it should have been. Pheasant shooting was, in the real world of banking, at least as important as providing bank officers with antique-furnished offices or any other expense that could only be justified as "corporate relations."

Pheasant shooting was so important that CONTBANK, as part of a deal with American Maize & Land Corporation (in which CONTBANK had made available $6.3 million on a ten-year 6.75% note for the acquisition by AM&L of the Herman Shoerr Estate) had insisted on reserving for itself exclusive hunting rights on the 6,400 acres involved. Long before Denn had joined CONTBANK, "the South Dakota Farm" had been organized for the entertainment of CONTBANK customers:

The largest and nicest of the farmhouses had been retained (AM&L had bulldozed the others flat) for use as a hunting lodge. A full-time caretaker had been engaged, who had very little else to do during the year except maintain the farmhouse (he and his family were furnished with a cottage a half mile away) and make sure that whatever AM&L was up to did not interfere with the pheasant population. During hunting season, however, he was expected to make himself available twenty-four hours a day to insure the comfort of CONTBANK's guests. His wife was pressed into duty then as cook for the guests.

All this was expensive, of course, but a justified expense, which satisfied not only the Internal Revenue Service but the bank's own internal auditors, who often took an even more critical view of entertainment expenses.

John H. Denn had not been surprised that CONTBANK wanted to entertain Craig, Powell, Kenyon and Dawes at the South Dakota Farm. But the telex sent to him on a CONTBANK "For Your Information" buck slip had surprised him:

CRAPOWBANK NY
CONTBANK CHICAGO

ATTN: J. B. SUMMERSFIELD, VICE CHAIRMAN OF THE BOARD
FOLLOWING LIST OF HUNTERS WILL ARRIVE SIOUX FALLS AIRPORT
BY AERO COMMANDER AFTERNOON OF OCTOBER 19:
BRIG GENERAL P. T. HANRAHAN
COL. P. S. PARKER III
LT COL. C. W. LOWELL
LT COL. R. G. MACMILLAN
1ST LT C. J. WOOD, JR.
MR. S. T. WOJINSKI
I APPRECIATE BOTH YOUR HOSPITALITY AND YOUR UNDERSTAND-
ING OF THE SITUATION. BEST PERSONAL REGARDS.
PORTER CRAIG
CHAIRMAN OF THE BOARD
CRAIG POWELL KENYON AND DAWES

J. B. Summersfield had not elected to tell John H. Denn who the soldier hunters were, or why their pleasure was important to the Continental Illinois Bank.

Whatever was the true purpose of the invitation, Denn had decided he would do whatever was required to insure these people shot pheasant and had a good time.

Unless there was an early blizzard, there was no reason they should not be pleased. The house was stocked with food, three cases of liquor and one of wine—labels not ordinarily available in South Dakota; and he had had special steaks sent air freight from Kansas City. In previous years, with some difficulty, he had managed to convince the caretaker's wife that economy was not a consideration when she was shopping.

When Denn had gone out to the Farm after his arrival from Chicago, the caretaker had assured him that sufficient plastic-insulated shipping containers were on hand, and that in the morning, he had been promised the first of the daily shipments of dry ice. You could never tell: Sometimes the hunters were really greedy for birds, and sometimes they didn't seem to care at all. But if these people did want them, they would leave with cleaned pheasant, frozen by dry ice, in plastic bags.

There were also at the Farm eight shotguns with ammunition, in case the hunters arrived without weapons. And the two Labrador retrievers would be handled by the caretaker's son.

In the house were telephones, a telex machine, and television sets. Everything but women. CONTBANK would not function as a procurer, even if that meant losing the chance to purchase the Bank of England at ten cents on the dollar.

Once he had checked things out at the Farm, there had been nothing to do but wait. The President of the Second National Bank of Sioux Falls, CONTBANK's correspondent, with whom he had touched base, had called the manager of the airport and had a word with him. The result of this was that the tower would call Mr. Denn the moment he knew an Aero Commander with a General Hanrahan aboard was approaching.

When, at eight o'clock, there had been no call from the airport, John H. Denn got into the rented station wagon and drove to the airport in Sioux Falls, leaving word with the caretaker to forward any calls to him at the airport manager's office.

At the airport, the manager told him there was no word of the Aero Commander.

"But there's somebody else waiting for them, Mr. Denn," he said, nodding across the small terminal building. "He's been here about an hour."

Standing erect, with hands folded against the small of his back, was a tall, dignified man in a fur-collared garbardine trench coat and a homburg. He wore a neatly cropped gray mustache. And he was black.

"You're sure?"

"He had the aircraft call sign," the manager confirmed.

John H. Denn walked over to him.

"Excuse me, sir," he said. "I understand we're waiting for the same airplane."

"We are?" the tall black man said.

"My name is Denn. I'm with the Continental Illinois Bank, and I'm here to meet General Hanrahan and his party."

The black man took off his gray glove and extended his hand.

"I am Colonel Parker," he said. "How do you do? Is there any news?"

The name was on the list, but he had not expected a black man.

"None so far, Colonel," Denn said.

"While I have yet to abandon hope, Mr. Denn," Colonel Parker said, "I have been seriously considering moving my vigil to the bar. Perhaps you would care to join me?"

"I think that's a splendid idea, Colonel," Denn said. "Give me a minute to tell the manager where we will be."

Parker nodded stiffly.

They had been in the bar half an hour, and had just ordered a second drink, when the airport manager's secretary came to them.

"Mr. Denn, the tower's got a report on your Aero Commander. It's five minutes out."

"Where can I meet it?"

She looked a little embarrassed.

"We tried to save a place close by for them," she said. "But somebody just parked there. It'll be way down at the end, I'm afraid."

She pointed down the airfield. Sioux Falls was jammed during pheasant season with hunters, many of whom came by private aircraft. There were, Denn judged, well over a hundred private aircraft already on the field, ranging from corporate jets to small Cessnas and Pipers.

"Colonel, I have a station wagon just outside. Why don't you come with me?" Denn asked.

"There are five of them, plus their luggage," Colonel Parker said. "I think it would be best if we took two cars."

As Denn retrieved the Hertz Mercury Park Lane station wagon from the parking lot, he saw Colonel Parker unlock the door of a black Cadillac Fleetwood. The car bore Kansas license plates, and Denn put that together with the coating of road grime and deduced that Colonel Parker had driven to South Dakota from Kansas.

As the security guard unlocked the hurricane fence to pass him through, Denn stopped and rolled down the window and told him the Cadillac was with him. Then he drove down the line of parked aircraft to the end of the access road pavement. Because the moon was nearly full, there was enough light for him to see a white-and-red Aero Commander (a six-place, twin-engined, high-winged airplane) coming in to land two hundred feet over the prison. The prison, he supposed, had been built in "the country" long before there were airplanes. And the airport had probably started as a dirt strip. The result was that on approaches from the west, aircraft passed directly over the prison yard. It was hardly, Denn thought, what you could call good public relations for Sioux Falls.

When the Aero Commander touched down and rolled past on the runway, he turned to see if Colonel Parker had made the connection, and for the first time noticed that the colonel was not alone in his Fleetwood. There were two passengers in the back seat, looking with dignified curiosity out the windows. Colonel Parker had brought his own Labrador retrievers with him.

The Aero Commander taxied back from the end of the runway, turned into line beside a Twin-Beech, and stopped. The rear door almost immediately opened, and a young man wearing a blue nylon insulated jacket got out. Without a word, he went to the tail of the airplane, turned his back to Denn and Colonel Parker, and relieved himself.

Next out was a pleasant-faced Irishman, in the act of zipping up a hooded parka. He too headed for the tail of the airplane.

Denn glanced at Colonel Parker. He was not smiling. He was obviously offended at open-air urination.

Next out of the airplane was a stocky, ruddy-faced man. Either he or the other one was General Hanrahan, Denn decided.

A fuel truck drove up, distracting Denn's attention. When he turned around again, another man had gotten out of the airplane. He was dressed in a tweed coat, sweater, and open-collared shirt. And he was enormous, probably weighing two twenty-five or more. Denn expected that he too would go to relieve himself, and he did. Last out of the airplane was a tall, handsome blond man. He saluted Colonel Parker and, looking somewhat sheepish, joined the others at the tail of the airplane.

When he had finished, the tall handsome officer went to Colonel Parker and offered his hand.

"Have we kept you waiting long, sir?" he asked.

"There are rest facilities in the terminal building," Colonel Parker said in reply.

He was really annoyed, Denn saw.

"There were extenuating circumstances, sir," the handsome one said.

"Indeed?" Colonel Parker asked stiffly.

"Our on-board facility, sir," he explained, "is an aluminum funnel attached to rubber tubing. If the funnel freezes, and ours did, the system not only fails to work but . . . I'm sure you're familiar, sir, with what happens when naked flesh touches freezing metal."

Denn was surprised at the almost formal respect paid Colonel Parker.

"It would seem that the system should have been checked before you took off," he said.

"Yes, sir," the handsome one said. "I should have done that."

"It's very good to see you, Craig," Colonel Parker said, finally relenting and offering his hand.

"You remember Mac, of course, Colonel," Craig Lowell

said, "but I don't believe you know General Hanrahan, Lieutenant Wood, or Mr. Wojinski."

General Hanrahan offered his hand.

"I'm glad to finally meet you, Colonel," he said.

"The honor, General, is mine," Parker said.

"And this is Lieutenant Charley Wood, my aide-de-camp," Hanrahan said.

"You, at least, Lieutenant," Colonel Parker said, "look young enough to retain bladder control."

Wood looked embarrassed. The others smiled discreetly at the starchy old soldier.

"It was a very long flight, Colonel," Lowell said.

"It would have been a short walk to the terminal," Colonel Parker said. He offered his hand to Wojinski, the enormous man in the tweed jacket.

"How do you do, Mr. Wojinski?" he said.

"I'm real pleased to meet you, Colonel," Wojinski said. "Phil's talked a lot about you."

"My son tends to talk too much," Colonel Parker said.

Denn walked up to them.

"General Hanrahan?" Denn asked.

The Irish-looking man seemed surprised. "I'm Hanrahan," he said. "But you're probably looking for him." He nodded toward the handsome man with the mustache.

"Who are you?" the man with the mustache asked.

"My name is Denn," he said. "I'm from Continental Illinois Bank."

The blond man also seemed surprised. "From the bank?"

Denn handed him his card. The handsome blond man glanced at it and handed it back. If he was impressed by being met by a CONTBANK vice president, it didn't show.

"I thought we'd get a caretaker," he said, offering his hand. "My name is Lowell."

His handshake was warm and firm.

"We're happy to have you with us, Colonel," Denn said. "Gentlemen."

Denn had decided quickly that the tall officer with the blond mustache was in charge of this group, though he didn't quite

understand why. There was a general, and generals ranked
much higher in the army than lieutenant colonels. Still, Lowell
was behaving with the assurance that came only with a great
deal of clout.

"Thank you," Lowell said. "What's the schedule?"

"Well, I thought we'd have dinner. . . . You are hungry?"

"Starved," Lowell said.

"Well, there's a place called the Copper Kettle here," Denn
said. "We can get dinner there, and then go out to the Farm."

"Licenses?" Lowell asked.

"All taken care of," Denn said.

"Well, you guys get the stuff out of the airplane," Lowell
said. "And I'll get the bird topped off."

That proved it, Denn decided. Lieutenant Colonel Lowell
was obviously the man in charge. General Hanrahan was the
first of them to start unloading baggage.

"Put what luggage will fit in the trunk of my car, Lieutenant,
please," Colonel Parker ordered. "With the general's permission, he and Colonel Lowell will ride with me."

"Thank you, Colonel," General Hanrahan said.

"Yes, sir," Wood said.

Denn corrected himself, wryly. The old black man was in
charge. He issued orders with assurance.

He wondered again who Lowell was, and the explanation
came immediately. Lowell handed a credit card to the gas truck
driver, who dropped it. Denn quickly picked it up. It was an
American Express card, and it bore the raised legend, "CRAIG
W. LOWELL Vice Chairman of the Board, Craig, Powell,
Kenyon & Dawes, Inc."

Then what the hell was this "Colonel" business?

Thirty minutes later, three tables had been pushed together
to accommodate all of them at the Copper Kettle restaurant.

"I don't know about Mr. Denn," Lowell said, "but bring
the rest of us Johnny Walker Black." Then he looked at Colonel
Parker. "Excuse me, Colonel," he said. "Is that all right?"

"Fine," Colonel Parker said.

"Fine with me, too," Denn said.

"And run separate checks, please," General Hanrahan said.

"Gentlemen, you're guests of Continental Illinois Bank," Denn said quickly.

"One check, and give it to me," Lowell said.

"One check," Colonel Parker said. "And give it to me."

"I really insist," Denn said.

"I will pay the bill," Colonel Parker said, flatly.

"Want to flip for it, Colonel?" Lowell asked mischievously.

"No," Colonel Parker said. "I will not 'flip' for it. I will settle it."

"Yes, sir," Lowell said.

"I see it's true, Colonel," General Hanrahan said.

"What is true, General?"

"That you're one of the two officers who can tell Lowell what to do—the other being E. Z. Black—and not get an argument."

"General Black," Colonel Parker said dryly, smiling at Lowell, "leads me to believe that is not always the case."

"Well, since the colonel is paying for this," Lowell said, "bring me the largest steak on the menu. Anything but a filet mignon. Pink in the middle."

"Unless there is objection," Colonel Parker said, "bring us all the same thing."

There was no objection.

"I'm sorry Colonel Felter couldn't come with you," Colonel Parker said.

"Felter thinks the slaying of pheasant is beastly," Lowell said.

"Did he say that?" Parker asked.

"No, sir," Lowell said, "what he said—and I forgot to relay his compliments, sir—is that when he has time off, he feels obliged to spend it with Mrs. Felter."

"The President keeps him pretty busy, Colonel," General Hanrahan said.

John H. Denn decided Hanrahan could not mean the President of the United States. He was wrong. Lieutenant Colonel Sanford T. Felter was for President Kennedy what he had been for President Eisenhower: He had been appointed (the appointment itself classified "Top Secret-Presidential") the "President's

Personal Liaison to the Intelligence Community with Rank as Counselor to the President."

"I'm surprised, considering the state of events in Cuba, that any of you could get away to go hunting," Colonel Parker said. He saw General Hanrahan's eyebrows go up, and added, "No offense, certainly, sir."

"None taken, Colonel," Hanrahan said. "But I spoke with Felter several days ago, and he told me that nothing's going to happen just now."

He thought—hoped—that was true. He was the Commandant, U.S. Army Special Warfare Center, and nothing big "officially" was happening. And even if Felter, who was pretty damned closemouthed, hadn't said anything, Hanrahan had other sources. Colonel Mac MacMillan, for instance, had friends in the 82nd Airborne Division (the guys who would certainly go in first), and they would have told him. It might not be what the Counterintelligence people liked, but when a Medal of Honor winner asked questions, he almost always got the answer, no matter what the security classification. An invasion of Cuba without Green Beret involvement was unthinkable.

"I surmised as much when you came out here," Colonel Parker said. "But I wonder if delaying the inevitable makes much sense."

"You think we'll have to invade, Colonel?" MacMillan asked.

That seemed to prove it, Hanrahan thought. Mac didn't know anything, or he would not have asked that question.

"I think we should have put the 82nd Airborne into Havana on January 3, 1960," Colonel Parker said. "If they had done that, the Bay of Pigs fiasco would not have been necessary. No civilization that has employed mercenaries has ever endured for long. You've read Gibbon, General. Certainly you agree?"

General Hanrahan looked uncomfortable.

"They weren't mercenaries, sir," Lowell said. "There were some, of course, but the bulk of the people we tried to put ashore were Cubans."

"They weren't Americans, Craig," Colonel Parker said. "We should have sent Americans."

"We sent some Americans," MacMillan said. "At the end, even Felter went in."

"And so did these two," General Hanrahan said, pointing at Lowell and Mr. Wojinski. "They went in and got Felter out."

Colonel Parker's eyebrows raised. "Indeed?" he asked.

"To get back to where we were," Hanrahan said. "I checked with the acting post commander before we left to come out here. He gave me absolutely no indication that anything is going on."

"If Kennedy believes the Russians are not as quickly as they can going to turn Cuba into a military base capable of controlling the Caribbean basin, he is more a fool than he appears on the surface," Colonel Parker said.

"Well, I don't think anything's going to happen soon," Hanrahan said.

"You would not tell us if there was," Colonel Parker said.

"No," Hanrahan said, with a smile. "But I wouldn't be here if there was."

"Someone," Colonel Parker said, "should give Kennedy a copy of Clausewitz and underline for him the passages about the longer you give the enemy to prepare the greater your casualties when you finally attack."

"I think we're embarrassing Mr. Denn," General Hanrahan said. "May I suggest that we change the subject."

It was a very tactfully put reproof, Denn realized, to Colonel Parker.

"I beg your pardon, sir," Colonel Parker said.

"Some information has just come to my attention," General Hanrahan said, "that bodes ill for the Army of the future."

Colonel Parker took him seriously. "Indeed?"

"The bottom of the barrel has been scraped; we have another Craig in the officer corps."

Lowell looked at him with fresh interest. "He got a commission?" he asked, obviously surprised.

"After successfully defending a mountain redoubt against far superior forces, assuming command of a mixed U.S.-Indigenous command when its officers were killed."

"I think this is where I came in," MacMillan said.

Wojinski chuckled. "It must run in the family. They're queer for sticking their ass out."

Lowell gave both of them a dirty look. "Did he get hurt?" he asked.

"Superficial wounds to the face," Hanrahan said.

"Christ, wait till his father hears about this," Lowell said. "I'll be drummed out of the family."

"I had a talk with Dave Mennen on MARS*," General Hanrahan said. "He was in the highlands—"

"Mr. Denn," Lowell interrupted, "to bring you in on this, we're talking about Porter Craig's boy. He's a Special Forces sergeant—"

"He's a Special Forces *lieutenant*," MacMillan corrected him.

"—in the highlands in Vietnam," Lowell finished.

"Splendid troops," Colonel Parker said, "and a fine idea!"

The idea that Porter Craig's son was an enlisted man, much less in Special Forces, took some moments for John H. Denn to get used to.

"You're talking about the ones who wear the berets, the green berets?" Denn asked.

"Yes, indeed," General Hanrahan said, and then resumed his story. "Dave told me to tell you, Craig, that he really did a good job."

"I'll be damned," Lowell said. "Could he stop the telegram?"

"That's why he got on MARS," General Hanrahan said. "He thought it would be better if either you or I told his father. If you don't want to, I'll call them."

Lowell thought that over. "I'll call him," he said. "If you called him, Porter would call me anyway."

"I've heard," John H. Denn said, "and read about the Green Berets. Are they really what they say they are?"

Military Amateur Radio Service, a worldwide network of amateur radio operators, who relay personal messages for military personnel.

Lowell looked at him. "You're asking, 'Do they really eat babies for breakfast?' That sort of thing?"

Denn was a little uncomfortable. "Well, some of the stories one hears. . . ." he said.

"Why don't you ask General Hanrahan? He's the head Green Beret, *ex officio* the chief baby-eater," Lowell said.

From the look on General Hanrahan's face, Denn saw that Lowell was telling the truth.

"Not very funny, Craig," Hanrahan said, a little stiffly. "But we only eat babies, Mr. Denn, when we're on duty."

"But an officer is never off duty," Lowell went on. "Isn't that so, Colonel Parker?"

"An officer is never off duty until he retires," Colonel Parker agreed, but sensing it was time to do so, he was willing to change the subject. Not completely off the Army, but to a previous war.

"I got out my great-grandfather's maps when I found we were coming here," he said. "I'll show them to you tonight, if you're interested."

"I'd be fascinated," Lowell said.

"Me, too," Hanrahan said.

"What maps?" MacMillan asked, confused.

"My great-grandfather, Colonel," Colonel Parker said with quiet pride, "served with the 10th Cavalry, 'the Buffalo Soldiers.' They campaigned through this part of the world in the Indian Wars."

"And you have his maps?" Denn asked. "I'd love to see them."

"Why did they call them 'Buffalo Soldiers,' Colonel?" Lieutenant Wood asked. "Because they lived off buffalos?"

"Actually, Lieutenant," Colonel Parker said, "the name was given to them by the Sioux, or else the Chiricahua, no one seems to be sure. It made reference to the similarity between the fur of the buffalo and the curly hair of the Negro troopers."

"Oh," Wood said. "I'm sorry, I didn't know."

"They weren't offended by it," Colonel Parker said. "It was a proud thing for a Negro to be a Buffalo Soldier."

(Two)
Near Wessington Springs, South Dakota
1430 Hours, 22 October 1962

The days had been good, and just about identical. Everyone rose about nine-thirty and sat down to enormous breakfasts of ham, eggs, sausage, and pancakes. At half past eleven, they got dressed, assembled outside, and were driven to where they would shoot.

Most of the shooting was through cornfields. The hunting party would walk ("beat") their way through corn higher than they were tall, with the Labradors trotting after them, toward the end of the field. Two or three hunters served as backup there. Backup was usually considered the best spot, for that was where most of the shooting happened, but that was not the way it was with these people.

Because of the thickness and height of the cornstalks (though they could be heard scurrying ahead of the hunters) pheasant were visible when they flushed for only seconds. Then they flew away, most often toward the far end of the field, where the backup hunters waited. In the moment the bird was visible, the beaters had to throw their shotguns to their shoulders, determine that the bird was not a hen but a legal cock, and fire. Despite the difficulty of the shots, these beaters were taking pheasants three times out of four. And they were taking them clean: there would be a small cloud of feathers, and then the birds would drop like stones. The backup hunters had very few shots.

Each day by four o'clock, they were back at the farmhouse, where they made themselves as useful as they could cleaning and freezing the birds. Colonel Parker had impressed both John H. Denn and the caretaker with his surgeonlike skill in skinning his catch. Most hunters ran the birds through a pot of melted paraffin so they could easily pluck them.

Colonel Parker's Labradors, a bitch and a male, also impressed John H. Denn. They were superbly trained, much better dogs than the Labs on the Farm. When Denn asked the colonel how he'd managed to produce such terrific animals, Parker replied that retirement gave him time to properly train dogs. There was also time to sew canvas seat covers to protect the brocade upholstery in the back of his Cadillac Fleetwood.

"When I was a young officer, Cavalry was still mounted," Parker said. "We had a saddler who taught me what he could of his trade. I found it a very useful skill."

By five o'clock each day, everyone had bathed and was into his whiskey. Vast quantities of it disappeared with surprising speed, but no one (except Lieutenant Wood, who demonstrated a tendency to drop off to sleep) seemed to feel it. They ate enormous dinners, roast beef the first night, roast pheasant the second, and they stayed up late talking and playing a game with dollar bills called "Liar's Dice."

John H. Denn had never served in a uniform, and had up until now little regard for the military, yet he found the nightly conversations fascinating. There was apparently much more to the Army than he'd been aware of. And he was more than a little surprised to learn that there was just as much politics in the Army as there was in the corporate corridors of CONT-BANK. The difference seemed to be that their political battles were punctuated from time to time with genuine battles.

Denn learned further that "blown away" meant "to be shot to death"; that "bought the farm" meant "blown away"; and that "nervous" meant "frightened," or more probably "terrified."

And late the second night, Colonel MacMillan's even more obscure remark about "this is where I came in" was explained when General Hanrahan, his tongue slightly loosened by a good deal of Scotch, related the story of then–Second Lieutenant Lowell's exploits in Greece. The man whose American Express card identified him as vice chairman of the board (for tax purposes, Denn understood) of Craig, Powell, Kenyon and Dawes, Investment Bankers, had once, while severely wounded, defended a position in the mountains on the Greek-Albanian border with sufficient valor and skill to be personally decorated by the King of Greece.

Lowell tried to make light of that, but Wojinski, who had

also been there, wouldn't let him. "Come on, Duke," he said.
"You can't forget that any more than I can. All those dead
Reds all over the place. There was no way to bury that many
people there, nothing but goddamned rocks, we would have
had to blast graves, and we couldn't get the Greek monks to
take them . . . they wouldn't bury the Communists, said they
were godless, wouldn't even touch them. . . . So what we did
was make up a convoy of trucks and carried them to Athens
and left the trucks in the Military Assistance Command motor
pool and disappeared. By then they was starting to smell. When
we showed up a couple of days later, they were madder than
hell, but the bodies were gone."

John H. Denn, Colonel Philip Sheridan Parker III, and Lieutenant Charles J. Wood, Jr., stood ten yards from the end of a
cornfield, holding their shotguns at the ready.

Colonel Parker was lightly holding in his hands a Sauer und
Sohn *Drilling*, two side-by-side 16-bore barrels above a rifle
barrel. John H. Denn knew a little something about shotguns,
and he knew the *Drilling* was worth more than three thousand
dollars.

And the *Drilling* was not the most valuable of the shotguns
being used by the party. Lieutenant Wood was armed with one
of two shotguns Lieutenant Colonel Craig W. Lowell had brought
to South Dakota in a leather case. They were a matched pair.
The numerals "1" and "2" had been inlaid in gold on the opening
lever of each gun. The guns were Holland and Holland's "Best
Grade," and were worth somewhere in the vicinity of twelve
thousand dollars. Denn suspected that Wood had no idea of the
worth of the gun he had been using for the past three days. He
knew it was a fine gun, of course, but not quite how fine.

There had been shooting now for five minutes, and every
once in a while the rainlike sound of spent shot falling onto
the cornstalks, but the cornfield was half a mile in depth, and
the beaters could neither be seen nor heard.

Then there was the crunching, whistling sound of men and
dogs moving down corn rows, and pheasants began to flush as
they were beaten toward the end of the field. They had several

minutes of good shooting, but then MacMillan's voice sounded from inside the field.

"Keep those muzzles up! Here we come!"

The beaters appeared a minute later, their jackets heavy with pheasant.

"I'm sure that's the limit," Lowell said. "We should have probably stopped shooting a couple of minutes ago."

"Why didn't you?" Colonel Parker demanded coldly. "I don't like taking more than the limit."

Lowell was embarrassed. "Let's count them," he said. "Maybe I'm wrong."

When the birds were laid out he was visibly relieved that they were one bird under.

"Let's not start anywhere else for just one bird," Lowell said. "I need a drink and a bath, in that order."

Wood and Wojinski began collecting the pheasants from the others. They carried the birds by their necks to the Mercury, whose back seat had been put down and covered with plastic.

"General Hanrahan," Colonel Parker said, "may I suggest that you and I leave these gentlemen to their labors? I recall hearing somewhere that rank is supposed to carry with it certain privileges. I would like first shot at the shower, before certain unnamed officers and alleged gentlemen again exhaust the hot water."

Parker, Hanrahan, and John H. Denn got in the Cadillac and drove off.

The others finished loading the birds and crowded into the Mercury station wagon.

A half mile down the dirt road, they saw Colonel Parker's Cadillac stopped by the side of the road.

"I wonder what the hell that's all about?" MacMillan asked, concerned.

As they approached, an arm came out of the driver's window of the Cadillac. Hand open, it extended upward, as a child extends its arm asking to leave the classroom. Or the commander of an armored cavalry troop signals the troops behind to halt.

MacMillan got out and walked quickly to the Cadillac, bent

down to the window, listened a moment, straightened, made a
gesture for those in the Mercury to join him, and then bent to
the window again.

By the time they had gotten out of the Mercury and walked
to the Cadillac MacMillan was standing straight again.

"What's going on?" Lowell asked.

"You just missed it," MacMillan said, gesturing toward the
radio.

"What?" Lowell demanded, impatiently.

"Kennedy," MacMillan said. "He was on the radio. The
Russians have missiles in Cuba. He just ordered a naval block-
ade."

"Good God!" Lowell said.

"Perhaps," Colonel Parker said thoughtfully, "someone has
read some Clausewitz to him after all."

"The nearest phone, I suppose, is at the farmhouse," General
Hanrahan said.

"Yes," Colonel Parker said. He put the Cadillac in gear and
stepped hard on the accelerator. The Cadillac's wheels spun
getting out of the small ditch. The others, left standing in the
road, ran in a moment to the Mercury.

(Three)

"Army Aviation Board," Mrs. Ann Caskey said. "Office of
the President."

"Ann, this is Colonel Lowell. Let me speak to Colonel
Martinelli."

"He's on the phone, Colonel," Mrs. Caskey said.

"Break in," Lowell said.

"All right," she said. "We've been looking all over for you,
Colonel."

There was a moment's pause.

"Where the hell are you?" Colonel Jack Martinelli asked.
"We've been looking all over North Dakota for you."

"I'm in *South* Dakota," Lowell said. "And Hanrahan's people knew where we are."

"Obviously not," Martinelli said. "How long will it take

you to get to MacDill Air Force Base?"

Lowell did the arithmetic in his head.

"Six hours, maybe a little longer."

"Report to General Jiggs," Martinelli said. "I'll call and let him know you finally turned up."

"What's going on?" Lowell asked a dead telephone.

He put the telephone in its cradle and looked at Paul Hanrahan, who was on the other telephone.

"Hold on," Hanrahan said to whomever he was talking to and covered the microphone with his hand.

"I'm to report to Jiggs at MacDill," Lowell said.

Hanrahan looked thoughtful a moment.

"Can you drop us at Bragg?"

"It would take me another two hours," Lowell said, adding bitterly, "and I'm already apparently AWOL."

Hanrahan thought that over a moment, then removed his hand from the microphone.

"Send an L-23 to MacDill," he said. "Have the pilot report to General Jiggs."

There was a reply. Hanrahan's face tightened in fury.

"Well get one of them back from the Corps fleet," he snapped. "By force if necessary."

There was another reply.

"Colonel, until such time as either you or I are relieved by proper authority, you are subject to my orders. Now do what I tell you, and don't argue with me about it."

He took the telephone from his ear and put it in the base with such slow precision that it was obvious he very much wanted to slam it down.

"I have been sandbagged," he said to Lowell. "I am being 'represented' by XVIII Airborne Corps at MacDill. My ass of a deputy has seen fit to turn my airplanes 'temporarily' over to XVIII Airborne Corps. He has justified this action with the 'explanation' that he 'believes' they have a higher operational priority."

"That sonofabitch," MacMillan exploded. "I never trusted him."

"As soon as I'm at MacDill, Paul," Lowell said, "you and

Mac can have the Aero Commander. If I need wings, I can get them from Rucker."

"Just get us to MacDill, Craig," General Hanrahan said. "As quickly as we can get there."

(Four)
MacDill Air Force Base
Tampa, Florida
2145 hours, 22 October 1962

"MacDill," Craig Lowell said to the microphone, "Aero Commander One Five, descending from one zero thousand, estimate five minutes north northwest of your station. Requesting landing instructions."

"Aircraft calling MacDill, say again," the MacDill tower replied.

"MacDill, Aero Commander One Five, five minutes out, north northwest, request landing."

"Aero Commander One Five, MacDill is closed to civilian traffic at this time. Permission to land is denied. I say again, denied."

"Oh, shit, that's all we need," Wojinski, kneeling on the floor between the pilot's and copilot's seat, said.

"There it is," MacMillan said. He was in the copilot's seat and pointing out the left window.

Lowell looked over him, then pushed the nose down, and turned to the left.

"What do we do, go into Tampa?" MacMillan asked.

There was a lot of traffic at MacDill. Lowell could see two Air Force fighters taking off simultaneously on one runway, while a C-131 made its landing roll on a parallel runway.

"MacDill, Commander One Five is on official business, we have a Code Seven* aboard."

"Commander One Five, MacDill. Advise landing at Tampa International. This field is temporarily closed to civilian traffic."

---

*Code Seven: Brigadier General

"MacDill, did you hear what I said about a Code Seven aboard?"

"Affirmative, One Five. I say again, this field is temporarily closed to civilian traffic."

"MacDill, Aero Commander One Five declares an emergency. Request immediate straight-in approach to Runway Two Seven Left."

"Jesus!" MacMillan said.

"Attention all aircraft in the MacDill approach and departure patterns. We have a declared emergency. The aircraft is a civilian Aero Commander, approximately three miles north of Runway Two Seven. We have a declared emergency. All aircraft in the approach pattern will execute one minute three hundred sixty-degree turns at their present altitude until further notice. MacDill clears Aero Commander One Five to make an emergency straight-in approach to Runway Two Seven. The winds are five from the north. The altimeter is three zero zero zero."

"Understand Two Seven," Lowell said. "One Five on final." He turned to MacMillan. "Put the wheels down, Mac," he said. "It's smoother that way."

"Jesus," MacMillan said again, as he put his hand on the lever.

"Aero Commander One Five, you will stop at the end of your landing roll. You will not, repeat not, depart the runway. You will be met."

"I'll bet we will," MacMillan said.

"Understand Taxiway Two Seven Left," Lowell said.

The tower was back on the air instantly. The operator seemed upset.

"One Five, negative! I say again, negative! Commander One Five, you are directed to stop in place at the completion of your landing roll. I say again, you are ordered to stop in place at the completion of your landing roll."

As they came in over the outer marker, they could see a procession of airfield vehicles, huge red fire trucks, two ambulances, a sedan painted in a black-and-white checkerboard pattern, and three jeeps, all with flashing red lights, racing down the taxiway parallel to the runways.

There was a chirp of rubber as the Commander touched down, and then a roar of the engines as Lowell reversed the pitch of the propellers, turning them into brakes.

He allowed the plane to run to the end of the runway, past the painted markings indicating the beginning of the active runway, onto the paved area beyond.

"MacDill," he said. "Aero Commander One Five, just past the threshold of Runway Two Seven Left. My emergency seems to have disappeared. It was probably a loose wire on the main power buss."

"Aero Commander One Five, hold your position," a new voice, this one cold and heavy with authority, came over the radio. "I say again, hold your position. Failure to do so will result in your aircraft being fired upon by base security personnel."

"My, they are annoyed, aren't they?" Lowell said.

"What the hell is going on?" Paul T. Hanrahan asked, sleepily.

"Sleeping Beauty is heard from," MacMillan said, laughing.

"We had a little problem, Paul," Lowell said. "But it's cleared up. We're at MacDill."

"You could say we have just jumped from the frying pan into the fire," Wojinski offered.

Hanrahan looked out the window. The airplane was surrounded. There were two fire trucks, from which were emerging firefighters in aluminum suits carrying large-mouth foam hoses. Air Force Military Police in two of the jeeps trained machine guns on the airplane. An officer carrying an electronic megaphone and wearing an MP armband jumped out of one of them and went to the checkerboard staff car.

"Attention in the aircraft!" the MP officer ordered through his microphone. "Shut down your engines and emerge from the aircraft with your hands in the air!"

"What the hell?" Hanrahan asked.

"When they said the field was closed to civilian airplanes," Lowell said, "I had an emergency."

"You go out first, Wood," Wojinski said. "Lieutenants are expendable."

"Don't you move, Charley!" Hanrahan snapped. He rummaged around until he had found his green beret and put it on, then walked to the rear of the cabin, pushed open the door, and stepped into the glare of the lights.

"I am General Paul T. Hanrahan," he announced. "Take that floodlight out of my eyes."

III

(One)
Office of the Commanding General
Headquarters, U.S. Joint Assault Force (Provisional)
MacDill Air Force Base
Tampa, Florida
2220 Hours, 22 October 1962

It is not really true, as folklore has it, that general officers are permitted to design their own uniforms. They are subject to the same uniform regulations as any other member of the Army. On the other hand, the more stars one has on one's epaulets, the fewer people there are in a legal position to correct one's dress.

Brigadier General Paul T. Hanrahan was meditating on that point as he marched into the office of the JAF CG. The fur-collared zippered nylon jacket General James G. Boone was wearing was intended by Army Regulations for wear by aviation personnel when engaged in flight activities. It was, in fact, specifically prohibited to nonaviation personnel, as well as to aviation personnel when not engaged in, or en route to, flight activities.

But there were four silver stars on each of the jacket's epaulets, which meant that there was virtually no chance of anyone suggesting to General Boone that he was out of uniform.

There were only two generals in the Zone of the Interior (the Continental United States) senior to General Boone: the Chief of Staff and the Commanding General of CONARC (Continental Army Command) and Hanrahan thought it very unlikely that either would say anything to him.

General Boone was also under arms. He was wearing a "Pistol, General Officer's, w/accoutrements." The pistol was a Colt automatic, caliber .32 ACP. The .32 ACP cartridge was, in General Hanrahan's judgment, only marginally more effective than a .22 long rifle cartridge. That is to say, hardly useful for anything more serious than shooting squirrels or holes in beer cans. The general officer's .32 Colt was carried in a soft brown leather holster suspended on a soft brown leather belt. The belt carried three lines of stitching lengthwise and was clasped by a gold-plated buckle, which, when closed, formed a circle stamped (engraved?) with the National Seal. These were the general's accoutrements.

Hanrahan thought the "General Officer's Pistol w/accoutrements" was something of a joke, something that would appeal to a recently appointed brigadier general of the Quartermaster Corps, or maybe the brigadier who served as Chief of the Medical Service Corps, who commanded the non-M.D. administrators and technicians who ran the Army's hospitals. At the time of his own promotion to brigadier general, when he had been presented with his "Pistol, General Officer's, with accoutrements," Hanrahan had looked at it, cleaned it, and then put it in a drawer. He had never worn it, never intended to wear it, and was genuinely surprised to see General James G. Boone wearing his. General Boone, in Hanrahan's judgment, was one hell of a soldier, and not given to affectations.

Boone, a tall, heavy man with a pockmarked face and short gray hair, had been a major of Engineers when the Philippines fell in World War II. Refusing to give up when Wainwright gave the order to surrender, he took to the hills of Mindanao, where he proclaimed himself "Commander, U.S. Irregular Forces in the Philippines" and promoted himself to colonel— in the correct belief that only a colonel had sufficient prestige to successfully enlist Filipinos to his cause. When MacArthur was finally able to send troops back to Mindanao, they landed to the strains of "The Washington Post March" played by the band of the thirty-thousand-man-strong U.S. Irregular Forces in the Philippines, Colonel J. G. Boone (his promotion by then having been confirmed and made a matter of record by General of the Army Douglas MacArthur) commanding. There was no doubt in General MacArthur's mind (he, in fact, would have done the same thing himself) that Boone was one hell of a commander and a soldier, even if he had refused a legitimate order to surrender and had the unspeakable arrogance to proclaim himself a colonel.

Boone had gone into Korea as an Infantry colonel, and came out eighteen months later as a major general, in command of a division. He was now deputy commander of CONARC (Continental Army Command) and Hanrahan had not been at all surprised when Boone had been named commander of the forces that were going to invade Cuba.

Hanrahan was deeply ashamed to come before General Boone in the present circumstances.

"General Hanrahan reporting to the commanding general as directed, sir," Hanrahan said, and raised his hand in salute.

General Boone's jowls had begun to sag. His eyes were slightly bloodshot and cold, and there were bags beneath them. He returned Hanrahan's salute, and said, softly, "You may stand at ease, General."

Hanrahan assumed a position just slightly less formal than "Parade Rest," but stiffer than "At Ease."

"Your reputation precedes you, General," General Boone said.

"I regret the circumstances, sir."

"I have heard the Air Force's version of what they feel is your 'inexcusable' conduct," General Boone said. "I will now listen to yours."

"No excuse, sir," Hanrahan said.

"This isn't West Point, General," Boone said. "That 'no excuse' business doesn't wash with me."

"I assume full responsibility, General," Hanrahan said.

"You're beginning to annoy me, General," General Boone

said. "I did not ask for a paraphrase of 'no excuse, sir.'"

"I was asleep when the incident occurred, General," Hanrahan said. "If I had been awake, I would have forbidden Colonel Lowell to do what he did."

"So it's Lowell's fault?"

"If I may continue, sir," Hanrahan said. "I would have forbidden him to do what he did, and I would have been wrong."

"That's interesting," General Boone said. "You're saying you believe what Colonel Lowell did was justified?"

"Yes, sir."

"Explain that, if you will."

"Colonel Lowell was directed to report to General Jiggs as soon as possible. Twenty minutes ago, he was told the field was closed even to an aircraft with a Code Seven aboard. If he had complied with that order, he would have had to land at Tampa International. If he had done that, I would probably be just now arranging for a vehicle to bring us here. It would be another hour and a half before we would arrive. And his aircraft, should I need it, would be at Tampa International, not here. Both we and the airplane are here, now."

"Why would you need his airplane?"

"Colonel Lowell has offered me his airplane, if I should need one," Hanrahan said. "I don't know that I will, but that was, I am sure, part of his reasoning."

"The end justifies the means?" Boone said, and without giving Hanrahan a chance to reply asked, "Are you sure MacDill was notified a Code Seven was aboard the aircraft?"

"Yes, sir."

"They neglected to inform me of that," Boone said. "But there was no bona fide emergency?"

"No, sir, there was not."

"Lowell just decided he was going to land whether or not the Air Force wanted him to, is that it?"

"Yes, sir," Hanrahan said. "In compliance with his order."

"He was a little late in complying with his orders, wouldn't you say, General? General Jiggs has been looking for him for three days."

"There was some kind of a communications breakdown,

General," Hanrahan said. "For which I am sure Colonel Lowell feels personally responsible. But I must say in his defense that I don't hold him responsible for that, and that I don't think there was thirty seconds wasted once he understood that he was supposed to be here."

"That brings us to you," General Boone said. "Inasmuch as Special Forces is being represented by the XVIII Airborne Corps liaison officer, what are you doing here?"

"I am the senior Special Forces officer, General," Hanrahan said. "I believe it is my place to be here."

"The XVIII Airborne Corps liaison officer was among the first to arrive," General Boone said. "Three days ago. When did you change your mind, General, about your place being here?"

"I was not aware of the situation until this afternoon, General."

"And what is it that you feel Special Forces can contribute to this operation with you here that it could not represented by XVIII Airborne Corps?"

"We have had recent experience in Cuba, General. If nothing else, we should be the pathfinders for the parachute drop. We are also prepared to harass the enemy's rear lines, sir. What we can do is proportional to the airlift capability that can be made available to us."

"XVIII Airborne Corps feels that the airlift capability we can give them is marginal, and they have informed me they are perfectly capable of using their own pathfinders."

Hanrahan said nothing, afraid to sound argumentative.

"Presumably, you left someone in command when you went off hunting?"

"Yes, sir."

"But you did not instruct him regarding what you regarded the duty of the Special Forces commander to be? Vis-à-vis coming here, I mean?"

"I apparently failed to make it sufficiently clear, sir."

"Or was it possibly a case, General, of your deputy deciding his greater loyalty lay with the commanding general of XVIII Airborne Corps?" Boone asked.

"I have not had the opportunity as yet, General, to discuss the matter with him at any length," Hanrahan said.

"Good man, is he?" Boone asked.

"I have found him to be more than satisfactory so far, sir."

"Excluding this? This failure to comprehend your desires?"

"Excluding this, sir. As I say, I have not had the chance to discuss this with him at any length."

"I feel sorry for him," General Boone said.

"Sir?"

"From what I know about you, General," General Boone said, "as I said, your reputation preceded you, I would not like to be an officer whom you felt had betrayed you."

"I don't know that to be the case, sir," Hanrahan said.

General Boone pushed a button on his intercom.

"Would you ask General Delahanty to step in here, please, Sergeant?"

There almost immediately came a knock at the door. Boone called "Come in," and an Air Force major general stepped into the room.

"General, this is General Hanrahan," Boone said. "General, this is General Delahanty, the base commander."

"General," General Delahanty said, stiffly.

"Sir," Hanrahan said.

"General, I have heard General Hanrahan's version of the incident that's bothering you," General Boone said. "General Hanrahan deeply regrets the inconvenience to your people, and so do I. Is that going to be sufficient?"

"Sir?"

"General Hanrahan has apologized. I apologize. Is that sufficient, or do you desire any additional action be taken?"

General Delahanty obviously desired additional action be taken. Even more obviously, he was not prepared to demand it from the man looking at him with cold bloodshot eyes.

"So long as General Hanrahan deals with the pilot, to preclude a reoccurrence of such an irresponsible act, as I'm sure he will, I can see no value in making anything official of this, sir."

"Thank you, General," General Boone said. "That will be all."

(Two)

The two officers walked into the commanding general's somewhat spartan office and saluted simultaneously.

"General Boone, this is Colonel Lowell," Major General Paul T. Jiggs said.

"Oh, yes," General Boone said, coldly eyeing Lowell. He returned their salute.

"How do you do, sir?" Lowell asked.

"I'm fascinated to meet you, Colonel," Boone said. "I have heard a good deal about you, most recently from our Air Force hosts."

Lowell did not reply.

"I am pleased to learn that your emergency ended without disaster," General Boone said.

"There was no emergency, sir," Lowell said.

"But you declared an emergency?"

"I wanted to land, sir," Lowell said. "I believed that they would bring us under fire if I just came in, after being denied permission to land."

"Colonel, I presume you are aware of your rights as expressed in the Thirty-first Article of War against self-incrimination?"

"Yes, sir."

"And certainly an officer of your service must understand that falsely declaring an emergency constitutes some sort of violation of the Code of Military Justice, so the question therefore is why you are not seeking the protection of the Thirty-first Article of War."

Lowell did not reply.

"I asked you a question, Colonel," Boone said.

"The facts are before you, sir," Lowell said. "I will not contest any decision you make in the matter."

General Boone glowered at Lowell and let him stew for

almost sixty seconds before he spoke.

"General Jiggs tells me you're a pretty good shaker and mover," Boone said.

"That's very kind of the general, sir," Lowell said.

"He wants to send you to Fort Hood," Boone went on. "The 2nd Armored may have bona fide problems that we don't know about, or it may have lead in its ass, but whichever, it's not getting its show on the road as fast as it has to."

"So General Jiggs has recently led me to believe," Lowell said.

"Under other circumstances, Colonel, you would spend the next two weeks devoting what General Jiggs tells me are your considerable literary talents to replying by endorsement to a letter I would like to write you asking you to explain this latest escapade of yours," General Boone said. "But the priority is getting the 2nd Armored out of low gear."

"Yes, sir."

"You will not, Colonel," General Boone said, "consider that the exigencies of the service have once again kept your neck out of the noose, but rather that I am delaying my final decision about what to do about you until I have a chance to weigh your sins against the service you will render at Fort Hood. Do I make myself clear?"

"Yes, sir," Lowell said.

Then General Boone read from a paper on his desk: "Your appointment as Deputy Inspector General, Headquarters, U.S. Joint Assault Force (Provisional), by authority of the verbal order of the commanding general, is effective immediately. You will proceed to Fort Hood, Texas, to investigate and if possible resolve certain logistic and transportation problems in the 2nd Armored Division by the quickest available means. You will identify yourself and explain your mission to the commanding general of the 2nd Armored Division on your arrival, making it clear to him that while you will report directly to this headquarters, your mission is to get the division moving, rather than to find fault with its commander or any of his officers."

"Yes, sir," Lowell said.

"Why is it, Colonel," General Boone said, "that I feel I have just put a loaded pistol in the hands of a ten-year-old?"

"I'm sorry you feel that way, General. All I can say is that I will try to justify your and General Jiggs's trust in me, sir."

"My confidence, at the moment, is in General Jiggs, Colonel, not in you."

"Yes, sir."

"That is all, Colonel," General Boone said. "I'll have a word with you, General, if you please."

"Yes, sir."

Lowell saluted.

"Permission to withdraw, sir?"

"You are dismissed, Colonel," General Boone said.

Lowell saluted, did an about-face, and marched out of the office, closing the door behind him.

"I wasn't kidding about that loaded-gun business, Paul," Boone said. "I'm sure your Colonel Lowell, who is a guardhouse lawyer if I ever saw one, is fully aware of the power I just handed him."

"He'll get the division on-loaded, General," Jiggs said. "There may be some bruised feelings, but he'll get it moving."

"I hope that's not auld lang syne speaking," Boone said.

"No, sir," Jiggs said.

"I felt sorry for Hanrahan," Boone said.

"Sir?"

"Triple H Howard has been off planning the Airmobile Army, and has left Ken Harke in charge of Bragg while he's gone. Harke let Hanrahan go off hunting without a word about what was going on about Cuba," Boone said. "And Hanrahan's deputy commander, who is Harke's man, just turned over Special Forces to XVIII Airborne Corps. He then did not consider it necessary to get in touch with Hanrahan."

Jiggs had a lot of respect for Lieutenant General H. H. Howard, XVIII Airborne Corps Commanding General, one of the Army's most intelligent—and most colorful—officers. Howard was already being talked about for Chief of

Staff. Jiggs thought rather differently about Major General Kenneth Harke and Colonel Roland Minor who was Hanrahan's deputy.

Harke had one priority, the advancement of the career of Major General Kenneth Harke. Since his career was tied to Airborne, Harke regarded the "threat" Special Forces posed to conventional parachute troops as a threat to him personally, and would do anything he could to reduce that threat. If he felt he needed to stab Paul Hanrahan in the back, then he would stab Paul Hanrahan in the back. Harke was a prick. Worse, Jiggs thought—an intelligent prick.

Colonel Roland Minor was something else. He had early on decided his path to advancement lay in attaching himself to a superior's coattails. Since he now had his nose way up Harke's rear end, he would easily convince himself that his loyalty was due to "the Army," that is, to Harke, and not to his immediate commander, Hanrahan.

"You're sure it was intentional?"

"Goddamn right it was intentional," Boone said. "Except for Triple H, those Airborne bastards want Special Forces, and if they can hang Hanrahan in the process so much the better. Christ, how I wish E. Z. Black hadn't gone to the Pacific. Do you realize that he and I are the only four-stars who don't jump out of airplanes?"

"I never thought of it, but it's true, isn't it?"

"And only the Secretary of Defense thinks I should be here," Boone said. "Everybody else is muttering it's an Airborne operation and should be commanded by an Airborne officer."

"Maybe that's why you got the job," Jiggs said.

"Unless your Colonel Lowell can get the 2nd Armored moving, it's going to *be* an Airborne operation. And when they get all shot up, as they will if we can't get the 2nd Armored there in time, I'll take the rap. Not personally, but because I am not Airborne, and Q.E.D. not really bright."

Jiggs was surprised by the bitterness of this speech. Boone had a reputation for being closemouthed.

"You think we're going?" Jiggs asked.

"Yeah, don't you?"

"It was twenty, thirty miles across the English Channel," Jiggs said. "It's ninety from Key West. And the Channel was ours. So was the air, for all practical purposes. I hope we don't have to go."

"I think we'll have to go," Boone said. "I think the Russians will call Kennedy's bluff. He backed down at the Bay of Pigs, and he acts like he never heard of the Monroe Doctrine. We had every right, under the Monroe Doctrine and international law, to stop those Russian ships months ago, but we didn't. We didn't open our mouths until they had their damned rockets nearly operational. I don't think the Russians are going to give them up without a fight, and if they succeed in knocking out the 82nd, or maybe the 82nd and the 2nd, that's the ball game, Paul. It's either kiss their ass or blow the world up."

He looked at Jiggs and then seemed to realize he had said more than he should have.

"Talking about minding the store, have you talked to home lately?"

"Yes, sir."

"And you're sure Army Aviation is not now under XVIII Airborne Corps?" Boone asked.

"We have Bob Bellmon and William Roberts guarding our interests in Washington," Jiggs said.

Boone grunted.

"Sir?" Jiggs asked.

"I just paid the both of them a left-handed mental compliment," Boone said. "I thought, 'Well, those two are pretty good politicians.' Isn't that a hell of a thing to think? Christ, I hope they're not telepathic."

Jiggs laughed. Brigadier General Robert Bellmon was the second general officer of his name to serve as a cavalryman. He had been captured at the Kasserine Pass in Africa in War II, and spent a terrible period as a POW. William Roberts had done more than any other single individual to provide the Army with its own aircraft. A West Pointer, and a lieutenant colonel at twenty-four, he was one of the Army's brightest officers. It had been a long wait for his colonel's eagle, but he finally got it, and soon after that he exchanged it for a general's star.

Bellmon and Roberts were what Jiggs thought of as fine officers: They *lived* the business about officer's honor and duty, no matter what it cost them. They would be offended to be thought of as politicians, but the fact was that they *were* very good at politics.

"Who's your deputy?" General Boone asked.

"I don't really have one," Jiggs said. "Jack Martinelli is at the Aviation Board*, so Bill Roberts had him put on TDY orders to the post. That made him the senior colonel present for duty, and he's acting commander."

"He's all right? He's not a closet parachuter?"

"No," Jiggs said. "He's one of the few Regular aviators. If anything, he's more of a danger to Airborne than they are to him. When he gives his speech about the way to put men safely on the ground is with helicopters, he makes Billy Graham sound tongue-tied."

Boone laughed.

"Go back to work, Paul," he said. "I'm going to get on the horn and call Stu Lemper at Hood and lie through my teeth about the faith and confidence I have in your man Lowell."

(Three)

"May I use your typewriter for a few minutes?" Lieutenant Colonel Lowell asked the chief clerk of the J-3 Section of Headquarters, U.S. Joint Assault Force (Provisional).

The chief clerk, a man in his late thirties, stood up.

"Colonel, I'll be happy to have anything you want typed up, I'll type it myself. . . ."

The chief clerk wore the insignia of a Specialist-Seven, six arcs and a representation of the national seal. The enlisted ranks

---

*The Army Aviation Board is charged with testing aviation equipment, from radios to entire aircraft, proposed for Army use. There are similar Boards for Armor, Artillery, etc.

of the army were divided into noncommissioned officers and
specialists. A Spec-7 drew the pay and allowances of a master
sergeant, and enjoyed just about as much prestige.

"If you don't mind," Lieutenant Colonel Lowell said, smiling, "I'm the best clerk-typist I ever met."

"Yes, sir," the Spec-7 said, and reluctantly got up from his
chair and stood to one side.

Lieutenant Colonel Lowell sat down.

"Paper?"

The Spec-7 leaned over and pulled out a drawer. Lieutenant
Colonel Lowell took a sheet of paper from it, put it in the
typewriter, and rapidly typed three lines.

HEADQUARTERS
U.S. ARMY SPECIAL WARFARE CENTER AND SCHOOL
Fort Bragg, North Carolina

Then he ripped it out of the typewriter, snatched a pencil
from an array in a Planters Salted Peanuts can, and counted
the letters in the second and third lines.

"I'll need serial numbers," Lowell said, handing a sheet of
paper to General Hanrahan. "Yours, Mac's, Wood's, and What-
sisname's name plus his serial number."

He reached for paper and carbon and second sheets, stacked
them quickly together, and rolled them into the typewriter. He
looked at the Spec-7.

"I need a Special Order number," he said. "Today's."

"We started numbering when we were activated," the
Spec-7 said. "Let me look for somebody else's."

Special Orders are numbered consecutively, starting 1 January. They are not normally issued on Saturday and Sunday.

"Here's one from Benning," the Spec-7 said. "Dated
20 October. The number's 233."

"That's close enough," Lowell said.

He moved the carriage of the typewriter to the center of the
page, backspaced six spaces and rapidly typed HEADQUAR-
TERS. Then he consulted the page on which he had counted
letters, backspaced accordingly, and finished typing the head-

ing. By then Hanrahan handed him the serial numbers and
names he had asked for.

Lowell's fingers flew over the typewriter keys. When he
was finished, he jerked the interleaved paper and carbon out
of the machine, handed it to Hanrahan, and reached for more
paper.

HEADQUARTERS

U.S. ARMY SPECIAL WARFARE
CENTER AND SCHOOL

Fort Bragg, North Carolina

Special Orders   22 October 1962

Number   235:

SUPPLEMENTAL

1. VO Commandant USASWC&S 22 Oct 62 confirmed and made a matter of record: COL MINOR, Roland G. Inf 0-345611 Hq USASWC&S Ft Bragg NC is
placed on TDY and WP Hq XVIII Airborne Corps Ft
Bragg NC eff immediately for an indef period. Off will
rpt NLT 0530 Hours 23 Oct 62 and hold himself in
readiness for further orders to follow.

2. VO Commandant USASWC&S 22 Oct 62 confirmed and made a matter of record: Following off Hq
USASWC&S Ft Bragg NC placed on TDY and WP Hq
US Joint Assault Force, MacDill AFB Fla for an indef
period.

BRIG GEN HANRAHAN, Paul T 0-230765
1/LT WOOD, Charles Jr Inf 0-236454
CWO(2) WOJINSKI, Stefan T W-330078

PAUL T. HANRAHAN
Brigadier General, USA
Commandant

"You better sign all the copies, Paul," Lowell said. "In case one should get lost."

He took more paper and carbon from the drawer, stacked it, and typed rapidly again.

HEADQUARTERS

U.S. ARMY SPECIAL WARFARE CENTER AND SCHOOL

Fort Bragg, North Carolina

General Orders: 23 October 1962

Number 5:

The undersigned herewith assumes command of the U.S. Army Special Warfare Center and School.

> RUDOLPH G. MACMILLAN
> Lieut. Colonel, Infantry
> Commandant

"Unless you have to, Mac," Lowell said, "don't let that assumption of command get out any sooner than it has to. Send it over to the XVIII Airborne Corps in the last message center pickup tomorrow. Or even the next day. Say it got lost."

MacMillan looked at General Hanrahan for orders.

Hanrahan nodded.

Lowell took one of the copies of the first order and handed it to the Spec-7.

The Spec-7 read the orders. He was an old soldier and reading what was not written down came automatically to him: Colonel Minor, whoever he was, was getting his ass booted out of Headquarters, U.S. Army Special Warfare Center and School.

"Yes, sir," the Spec-7 said.

"Just go to Colonel Minor, Mac," General Hanrahan said, "at his quarters if necessary, and hand him one of these. Don't talk to him about it, and for Christ's sake, don't let your mouth run away with you. Just give it to him, salute, and leave."

"OK," MacMillan said.

"I'll call you in the morning," Hanrahan said. "You better get going."

MacMillan saluted, and marched off.

"Well," Lowell said to Hanrahan, "Mac finally gets to command something larger than a platoon."

Hanrahan looked at him and saw that Lowell was not being sarcastic.

"I'm still a little worried about this," he said.

"You couldn't leave Minor in command," Lowell said. "How many times do you want to get stabbed in the back?"

"You going to Hood tonight?" Hanrahan asked.

"As soon as the Air Force fuels, ever so reluctantly, the Commander," Lowell said.

"You almost went to the stockade," Hanrahan said.

"*'L'audace, l'audace, toujours l'audace, mon général,'*" Lowell quoted.

"*Merde*," Hanrahan said, laughing, and then: "Craig, I want you to take Ski with you to Hood."

Lowell's eyebrows rose in question.

"He'll be useful to you," Hanrahan said. Lowell nodded. "And I want to keep him as far out of the line of fire as I can."

Lowell nodded again.

"I may lose this battle," Hanrahan said. "There's no sense in taking Ski down with me."

Lowell turned to the Spec-7.

"When you get around to cutting orders sending me to Hood," he said, "put Mr. Wojinski on them."

"Yes, sir."

"If I were you, Paul," Lowell said, "I'd get on the horn to Felter. If you don't want to call him, I will."

"I think Felter's got enough to keep him busy right now without worrying about Paul Hanrahan," Hanrahan said. "I'd like to keep him in reserve for something more important than my problems."

"Don't close out that option," Lowell said.

"Have fun in the mud at Hood, Craig," General Hanrahan said, and put out his hand.

He left the room. Lowell got on the telephone and asked for in-flight weather across the Gulf of Mexico. When the Air Force forecaster started reciting the known weather at thirty thousand feet, Lowell had to stop him and tell him he was interested in low-altitude weather, nothing over twelve thousand. He was flying an Aero Commander, not an F-101.

When he had the low-altitude weather, and started to walk out of the office, the Spec-7 called after him: "Colonel?"

Lowell turned to look at him.

"If you should ever need a job as a clerk-typist..." the Spec-7 said.

"I take that as a compliment of the first degree," Lowell said.

"That was my intention, sir," the Spec-7 said.

(Four)
The Officers' Open Mess
Fort Hood, Texas
0605 Hours, 23 October 1962

Chief Warrant Officer (W-2) Stefan T. Wojinski, like most long-time enlisted men, was seldom comfortable when general officers were looking at him. And he was especially uncomfortable now, for there was a major general looking at him in a way that clearly indicated he was annoyed, and perhaps even worse.

The major general was having his breakfast at the head of two four-man tables pushed together in the cafeteria of the Officers' Open Mess. He was dressed in fatigues; and as if to symbolize that the 2nd Armored Division was very likely on its way to war, he wore a .45 Colt pistol in a shoulder holster.

The only officers in the room not wearing pistols and fatigues were Lieutenant Colonel Craig W. Lowell and CWO Wojinski, who were in class "A"s.

Wojinski wasn't even sure what he was doing here. He had no idea why General Hanrahan had not sent him back to Bragg with Colonel Mac. The general had given him an explanation and all that. He'd told him Lowell was going to need him to help get the 2nd Armored Division moving. But that didn't make much sense, Wojinski thought, since General Hanrahan was as aware as he was that what he knew about armor could be written in large letters with a grease pencil inside a match book.

The real reason, Wojinski had finally realized, was that when Colonel Mac told that asshole, Colonel Minor, that he's on TDY to XVIII Airborne Corps (Get your ass out of here!), the shit was going to hit the fan, and the general didn't want him to get splattered with any of it.

Now yesterday had been a good time. No staring generals. No trouble. Just plain fun. What happened was that on the way over, Wojinski—sort of stretching the point since he knew even less about flying than he did about armor—had flown the Commander for almost two hours. Colonel Lowell, shortly after they took off, started to yawn.

"Pity you can't crap out, Duke," Wojinski said. "You must be beat."

"And you're bushy-tailed and wide awake?"

"I slept all the way, mostly, from South Dakota."

"Let me show you how this thing works," Lowell said. "And then you sit here and wake me up in case something goes wrong."

The Duke had shown him how to read the altimeter and how the Radio Direction Finders worked, and what a blip on the radar meant, and then announced he was going to "doze a little." He told Wojinski to wake him if anything went wrong, and particularly if "any little red lights come on."

Wojinski didn't touch anything except the ashtray lid while he was at the controls. He just sat there and watched the needles, and watched for red lights to come on. But if there are only two guys in an airplane flying at twelve thousand feet right across the Gulf of Mexico from Florida to Texas, and one of them is sound asleep, who's flying?

When they landed at Houston, the Duke told him to "follow me through," which meant that Ski kept his hand on the wheel and his feet on the rudder pedals as the Duke landed the airplane. Though they had enough fuel to make Fort Hood without stopping, Lowell told him they were landing at Houston so they wouldn't be almost out of gas when they got there, because he wasn't sure they'd be able to get any at the Army Air Field, and because he wanted to file a flight plan, which would let Hood know they were on their way.

They had come across the Gulf of Mexico without a flight plan.

"Why no flight plan then," Wojinski asked, "and then we make one now?"

"That gets complicated, Ski," the Duke said. "Unfortunately, we are not as well equipped as the authorities would like with over-the-drink gear. And making a dog-leg over land would cost us a couple of hours."

Translated, that meant if they went down in the Gulf, they would drown. It was something that Wojinski had thought about as he "flew." On the one hand it seemed stupid and dangerous, but on the other, he knew the Duke well enough to know he would not have done it if he thought there was more than a very slight chance that something would go wrong.

He "followed through" again when they took off from Houston, and when they landed at Fort Hood. His imagination took over, and he began to think about maybe applying for pilot's school. A fantasy he quickly talked himself out of. He liked being where he was.

When he went into the Army he never dreamed he would make warrant officer. And he knew, too, that if they'd ever made him take the written exam, he would still be running around with six stripes on his sleeves. He'd gotten the warrant when the Duke got his silver leaf, after they'd gone to Cuba and bailed Colonel Felter's ass out of the soup. The promotion was more like a medal than anything else, the big difference being that it meant he could retire on the same pay as a first john right now, and if he kept his nose clean, he could make W-4, and retire on a major's pay. Medals didn't pay a god-damned thing, except that there was some kind of a pension connected with the Congressional, and you got to send your kids to West Point. Two of Colonel Mac's were at the Point, and that saved him a bunch of money.

So now, anyhow, he was a chief warrant officer of Special Forces. He was somebody. He didn't think there were many aviation warrants who got to go hunting with the general and a bunch of colonels. In aviation, he would be just one more anonymous warrant who had somehow managed to get through flight school. The grass was not always greener.

When they landed at Hood it was almost three o'clock in the morning. By the time they got from the airfield to the post and into a BOQ, it was almost four.

"We have time for an hour and a half in the sack," Colonel Lowell told him. "Use it."

He woke up to the sound of the Duke having it out with Avis Rent-A-Car in Killeen, Texas. They were willing to send a car out to him, but they insisted that he drive the man who delivered the car back to Killeen. Colonel Lowell told them he didn't have time for that. He was polite at first, but when he didn't get his way, he jumped all over their ass. When the Duke was crossed, he could eat ass as well as anybody Ski had ever met. So he was not at all surprised when Avis sent two cars.

They went to 2nd Armored Division Headquarters, where Lowell got into another argument, this time with the staff duty officer. When the staff duty officer told him that the way he was supposed to report in was to go to the secretary of the general staff (who would come on duty at 0730), Lowell told the guy he was under orders to report to the commanding general immediately on arrival and that it was his intention to comply with his orders.

"I'm an inspector general on the staff of General Boone, Colonel," Lowell said. "And if you refuse to put me in touch with the commanding general right now, that fact will be par-agraph one in my report."

The staff duty officer turned white in the face.

"The general is having breakfast at the Officers' Open Mess, Colonel," he said. "If you wish to go there, I cannot, of course, stop you."

Ski wondered if the staff duty officer had gotten on the phone the minute they'd left his office. The *very* pissed look the general was giving them now made that seem a very likely thing.

"Are you trying to attract my attention, Colonel?" Major General Stuart G. Lemper asked.

"I had hoped to, sir," Lowell said. He walked closer to the table where the general was having a breakfast of scrambled eggs, sausage, and toast, came to attention, and saluted. Ski, three feet behind, copied him.

"Lieutenant Colonel Lowell reporting to General Lemper at the orders of General Boone, sir," Lowell said.

General Lemper returned the salute.

"And who is this gentleman?" he asked, thickly sarcastic, nodding at Ski. "Is he with you? Yet another expert to help us through our problems?"

"Sir," Lowell said, "may I introduce Chief Warrant Officer Wojinski?"

General Lemper almost immediately regretted his sarcasm. It was not this lieutenant colonel's fault that he had been sent here. General James G. Boone had sent him. He should not hold that against Lowell.

"Have you gentlemen had your breakfast?" General Lemper said, with considerably less venom. "Will you join me?"

"Thank you, sir," Lowell said.

There was a cafeteria line rather than waiter service.

"I'll get it, Colonel," Ski said. "What would you like?"

"Anything but grits," Lowell said.

When Ski had gone off to join the line, General Lemper looked at Lowell.

"All else having failed, General Boone sent a couple of snake-eaters?"

"Ski's a professional snake-eater, sir," Lowell said. "I'm

more of a paper pusher. Not that I want to be, but that's how it's turned out."

"What kind of paper?" General Lemper asked.

"When this came up, I was helping General Howard with the Howard Board," Lowell said.

"And he sent you to MacDill?"

"No, sir," Lowell said. "He's probably wondering where I am. General Jiggs is at MacDill. He asked for me."

"You're acquainted with Jiggs?"

"I once worked for him, sir."

"I have explained to General Jiggs our problems here," General Lemper said. "Would you say that your presence here, Colonel, indicates that my explanation was unsatisfactory to him? Or perhaps he understands, but General Boone is unable to?"

"Sir, General Boone instructed me to tell you that I am not here to find fault with any officer, but rather to help in any way I can."

"That's what is known as coating the cyanide pill with chocolate," General Lemper said. "Unless, of course, you are some sort of expert. Are you some sort of expert, Colonel?"

"No, sir," Lowell said. "I have never been assigned to an Armor unit larger than a battalion."

"But here you are to find fault with us, right?"

"I'm here to help in any way I can, General."

"When you're not writing science fiction for Triple H Howard, what do you do, Colonel?"

"I'm at the Aviation Board at Rucker, sir."

"General Boone must really think highly of me," General Lemper said. "To send an aviator and a Green Beret warrant officer to get me out of the rough."

Ski returned with two trays, set one in front of Lowell, and then sat down.

"I can only repeat, sir," Lowell said, "that my orders are to make myself useful in any way I can, and that I am not here to find fault."

"And you can make me a good price on a bridge in Brooklyn, right?" General Lemper said. And then he looked over Lowell's head. "You want to see me, Wallace?"

A huge chief warrant officer, a W-4—the most senior warrant—broad-shouldered, barrel-chested, and crew-cut, was standing almost at attention behind Lowell.

"I had hoped to have a word with the colonel, sir," he said, in a deep gravelly voice. "That is, if the colonel remembers me."

Lowell looked over his shoulder and got quickly to his feet. He was smiling broadly.

"Prince!" he said. "How the *hell* are you?"

He put out his hand, and it disappeared in the huge hand of Chief Warrant Officer Prince T. Wallace, and then the handshake turned into an embrace. They pounded each other on the back. It was an extraordinary demonstration of affection.

"I gather the colonel does indeed remember you, Wallace," General Lemper said dryly. "Curiosity overwhelms me."

"I was with the Duke in Task Force Lowell, sir, in the Pusan Breakout," Wallace said with quiet pride. "And then I went to the Yalu and back with him."

General Lemper, who had been a colonel in Europe at the time, had heard of Task Force Lowell. It had been a classic use of Armor in the breakthrough and the old Cavalry task of disrupting the enemy's lines of supply and communication. Lemper had gone from Germany to duty as an instructor at the Command and General Staff School at Fort Leavenworth, where he had replayed Task Force Lowell on the sand tables a dozen times. Task Force Lowell had made the textbooks.

"You're that Lowell?" General Lemper asked.

"Yes, sir," Chief Warrant Officer Wallace answered for him. "It had a bullshit name, Task Force Bengal, but we changed it."

"We had a stowaway, General," Lowell said. "In direct disobedience to orders, Prince, who devoutly believed I couldn't find my way across the street without his help, pulled a driver out of his hatch in an M46, threw him fifty feet into the bushes, and climbed in."

"I didn't throw anybody anywhere," Wallace corrected him. "I told him the chaplain wanted to see him. By the time he found the chaplain, we were gone."

"Maybe Paul Jiggs believed that," Lowell said. "I never did. I believed the kid with the pine cones in his nostrils. Say hello to Mr. Wojinski, Prince. I've known Ski even longer than I have you. Ski, this is Prince Wallace."

The two warrants shook hands.

"You *did* say, didn't you, Colonel," General Lemper said, "that you were acquainted with General Jiggs? But I *didn't*, did I, ask you how *well* acquainted?"

It was not the sort of question to which a reply was expected.

"Wallace," General Lemper said, "General Boone, very likely at the suggestion of General Jiggs, has sent Colonel Lowell over here to point out our errors to us."

"Well, sir," Wallace blurted, "if anybody can get us out of low gear, the Duke can."

Lowell's face tightened, almost into a wince. But to his surprise, General Lemper did not take offense.

"Our basic problem, Lowell, is rail transportation," General Lemper said. "That can be further defined as follows: (a) The Congress has not seen fit to fund the construction of an adequate rail yard here, or to provide sufficient switching locomotives. (b) The railroads, although I am sure they are doing their best, have not been able to furnish us with enough flatcars, particularly of the type without braking wheels at one end, which means we cannot simply form a train of flatcars and drive tanks and other heavy vehicles onto it. (c) In their haste to provide us with the cars we have requested, the incoming empty trains are mixed: flatcars and boxcars. This necessitates our forming new trains, composed of cars in the order we need them."

"Yes, sir."

"With our limited rail yard facilities, this is time consuming. And so is the necessity of backing up one car at a time to a ramp, so that a tank can be loaded. Do you see the problem?"

"Yes, sir."

"We are working two shifts, each of twelve hours," General Lemper went on. "The enthusiasm of the men is such, Colonel, that I have had to threaten disciplinary action against any commanding officer I catch permitting his men to work more than sixteen hours."

"Yes, sir."

"Can you see a solution to this problem, Colonel, right off the top of your head?" General Lemper asked.

"No, sir," Lowell said. "I cannot."

"Would you like to have a look around, Colonel? You *might* just *think* of something if you saw the system in operation."

"If that is the general's desire, sir," Lowell said. "Perhaps I could make a suggestion, here and there."

"I think Generals Boone and Jiggs expect more of you than that, Colonel," General Lemper said. "Wallace, I want you to take Colonel Lowell and his people around, anywhere they wish to go. If Colonel Lowell sees any means to speed up our loading, I want it implemented, then and there. You will inform anyone who questions this that Colonel Lowell is acting at my specific orders, and that any objections to his suggestions will be made to me personally, *after the fact*. If General Boone and you both believe that Lowell is the man to get us out of low gear, far be it from me to stand in his way. Is that clear to you?"

"Yes, sir," Chief Warrant Officer Wallace said.

(Five)
Fort Bragg, North Carolina
0715 Hours, 23 October 1962

Master Sergeant Peter C. Crowley, who was operations sergeant of "A" Team Number Seven of Company "A," Fifth Special Forces Group, was a squat, crew-cut man of thirty. He had been in the Army since he was seventeen, and he could not remember ever having been as pissed at the dumb sonsofbitches in charge as he was at this moment.

At the moment, he was behind the wheel of a GMC six-by-six, in a small convoy consisting of a jeep (up front with a sign reading CONVOY FOLLOWS hanging from its bumper), two three-quarter-ton Dodge trucks, another six-by-six GMC, and a jeep trailing (with a sign reading END OF CONVOY hanging from its rear bumper).

In the "Regular" army, which, from Master Sergeant Crowley's point of reference meant anything but Special Forces, master sergeants did not normally drive trucks. Trucks were driven by PFCs or corporals, who had the appropriate MOS*, and did nothing else but drive trucks.

Master Sergeant Crowley was at the wheel of the GMC six-by-six because there were no PFCs or corporals around to drive it. The junior member of his "A" Team was a staff sergeant. There were six vehicles assigned to the "A," which had a strength of two officers and seven enlisted men. Only the officers (one in each jeep) and one of the noncoms (Sergeant First Class Willy Stern) did not have the additional duty of "Wheeled Vehicle Operator."

SFC Stern knew something about jeeps and trucks, and so he had the unofficial responsibility of fixing them when they broke. He was carried as a passenger in one of the three-quarter-tons, from which he could be dropped off to aid a stalled vehicle. That was convenient, because following an incident in which the North Carolina State Police had charged SFC Stern with exceeding the posted sixty miles per hour speed limit by fifty miles per hour, the judge in Fayetteville had suspended his license for six months, and the Army, in a spirit of cooperation with civilian authorities, had pulled his GI license "permanently."

At approximately 0345 hours that morning, Master Sergeant Crowley had been wakened in his quarters by a telephone call from first Sergeant Tom Spencer of Company "A," Fifth Special Forces Group. Mrs. Crowley was like a wet cat when wakened from her sleep by a ringing telephone, and she had hissed and muttered and raked her claws along the sheets while First Sergeant Spencer informed Master Sergeant Crowley that an alert had been called, and the log would show that Master Sergeant Crowley had been notified at 0347 Hours.

*Military Occupational Specialty.

"Where we going?" Crowley asked.

"Camp McCall, where else?" Spencer said, and hung up.

That was so much bullshit, of course. The Cuban thing was about to happen, and they were obviously going to be involved. Camp McCall was the Special Forces training area, an otherwise deserted World War II Army base where what barracks and other buildings had not collapsed of old age had been torn down as health and safety hazards. Wherever the team was being sent, it was not being sent to the Carolina Boonies. Spencer couldn't say anything on the phone, of course, and it had been dumb to ask.

The only thing that surprised Master Sergeant Crowley was how long it had taken the bastards to blow the whistle.

He had then turned the bedside table lamp on, which normally caused Mrs. Crowley to arch her back, show her teeth, and bare her claws even more than the ring of the telephone.

"Where you going?" Mrs. Crowley asked, almost civilly.

"McCall," he said.

"Like hell," she said, and pushed herself out of bed. She went into the kitchen, and he could hear the sound of the teakettle on the stove as he dialed the two numbers he was responsible for in the telephone alert procedure, those of the two officers.

That worked like sort of a pyramid. Headquarters—usually Sergeant Major Taylor, once the word was given—called two numbers at Headquarters, Fifth Group. One of the two people he called relayed the word to somebody else at Fifth Group, the other one called somebody at one of the companies. If there was no answer, there was an alternate name. Everybody that got called was responsible for calling two other people. In a matter of minutes, everybody had the word.

One of the people Crowley called was the "A" Team commander, Captain Dick Brewer, who had just got his railroad tracks and who, because he wasn't eligible for housing on the base, lived in Fayetteville. Brewer would call the other officer, Lieutenant Bob McGrory, who also lived in Fayetteville. Then, since they had reached the bottom of the pyramid, and there was nobody else to call, they would each call one other guy to make sure he'd gotten the word. Then one or the other of them would pick up the other officer (and whoever else on the team who lived in Fayetteville and needed a ride) and drove to Smokebomb Hill on the post.

Master Sergeant Crowley was prepared for an alert. The hall closet held a completely packed set of field gear, everything but a weapon and ammunition, and a small web bag packed with Master Sergeant Crowley's creature comforts, ranging from Band-Aids and Preparation H to a sealed can of cigars and two well-wrapped quart bottles of Jack Daniel's Old Number 7.

All he had to do for an alert was put on his fatigues, grab the field gear, and go.

This wasn't an ordinary alert, however, and when he had his pants and boots on he went to the bedroom closet and took from it a shoulder holster and a Colt Trooper Mark III .357 Magnum revolver. Taking your own weapon with you was expressly forbidden, and Crowley supposed that here and there there were probably a couple of guys who didn't. He devoutly hoped that he would never have to use the .357, but it was nice to have in case something came up.

Mrs. Crowley, carrying a cup of instant coffee, came into the bedroom as he was putting his arms into the shoulder holster's loops.

"You want a doughnut or something?" she asked.

"No, thanks," he said.

"Camp McCall, like hell," she repeated.

"This is what I do for a living," he said.

"I noticed," she said.

He put on his fatigue shirt and tucked it in his trousers, then picked up his field jacket and his beret and put them on.

"Don't get her all excited," Mrs. Crowley said when he stepped past her into the corridor, obviously headed for the kid's room.

The kid was sleeping like a log, and only stirred when he bent over and kissed the top of her head.

"You all right for dough?" he asked as he walked into the kitchen.

"Yeah. How long are you going to be gone?"

"I've done this before," he said. "We go out to McCall, pitch tents, run around in the woods for a couple of days, and come back."

"Do you know and just won't tell me?"

"Spencer said McCall," he said. "Now you know as much as I do."

They looked at each other a moment, until he bent and kissed her, allowing his hand to drop down and cup her buttocks, and then he pulled open the kitchen door and went out to the carport.

As he pulled the Olds's door closed, he heard her say, softly, "Take care of yourself, Peter."

When he got to Smokebomb Hill, Spencer gave him the requisitions. He looked at them in disbelief.

Blank ammunition; inert shells for the rocket launchers; artillery simulators; explosive charge simulators, inert.

"What the hell is this?"

"So far as I know, you can read."

"You mean we're really going to *Camp McCall?*"

"So they tell me."

"Is this another of Minor's nutty ideas? Where's the general?"

"I dunno, and I dunno," First Sergeant Spencer replied.

"Jesus H. Christ!" Crowley said.

"Do me a favor, Pete," First Sergeant Spencer said. "Shut up and load up."

It was not necessary to go to the ammo point for the "ammunition" and "explosives," because, since the stuff was hardly any more dangerous than fireworks, permission had been granted to store it in a bunker near Smokebomb Hill. By the time the officers arrived, Crowley's "A" Team was ready to roll.

The officers were summoned to a meeting, and returned with the information that they were to fill the Jerry cans.

"What the hell for? We can go back and forth to McCall a half dozen times on a tank of gas."

"*Ours* not to reason why, Sergeant Crowley, *yours* but to fill the goddamned cans."

Filling the cans was a pain in the ass, and the goddamned things would have to be unfilled when the alert was over. Which meant returned to a MOGAS storage tank by pouring them through a filtered funnel. That took forever and was another genuine pain in the ass.

Thirty minutes later, after the Jerry cans were filled and the CONVOY signs hung on the jeeps, Crowley's "A" Team rolled slowly away from Smokebomb Hill toward the Range Road, and the back gate that offered the shortest route to Camp McCall.

The Fifth Special Forces Group was about to run around in the woods at McCall, eating snakes and making warlike noises, while the Regular army was gearing up to kick the Cuban ass. Crowley had never been so pissed in his life.

And not only that, he had been so eager that he hadn't had a goddamned thing to eat since an early hot-dog-and-beans supper.

And then he saw the Beret standing by the side of the road making MP arm signals. They were being directed off onto a dirt road.

Crowley knew what this was, he'd bet a dime to a doughnut. The minute the general was out of sight, Colonel Minor was always up to something chickenshit like surprise inspections or unscheduled alerts. Today he was putting the two together. First he called an alert, and now he was going to have the Ordnance creeps from the post on a back road. They would check the vehicles to see when they had last been serviced. They'd measure the depth of the tread of the tires, and make sure the MOGUS ONLY sign painted over the gas tank cap was legible. And issue formal inspection reports, which had to be answered.

A quarter mile down the dirt road there was a field on which was a collection of vehicles that at first confirmed Crowley's darkest suspicions. But then it turned out that this was not an Ordnance inspection team. Everybody out here was wearing a green beret. He saw Sergeant Major Taylor and Lieutenant Colonel Mac MacMillan, in fatigues. But no Colonel Minor.

A sergeant Crowley recognized as one of the candy-asses

at Center Headquarters stepped up on the GMC's running board.

"The first thing you do is drive down to the end of the field and dump the blanks and the rest of that shit," he said. "Then you go to those trucks over there and pick up live ammo and explosives. When you've done that, you get in line over there and go up to the guys at the tables. They'll give you your pay records, fuel vouchers, meal vouchers, and the rest of it. And road maps."

"Where the hell are we going?"

"MacDill Air Force Base," the sergeant said. Then he added, in what he thought was a credible Cuban accent, "Hey, GI, you wanna fook my seester?"

IV

(One)
Rail Marshaling Yards
Fort Hood, Texas
1015 Hours, 23 October 1962

"Sir," Captain Dwayne Smitherman's first sergeant said, opening the door of Captain Smitherman's compartment a crack. "There's a light colonel from the I.G.'s office out here to see you."

"Jesus!" Captain Smitherman said, removing his feet from their resting place on the table. He was a tall, lanky, loose-limbed young man with a pleasant, easygoing look. He stood up, quickly checked the buttons on his fatigue shirt to make sure they were buttoned, looked down at his boots, saw that they were scuffed, and decided it was too late to do anything about them now. He went out of the compartment into the corridor.

There were two officers with the light bird in the corridor, a chief warrant Smitherman had seen in G-3, and another chief warrant wearing a green beret. The presence of an I.G. worried Smitherman. There was nothing for which he could be called to account that he could think of. But some of his troops had discovered a new guardhouse lawyer technique that he could think of no legal means to counter. They ran to the I.G. the moment someone talked rudely to them and complained of "racial or ethnic discrimination."

That Captain Smitherman was himself what his grandfather had called "colored," his father "Negro," and Smitherman "Black" didn't get him off the hook any easier than if he had been a freckle-faced redhead named O'Grogarty. Investigations were called for, and long letters headed "Report of Investigation Into Allegations of Racial Prejudice Claimed by Sp-4 JONES, Franklin D." had to be written.

Smitherman came to attention and saluted.

"Sir, Captain Dwayne Smitherman, Commanding, 4027th Engineer Light Equipment Company."

"Good morning, Captain," the light bird said. "My name is Lowell. This is Mr. Wojinski and Mr. Wallace."

He was an elegant sonofabitch, Smitherman thought. That uniform hadn't come off the "Slightly Irregular-Reduced Price" racks in the clothing sales store.

"I know Mr. Wallace, sir," Smitherman said, as he shook their hands. "My first sergeant, Colonel, tells me that you're the inspector general."

"I'm *an* inspector general," Lowell said, "from JAF."

"JAF, sir?"

"The Joint Assault Force, at MacDill," Lowell explained.

"I believe you'll find everything is in order, sir. We're loaded and waiting to be hauled off. But perhaps there's something in particular the colonel would like to see?"

"Some of those steaming cups of coffee we saw your mess sergeant passing out, Captain, would be very nice," Lowell said.

"Yes, sir. My pleasure, sir. First Sergeant?"

"I've already sent for coffee for these gentlemen, sir," the first sergeant said.

"As you can see I have a first sergeant who looks ahead," Smitherman said.

"And is there someplace where we could sit down?" Lowell asked. "I have walked farther this morning than the sum of the distance I've walked in the last two years."

"Yes, of course," Smitherman said. "The seats are a little

dusty—I don't think this car has rolled in years—but they're soft."

He led them into his compartment.

A moment later, a fat little man in cook's white bustled in with a stainless pitcher of coffee and a handful of mugs. On his heels was a skinny young man in whites with condensed milk and sugar and a bowl full of spoons.

"If the colonel would like some, I'm about to make doughnuts, it'd just take a minute."

"We accept," Lowell said, "with profound gratitude."

"Now, how may I help the colonel?" Captain Smitherman said.

"You're loaded, you said, and ready to be hauled off?"

"Yes, sir."

"All of your equipment?"

"Everything but the rock crusher, sir. I have been told there is one in crates which will be furnished to us at the port of embarkation."

"That's quite an accomplishment, Captain," Lowell said.

"Well, sir, it's easy to move things if you have the equipment to move them."

"I suppose it is," Colonel Lowell said, smiling. "I was just thinking, Captain, that I've never seen an Engineer *Heavy* Equipment Company."

"Sir?"

"You, Ski?" Lowell asked.

"No, sir," Wojinski said.

"Maybe when they put in the floating harbor on D-Day in France, *that* was a Heavy Equipment Company," Warrant Officer Wallace suggested.

"What I was leading up to, Captain," Colonel Lowell said, "is that I don't suppose there's anything that an Engineer *Light* Equipment Company couldn't pick up and move around, is there?"

"No, sir," Captain Smitherman said, "I don't suppose there is."

Lowell smiled at him.

"Fifty tons, maybe?" he asked.

"Colonel, two months ago, we picked up the whole Combat Command "A" Headquarters Building, two stories tall, fifty two point five feet by one hundred twelve, and moved it two miles."

"Fascinating," Wojinski said.

"In other words, for the sake of conversation," Colonel Lowell said, "you could pick up and move an object, say twenty-five feet long, twelve feet wide, eleven feet tall, and weighing forty-seven tons?"

"Yes, sir," Captain Smitherman said.

"You could pick it up, say, six feet, and move it, say, twenty feet sidewards over an obstacle?"

"Yes, sir," Captain Smitherman said. He was beginning to smell a rat. "That would depend, Colonel, on the size of the obstacle."

"Say six feet tall and twenty feet wide."

"Yes, sir," Smitherman said. "We could handle that."

"Let's carry this a little further," Colonel Lowell said. "How long would it take you to set up to move such an object?"

"Not long. No more than an hour, sir."

"And let us suppose that after you moved this object, you wanted to put it back where it was. How long would that take you?"

"Once we were set up, Colonel, it wouldn't take us more than a couple of minutes."

"And how long could you keep this up?"

"Indefinitely, sir."

"Now, suppose there were several objects that had to be simultaneously lifted and moved the way we've been talking about. How many objects could you move at one time with the equipment you have presently available to you?"

It took Captain Smitherman a moment to come up with the answer to that one. "Four, sir," he said finally.

Colonel Lowell smiled almost fondly at Captain Smitherman.

"Now, understand that I don't doubt your word, Captain, but Mr. Wojinski is a snake-eater who deals with nothing more complicated than spears and rocks. One has to explain things to Green Berets in simple terms, as to a child. Would you very much mind taking a piece of paper and showing Ski how you would do this, step by step?"

"Not at all, sir," Smitherman said. He was now convinced that he was about to be had, but he had no idea how.

He took several sheets of paper from his attaché case, and using that as a desk, sketched how he would solve the problem posed to him by Colonel Lowell.

He would place a "Drag Line, Self-Propelled, 25-ton Capacity" at each corner of the object to be moved, and a "Tractor, Caterpillar, D3," on the other side of the six-foot-tall, twenty-foot-wide obstacle.

"I would then devise some sort of a lifting cradle of steel cable—"

"Let's just say," Colonel Lowell interrupted him, "that the object has lifting hooks."

"In that case, sir, it would be much easier. The drag lines would lift the object to a height greater than the height of the obstacle. The Cat would then, by a cable attached to the object, pull it over the obstacle. The drag line operators would permit their booms to swing as the object was being pulled away from them."

"And could they, if they wanted, lower the object gently onto the obstacle itself?" Colonel Lowell said.

"Yes, sir," Captain Smitherman said.

"Mr. Wallace," Colonel Lowell said. "I hope that you have been paying close attention to this."

"Yes, sir."

"There are several morals to be learned," Lowell said. "First, that if you don't know what you're doing, ask somebody who probably does. Second, that if there's a will, there's a way. And third, virtue is very often its own reward."

"Yes, sir," Wallace said, solemnly. "I will try to remember that, Colonel."

Lowell turned to Captain Smitherman.

"Congratulations, Captain," he said. "A kind fate has put you in a position to get the 2nd Armored Division off the dime."

"Sir?"

"Will you please call your first sergeant in here and tell him to get the troops off their racks? They're about to load some tanks."

Now that it was out in the open, Smitherman wondered why he was surprised. The colonel probably fondly believed he was the first one to think of loading tanks on flatcars using heavy Engineer equipment. Smitherman had thought of it often himself.

"Sir," Captain Smitherman said uncomfortably, "it's specifically forbidden by regulation to use drag lines to lift tanks."

"Is that so?" Colonel Lowell asked. "Do you happen to know why?"

"The danger to the equipment is too great."

"You mean the weight could snap the cables?"

"Either snap the cable or cause the booms to fail, sir," Smitherman said.

"Explain that to me, please," Lowell said.

"There's a thirty-three and one-third percent safety factor built into the equipment, sir. In other words, equipment with a ten-ton capacity can really lift about thirteen point three tons. I don't know exactly what an M48A5 weighs—"

"Ninety-four thousand, six hundred pounds, give or take a couple of hundred," Colonel Lowell said. "Right at forty-seven tons."

"Yes, sir. What I'm trying to point out, Colonel, is that that much weight exceeds the combined rated load of four drag lines by seven tons."

"But with the safety factor, four of your machines should be able to lift fifty-two tons. As a matter of fact, fifty-three point two tons."

"Yes, sir, but, in this case, if just one cable should snap, or any other part of one machine should fail, that would divide the weight between the remaining three. Let's see, that would put a little under sixteen tons on each of the remaining machines, and they could be expected to fail. And when I say fail, sir, I mean they'd more than likely be destroyed."

"You're going to just have to take that risk," Lowell said.

"Tell your men to be careful. Take the strains cautiously, work together."

"Sir, I respectfully repeat that it's against regulations," Captain Smitherman said, "and I can't do it."

"Your intact drag lines would look pretty silly on a Cuban beach when the division's tanks are sitting in Texas," Lowell said. "Has that occurred to you?"

"Sir, respectfully, regulations are regulations."

"Captain, are you familiar with the name E. Z. Black?"

"General Black? Yes, sir."

"General Black is famous in the service for a number of things," Colonel Lowell said. "But perhaps most famous for his temper when aroused. I have been reliably informed that an incident in Korea triggered his rage almost as much as when he had elements of your own division across the Elbe, was about to take Berlin, and received a radio call to halt in place and let our Russian allies take it."

"I've heard that story, sir," Smitherman said.

It was division legend that General Black had methodically kicked each of the windows out of his van while he was warming up to a full rage.

"As I was saying, Captain, he was angered almost to the same degree in Korea. Have you heard *that* story?"

"No, sir."

"A colonel told General Black that he couldn't do something he wanted to do because it was against regulations," Lowell said. "The gist of General Black's remarks on that occasion, which no one who heard them will ever forget—phrased as they were in the somewhat colorful language of the cavalryman—is that regulations are for the *guidance* of the commander, *only;* that they did not come off Mount Sinai graven on stone; that the only order or regulation binding on a commander is the execution of his mission. And that any officer who doesn't know that should not be entrusted with the command of anything more important than a Quartermaster Corps mess-kit repair platoon. Am I making my point, Captain?"

"Sir, with all respect—"

"In the worst possible scenario here," Lowell interrupted him, "we would load zero tanks before your equipment failed. We would then be no worse off than we are now. Your equipment, by itself, has zero value to this operation. On the other hand, depending on how well you have trained your people and maintained your equipment, and with a little bit of luck, we can perhaps load a lot of tanks without destroying all of your equipment. So far as I'm concerned, that's it."

"Sir, is that your decision to make?" Smitherman asked.

"Tell him, Wallace," Lowell said.

"Sir," Wallace said, "General Lemper asked me to come along with Colonel Lowell, and to tell anyone who questioned Colonel Lowell's authority that he was to first comply with Colonel Lowell's orders, and then complain about it, personally, to the general later."

"Actually," Lowell said, "the general's words were 'after the fact.' Now, are you going to take Mr. Wallace's and my word about that, or do you want to run over and ask General Lemper yourself?"

Captain Smitherman looked at Lowell, whose eyebrows were raised in amusement and question.

"First Sergeant!" Captain Smitherman bawled.

(Two)
Office of the Commanding General
XVIII Airborne Corps
Fort Bragg, North Carolina
1845 Hours, 23 October 1962

Major General Kenneth L. Harke, Chief of Staff, XVIII Airborne Corps, in the absence of Lieutenant General H. H. "Triple H" Howard, XVIII Corps commanding general (who was off at Benning as Chairman of the Howard Board, which had been charged by Secretary of Defense McNamara with developing an airmobile division), was now for all practical purposes the XVIII Corps commander.

Things were bad in Vietnam and getting worse, and McNamara saw in the concept of an Army division equipped with enough helicopters and other aircraft to be entirely self-transportable by air a way around MacArthur's fears about the United States getting involved in a war on the Asian land mass.

The United States was daily getting more and more involved in such a war, so the question was not *whether* such a war should be fought, but *how*. Howard, the third H. H. Howard to wear the three stars of a lieutenant general, and a man generally recognized as one of the Army's few really brilliant officers (some said only Max Taylor was brighter, and Taylor—now the President's military advisor—was long retired) had been given the job of designing an airmobile division. And he had gotten an extraordinary amount of authority in order to do that.

While Howard had not been relieved of his command of XVIII Airborne Corps and Fort Bragg, he was spending just about all of his time at Benning. There the Howard Board—lavishly funded—was finding out just how quickly platoons and companies and battalions could be moved by helicopter from one place to another. This was done by actually moving the troops around in as realistic tests as could be developed.

When he wasn't at Bragg, Triple H Howard was in Washington, fighting an enemy attired in Air Force blue. The Air Force bitterly resented the notion of the Army having its own in-theater airlift capability, and grew hysterical at the notion that it might be a good idea to arm Army aircraft.

The result of all this was that Major General Harke found himself running XVIII Airborne Corps. That would have been a prestigious assignment under any circumstances. But now, since the invasion of Cuba was just days away, and since that invasion was to be led by the 82nd Airborne Division, which was assigned to XVIII Corps, it was arguably the best place Major General Kenneth L. Harke could find himself.

Secretary of Defense McNamara placed such a priority on the Howard Board that it was likely that Triple H Howard would not be permitted to leave Benning and resume command of XVIII Corps. Harke would thus be in a position to demonstrate his ability to command a corps by actually commanding it in action in Cuba. If he did that, he was assured of at least a third star, and probably later a fourth. So for him Commander in

Chief, Pacific, or C-in-C, Europe, or NATO Commander, or even Chief of Staff was no longer simply a fantasy.

Major General Harke had been away from his office all day, and was tired when he got out of the Ford staff car at the rear of the building, a converted three-story brick building directly across from Post Theater #1 on the main post.

When General Harke walked into the reception room outside his office, everyone in the room stood up. In the red-leather-upholstered chair nearest the sergeant major's desk was Colonel Roland G. Minor, Deputy (at the moment "Acting") Commander of the U.S. Army Special Warfare Center and School.

"Is it important, Minor?" General Harke said. "I'm bushed."

"I have been presented, sir, with Special Orders personally signed by General Hanrahan placing me on TDY to Corps, sir. MacMillan has assumed command. For all practical purposes, sir, I have been relieved."

A wave of anger flushed through General Harke.

Goddamn Hanrahan! I will have that insubordinate, disloyal sonofabitch's head on a pole or die trying.

"I guess you had better come in, Colonel, and tell me about it," General Harke said. His voice was level and calm, as if Colonel Minor had come to tell him about arrangements for the post bowling tournament.

"Excuse me, General," the sergeant major said. "The general is here."

He looked at him in surprise.

"He came in about an hour ago, sir," the sergeant major said. "I told him where you were."

"Stay where you are, Minor," General Harke said.

"Yes, sir," Colonel Minor said.

Harke went to the door to the office of the commanding general and knocked, the act reminding him painfully that it was Triple H Howard's door, not his, and that he had been a fool to believe that Triple H Howard could be kept from the command of his corps if it was going to war.

"Come in," Howard called. Harke went inside and saluted.

"I hope I haven't kept you waiting long, sir."

"Not long, Ken," Howard said. "What's going on?"

General Howard was in fatigues. They were impeccably tailored and stiffly starched, to be sure, but they were fatigues. Over them he wore an olive drab zipper jacket with a fur collar. It was an aviator's jacket, and it was, by regulation, restricted to use when personnel were engaged in flight operations. General Howard had his own ideas about proper uniforms. He also had a World War II horsehide Air Corps jacket that he wore when the mood struck him.

The epaulets of the OD aviator's jacket carried the three stars of his rank. To the breast of the jacket were sewn a name tag, the XVIII Airborne Corps patch, and embroidered representations of three of General Howard's military qualification badges, his Combat Infantryman's Badge, his Aviator's wings (recently obtained; Howard figured that he better be able to fly planes if the Howard Board was going to be able to do the job it was supposed to), and his parachutist's wings. General Harke did not like the precedence General Howard had elected to give them, correctly believing it reflected General Howard's own opinion of their relative importance. His Combat Infantry Badge was on top. His aviator's wings were below the CIB, and the jump wings were on the bottom.

"Hanrahan sent Minor here on TDY, sir," Harke said. "In effect, he relieved him. He put MacMillan in charge over there."

"Over there" was Smokebomb Hill, the U.S. Army Special Warfare Center and School. Harke obviously didn't even like to use the name. General Howard made a disparaging "that's not important" gesture with his hand.

"What's happening with the Corps?" Howard said. "I'd like to have a look at the maps, get briefed."

"Yes, sir," Harke said. "I have the maps set up in the War Room, sir."

Howard led the way to the War Room, a conference room equipped much like a small theater: There was a small stage, a lectern, and a device that held more than twenty maps.

General Howard sat in one of the theater-type chairs and signaled General Harke to begin.

"I've been in Washington, General," Harke said, "where I met with the Deputy Chief of Staff for Operations and the Chief of Transportation, and in Fort Monroe, where I talked with the CONARC CG and his staff. The problems in both cases are logistical."

General Howard slumped low in his seat, took a light green panatela from his fatigues, lit it, and held it between his teeth.

"With the Air Force aircraft which have been made available to us, sir, we are prepared on thirty minutes' notice to move in one lift the forward element of 82nd Airborne Division Headquarters, the 505th Parachute Infantry Regiment, plus some supporting Artillery, Signal, Engineer, Ordnance, Medical, and Transportation personnel."

"The airlift is here? In place?" General Howard asked.

"Yes, sir," General Harke said. He went to the row of maps, pulled out a large-scale map of the north coast of Cuba, and pointed to it with a three-foot pointer as he continued.

"The first drop, on the plain between Cárdenas and Varadero, has as its mission the capture of the airport, and the elimination of any Cuban forces which would hinder the amphibious landing of initial elements of the 2nd Armored Division near Varadero. This is essentially the war plan DCSOPS drew up last year."

"I understand 2nd Armored has rail problems," Howard said.

"Yes, sir, my liaison officer has kept me abreast of that. It would appear General Lemper has some egg on his face."

"Is there anything we can do for them?" Howard asked.

General Harke reacted as if the question surprised him.

"I don't see how, sir. And it is General Lemper's problem, not ours. And as you will shortly hear, General, we have our own problems."

Howard just perceptibly nodded his head.

"Go on, Ken," he said.

"As you know, sir, as reinforced, the 505th Regiment, although it has not been formally designated as such, is actually a brigade—a pocket division—able to completely support itself in the initial stages of the operation. I have little concern that Phase One will go off as scheduled, and pretty much as it's supposed to.

"Phase Two, however, may cause trouble. Immediately after dropping the 505th, the Air Force aircraft are to return to Florida to enplane the 508th PIR. Then, depending on whether or not the airport has been secured, the 508th will either land at the airport, or parachute into the original drop zone.

"At present, we do not intend to send in the 502nd PIR, which is Corps Reserve, until the airport is secure."

"Is that a polite way of saying the 502nd won't go in until it's perfectly clear that *both* the air landing and the amphibious assault have gone off more or less successfully?"

"Yes, sir," Harke admitted.

"Well, then, let's hope General Lemper can somehow get 2nd Armored off the dime," General Howard said.

"It will be the mission," General Harke went on, "of the 502nd to accompany, as infantry, the by-then-landed balance of the 2nd Armored, which will advance along the coast road to Havana. The 505th and 508th will insure that no Cuban reinforcements are brought up against the port, or the 2nd Armored Division's rear."

"Sounds fine, Ken. What are our problems as you see them?"

"In my judgment, sir, we have been allocated shamefully insufficient sea-lift capability, and grossly inadequate heli-lift capability."

"'Shamefully'? 'Grossly inadequate'?" General Howard quoted. It was a question, not a challenge.

"Yes, sir. And conversely, I believe the heli-lift and sea-lift capability assigned by S-3 JAF to the 2nd Armored is in excess of its reasonable requirements. The JAF S-3 is General Jiggs, and predictably he has seen fit to take care of Armor. Even though they have far more TO&E* trucks than we do, they, nevertheless, have been augmented by General Jiggs with three TC** truck companies."

"They also have more tanks than we do," Howard said.

---

*TO&E: *T*able of *O*rganization & *E*quipment, prescribing the type and amount of equipment a unit is authorized.
**TC: *T*ransportation *C*orps.

"Tanks require vast quantities of fuel. Fuel has to be transported."

"The point is, sir, that we simply have to have more helicopters and more Otters and Beavers than we've been given by Jiggs. There is no way we can move rapidly toward Havana if we can't keep the 502nd supplied, and there is no other way to do it than by light aircraft. Would you like the tonnage figures, General?"

"I'm familiar with the tonnage figures, Ken," General Howard said.

"It is not a question of any problem getting light aircraft to Cuba," Harke went on. "Even an H-13 can make it across from Florida, if necessary. It poses no problem whatever for large helicopters. Beavers and Otters taking off from Key West can arrive in Cuba with three hours plus of fuel in their tanks."

"You're preaching to the saved, Ken," Howard said. "I presume you discussed this with Paul Jiggs?"

"General Jiggs rather bluntly informed me that the situation had been considered before his decisions were made, and that he did not have the time to enter into a debate with me about his decisions. I then attempted to bring our position to General Boone's attention, sir."

"And?"

"General Boone said he didn't have the time to discuss it with me, that I'd have to work it out myself with Jiggs. At that point, I felt the situation required that I discuss it with OCT* and DCSOPS**."

"What happened?"

"OCT agrees that 2nd Armored can do without some of its aviation assets, but DCSOPS wouldn't even listen to me. I was told rather bluntly that the decision was properly that of the Joint Assault Force commander, General Boone, and that DCSOPS would not presume to interfere."

"Did you really think they would?" Howard asked conversationally.

---

*OCT: *Office of the Chief of Transportation.*
**DCSOPS: *Deputy Chief of Staff for Operations.*

"Under the circumstances, General, I was prepared to take the heat for going out of channels. You're aware I went to CONARC, sir?"

"I heard about it," Howard said. "Let's hear your version of what happened."

"I went to CONARC because they have authority to allocate all Army aircraft in the country, those which have not already been assigned to JAF or the CONARC Reserve."

"And what did CONARC say?" Howard asked.

"The CONARC commander said that I could 'talk to Rucker' and see what fixed- and rotary-wing aircraft could be spared from the Aviation Center's training fleet 'in a pinch.' When I called Rucker, Rucker told me every aircraft which could be spared had already been sent to Florida, and that 'contingency plans' called for the shutting down of the school training program and sending what was left of the fleet to Joint Assault Force if necessary. And to change to that program, I was told, would require authority from JAF at MacDill."

"So you were back where you started?" Howard asked.

"Yes, sir. I didn't really expect to get anything from Rucker. Paul Jiggs left a Colonel Martinelli in command of Rucker when he went to MacDill to become Joint Assault Force J-3. Martinelli knows where his bread is buttered. If he was going to make extra aircraft available, he would make them available to JAF, not XVIII Corps."

General Howard shrugged. General Harke took the gesture to signal agreement.

"All of this," he said, "could have been avoided if XVIII Airborne Corps had been given the mission of invading Cuba, instead of some super-duper *ad hoc* Joint Assault Force which wasn't even in existence three weeks ago."

General Howard looked at him curiously, which again encouraged General Harke to continue.

"By definition, a corps is a headquarters under a lieutenant general commanding two or more divisions. Corps can be, and have been, a hell of a lot larger than two divisions, too. In Korea, I. D. White's X Corps (Group) had one American and three Korean corps under it, and he was only a lieutenant general. X Corps (Group) was an army in everything but name. There's no damned reason to have this demand Joint Assault Force under a four-star general, except that Armor doesn't want to find itself under an Airborne commander. If Armor had its way, they would invade Cuba the way Cavalry did in 1899, by lowering horses over the sides of ships into the ocean and swimming them ashore."

General Howard did not immediately reply. Harke realized that he'd got a little carried away.

"Got it all out, Ken?" Howard said.

"I guess I got a little carried away, sir."

"Yes, I think you did," Howard said. "You said something a moment ago about how this could all have been avoided."

"Yes, sir."

"It could have been avoided if you had done what I expected you to do, Ken, which was to get in touch with me when you were faced with a problem you didn't know how to handle."

Howard looked to his side, and pushed a telephone with his fingers. "I was no farther away than that."

"I was aware of how busy you were, sir, and didn't want to bother you."

"That was an error in judgment, Ken. I'm afraid it's going to prove costly."

"Sir?"

"I had a telephone call from the Chief of Staff about two o'clock. He told me that he had heard from General Boone. Since you had been running around the country out of channels, like a headless chicken, General Boone wanted to know if I could not be sent back here to take over from you. With the concurrence of the Secretary of Defense, here I am."

"I don't quite understand, sir."

"That, I'm afraid, is your basic problem, Ken. You go off half-cocked. You went off half-cocked here. The reason you're at the moment a little light on Army aviation is because, among other things, I have formed a provisional aviation battalion from the assets of the Howard Board. If we go to Cuba, there will be three helicopter transport companies, and one company each of Beavers, Otters, and Caribou. When I made these assets available to General Jiggs, he assigned them to XVIII Airborne Corps. He was fully aware that you needed more transport. He was prepared to close down the Aviation School and confiscate the Aviation Center Fleet to get it for you, if that was necessary."

"He said nothing to me, sir."

"He kept the XVIII Airborne Corps commander advised. I am the XVIII Corps commander, a fact that seems to have slipped your mind."

Harke's face stiffened.

"All you had to do, Ken," Howard went on, "was get on the phone to me, and you would have been told what was going on. I put off telling you about the provisional aviation battalion, because I wanted you to do as much as you could with what you had. I hoped, still hope, that I will be able to return to General Jiggs for use elsewhere some of the aircraft he has assigned here. In my judgment, the assignment of all of them here is over-generous."

Harke did not reply.

"I presumed, Ken, that you would have the common sense to understand that Paul Jiggs was named JAF S-3 because he was the best man for the job, and that he would allocate available assets with the mission in mind, and nothing else. I also presumed that you knew what is expected of a chief of staff. He is to do only those things in the name of his commander that he knows, without any question, the commander would do himself. And that when he doesn't know what to do, he is to ask the commander, not confuse being left in charge with assuming command."

General Harke's face was white.

"Obviously, I was wrong on both counts. And there is, unfortunately, more. When I tried to cover for you with General Boone, he put a question to me I was hard pressed to answer," General Howard said. "He asked me if I could not trust you to do what you were told, why should he?"

"I was acting as I believed the general would wish to me act, sir," Harke said.

"Did you listen to what you just said? It's an admission that you really believe if I had been here, and didn't get all the assets I thought I needed, that I would have jumped in an airplane and left my command with the balloon about to go up and rushed off to DCSOPS and told them those nasty boys in JAF were picking on me. For Christ's sake, Ken, you're an officer. When an officer gets an order he doesn't like, he salutes and says 'Yes, sir' and tries his damnedest to carry it out."

"Am I to understand that General Boone believes I should be relieved, sir?" Harke said.

"I'm sure he thinks you should, but if you're really asking did he tell me to relieve you, no. He left that decision to me. To be truthful, Ken, I would relieve you if I had somebody to replace you. But I don't. Until this Cuban thing is over, I need you. You will not be relieved for the moment."

"In that circumstance, sir," Harke said, angrily, "I can see no alternative but to respectfully demand, since you do not trust me, that I be relieved of my duties."

Now Howard's face tightened in anger.

"'Demand'?" he quoted furiously. "'*Demand*'? For Christ's sake! Sitting in my chair really went to your head, didn't it?"

Howard stopped, and it was a moment before he trusted himself to go on.

"General," he said, finally, speaking calmly and perhaps even a bit more slowly than normal, "the question of your trustworthiness and misapplication of the authority entrusted to you came up in another connection. General Boone asked me if I wasn't carrying my animosity toward Special Forces a little far. I told him that not only did I bear Special Forces no animosity, but that I had no idea what he was talking about. It was then I learned that in direct violation of my instructions to do nothing with the Special Warfare Center without my express permission you took it upon yourself to exclude them from this Cuban business. And you did that in a sneaky manner, by permitting General Hanrahan to go off hunting without telling him what was going on, and then 'by not being able to get in touch with him.'"

"Sir—"

"Be silent!" Howard snapped. "It was my intention to permit you to retire gracefully, General, in consideration of your past service, and because it does the Army no good when it becomes known that it has been necessary to relieve a general officer. I have now concluded neither I nor the Army can afford that gesture. You stand relieved, sir. Get out of my headquarters, and get out within the next three minutes, and on your way out, take your Colonel Minor with you. You might suggest to him that when Hanrahan writes and I endorse his efficiency report, it might well behoove him, too, to plan for immediate retirement."

General Harke, white-faced, marched stiffly up the aisle and out of the War Room.

General Howard's stomach churned. He looked at his cigar, and then lit it with a shaking hand.

Then he picked up the telephone beside him, and dialed a number from memory.

"General Howard for General McKee," he said. General McKee, the 82nd Division commander, came immediately on the line.

"I don't want to discuss this, Mac, and I don't want you to play games with me. I just relieved Ken Harke, and I need a chief of staff, right now. You can't have the job because I need you where you are, and I don't want your chief of staff. Now, who can you give me?"

He knew, as he had known on the trip from Benning to Bragg (realizing then that he might have to relieve Harke), that he had just the man for the job, but couldn't have him. One of Paul Jiggs's protégés, a lieutenant colonel named Lowell. Lowell would have been an ideal chief of staff. The problem was that he was a lieutenant colonel; the TO&E called for a major general. While Howard could dip to a promotable full colonel, he could not have an officer as junior as a lieutenant colonel.

Thirty minutes later, a young colonel, who had begun the day fully expecting that he might today parachute into Cuba in the command of his regiment, was ordered to report to XVIII Airborne Corps Headquarters. His bitter disappointment at being denied command of his regiment in a combat jump was only partially alleviated by his realization that there was probably no quicker way for a colonel to become a brigadier general than to do a good job in the next week or ten days as Chief of Staff, XVIII Airborne Corps.

(Three)
Headquarters
2nd Armored Division
Fort Hood, Texas
0645 Hours, 24 October 1962

"General," the post transportation officer, Colonel L. L. Sapphrey, said, "Major Gubbins has brought something to my attention that I thought I should bring to your attention, sir, as soon as possible."

Major Gubbins was the 2nd Armored Division's transportation officer. He had, General Lemper thought, obviously carefully arranged for Colonel Sapphrey to make his pitch for him. Colonels have more influence with generals than majors. He thought that was a clever thing for Gubbins to do, and wondered if Sapphrey had done it because he had been tricked into it, or because he was as annoyed with Lieutenant Colonel C. W. Lowell as Gubbins obviously was. There was no question in General Lemper's mind that Lowell was at the root of whatever it was.

There had been a telephone call from Major Gubbins the previous afternoon: "Does the general know that the Engineer Light Equipment Company has been off-loaded? At the orders of a Lieutenant Colonel Lowell?"

"No, I didn't," General Lemper had said.

"Does the general approve?" Gubbins had asked.

"I think we have to presume that Colonel Lowell had his reasons," Lemper had said.

He had no idea what Lowell was up to, but he had decided to give him twenty-four hours. That twenty-four hours was just about up.

"General," Colonel Sapphrey said, "these are the reports from the yardmaster." He waved a sheaf of paper. "In the twelve-hour period from 1200 yesterday until 2400, at the orders of Colonel Lowell, one hundred and eighty-two railcars, mixed flat, box, and tanker, have been ordered unladen to New Orleans."

"Let me see that," General Lemper said. As much trouble as they had getting railcars, something sounded wrong about sending any of them away unladen. And 182 railcars was a *lot* of railcars.

The yardmaster's report consisted of long columns of car numbers and some sort of a code General Lemper didn't understand.

"I don't understand this," he said.

"I understand the same pattern is continuing, sir, in the period between the end of this yardmaster's report and now," Colonel Sapphrey said.

"Can you look at this, Sapphrey, and tell me how many tanks have left?"

"Yes, sir," Sapphrey said. "It will take me a moment, sir."

Two minutes later, he reported that, if the figures could be believed, 217 tanks had left the yards on the trains in question.

"And there would be more, you would say, Colonel, in the time since the end of this report?"

"I would presume so, sir."

Lemper doubted that figure. As a logistic rule of thumb, under ideal conditions, he had always figured ten minutes per tank before the train was ready to roll. Six tanks per hour, twelve hours, seventy-two tanks. Two sidings capable of handling that, 144 tanks. Lowell was supposed to have loaded 180% of that figure.

"I think I'll go have a word with Colonel Lowell," General Lemper said. "Perhaps you gentlemen would like to accompany me?"

The Fort Hood rail marshaling yard was beyond the troop housing area and the tank parks. Beside the two-lane macadam road that ran from the tank parks was a dirt road, capable of handling two-way tank traffic. Tanks, because of their weight, cannot travel on macadam roads without almost immediately destroying the macadam surface and the base beneath it. On the other hand, because tanks are tracked vehicles, they can move with ease along badly chewed-up dirt roads. General Lemper saw that the dirt tank road was badly chewed up, which was not surprising, considering how many tanks were being moved along it, six feet apart, two abreast. The tanks were dusty, and muddy, and there was the smell of diesel fumes in the air.

When he got to the rail marshaling yards themselves, he saw that the double column of tanks did not turn into the marshaling yards. He was curious about that. At first he thought both columns were moving straight ahead, but as he got closer he saw that the left column, closest to the rail yards, split off and disappeared in the direction of the two loading docks in the marshaling yards.

The rest of the column continued on, reforming itself into two columns, and disappeared from sight down the road along the tracks that left the marshaling yards.

General Lemper saw a sergeant giving arm signals to one tank to turn off into the marshaling yard, and then to the tank behind it to continue moving straight ahead.

"Jerry, go straight," General Lemper said to his driver, a young and natty sergeant. Next to him sat Lieutenant Bill Cole, General Lemper's aide-de-camp, and Major Gubbins. Colonel L. L. Sapphrey sat beside the general in the back of the olive-drab Chevrolet.

The double line of tanks continued for a quarter of a mile, where it merged, under the hand signals of a sergeant, into one column. On the other side of the column, General Lemper spotted the observation windows of a caboose. As he watched it, it jerked into motion. He heard the crashing sound of a train starting up, and then, ten or fifteen seconds later, the sound of couplers crashing together as they do when a train stops.

The train itself was mixed flatcars and boxcars. There was nothing on the flatcars, and the doors of the boxcars were open. In perhaps half of the box cars, General Lemper could see jeeps, three-quarter-ton trucks, their cargo and water trailers, wooden crates, and palletized cargos. Soldiers in fatigues were also in these cars, either leaning against the open doors, or on the floor dangling their legs over the side. In one car he saw two sergeants sitting in folding aluminum-and-plastic-webbing lawn chairs, holding what looked very much like cans of Schlitz in their hands.

Most of the boxcars were empty, and all of the flatcars were unladen. The reason for that became evident a moment later when they came to four drag lines, parked on the far side of the column of tanks and the railroad tracks.

"Stop!" General Lemper ordered. He was out of the car the moment it halted.

Colonel Sapphrey started to follow him, as did the officers in the front seat.

"Stay," General Lemper ordered, and gestured with his hand.

Then he trotted along the column of tanks.

He heard some soldier say, "Jesus, there's the general."

He reached the end of the column of tanks.

Its four-man crew was standing to one side.

One of them spotted him.

"Atten-hut!"

"As you were," General Lemper said.

A heavily perspiring master sergeant was standing on the hood of a three-quarter-ton truck. His fists were held balled at waist level, with the thumbs sticking up.

As General Lemper watched, he began to make a slow up-and-down movement with his hands. There was the sound of diesel engines revving, and a moment later the ponging sound of steel cables being put under strain. The master sergeant raised his balled fists, thumbs extended, to the level of his ears. There was another roar of diesel engines, and then creaking; and the tank beside General Lemper rose, somewhat unsteadily, six feet into the air.

The master sergeant gave another arm signal, and the tank moved sideward. The master sergeant swung his hands before his face, palms now open, and the sideward motion stopped.

A horn blasted behind General Lemper, startling him. He turned and saw another M48A5 moving up where the lifted tank had been. All he could see of the driver was his head sticking out of the hatch. The kid looked torn between fear of the consequences of having blown his horn at the division commander and delight that he had made the old bastard jump.

General Lemper moved out of the way.

When he looked again, the M48A5 on the end of the cables was touching down on the flatcar.

The master sergeant crossed his hands, palms down, in a horizontal movement at the level of his waist. For the first time he noticed General Lemper. He came to attention, saluted crisply, and then climbed off the hood of the three-quarter-ton truck.

"What are you waiting for, an invitation?" he snarled at the tank crew. They ran quickly to the flatcar, freeing the cable hooks from the hoist points on the tank. Lemper saw a sergeant first class, presumably the tank commander, signal the heavy equipment operators that the cables were free, and as the train began to move a moment later, the four hooks rose into the air.

"Excuse me, sir," the master sergeant said, walking quickly past him. Lemper turned to watch him. First he signaled the driver to cut his engine, and he made a signal for the crew to get out.

"I'll go over this one more time," the master sergeant said. "When the hooks come down, grab them and put your weight on them. Otherwise they won't come all the way down. Then hook them up and get out of the way. As soon as it's on the flatcar, climb on and unhook them. Then chain the tank in place with your own chains. If you don't have your own chains, there's a six-by-six a hundred yards down that has chains. Any questions?"

There were no questions. The master sergeant walked quickly back to the three-quarter-ton truck and climbed onto the hood again.

Which explained why he was sweating so much, General Lemper thought.

He raised his wrist and pushed a button on his stainless steel chronometer.

The train crashed into movement again. Two boxcars passed. One was empty. The next was the one with the two sergeants sitting in their lawn chairs. The train crashed to a stop again when a flatcar was in place.

General Lemper watched as three more tanks were loaded, and then pressed the chronograph button again. When he looked at it, the elapsed-time dial showed fifteen minutes, forty-eight seconds.

Call it sixteen minutes, the general thought. They were loading tanks at a rate of one every four minutes. Fifteen an hour, presuming they had another train ready to roll up the tracks following this one. One point five times as fast, under lousy conditions, as what he considered to be a satisfactory loading time under ideal conditions.

Presuming he was still in command when this was over, General Lemper decided the division was going to spend a good deal of time practicing loading up. And he was going to look like a horse's ass when this got back to General Boone.

He walked to the three-quarter-ton and waited for the master sergeant to climb down off the hood.

"Very impressive, Sergeant," he said, as he returned the sergeant's salute.

"We're really loading the fuckers, General," the master sergeant said, with quiet pride.

"Keep it up," Lemper said. "Do you know where I can find Colonel Lowell?"

The sergeant looked distinctly uncomfortable.

"Where is he, Sergeant?" Lemper insisted.

"I believe the colonel went to ask the quartermaster to reconsider refusing to loan us his big forklifts, General," the sergeant said, formally.

"Do you know why Colonel Lowell wanted the forklifts?"

"I think he wants to load six-by-sixes with them, sir. I mean, onto flatcars, not the six-by-sixes theirselves."

"He'd probably be at the quartermaster warehouses?"

"Yes, sir, probably," the master sergeant said. He was obviously impatient to get back to work.

"Carry on, Sergeant," General Lemper said.

"Yes, sir," the master sergeant said.

Why the hell did I say that? "Carry on, Sergeant"? *I sound like David Niven in a movie about the British Army in India. All I need is jodhpurs and a riding crop.*

He walked back to the staff car. The driver held the door open for him, and he got in beside Colonel Sapphrey.

"What's going on here, sir?" Colonel Sapphrey asked.

"I'm not sure," General Lemper said, "but I am a devout believer in the philosophy that if it ain't broke, don't fix it. Jerry, take us to the QM warehouse area, please."

"Yes, sir," his driver said, and made a U-turn so he could head back toward the post.

"General," Colonel O. Richard Ambler, the post quartermaster, said, "I asked Colonel Mize to ask you to call me when you had a moment free. I know how busy you are. I didn't expect you to come over here."

Lieutenant Colonel W. W. Mize was secretary of the general staff.

"And what, Colonel," General Lemper asked, guessing correctly what that was all about, "has Colonel Lowell done to the Quartermaster Corps?"

"Colonel Lowell stated that he was acting with your full authority, sir, and that I was free to raise any objections I wished after I had complied with his requests."

"That's the way it is," General Lemper said.

"I checked, of course, with Colonel Mize," Colonel Ambler said, "and he said that was his understanding of the situation. So I permitted Colonel Lowell to take our forklifts."

"And?"

"He has already rendered seven of them inoperable, General. They are not designed to lift the weight of a loaded six-by-six."

"Anybody hurt?"

"Not so far, sir."

"Where is Colonel Lowell now?"

"He's here, sir," the quartermaster said.

"Here, where?"

"He has men from the Engineers loading six-by-sixes on flatcars, sir."

"I thought you said that the forklifts won't handle the load?"

"They will not, sir," the quartermaster said. "Eventually,

the hydraulic hoses just give way. Or the tires. The tires literally explode, sir."

"Eventually" means that Lowell is managing to load probably more than one six-by-six before the hydraulic hoses or the tires fail, General Lemper thought.

"Let's go have a look, Colonel," General Lemper said.

"Colonel Lowell has been loading tanks with drag lines from the Engineer Light Equipment Company," Colonel Sapphrey said to his friend Colonel Ambler.

"I didn't think they'd handle that much weight," Colonel Ambler said.

"They're not supposed to," General Lemper said, as he pushed open the door.

He found Lowell four buildings away. The group arrived just as, with a sharp crack, a hydraulic line on a large yellow warehouse forklift burst, spraying purple hydraulic fluid into the air.

At the moment the line burst, the lift's forks were eight feet in the air, suspending a six-by-six over a flat car. When the lines failed, the six-by-six dropped like a stone onto the flatcar, a vertical drop of about five feet. It bounced wildly on its springs.

"Aw, shit!" the corporal driving the forklift said bitterly, wiping hydraulic fluid from his face. "Another one!"

General Lemper wondered why the truck had been raised so high in the first place. Then he saw why. There was a line of six-by-sixes on the rail-car loading platform of one of the QM warehouses. A ramp had been built for them out of railroad ties. The forklifts were taking the trucks down from the loading platform, rather than up from the ground. The greatest strain on the hydraulic hoses came when the loaded forks were raised. By taking the trucks down from the loading platform, the forks had to be raised only a foot or so in order to clear the wheels. They would have had to be raised to five feet if the trucks had been picked up from the ground.

The forklift driver backed the lift away from the flatcar. There was a screeching noise as the forks dragged across the flatcar; and then when the tips cleared the flatcar, the forks crashed to the ground.

Colonel Ambler looked at General Lemper as if pleasantly anticipating an angry order to cease and desist.

General Lemper watched the forklift with the ruptured lines back around the corner of the building, dragging the forks along the ground. Lemper followed it.

A repair operation had been set up. Mechanics drenched with hydraulic fluid were replacing ruptured hydraulic hoses. Other mechanics were changing tires using one now-tireless forklift as a jack.

Lowell was overseeing this operation, his hands on his hips. As General Lemper walked over to him, he saw dark spots on both his tunic and trouser legs. It was not a criticism of his appearance. The spots had obviously been caused by hydraulic fluid. Since the stuff didn't come out, Lieutenant Colonel Lowell's very expensive, tailor-made uniform was ruined. And so, Lemper saw, were his boots.

"What are you going to do, Colonel, when you run out of forklifts you can cannibalize?"

Lowell turned around and saluted crisply.

"Good morning, sir," he said, and then answered the question: "I sent a sergeant on a scrounging mission, sir. He seemed quite confident of success."

Lemper introduced the officers with him. They eyed Lowell suspiciously.

"Colonel Sapphrey is concerned, Colonel, with reports that we have been dispatching empty boxcars," Lemper said.

"Yes, sir, I have been," Lowell said. "One of the holdups was the switching around of cars; segregating, I suppose, is the word. It takes forever with trains."

"So I've learned," Lemper said. "What was your solution to that? Just ignoring the cars you couldn't use?"

"Not exactly, sir," Lowell said. "I had a talk with a couple of the railroad engineers and conductors. They came up with a solution to the problem, and I put it into action."

"And what was that solution, Colonel?" Colonel Sapphrey asked.

"New Orleans has got a really efficient car distribution center, or so they told me. It's supposed to be the fastest place in the country to make up trains. So I've sent them the job. They're going to make up trains, some for New Orleans, some for Mobile, some for Miami, and then make up trains of the empty cars and send them back here."

"Just like that?" Colonel Sapphrey said. "You sent them the job? Just who do you think you are? And what makes you think they'll oblige you once the trains you've ordered to New Orleans get there?"

"Well, I sent Mr. Wojinski with one of the train men, some sort of a district supervisor, I didn't get his exact title, but he understands our problem and is willing to help. Between them, I'm sure it'll work."

"We'll have to wait and see, won't we?" Colonel Sapphrey said.

"When will these people get to New Orleans?" General Lemper asked. "When will you know for sure?"

"I would have heard by now if there were problems, sir. They've been there six, probably seven hours. The first trains from here should be arriving in New Orleans about now."

"How did you get them to New Orleans?" Lemper asked.

"They flew, sir."

Lemper was mildly annoyed. To keep his staff people from flying in all directions, he had ordered that no aircraft be dispatched out of the local area except with his express permission.

"I'm surprised my aviation officer gave you an airplane," he said.

"He loaned me a couple of pilots, sir," Lowell said. "They went in my airplane."

"You have an airplane assigned to you?" Lemper asked.

"No, sir, I meant *my* airplane. I own one."

"How much permanent damage are you doing to these forklifts?" Lemper asked.

"They're pretty tough, sir," Lowell said. "I don't think very much."

"In my judgment," Colonel Ambler said, "after the abuse

to which they are being subjected, they'll require complete depot-level overhaul."

"I would have to defer to your judgment, Colonel," Lowell said, politely.

"Gentlemen," General Lemper said, "I would suggest that Colonel Lowell has more important things to do than chat with us." Then he gave in to the impulse: "Carry on, Colonel."

"Right you are, sir," Lowell said, with just a hint of a phony English accent.

General Lemper quickly turned, so the others would not see his smile.

When he got back to his office, he called Major General Paul T. Jiggs, J-3, Joint Assault Force, at MacDill Air Force Base in Florida.

"Stu, Paul," he said when Jiggs came on the line. "Got a minute to chat?"

"In other words, you have a few comments vis-à-vis Craig Lowell that you would rather not make official? How mad are you, Stu?"

"Mad isn't the word. Embarrassed."

"You're not mad?"

"The Transportation Corps is mad; the Quartermaster Corps is mad; and I suspect if I talked to the Engineer, he would be mad. But I'm embarrassed. Lowell has got us off the dime. That shouldn't have been necessary."

Paul Jiggs and Stu Lemper were a year apart at the Point, Jiggs having graduated a year earlier. They had been friends for a long time.

"As long as you're off the dime, that's all that counts," Jiggs said. There was more than a hint of criticism in the sentence, Lemper thought.

"Yes, it is," Lemper said. "I would hate to see this affect my taking the division to Cuba, Paul."

"That hasn't come up," Jiggs said. "Don't worry about that."

"You have to send somebody to help me do what I should have been able to do myself, and I worry."

"What you saw is what you got. I thought Lowell could

help. If he has, fine. That's all there is to it."

"He work for you? I saw the Aviation Center patch."

"He's assigned to the Aviation Board."

"Can I take him with me? Or have you got something else for him to do?"

"You think he would be useful?" Jiggs asked, and then went on without waiting for a reply: "If you want him, Stu, he's yours."

"Thank you."

"What are you going to do with him?"

"Just what he's doing now," Lemper said.

There was a pause, and then Paul Jiggs said: "Stu, if you should come to need a battalion commander, or, for that matter, a combat command commander, Lowell is one hell of a combat commander."

"So I understand," General Lemper said. "You had the 73rd Tank."

"It was his show, and he really did it right. He was twenty-four."

"I played Task Force Lowell on the sand tables at Leavenworth," Lemper said. "How did somebody with that behind him wind up driving an airplane?"

"It's a long and sad story," Jiggs said. "He can fuck up spectacularly in a moment's time. Not when it counts—don't misunderstand me—but when the mongrels nipping at his heels can get at him. I've often thought Craig should be kept in a deep freeze, and thawed only when there's a war."

Lemper didn't respond to that.

"Is this just between you and me, or can I have him officially?" he asked.

"I'll have orders cut this morning, putting him on TDY, if that's what you want."

"Please, Paul."

"You got it. I'll see you in a couple of days, I expect."

"Yeah. Thanks, Paul."

General Lemper hung up the telephone and then raised his voice.

"Lieutenant Cole!"

The general's aide-de-camp promptly appeared at the office door.

"Bill," General Lemper said, "Colonel Lowell is probably still swimming around in hydraulic fluid in the QM warehouse area."

"Yes, sir?"

"Lieutenant, you will present my compliments to Colonel Lowell, and inform him that he is now on temporary duty with this division for an indefinite period. You will inform him that he is now occupying the position of special assistant to the commanding general, and you will inform him that the commanding general wishes him to understand that the order restricting personnel to twelve hours' duty per day applies to him."

The young officer smiled.

"He's really been lighting some fires under people, hasn't he, sir?"

"And then you will tell Colonel Lowell that the commanding general would be pleased if Colonel Lowell could take dinner with the commanding general at his quarters at 1800."

"Yes, sir."

"Mrs. Lemper, I'm sure, would be pleased if you and Mrs. Cole could join us. And I hope you're free. I think that you might find it educational."

"Yes, sir. We're free, sir. Thank you, sir."

"Set it up with my wife, Bill, please, and tell her, please, no Indonesian buffet or anything else exotic. I don't want Lowell to think I'm trying to poison him."

"Yes, sir."

V

(One)
Brookley Air Force Base
Mobile, Alabama
1430 Hours, 28 October 1962

Brookley Air Force Base was considered by logisticians to be the most ideally situated military supply facility in the world. Its eastern border was Mobile Bay, thus Brookley had "on-station" piers and wharfs for deep-water shipping. Brookley was also connected to the rail yards half a mile away, which were the terminus of four major railroad lines. And when the National Defense Highway System ("The Interstate")—fought through Congress by President Eisenhower—was completed, I-10 (East and West) would run past Brookley's west fence, and I-65 (North) would begin two miles from Brookley. Brookley's runways were capable of handling any existing or projected fighter, bomber, or transport aircraft. Its maintenance hangars and its thousands of employees could perform any maintenance required by any aircraft in the Air Force inventory. And its enormous warehouse facilities contained stores of supplies for just about every Air Force maintenance need.

As the Aero Commander approached Brookley from the west, it was overtaken by two Air Force fighters descending

through ten thousand feet to Brookley. Lieutenant Colonel Craig
W. Lowell heard the Brookley tower warn the flight leader that
there were five aircraft in the vicinity; two C-130 transports at
eight thousand, approaching Brookley from the west; two C-
130s at five thousand, departing Brookley to the southeast; and
one small civilian twin at four thousand, approaching Brookley
from the west.

"Roger, Brookley, we have the civilian twin in sight."

"Brookley clears Air Force Six Oh One and Six One Nine
for simultaneous landing as Number One on Three Four. The
winds are negligible, the altimeter is two niner niner niner."

Lowell reached over his head, slid the curtain out of the
way, and looked through the Plexiglas panel for the fighters
descending on him. A minute or so later, they flashed over
him, their flaps, wheels, and speed brakes extended to dirty
them up and slow them down.

"Brookley, Air Force Six Oh One over the outer marker,"
the Air Force flight leader reported.

Lowell saw the two gleaming fighters land side by side on
one of Brookley's major runways. There were few places in
the world with runways wide enough to handle two supersonic
fighters landing simultaneously. Brookley was one of them.*

Lowell slid the curtain back in place.

"Brookley, Aero Commander One Five, at three thousand,
two miles west, for landing."

"Aero Commander One Five, Brookley. Brookley is a military facility, closed to civilian traffic at this time. Suggest you
divert to Mobile Municipal, six miles northwest."

"Brookley," Lowell announced, somewhat pontifically, "Aero
Commander One Five is in the military service of the United
States. Request landing instructions."

There was almost a minute's delay before Brookley came
back on the air.

"Aero Commander One Five, you are cleared as Number

---

*Brookley Air Force Base was ordered closed, as "an economy measure,"
as the Vietnam War escalated in late 1964, shortly after the re-election of
President Lyndon B. Johnson. Mobile, Mobile County, and Alabama had
voted, two to one, for Senator Barry Goldwater.

One on Three Four, after the C-141 on its takeoff roll. Beware of jet turbulence. The winds are negligible, the altimeter is two niner niner niner. On landing, take the first available taxiway and hold in place. A Follow Me will meet you."

"I see the 141, thank you," Lowell said, and reached for the throttle quadrant, and then for the flaps and the wheels.

He touched down just past the threshold, reversed his props, and slowed enough to make the first taxiway turnoff.

The Follow Me Chevrolet pickup, painted in a black-and-white checkerboard pattern and flying two huge checkerboard flags, raced down the taxiway to him, turned around, and then led him to a parking ramp. An Air Force ground crewman jumped out of the truck, as an AP—Air Police—pickup truck drove up, and directed him to a parking place beside a huge C-141.

When he opened the door and got out, one of the APs saw he was in uniform and almost visibly relaxed. He saluted.

"Would you come with me, please, Colonel? They'd like to talk to you in Base Ops."

Just inside the double glass doors of Base Ops a gray-haired man in a flight suit, holding his helmet under his arms like a basketball, looked at Lowell in surprise. Lowell saluted. There were the silver stars of a brigadier general on the flight suit.

"Good afternoon, Colonel," the Air Force brigadier said. "That was you in the Commander?"

"Yes, sir."

"May I ask you a personal question, Colonel?"

"Yes, sir, of course."

"What the hell have you been rolling around in? That uniform is the dirtiest one I can remember."

"Well, first, sir, there was a flood of hydraulic fluid, and then I spent the last two days in the rail yards in New Orleans."

"Steam cleaning the trains, no doubt?" the general asked. He seemed more amused than offended. "How can the Air Force assist the Army, Colonel? My question may be interpreted as official. I'm the deputy base commander. My name is Winston."

"General, my name is Lowell. I'm with the 2nd Armored

Division. We're running trains by here."

General Winston nodded.

"In about an hour, there will be two sections—two enormous sections—of a special train carrying tanks and other heavy equipment. I've been able to arrange for messes aboard the troop trains, but the troops accompanying the equipment have been living on sandwiches for three days, and I'd like to get them a hot meal. Especially the men guarding the ammo; they've had a rough time, all the way in boxcars."

"You can stop the trains here?"

"I've arranged for each section to be stopped for an hour, sir. The second section is thirty minutes behind the first."

"Your concern for your men is as commendable, Colonel," General Winston said, "as your uniform is disgraceful. What I intend to do is get on the horn to my food service officer, and order up a meal—steak and eggs always seems to go well in this kind of situation—and then I will personally call the officer in charge of our dry cleaning plant and tell him he is about to get a priority job. We'll get you a flight suit to wear, and I don't suppose you would turn down a cold beer?"

"You're very kind, sir."

The best efforts of the Brookley Air Force dry cleaning facility, under the personal direction of the supervisor, could not do much with Lieutenant Colonel Lowell's uniform. It was indelibly stained with hydraulic fluid and railroad grease. But they pressed it up neatly, and he was wearing it again when the first section of the train ground to a halt at the west fence of Brookley.

The Air Force was waiting for the troops of the 2nd Armored Division, not only with steak and eggs and french-fried potatoes and all the milk they could drink, but with lines of buses to take them to the Air Force barracks for a quick shower and a change of underwear.

The first section of the train had just pulled out when an Air Force staff car drove up. It provided a radio link to Base Commo, and Base Commo was of course tied in to the military around the world.

Major General Paul T. Jiggs, J-3, Joint Assault Force, MacDill Air Force Base, was on the horn.

Khrushchev had blinked. The Russians would take their missiles out of Cuba. Aerial surveillance from Big Black Birds already had photographs showing that the disassembly process had begun. So the invasion was off. Second Armored was ordered to return to Fort Hood and stand down.

Lieutenant Colonel Lowell privately and professionally believed it would have been far better for 2nd Armored to route itself home via Havana. Castro was still in place, and there was no question in his mind how the Russians regarded the situation. They would see this as only a temporary setback. Just as soon as they thought they could get away with it, they would sneak missiles back into Cuba. In the meantime they could turn the island into a logistics and submarine base ninety miles off the enemy's shore.

As he watched the several hundred young men wolf down the steak and eggs, he had privately and personally been disturbed with his judgment that within a week one of five of them would likely be maimed or dead.

So he was of course pleased that that had been avoided. In a week, they would be back at Hood, all alive and in one piece. On the other hand, since they had not taken Castro out when the odds were in American favor, it was very likely that the confrontation had only been delayed, and that when it became necessary later to mount an invasion of Cuba, the casualties would be even higher.

He had the somewhat cynical thought that the sacred tradition that military officers scrupulously avoid politics was in effect not because of the necessity of the separation—like that between church and state—between the state and the military, but rather because officers with any knowledge of history or geo-politics could not avoid holding politicians, of whatever persuasion, in deep contempt.

(Two)
The Officers' Open Mess
Headquarters, Continental Army Command
Fortress Monroe, Virginia
1915 Hours, 12 November 1962

The post-operation critique of the aborted invasion lasted through four eight-hour sessions at Monroe. Mistakes had been made. The way to avoid a repetition of these mistakes was to get them out in the open and determine how they could be avoided in the future.

At 1630, when the final meeting broke up, there were several matters to be discussed, privately between Boone and the Chief of Staff. By the time that was over, and General Boone had driven the Chief of Staff to the airfield and seen him aboard his L-23 for the return flight to Washington, it was almost 1900. Boone then went to the Officers' Club where he hoped to be able to have a word with Major General Stu Lemper. As they left the conference room, Boone had overheard Triple H Howard invite Lemper to have a beer. Though he wasn't at all sure they would still be there—general officers usually do their drinking in their quarters, not in the O Club—he hoped they might.

There was an uncomfortable parallel for Boone between the critique and what Communists called "self-examination." Lemper had been forced to get up and confess his sins, and had, in some detail, explained what had gone wrong.

Things had gone wrong, but that was not the same thing as saying that what had gone wrong was Lemper's fault, and he suspected correctly that Triple H Howard was going to make this point, backed up by Paul Jiggs, over a beer in the O Club. Boone believed it his duty to make the same point. Lemper was a good man, and he had done all that could be expected of him.

He found Generals Howard, Lemper, and Jiggs sitting at a table in the bar. None of the adjacent tables was occupied. A covey of general officers sitting together over drinks had the same effect on their juniors as a trio of lepers.

The three of them stood up when he walked to the table.

"Is this a private gathering, or can any bull-thrower join in?" Boone asked.

"We're glad to have you, sir," Triple H Howard said.

A red-jacketed waiter—a moonlighting noncom—came up quickly.

"Since I'm buying," General Boone said, "give them whatever they want, Sergeant, so long as it's cheap. I'll have a Scotch, no ice, and a glass of soda on the side."

When the drinks had been delivered, and the waiter had gone (not too far, but out of hearing), General Boone said: "Before we start talking about women, Stu, and in case this hasn't been made previously clear, I think you did a hell of a job. I want you to understand that I'm aware of the problems you had, and that I think you handled them splendidly."

"That's very kind of you, sir, to say so," Lemper said. "But the bottom line is that it took me too long to get off the dime."

"Don't argue with me," Boone said. "I'm a general."

They laughed. A little too loud, Boone thought. They had been socking it away for an hour and a half. Whiskey, not beer.

"I have just been explaining to General Lemper, sir," Triple H Howard said, "about the battle than can never be won."

"Which one is that?"

"Against the mongrels that nip at your heels," Howard said.

Boone thought he understood what Howard was talking about.

"You think calling a Harke a mongrel is appropriate?" he asked, just a little stiffly.

"I was talking about DCSPERS*, sir," Howard said, undaunted. "What happened between General Harke and myself is between General Harke and myself. It was not under discussion."

"The Chief of Staff discussed it with me," Boone said. "He believes that you were a bit harsh dealing with the problem." He paused a moment, and then went on: "I told him that I

*Deputy Chief of Staff for Personnel.

supported your decision, that I would have done the same thing, under the same regrettable circumstances."

"Thank you, sir," Howard said.

"What about DCSPERS?" Boone asked.

"I was explaining to Stu why he can't have Colonel Lowell."

"Regarding Colonel Lowell," General Boone said. "I owe you an apology, Paul. When I sent him down to help Stu, I did so with great reservation."

"Oh, ye, of little faith!" General Jiggs said. "How could any officer trained personally by me fail to be anything but superior in every respect?"

"He did one hell of a job for me," General Lemper said. "That's why I want him."

"And you can't have him?" Boone asked. "And Triple H Howard is blaming DCSPERS?"

"Yes, sir."

"Never trust anyone who jumps out of airplanes, Stu," General Boone said. "The landing jolt scrambles their brains. They need people like Lowell to read and write for them. DCSPERS probably has nothing to do with it."

"Unfortunately, sir," Howard said, seriously, "the general errs. DCSPERS has everything to do with this."

"Tell me how 'the general errs,'" Boone said.

"Well, just before this thing started, I received an extraordinary communication from DCSPERS. They had discovered, with great glee, I must add, Colonel Lowell's shameful secret."

"I'm afraid to ask what that is," Boone said.

"Colonel Lowell was not graduated from an accredited college or university. Graduation from an accredited college or university is a prerequisite for a commission in the Regular Army. Therefore, the validity of Colonel Lowell's commission is in question."

"You're serious," Boone said. Howard nodded. "I thought you told me, Paul, that he had graduated from the Wharton School of Business?"

"Yes, sir, he did. Magna cum laude."

"Then how did he get into graduate school without a bachelor's degree?"

"I guess they make exceptions for people who own banks," Jiggs said.

"That's absurd," Boone said. "Is DCSPERS serious about this?"

"Yes, sir," Howard said. "I discussed it with DCSPERS personally."

"Then what's behind it?" Boone said.

"Equal treatment of all officers under Army Regulations, is the way he put it," Howard said. "If they grant an exception, everyone will want an exception. I am sure, of course, that it has nothing whatever to do with the fact that Lowell was nominated for lieutenant colonel by the President after having been twice passed over by DCSPERS's promotion boards."

"They're not actually suggesting his commission should be vacated?" Boone asked, coldly.

"No, sir. What they want is for Colonel Lowell to be enrolled in the Boot Strap Program."

"What the hell is that?"

"It is a program under DCSPERS in which officers who for some reason or another do not have the required formal education are given the opportunity to get it. They are placed on TDY for up to a year, sent to college, and the Army pays for it."

"They want to send a *lieutenant colonel* with that much service back to college?" Boone asked, incredulously. "On *duty?*"

"They do it all the time, General, or so I have been informed," Howard said.

"I'll look into this," Boone said.

"With all respect, sir, I have already carried the appeal to the highest court, and it has been denied," Howard said.

Boone's eyebrows went up in question, and he made a "come on" gesture with his hands.

"I told DCSPERS that I thought he was out of his mind, and that if necessary I would personally go to the Secretary of the Army with it. I need Lowell for the Howard Board. He then informed me that considering Lowell's 'unusual status,' he had already brought the matter to SECARMY, and SEC-

ARMY had agreed that there could be no exceptions."

"Unusual status meaning his work on the Howard Board?"
Boone asked.

"That and his political influence, I think," Howard said.
"And then I went to the court of highest appeal. McNamara."

"Directly?" Boone asked.

"He—unofficially, of course—keeps a pretty close eye on
the Board," Howard said. "He drops in from time to time. And
one time when he dropped in, I found the opportunity to bring
this to his attention. He was not very sympathetic. He told me
he was reluctant to step in and countermand SECARMY, and
then he warmed to the subject, and told me if he had his
druthers, Lowell would resign from the Army and go to work
for DOD* as a civilian. He left me with the impression, sir,
that he thinks Lowell is a fool for being an officer in the first
place, when he has the choice to be either a banker or a Deputy
Assistant Secretary of Defense, and that if he persists in in-
dulging himself playing soldier, he will have to play by the
rules."

"If he turned you down, he'd turn me down," Boone said.
"What does Lowell have to say about this?"

"I don't know, sir," Howard said. "I haven't told him about
it. Now, of course, I'm going to have to tell him."

"What do you think, Paul—he's your protégé—he'll do?"

"One of two things, sir. He'll either cheerfully obey his
orders or tell us to go piss up a rope. I just don't know. If I
were him, I'd be furious. And it's not as if he has to stick
around so he can qualify for a pension in his old age."

"Well, we're not going to beg anyone to stay in the Army,"
Boone said. "But is there some way we can sugarcoat the pill?"

"I was thinking of that, sir," Jiggs said. "I thought about
calling General Harmon at Norwich*, and explaining the situation to him."

---

*Department of Defense.

**Norwich, the Military College of Vermont, has a long tradition of pro-
viding Cavalry (and later, Armor) officers to the Regular Army. Its pres-

"Good idea," General Boone said. "I think Ernie Harmon will be as appalled as I am that a light colonel with a combat record like Lowell's has to turn into an undergraduate. Would you like me to have a talk with Lowell?"

"No, sir," Howard said. "If there's anybody who could talk him into enduring this humiliation for the good of the service, it would be Paul."

"You're probably right," Boone agreed. "Make the point to him, Paul, that stars have a price. In his case, that's going to mean going to Vermont and wearing a collegiate beanie. And a smile, as if he likes it."

---

ident traditionally is a West Point graduate of distinguished service in the Army. Norwich President Major General Ernest Harmon (USMA '16), USA, Retired, led the 2nd Armored Division in World War II until turning command over to Major General I. D. White (Norwich '20), USA.

VI

(One)
Soc Trang (Mekong Delta)
Saigon, Republic of Vietnam
0305 Hours, 19 February 1963

It had been raining all night, a steady, drenching, windswept downpour. The Marines guarding the flight line walked their posts with the muzzles of their M-14 rifles pointing downward. They wore helmets (against which the rain drummed not unpleasantly) and what the Marines called "utilities," which were a Marine version of Army fatigues; and a poncho, a plasticized cloth with a hooded hole in the center for the head and snaps along the edges. These could be closed to form sleeves or snapped together with another poncho to form a shelter half or a tarpaulin.

The ponchos were as impermeable to air as they were to water, and within half an hour of putting one on, a wearer could expect to be nearly as wet from his own sweat as he would have been from the rain. Under the right conditions, the sentries could be seen giving off steam.

All the aircraft on the flight line with one exception were Marine versions of the Army's Sikorsky H-34 helicopter, a single-rotor, larger version of the Sikorsky H-19. The exception

was an Army airplane, an OV-1 Mohawk. This one was equipped
with a side-looking radar antenna hung below its fuselage and
with other sensing devices. The Mohawk would participate that
day as the electronic eyes and ears for a Marine operation: A
mixed force of ARVN soliders and Marines were to be transported to an island in the delta, where Intelligence said there
was a cache of Vietcong weapons, food, and other supplies.

Somebody had fucked up, and there was no JP-4 fuel for
the Mohawk's twin turboprop engines when the plane arrived.
Some ass was eaten, some embarrassed telephone calls made,
and a six-by-six tanker with an escort of armed jeeps was
dispatched from the nearest source of JP fuel.

It arrived at 0300, was duly challenged by the sentry, who
then got in the cab with the GI driver and his Vietnamese
assistant and rode down the flight line to the Mohawk. Under
the circumstances, it was perhaps understandable that he elected
to stay in the closed cab of the fuel truck and catch a quick
smoke while the fuel truck guy and the flight line chief fueled
the Mohawk. (JP-4 was diesel fuel, sort of; you couldn't smoke
around fuel trucks when they were fueling the Sikorskys with
av-gas, but fueling a Mohawk with JP-4 in a driving rain was
something else.)

Nobody was going to blow up the Mohawk while people
were working on it.

The Vietnamese assistant fuel truck driver, in order to make
sure that no fuel somehow leaked into the aircraft fuselage,
opened an inspection port in the starboard wing near the root,
and shined his flashlight inside.

When he was sure that no one was looking, he reached
inside his poncho and took from it a clever American tool,
which he had stolen two weeks before. It was a battery-powered
electric drill. He had already chucked a drill into it, the kind
used by the American technicians who repaired the electronic
components of the Mohawk's black boxes. It drilled very tiny
pin holes.

With it, in the time he thought he had available without
being caught, he drilled holes in whatever hydraulic lines he

could identify by their color. The holes were so tiny that the purple hydraulic fluid within the lines did not even drip out, but simply formed tiny beads at the holes. Even if they were spotted during the preflight, it would be supposed that they were nothing more than the expected leaking ("oozeage") from connections to the hydraulic system.

Then the Vietnamese assistant fuel truck driver stuck the battery-powered drill back into his trousers under his poncho, closed the inspection port, and went to see of what other use he might be.

(Two)
*Coordinates Fox Three Baker, Baker Six Whiskey
AirNav Chart 407 (Mekong River)
Republic of South Vietnam
1015 Hours, 19 February 1963*

Charley had not left his cache of weapons and supplies unguarded. The Marines on Island 237 were taking mortar fire from the mainland to the west.

This information had twice been relayed to superior head-quarters, once by the Marine officer in command on the ground, and again by the pilot of the Mohawk accompanying the operation. For forty-five minutes he had been flying an endless oblong pattern: a mile west to east, a steep 180° turn, a mile east to west, and then another steep 180° turn. The roll of somewhat sticky paper spilling out of the black box in front of the copilot had not only pinpointed the presence of objects on the west bank, but counted them. Because the objects were radiating at 102° Fahrenheit it had concluded that these were individual human beings and made the appropriate symbol on the printout. The black boxes had also detected the position of the mortars, and by judging the duration and temperature of the gas ejected from their muzzles had determined that the mortars were four M-1937 82-mms and two M-1938 107-mms. The appropriate symbols were placed on the printout. All the data had been simultaneously transmitted by radio to superior headquarters, which had taken the appropriate action.

A six-plane flight of Douglas "Skyraiders" was en route to coordinates Fox Three Baker, Baker Six Whiskey, where they would bring the Vietcong mortar positions under attack by rockets, machine guns, and napalm.

The trouble, the Mohawk pilot, Major Philip S. Parker IV, concluded, was that the Skyraiders were six to eight minutes away. Six to eight minutes was a very long time when you were on the receiving end of a heavy mortar barrage.

Under the agreement worked out—semi-officially—between the U.S. Army and the U.S. Air Force, armed Mohawk aircraft were permitted to engage enemy targets only when they had been first attacked. Armed Mohawks were expressly forbidden to engage the enemy unless that response was necessary for self-defense.

"I've got it," Major Parker said to his copilot. "Let's go make them keep their heads down."

He flipped off the automatic stabilization system and flipped up the toggle switch (under a red protective cover) that energized the machine guns in the pods beneath each wing.

He was not aware of course that each time he had energized the Mohawk's hydraulic system during the steep 180° turns, the fluid in the system had come out of the hydraulic lines through barely visible holes with force enough to vaporize it.

The HYDRAULIC FAILURE warning lights had blinked on and then off as he made the recovery from his first strafing run. He'd seen them, but hadn't paid much attention. Warning lights tended to blink on and off. It was only when they stayed on that there was genuine cause for concern.

The HYDRAULIC FAILURE warning lights came on again as he lined up for his second strafing run, went off again, and then came on again and stayed on.

"Shit, we've got hydraulic failure lights," the copilot said.

Whatever was wrong with the hydraulic system, Parker decided, could wait until he had finished the strafing run. As he pressed the trigger on his stick, the lights went off, and he relaxed again.

He was at five hundred feet, making two hundred knots.

He saw the one-in-five tracers spraying the forest. He took his finger off the trigger and watched the warning lights panel. The HYDRAULIC FAILURE lights remained off. But Major Parker was an experienced, which is to say cautious, pilot. He decided not to pull up and make a steep 180°, so he could dive again quickly on the mortar positions. Instead he'd make a wide, slow turn at his present altitude, and then make a final strafing run. That would exhaust his ordance, and the Skyraiders would be on target by then.

He was in a slightly nose-down position when the HYDRAULIC FAILURE lights came on again, and this time they stayed on.

When he tried to raise the nose after the run—gently, not an attempt to zoom up dramatically—he found he had neither rudder nor aileron control. The Mohawk was headed for the ground, and there was nothing whatever he could do about it.

"We're going to have to eject," he announced, reasonably calmly, "and right now."

Then he pressed the microphone switch.

"Mayday, mayday, Army One Oh Four has lost all hydraulics. Am ejecting at this time. I hope you guys have got me on the radar."

Major Parker looked at his copilot and nodded. Then, very frightened, he reached over his head and pulled down a device which both covered his face against the shock of ejection and triggered the mechanism. He felt the blast as explosive bolts sent the cockpit canopy off into the windstream. There was a brief moment when he felt the airstream, and then, as a 20-mm blank shell in the Martin-Baker ejection seat went off, he felt the blow to his back and buttocks as the seat was blown free of the aircraft.

It was even worse than he had anticipated, and he had worried a lot about actually having to eject.

He felt himself spinning through the air, sensed his parachute deploying, felt the seat separate from him, and then there was a pop as the canopy of the parachute opened and he was swinging back and forth under it.

In the last moment before his feet struck the tops of the

canopy of trees in the forest, he saw—chilled and horrified—
his copilot. His chute had not deployed. Waving his arms as
if this somehow would brake his fall, the copilot disappeared
into the treetops.

(Three)
Fort Riley, Kansas
0930 Hours, 21 February 1963

The situation was unusual. Army Regulations prescribed
that a notification team (an officer of grade equal to, or superior
to, that of the casualty; a chaplain of the appropriate faith; and
a medical officer, if available) would call upon the immediate
next of kin. If the casualty was married, the parents were no
longer next of kin. Major Philip S. Parker IV was married.

But in this case, by the direct order of the Deputy Commanding General, CONARC, a notification team would call
upon the casualty's parents. And not the regularly assigned Fort
Riley notification team alone. The commanding general had
been informed that a Lieutenant Colonel Lowell and party would
arrive at Fort Riley at approximately 0930 hours, and would
be afforded every courtesy in their mission.

Inasmuch as the Deputy Commanding General, CONARC,
was personally involved, the commanding general of Fort Riley
decided that it was appropriate for him to be at the airfield
when the aircraft carrying Lieutenant Colonel Lowell and party
arrived. He had ordered the notification team, of course, to be
on hand with an extra staff car and orders to be wholly co-
operative. But if this Lieutenant Colonel Lowell was important
enough to be sent by the deputy CONARC commander personally, he was important enough to be met by the Riley CG.

He was surprised when the aircraft that landed turned out
to be a civilian Aero Commander. And when the door opened,
he was surprised again that the first person out turned out to
be a tall, sharp-featured black woman in a knee-length mink
coat.

She turned around, and two children, a boy and a girl encased in hooded nylon jackets against the cold, stepped to the ground. Then an officer, out of uniform in old-fashioned and now proscribed pinks and greens, got out. The general was so surprised at the old uniform that it was a moment before he saw that the wearer of the uniform was also wearing his medals— a solid mass of them covering his breast—not just the ribbons. There was a 2nd Armored Division patch on his sleeve, and the stars of a major general on his epaulets.

And then he recognized the general. He had been in North Africa as a young major when General Harmon was commander of the 2nd Armored Division.

The general brushed by his notification team and saluted.

"Welcome to Fort Riley, General," he said. "I regret the circumstances."

"Thank you," General Harmon said. "May I present Dr. Parker? Dr. Parker is Major Parker's wife."

She nodded and made a failing stab at a smile.

"This is Colonel Lowell," Harmon said, gesturing to the officer coming out of the door of the Aero Commander. Colonel Lowell was in uniform, and his breast too was covered with medals, not ribbons. An enormous gold medal, the size of a coffee cup saucer, was pinned to a purple sash running diagonally across his chest. The general had never seen one like that before.

Lowell saluted, a crisp gesture. Good-looking officer, the general thought. He wondered where he had gotten the expensive civilian airplane.

"Riley is completely at your disposal, General," the general said. "I believe you once commanded here?"

"Yes," Harmon said. "Thank you."

"This is our notification team," the General said.

Harmon looked them over.

"I appreciate your interest, gentlemen," he said, in his gravelly voice, "but I don't think we'll need you. If you, General, on the other hand, can spare the time from your duties to accompany us, I would be grateful."

"Certainly, sir."

"We have to make a rest stop for the children," Harmon said. "There used to be facilities in that hangar." He pointed.

"Yes, sir," the general said.

"If I may ride with you, General," Harmon said. "Colonel Lowell can ride with Dr. Parker."

"Yes, sir, of course," the general said.

The day was clear and bright, after several days of snow. The surface of the snow at the Parker farm was unbroken, save for a field to the left of the rambling wooden farmhouse, where Colonel Philip S. Parker III, Retired, had been exercising his Labradors.

They were easily seen from the road. The Labradors were black against the snow, and Colonel Parker was wearing a bright red tufted kapok nylon jacket.

When Colonel Parker saw the two staff cars turn off the highway into the drive, he started walking toward the house. By the time he got there, the staff cars had stopped before the house on the circular driveway. An American flag hung listlessly from a thirty-foot pole.

When he saw Toni and the children, he had a very good idea what was going on. When he saw Ernie Harmon and Craig Lowell wearing their medals, as well as the Fort Riley commanding general, there was little question at all.

Lowell saluted as Parker approached. Parker nodded, but did not return it. Only military personnel in uniform were entitled to salute.

"Gentlemen," Colonel Parker said. "Please come directly to the point of your visit."

There was a pause, then General Harmon broke it.

"Phil, I'm afraid we have to put the colors at half-mast."

"Philip has fallen," Colonel Parker said.

"No, sir," Lowell said, quickly. "He went down, but he got out. His chute opened."

"A prisoner, then?" Colonel Parker asked.

"Yes, sir," Lowell said. "We believe that to be the case."

"In that case, sir, with respect," Colonel Parker said, "I do not think it appropriate to half-mast the colors."

"Of course not, Phil," General Harmon said. "That was stupid of me."

"One has difficulty finding the appropriate words at a time like this," Colonel Parker said. He looked at his daughter-in-law. "My dear Toni," he said. "How terrible for you, and how good of you to come."

"Oh, Jesus, Dad!" Dr. Parker said.

Colonel Parker saw his wife on the porch.

"Philip's aircraft went down," Colonel Parker said. "His parachute opened. They believe him to be a prisoner. I'm sure there are some other details, but they can wait, I believe, until we get the children out of the cold."

Mrs. Parker came off the porch and scooped up the younger child. Dr. Parker picked up the older and the women went in the house.

"After you, gentlemen, if you please," Colonel Parker said to the others.

There were a number of photographs of Philip Sheridan Parker IV on the mantelpiece of the library. There was one of him as a Boy Scout; another of him in cadet uniform at Norwich; another in a brand-new second lieutenant's uniform on his graduation; another as a captain with an M4A3 tank in Korea; and one with his Mohawk in Vietnam.

"General Bellmon sends his compliments, sir," Lowell said. "He just couldn't get away. General Hanrahan is in Vietnam."

"I was privileged to command the unit which released Bellmon from captivity," Colonel Parker said.

"Yes, sir, General Bellmon asked me to remind you of that. He said he will remind you again when he telephones."

"That's very kind of him," Colonel Parker said. "What details can you give me?"

"All that General Hanrahan had, sir," Lowell said, "was that Phil was flying a Mohawk in support of a Marine operation. The Marines came under fire from VC mortars. Phil was strafing them when he went in. There was one brief radio message, a Mayday, saying he'd lost his hydraulics and was ejecting."

"And what have you of a concrete nature to support your belief that he is a prisoner?" Parker asked.

"The Marines went after him, Colonel," Lowell said. "They found the body of Phil's copilot. His chute didn't open. Navy pilots coming on the scene reported the deployment of a parachute, which had to be Phil. The Marines on the ground found Phil's deployed chute in the trees. They reported signs which indicate Phil was captured and taken away."

Colonel Parker nodded.

"It was good of you, Craig, to bring Toni and the children here."

"My privilege, sir," Lowell said.

"I've spoken with Colonel Felter, sir," Lowell said. "He tells me that it is possible, repeat possible, that he will have some definite word on Phil within two or three weeks. If he is taken north, it may take a little longer."

Colonel Parker considered that.

"If anyone can find Phil, Felter can," he said finally.

"Would I be intruding?" Toni Parker said, coming into the room.

"You are, of course, quite welcome," Colonel Parker said. "Despite the hour, I was about to offer a libation. I don't suppose you—"

"Yes, I would, Dad," Toni said, "please."

Colonel Parker went to a liquor cabinet, took out a bottle of twenty-four-year-old Ambassador Scotch, lined up glasses, and poured Scotch an inch deep in each of them. He then passed out the glasses and raised his own.

"Absent companions, gentlemen," he said.

"Absent companions," they parroted, and drank it down.

"Colonel," the Fort Riley CG said, "if I have to say this, if there's any way Riley can be of assistance, or myself personally . . ."

"That's very kind of you, General," Parker replied. "But I can't think of a thing."

Colonel Parker ceremoniously refilled the glasses.

"I have a question of General Harmon," Colonel Parker

said. "Philip, I must tell you, Craig, was—is—rather amused at the notion of your being at Norwich as an undergraduate. I confess that I too find it, on the surface, rather amusing."

"Well, I'm glad that someone finds it amusing," Lowell said.

"How is Colonel Lowell doing as an undergraduate, General?" Parker asked.

"Well, Phil," Harmon said, "he posed a small problem for one of my colonels, who based his Armor Operations course on Task Force Lowell. He found it disconcerting to have Lowell there while he was playing it out on the sandtable. Aside from that, he seems to have adjusted well."

"I very much appreciate your coming here, General," Colonel Parker said.

"We're old friends, Phil," Harmon said. "I regret the circumstances."

"Phil'll be all right, Colonel," Lowell said.

"Yes, I have every confidence he will be," Colonel Parker said.

"He told me," Toni blurted, "that he'd rather be killed than captured."

The men looked at each other, but none of them could think of anything to say in reply.

VII

Personal Effects Storage Area
Camp Buckner, Okinawa
16 August 1962

"You got the wrong place, Lieutenant," the sergeant said, with the clear implication that here was yet another proof that officers couldn't read. "The sign says 'Stored Enlisted Gear.'"

"I went over there as a sergeant," the lieutenant replied. "Craig, Geoffrey, US 5260674."

The duffle bag was found and delivered, and he carried it to his BOQ.

First Lieutenant Geoffrey Craig, late of the First Special Forces Group, was now out-processed from Vietnam duty via Okinawa. What that meant was that, dreadfully hung over, he was flown out of Foo Two by helicopter one morning and taken to Da Nang. There, nursing a cold beer, he went through a brief in-Country out-Processing briefing. He was then told his next stop would be Okinawa. There he would reclaim his personal gear, undergo a physical, and could expect to be on a plane to the Land of the Big PX within no more than thirty-six hours. The briefing officer carefully pointed out that war souvenirs were forbidden. And fully automatic weapons, such

149

as the AK-47, placed their possessors in great jeopardy from the Bureau of Alcohol, Tobacco and Firearms. Lieutenant Craig had turned in his issue weapon, an M-1911A1 .45-caliber pistol, and then boarded a C-131 bound for Okinawa, carrying a barracks bag with a suspiciously AK-47–like bulge.

At Camp Buckner, he was provided with a steak dinner, shown temporary quarters, subjected to a rather detailed physical, and told that since a chartered American Overseas Airways jet had departed for San Francisco not long before his C-131 had landed, he would have the opportunity to wallow in the cultural attractions of Okinawa for at least twenty-four hours before the next one left. There would be plenty of time for him to get paid and collect his gear and have a couple of beers.

Two events made him profoundly aware that he had been for more than six months an officer and a gentleman. The first was the sight of the stack of twenty dollar bills counted out to him when he endorsed the check Finance gave him. It was as much cash as he could ever remember seeing at one time, even in the legendary poker games at Da Nang. Lieutenants, obviously, got paid considerably more than sergeants. He converted all but six hundred dollars of it into U.S. Postal Money Orders.

The second happened when he carried his duffle bag to the Transient BOQ and unpacked it. He had been taught to pack a duffle bag by his brother-in-law, and he marveled anew at Staff Sergeant Karl-Heinz Wagner's all-around soldierly skills. When he took his clothing from the duffle bag and shook it out, it was practically creaseless, even after thirteen months in the warehouse. There was sort of a wave in the trousers, but that would shake out.

There was only one problem with the uniform. It was an enlisted man's uniform. Not only did the sleeves carry the three stripes of a sergeant, but the blouse did not have the black stripe on the cuff, nor the trousers the black stripe down the seam that an officer's blouse and trousers did.

Fuck it, Lieutenant Craig decided. He was only going to wear the sonofabitch long enough to go home and resign anyway, and there was no sense buying a uniform to wear no more than he intended to wear it. He could think of no good reason why he couldn't resign the moment he hit the States.

He took a razor blade and very carefully slit the stitching of the chevrons, and then very carefully pulled all the little threads loose. You could still see where the stripes had been, but unless he ran into some chickenshit, he could get away with it. He started to throw the stripes away, and then decided against that. He would frame them. He took lieutenant's bars and the gold crossed rifles of Infantry from his toilet kit, and replaced the enlisted insignia with them. Headgear posed no problem. The only difference between enlisted and officer green berets was that officers wore their rank insignia pinned to the flash.

He examined himself in the mirror, decided he passed muster and that he could now go to the O Club for a medicinal beer and something to eat.

He almost made it before he encountered some chickenshit captain of the Adjutant General's Corps, who was officer of the day. Restraining the impulse to tell the captain to take a flying fuck at a rolling doughnut (the consequences of which would likely involve at least missing the next plane), he said, "Yes, sir, I'm on my way to the Officers' Sales Store at this very moment."

He smarted at the captain's condescending treatment of him.

"Now that you're an officer, you have certain obligations in manners of dress and in other ways."

He had been treated as if he had just got here from some desk in Saigon rather than as somebody who had completed a tour with the Montagnards in the Highlands. But when he got to the sales store and saw himself in the mirror, he found the explanation. There was nothing on his uniform but the bars and rifles. No Combat Infantry Badge, no parachutist's wings, no fruit salad. The only thing that identified him as a Highlands type was a bracelet made from strands of an elephant's tail, and that dumb shit from the AGC couldn't be expected to know what that was.

Fuck it, give in. He had a pisspot full of dough anyway.

An hour later, he emerged from the sales store wearing one new officer's uniform and carrying another. He had come to a deal with the young soldier in charge: old uniform and the price of a bottle of bourbon for instant tailor service. He had black stripes where there were supposed to be black stripes, and he had all his fruit salad and other doodads. He looked, he thought, not entirely modestly, like a recruiting poster. He had never worn his ribbons before, and he was astonished by how many, both American and Vietnamese, he had. He even had Vietnamese parachutist's wings, the result of having met a Vietnamese Beret while on a three-day R&R on the beach. Jumping with Vietnamese Berets had seemed like a splendid idea at three in the morning; and at half past five, when they woke him up to take him, it had been too late to back out.

He went to the PX and bought two suitcases, packed them, and then finally went to the O Club for several medicinal beers and another steak. Twenty-two hours later, he boarded a Northwest Orient Airlines airplane for San Francisco.

There were stewardesses aboard, lovely young women who smelled of erotic perfume and the swell of whose breasts were delightfully apparent as they served meals and otherwise made themselves hospitable. He could now afford to think again of Ursula in ways he had been wise not to do at Foo Two. He was headed at six hundred miles per hour for the sanctioned joys of connubial congress. He was married to the best-looking woman in the world, and three minutes after he got home, he intended to be fucking her eyeballs off.

It didn't go quite the way he envisioned over the Pacific, and later aboard TWA 105 from San Francisco to Idlewild, nor in the cab from Idlewild to the apartment of his parents on upper Park Avenue, where Ursula should be waiting for him.

For one thing, there was a new doorman. O'Hara was gone. The ruddy-faced, whiskey-nosed Irishman had been the daytime guardian of the portals for as long as Geoff could remember. A Latin-American of some species, with a pencil line mustache, had taken over O'Hara's post—and his overcoat, too, to judge by the way it fit him.

He could not, he said, permit Geoff to go upstairs without being announced. He seemed to relent, after Geoff showed him both his I.D. card and the key to the apartment, which he had carried all through Vietnam on his dog tag chain. But as Geoff got on the elevator (the elevator operator was new, too, this one an Afro-American gentleman with what looked like twenty pounds of hair) Geoff saw the doorman working the telephone switchboard.

Neither Ursula nor the housekeeper opened the door. The butler did.

"Welcome home, Mr. Geoff," Finley said, formally, and then abandoned butler protocol and embraced his employer's son in a bear hug.

Which somewhat dismayed Geoff. It was not that he was not glad to see Finley, for whom his affection was deep and lifelong, but Finley was supposed to be in the house in Palm Beach with his mother. If Finley was here, his mother was here, and that was going to interfere with his plans for connubial congress.

"Oh, my *God!*" his mother wailed as she appeared. "What have they *done* to you? You're as thin as a rail!"

It was five minutes before he learned that Ursula wasn't even in the apartment. She was living in Greenwich Village, his mother told him.

"No," his mother said somewhat tartly when she saw Geoff's look, "I have not lost my mind. It wasn't my idea that Ursula should live down there. I was of course opposed to the whole idea. But she was aided and abetted in the notion by your cousin Craig, who, as you know, owns an apartment there. And so she left because she 'felt bored to death by life on Park Avenue.'"

"Do you have a key?"

"Yes, as a matter of fact, I do. I try to drop in on her from time to time, so she gave me this one in case she wasn't at home."

He could have walked down Fifth Avenue, he thought, considerably faster than the cab carried him.

Washington Mews, all of which the family (or perhaps Cousin

Craig personally) owned, was a double row of old houses on
either side of a private, cobblestone street just north of Washington Square. When he stepped over the chain barring access
to the street, he realized he had no idea which of the houses
he was looking for.

He finally found a red-painted door to which a shiny cast-
brass plaque reading LOWELL was bolted. The key fit the door,
and he pushed it inward.

"Ursula!" he called.

There was no answer. He walked through the house. It was
elegantly furnished. Obviously, Craig and his dead wife Ilse's
furniture. There was a picture of the dead woman holding a
new baby, with a very proud-looking second Lieutenant Craig
W. Lowell beaming, in a silver frame on a table.

He went through the entire house, even down into the basement. In the bathroom of the master bedroom he found two
pairs of white underpants and two brassieres hanging on a
steam-heated towel rack. He found this highly erotic.

"Where the *hell* is she?" he asked, aloud.

He would, he thought, keep calm and collected, have a
drink, and Ursula, who was probably shopping, would come
home while he was drinking.

There had been a bar in the basement, a real bar with stools
and a sink and coolers and a large assortment of bottles, and
there was a portable bar in the living room mounted on huge
wheels. He went to it, poured Scotch in a glass, and just because
it was there, not because he expected that there would be ice
in it, raised the lid of a silver ice bucket.

There turned out to be a few nearly melted ice cubes inside,
and as he dropped them in his glass and added water, he was
curious about them. Ursula's drinking was generally limited to
a glass of wine. To whom had she been feeding booze?

He forced the question from his mind, then took his whiskey
and sat down in a stainless-steel-and-leather chair facing a wall-
mounted television. There was a cigar box on the table. It
certainly would not contain cigars, but what the hell, have a
look.

It was full of cigars. Big black cigars. Fresh big black cigars.
Cousin Craig was obviously spending time here.

He assured himself that he had a despicably suspicious mind.

He took one of the cigars and lit it.

He assured himself again that he had a despicably suspicious
mind. While Cousin Craig had an Army-wide—not to mention
family—reputation for fucking any female over fifteen who
could be induced to hold still for thirty seconds, he certainly
would draw the line at Ursula.

On the other hand, why was he being so nice to her?

He looked at the match box in his hand.

GASTHAUS BAVARIA 21 WEST THIRD STREET GREENWICH VILLAGE

The matches, at least, were Ursula's. He doubted that Cousin
Craig would spend much time in a Bavarian Gasthaus on West
Third Street.

That was why she was in the Village. Of course she was
bored with life in the uptown apartment. For a wild time, she
could look down from the garden at the cars going up and down
Park Avenue, and top that off with a quick trip to Gristede's
Grocery Store.

Was it possible that she was at the Gasthaus Bavaria now?
And if he went to look, wouldn't she walk in the door two
minutes after he walked out?

What the hell, it was only a couple of blocks away, just the
other side of Washington Square. It wouldn't hurt to look.

As he crossed Washington Square, an extraordinary thing
happened. Someone sitting on one of the benches, he wasn't
sure who, hissed "Baby killer!" at him.

He wondered what the hell that was all about.

There was a knot of people at the covered entrance to
Gasthaus Bavaria.

With a clear conscience—he wasn't after a table, just looking to see if Ursula was there—he shouldered his way through.

He got as far as the velvet rope before being challenged.

"This isn't the Army, Lieutenant," a man hissed at him.

"You have to wait in line like everyone else."

Geoff ignored him and looked around Gasthaus Bavaria. There was even an ooom-pah band. The waiters were in lederhosen.

"Did you hear what I said, Lieutenant?" the man said, petulantly, tugging at Geoff's sleeve.

Geoff looked at him.

"Fuck you," he said, clearly and distinctly.

He spoke loud enough for his voice to carry around the room. Heads turned, including that of the hostess, who was attired in Bavarian costume, with a white blouse and a pleated skirt and knee-high woolen stockings. She even had her hair done up in a bun. When she located the source of the obscenity, she dropped her menus and ran across the room, crying, *"Liebchen! Oh, Liebchen! Meine Liebchen!"*

Geoff thought Ursula looked really terrible in her Bavarian costume and hair in a tight bun. It didn't really matter, for ten minutes after he first saw her in it, he had her hair down, and Ursula was wearing her birthday suit.

(Two)

Ursula was tracing with the balls of her fingers the small white scars on his left leg (Purple Heart #2) and upper right chest (Purple Heart #3), when the door chimes sounded.

"If that's my mother," Geoff announced, "I'll pour boiling oil on her."

"You're terrible," she said, and jumped out of bed and went to the window, adjusted the Venetian blinds, and looked down.

Those boobs are absolutely perfect. And the tail ain't half bad either, Geoff thought.

"It's Mary and Luther," Ursula announced.

"OK, pour boiling oil on Mary and Luther, whoever the hell they are."

"They've brought us a present," Ursula said. She opened the window a crack and bent over it, which Geoff thought to be a remarkably erotic act, and called, "Just a minute."

She straightened and said, *"Ach, Gott,* we're not dressed."

"You noticed," he said.

"Get a robe from Craig's room," she said. "He wouldn't mind. Last room on the left."

He was a little disturbed that Cousin Craig was indeed living here, and considerably surprised at what he found in Cousin Craig's room. There was a large safe, a desk, a typewriter, dictating equipment, and three telephones.

In the closet were both uniforms and civilian clothing, and two filing cabinets. And of course, the robe Ursula had talked about.

He put on a silk dressing gown that looked like it had belonged to John Barrymore in Hollywood in 1930. Then he saw the monogram, and realized he hadn't been far off. The initials were those of Craig Lowell's father, who had died before Geoff was born.

Then he found slippers and went downstairs to meet Luther and Mary.

Luther and Mary had brought them a cake that looked to be one thousand calories to the bite and two bottles of white wine. Luther and Mary, he quickly found out, were the proprietors of Gasthaus Bavaria. They were, like Ursula, East Germans who had gotten out across the wall.

"Ven I zed, 'Gasthaus Pomerania,'" Luther said, "people zed it zounded as if it vas for dogs."

Mary had overheard Ursula speaking German at a vegetable stand and introduced herself. One thing led to another and Ursula became the hostess (and sometimes cashier) of Gasthaus Bavaria.

"So ven vee heard you vas over dere, and her brudder vas in Berlin, we sort of keep an eye on her, and den, like it says in duh Bible, casting bread on duh vater, ven Ursula tells de Herr Oberst dat duh landlort's giffing us drubble about duh lease, duh Herr Oberst knows zumbody, and fixes it."

The translation of that was that when the Herr Oberst, Mr. Colonel, Cousin Craig heard from Ursula that the people who had been so nice to her were having trouble with their landlord.

he had done something about it. Geoff didn't think that it had posed many problems for Mr. Colonel. He was almost positive that the family (in other words, either Geoff's father or Cousin Craig) owned that entire block of West Third Street. The Craig family had held large portions of that part of Manhattan Island since they had brought it from the Dutch. And the one unbent rule of the family was that once real estate was acquired it was never sold.

The next visitor (this place is like Grand Central Station, Geoff thought with annoyance) was a portly mustachioed man in a well-tailored suit smoking a foul-smelling pipe and carrying a briefcase.

"Major Brockhammer," Ursula announced proudly, "this is my husband."

"Welcome home, Lieutenant," Brockhammer announced. "Colonel Lowell's told me what a hell of a job you did over there."

"May we offer you a drink, Major?" Geoff asked.

"I'd love one, but I can't," Brockhammer said. "I sneaked in here without a copilot, and that's bad enough. I'll just drop this off and head back to Benning."

Without asking permission, he went upstairs, was gone three minutes, and came back without the briefcase.

"Ursula," he said. "The alarm is on."

"What alarm?" Geoff asked.

"I'll tell you later," Ursula said. "Just don't go in Craig's bedroom."

"Nice to have met you, Lieutenant," Brockhammer said, and was gone.

Herr Oberst arrived thirty minutes later, as Mary and Luther were finally leaving. He was wearing a flower-patterned sports coat and wide-brimmed straw hat. And carrying a briefcase.

There weren't very many people who could get away with wearing the coat and the hat, Geoff thought, but Cousin Craig carried it off splendidly.

Geoff got a handshake, and then an impulsive hug.

"Since he's wearing my robe," Lowell said, "I gather Brockhammer has not yet arrived?"

"He was here," Ursula said, "half an hour ago. The alarm is on."

"What the hell is this alarm?" Geoff asked.

"I'll have to leave this overnight," Lowell said, gesturing with the briefcase. "I don't know what else to do with it. And I'll have to come back early in the morning, I'm afraid."

"Come back from where?" Ursula asked.

"If all else fails, I can stay at his father's apartment," Lowell said.

"Why?" she asked. "Don't be silly."

He's not being silly, Geoff thought. He is being a perfect gentleman.

"How thick are the walls?" Craig Lowell said, immediately disabusing the perfect gentleman notion.

Ursula blushed. "Thick enough," she said, softly.

"Don't be silly," Geoff heard himself saying. "Stay here."

"I thought you might never ask," Craig Lowell said. "I accept. I will plug my ears if that would make you more comfortable. But I really have work to do, and you weren't expected until tomorrow."

"You knew I was coming?" Geoff asked. Lowell nodded.

"You didn't say anything to me," Ursula accused.

"He wanted to surprise you," Lowell said.

"He surprised me all right," Ursula said. "He walked in the Gasthaus and said a dirty word at the top of his lungs."

"Did you really?" Lowell asked, amused.

"What's with the alarm?" Geoff asked. "I keep asking and you keep ignoring me."

"There's some classified material, from time to time, in a safe upstairs. The room and the safe are wired to a burglar alarm. I set off the room alarm by mistake one time, and there were three cops here with sirens screaming in two minutes. I've been tempted to set off the safe alarm, just to see what would happen. We'd probably get the National Guard."

"What kind of classified material?" Geoff asked.

Lowell looked at him for a moment before replying.

"Right now, the plans for an air assault division," he said.

"A *division?*" Geoff asked.

Lowell nodded.

"That is classified, obviously, Lieutenant Craig," Lowell said. "And I didn't tell you."

"What's it doing here?"

"For four days a week, I am a devoted student of Basket-weaving I, Organized Grab Ass II, and other such subjects. On Thursday night, I fly down here from Vermont and work, on the QT, for the Army. Sunday night, I take it to Washington, and turn it over to somebody who carries it to Benning."

"Before Major Parker went down," Geoff said, "he told me what they were doing to you. Why don't you just tell them to go fuck themselves?"

"Geoff!" Ursula protested the language.

Lowell met Geoff's eyes. "And do what, Geoff? Go to work with your father?"

"Why not? Just as soon as I can resign, that's what I'm going to do."

"I think you will find as many horse's asses in the employ of Craig, Powell, Kenyon and Dawes as you have found in the Army," Lowell said.

"The pay will be a little better," Geoff snapped.

"That argument won't wash for you, Geoff," Lowell said. "You can't spend the money you already have. And you don't even have all of it yet."

"People won't be shooting at me on Wall Street," Geoff went on, sensing he was losing the argument.

"You may wish that somebody was," Lowell said. "When the great excitement of the day is deciding whether to eat the Dover sole at the Luncheon Club, the Executive Dining Room, or Fraunces Tavern."

"Dover sole is a hell of a better meal than what I have been eating for a year," Geoff said.

"Touché," Lowell said. "I turn over my king, sir."

He was not turning over his king at all, Geoff thought, with mingled anger and embarrassment. Cousin Craig had decided not to fight with him, either because he didn't want the argument to get out of hand, or because he had decided there was no point in arguing with a fool.

"I will now put on my Dutch uncle hat," Lowell said. "You will have to restrain your lust for several hours. Your father is too much of a gentleman to come busting in here without an invitation, and whatever it costs him, he will restrain your mother from doing the same. You can't do that to him, Geoff. Get on the phone and take your father and mother to dinner. Take them to the Harvard Club, why don't you? Let your father show you and your medals off. He's entitled."

"I don't belong to the Harvard Club," Geoff said.

"I do," Lowell said. "I'll call and make reservations."

"You'll come with us," Ursula said, deciding the argument.

"No, thank you," Lowell said. "For one thing, I shouldn't be there, and for another, I fortunately have the argument presented by this briefcase and the one in the safe for an excuse."

(Three)

Geoff's body cloak was out of synch. He had come halfway around the world in just a few hours. So he was wide awake at five-thirty. He raised himself on his elbow and examined his wife in the faint light of the bedside clock-radio. He debated and decided against seeing if he could wake her up. She was sleeping like a child.

Jesus, I love her!

He crawled with infinite care out of bed so as not to wake her and walked on tiptoe out of their bedroom, and then downstairs. There was a light on in the kitchen. Craig Lowell was sitting at the kitchen table, drinking coffee, two thick folders stamped SECRET and TOP SECRET on the table before him.

"Christ, what are you doing up? I heard your typewriter going at half past one."

"I get a lot of sleep in Vermont," Lowell said dryly. "And I wanted to get this done as quickly as I can. I'm just about finished, as a matter of fact."

Geoff helped himself to a cup of coffee and sat down.

"There was one argument I didn't use last night," he said. "Which is?"

"That I am a married man and want to start a family. Soldiers get killed, and that wouldn't be fair to Ursula."

"I won't argue the point," Lowell said, but then argued it: "Death is inevitable. You can get mugged on Washington Mews as well as shot in the service. When your number is up, it's up. And my experience has been that if you're going to get blown away, it happens in the first thirty days of combat. If you get through that first month, it has been my experience, you'll get through it all."

"The counterargument to that is that you can stick your neck out only so many times before getting it cut off," Geoff said. "And then I think of Parker. Christ, I don't want that to happen to me. Jesus, what it would do to Ursula."

"It would be tough on her," Lowell said. "I see Phil's wife—"

"She's a doctor, isn't she?" Geoff interrupted.

"Yeah," Lowell said. "The last time I saw her, she told me that she'd been offered a professorship at Harvard Medical . . . now that would drive your old man up the wall, a black woman in the Harvard Club."

Geoff chuckled.

"But, as much as she wanted to take it, she didn't think she could. It would be tantamount to admitting that she thinks Phil won't come back."

"Will he?"

"He's alive. We know that. Felter found out. But that's no guarantee that he'll come through it all right."

"Where is she?"

"Bragg. She wants to talk to you."

"Why?"

"I told her you checked out the site for me."

"I can't tell her anything I didn't tell you. Did you tell her what I told you?"

"Yes, of course. I don't think Toni expects anything new. It's just that you saw him over there, and just before he went down."

"He was in high spirits," Geoff said. "He had just heard what they had done to you."

"Phil and I were in Basic Officer's Course at Knox together. My son was born there. Phil and his father are his godparents. I had to go tell the colonel that Phil was down. That was tough. You make your point about what happens to a soldier being tough on his people. But I suppose that it's just as tough when your husband gets run over by a bus."

"Being dead is better than being in the Hanoi Hilton," Geoff said. "The day they made me a second john, my boss got carried off. A rough old Russian, a master sergeant named Petrofski. I think about him a lot."

"You were the only one left, is that right?"

"Only one left on my feet," Geoff said.

"Mennen was very impressed," Lowell said. "He's not big on battlefield commissions."

"Mennen said I could resign when I came home," Geoff said.

"Go to Bragg you mean?" Lowell asked. "When are you going?"

"I was hoping I could do it by mail," Geoff said.

"No, they'll want you there for a physical and the paperwork. Would you like to go today?"

"Today?"

"I'm going to Benning in the Commander to drop off the briefcases. Bragg's on the way. It might be fun to return in triumph where you once arrived such a fuckup."

"I'll ask Ursula," Geoff said. "The Village is not my idea of a romantic setting. We could rent a car and drive over to Hilton Head . . . that should be nice this time of year."

(Four)
Office of the Commanding General
U.S. Army Special Warfare Center and School
Fort Bragg, North Carolina
1440 Hours, 22 August 1963

"In the worst possible scenario for this situation," said Brigadier General Paul Hanrahan, "you would be here with Lieutenant Craig, Craig. You have a tendency not only to say dirty words when crossed, but to go off half-cocked and do and say things that should not be done or said."

"I think you better explain that, General," Lowell said.

"I am in receipt of instructions," General Hanrahan said, "which state that applications for resignation from Special Forces by qualified officers will be approved in only one of two circumstances. When a request for their services after separation has been made by the Central Intelligence Agency, or for compassionate reasons—*after* DCSPERS has considered the circumstances of the officer's personal troubles."

"General," Geoff said, "I had Colonel Mennen's word when I took the commission. He told me that I would be allowed to resign as soon as I came home."

"What's the second circumstance?" Lowell asked.

"Good of the service," Hanrahan said. "In lieu of court-martial. Queers, thieves, weirdos. Lieutenant Craig doesn't qualify."

"Then I'll have Sandy Felter get the CIA to request his services," Lowell said, immediately. "And then he can resign from the CIA."

"No," Hanrahan said, a little sharply. "This is what I had in mind when I thought the worst possible scenario would involve you."

"Look, Paul, he's paid his dues," Lowell said. "Mennen made him a promise. Screw whoever was responsible for your instructions."

"I am reliably informed that the source of my instructions was the White House."

"Then we're back talking about Sandy," Lowell said.

"Possibly," Hanrahan said. "That opens two possibilities. First that Sandy was responsible for the order. That seems to me likely. We don't have enough Special Forces types, and letting go the ones we have doesn't make sense. If Sandy is responsible, I doubt if he would go along with you sneaking around the rules."

"Sandy owes me," Lowell said, flatly.

"He doesn't owe Lieutenant Craig."

"*I* owe Lieutenant Craig," Lowell said. "I'm the one who sent him to you, remember?"

Hanrahan looked as if he was going to reply, but stopped himself.

"It doesn't bother you at all, does it, Craig, to circumvent the rules that apply to everybody else when you want something?"

"Not a goddamn bit," Lowell said. "If I had followed the rules that apply to everybody else, Paul, Colonel Sandy Felter would be eating beans and rice in a Cuban slammer instead of whatever they serve in the Senior White House Mess."

Hanrahan gave him a look that could have been resigned or contemptuous.

"It's not really a subject for debate," Hanrahan said. "He has been declared essential—all of us have. Since you are Special Forces qualified, Craig, that includes you, too. So I cannot accept his resignation. I'm sorry, Lieutenant, but that's the way it is."

"*I'm* essential?" Lowell said. "I suppose that's why I'm doing what I'm doing? The fate of the nation depends upon my passing 'An Introduction to Social Theory'?"

Hanrahan was unable to restrain a smile.

"How is college?" he asked. "Learning anything interesting?"

"For Christ's sake, Paul," Lowell said. "It isn't as if we're trying to get him out of hazardous service. He's paid his dues, to reiterate. And I presume there is a rotational roster for Vietnam service. . . . on which he would obviously be on the bottom?"

"Before he goes overseas, he would have to work his way up the roster, and then he would go either to Europe or Panama before he went back to Vietnam."

"What would he be doing?" Lowell asked.

"Well, first, he has to go to Officer's Basic Course at the Infantry School, and then we'll probably assign him here as a training officer."

"He already knows how to eat snakes," Lowell said. "Is that the best you can do for him?"

At that moment, Lieutenant Geoffrey Craig understood that he had been fucked by the fickle finger of fate. He was not going to be allowed to resign.

"What do you have in mind, Craig?" Hanrahan asked, slightly sarcastic.

"You have been given twenty-two slots at Rucker," Lowell said. "Give him one of those."

"I have been given twenty-two slots at Rucker?" Hanrahan parroted. He had, but he was surprised that Lowell knew about it.

"Twelve for Mohawk training," Lowell said. "Ten for Helio-Courier*. In addition to the pilots you will get from the regular program."

"How do you know about that?" Hanrahan said.

"Who did you think gave them to you?" Lowell said, "the tooth fairy?"

"You're still working for Triple H Howard?" Hanrahan asked. Now that he thought about it, he wasn't surprised.

"Perish the thought, sir. In cheerful, willing obedience to my orders, I pass my days in innocent academic pursuit."

"Well, if that's the case, Craig, thank you," Hanrahan said. "It's important, I think, that at least some of our pilots think of themselves as Green Berets first and airplane drivers second."

"They wanted to form a company, and assign that to you," Lowell said, "under the 'administrative control' of XVIII Airborne Corps. You know what that would have meant. I talked Howard out of that, too."

"You want a medal? You got one. I suppose I should have detected your Machiavellian hand in that. I would have thought, however, that your overwhelming modesty would have kept you from telling me about it."

---

*Helio-Courier: A special-purpose fixed-wing aircraft capable of operation from very short, unimproved runways.

"I thought I should make the point that you owe me, too," Lowell said. "You can pay me back by giving Geoff one of the Rucker slots."

"Don't you think it would be nice if we asked him if he wants to go to flight school?"

"He's a nice young lieutenant," Lowell said. "Nice young lieutenants don't question their superiors. They know we're never wrong, and have their best interests at heart."

"Oh, God!" Hanrahan laughed. He looked at Geoff. "Well, would you like to go to flight school, Lieutenant? I should warn you if you do, when you get to Rucker, and they find out you're related to this character, you will become known as 'Hanrahan's Revenge.'"

"Yes, sir," Geoff said, in a moment. "I would like that, sir."

"I own a house down there," Lowell said. "I think Ursula will like it."

VIII

(One)
Room BF-746
The Pentagon
Arlington, Va.
0915 Hours, 27 June 1965

The conference room of the Office of the Deputy Chief of Staff for Operations, U.S. Army, provides a table around which eleven people may sit. There are chairs for an additional ten persons around the wall. The DCSOPS Conference Room is equipped with two Vu-Graph machines; one 3.25-inch-by-4-inch slide projector; a 35-mm slide projector; a 16-mm motion picture rear-projection screen; two tape recorders; a lectern with a microphone; and closed-circuit television.

The meeting today was chaired by DCSOPS himself. Other participants included the Chief of Staff, CONARC; DCSPERS; the commanding generals, Fort Rucker, Alabama, Fort Benning, Georgia, and the 11th Air Assault Division (Test), based at Fort Benning; a major general representing Military Assistance Command, Vietnam (MAC-V); and the Director of Army Aviation.

All the chairs at the table were filled; and most of the chairs around the wall by the one assistant the Notice of Conference to Be Held had authorized each participant to have. There were two stenographers in attendance. One was at the head of the table with her Steno-Type machine. The other, who was behind the rear-projection screen, wore earphones.

The subject today was the Manning Chart, 11th Air Assault Division (Test). A Table of Organization & Equipment (TO&E) stipulates the number of officers and enlisted men assigned to a unit, and their ranks. A manning chart names the individuals.

The conference today would deal with the names of the three general officers, seven colonels, and forty-five lieutenant colonels who would man the 11th Air Assault Division (Test) as of 1 July 1965. At a lower level of command the names of the majors, captains, lieutenants, and enlisted men would be provided.

The newly appointed and newly promoted Vice Chief of Staff of the Army had been invited to the conference—more of a courtesy than anything else—but he was not really expected to show up.

He did, as the conference had just been called to order.

"Keep your seats, gentlemen," he said. He refused DCSOPS's offer of his chair at the head of the table. "And you stay where you are, Dick. I'll sit at the other end."

DCSOPS's briefing officer, a smartly attired, intelligent-looking colonel, went to the lectern, tapped his finger on the microphone to make sure it was working, and spoke: "If I may have your attention, please, gentlemen. The first chart shows just about everything. The subsequent charts will show the individual command structures."

He pushed two buttons on the lectern. The lights dimmed, and an organizational chart of the 11th Air Assault Division (Test) appeared on the rear-projection screen. At the top was an oblong box. It was labeled DIVISION HEADQUARTERS and it contained the names of the major general who would be the commanding general, and of the brigadier general who would be his assistant division commander.

A black line went from the oblong box to the right, where there were three boxes for the General Staff and Special Staff.

Each was filled with the names of the colonels and lieutenant colonels who would man those slots.

Another black line descended downward from the Command Box, and then split off so as to connect to boxes labeled with the names of the subordinate units. There was Division Artillery (under the third general officer, a brigadier); an Aviation Group; a Signal Battalion; an Engineer Battalion; five Brigades; an Air Cavalry Squadron; and a Support Command.

Each box contained the names of the colonels or lieutenant colonels who would fill the slot. Where applicable, there were "ghost boxes" without names showing. There were, for example, four Signal Companies within the Signal Battalion, four Engineer Companies with the Engineer Battalion, and so on.

Each of the participants at the conference had contributed to the manning chart. Most of them knew it from memory, and the briefing officer knew that.

"If there are no questions, gentlemen, I will go on to the next slide," the briefing officer said.

"Why don't I see Lieutenant Colonel Lowell's name on there anywhere?" the newly promoted to four-star general, newly appointed Vice Chief of Staff of the U.S. Army asked.

The briefing officer raised the lights in the room.

"Lieutenant Colonel Lowell's name will be on the Headquarters and Special Staff Chart, sir," DCSPERS said. "He is the Deputy Assistant G-3, sir."

"Bullshit!" the Vice Chief of Staff said. The vulgarity hushed the room. General Triple H Howard was fully aware of the shock value of an obscenity, especially from someone who rarely spoke one.

There was a long pause.

"I am waiting, General, for your reasoning," General Howard said.

"Sir, Colonel Lowell is singularly well qualified by rank and experience to be the Assistant G-3. It was further felt that in this assignment, he will be in a position to evaluate the division with an idea to being able to suggest further modifications to the TO&E, and in other ways."

There was another almost painful pause.

"That's it?" General Howard finally asked.

"Colonel Lowell was considered for various commands, sir," DCSPERS went on, somewhat uneasily, "and it was the consensus—he has commanded nothing larger than a tank company, sir, as I'm sure you're aware—that others were more highly qualified."

"Bullshit!" General Howard repeated. "I don't know what is the source of your animosity toward this officer, General, but I have had enough of it. The tank company which Lowell commanded was, in fact—and you could have learned this from General Jiggs—of battalion strength. And he commanded it with such skill that it is now being taught on the sand tables at the Point and at Leavenworth. He is a senior aviator as well. For the good of the service, not to mention in simple decency toward him, it is my desire that he be given a command within the 11th Air Assault Division. You have exactly one hundred and twenty seconds to make a recommendation, failing which, or in case I disagree with your recommendation, I will make the appointment myself."

(Two)

Now the Army had an Airmobile Division. The question remained what to name it. The Airborne establishment thought it would be nice to just drop the parenthetical (Test) from the name it now had, making the new division the 11th Air Assault Division, which would thus retain the traditions of the 11th Airborne Division.

There were those who felt that would produce the wrong image and suggest that Air Mobility was simply a version of Airborne. It was not. It was a new idea; and the Airmobile people, who had to wage a long and bloody bureaucratic campaign against Airborne to get an airmobile Division in the first place, were not now just going to hand it to them.

The Infantry establishment, agreeing with this opinion, thought it would be nice to add the parenthetical term "Airmobile" to the Second "Indianhead" Division then stationed at the Infantry Center, Fort Benning.

There were those who objected to this, some unwilling to tarnish the proud name of the Second Infantry Division by associating it with this wild Airmobile concept, and some Aviation types unwilling to turn it over to Infantry.

Several four-star generals involved themselves in the dispute. Generals E. Z. Black and Triple H Howard—coincidentally Cavalrymen—thought they saw the solution. The First Cavalry Division (Dismounted) was in Korea, where it was really nothing more than an ordinary infantry division. They were willing to admit that the Army really didn't need a horseborne Cavalry Division at this time, but a Cavalry Division that moved like Cavalry, using aircraft, was something else again.

Four-Star General I. D. White was heard from. When the new insignia for Armor was proposed, a modern tank replacing the World War I tank, it was I. D. White who insisted (it was reported, with something less than his usual calm courtesy) that Cavalry sabers be superimposed over the tank. General White offered the opinion that renaming the First Cavalry Division (Dismounted) the First Cavalry Division (Airmobile) would not offend him in the least. An Airmobile Division was in the classic sense Cavalry anyway, and the First Cavalry (Airmobile) could carry on the traditions of the Cavalry very nicely.

While Generals Howard, Black, and White were personally very nice fellows, there was no other group of officers in the Army willing to go up against them when they agreed with each other on something as important as this.

"Never Get Between a Cavalryman and His Horse" was a military truism dating back to the Roman Legions.

The order was finally published.

HEADQUARTERS

DEPARTMENT OF THE ARMY

WASHINGTON, D.C.

GENERAL ORDERS   1 JULY 1965

NUMBER   181

1. 2nd United States Infantry Division, Third United States Army, Fort Benning, Ga. (less personnel and equipment) is assigned Eighth United States Army, Korea.

2. 11th Air Assault Division (Test), Third United States Army, Fort Benning, Ga., is deactivated.

3. 1st United States Cavalry Division (Dismounted), Eighth United States Army, Korea, is redesignated 1st United States Cavalry Division (Airmobile) and assigned (less personnel and equipment), Third United States Army, Fort Benning, Ga.

4. Personnel and equipment formerly assigned 1st United States Cavalry (Dismounted) are assigned 2nd United States Infantry Division.

5. Personnel and equipment formerly assigned 11th Air Assault Division (Test), Fort Benning, Ga., are assigned 1st United States Cavalry Division (Airmobile), Fort Benning, Ga.

6. 1st United States Cavalry Division (Airmobile), Third United States Army, Fort Benning, Ga., is alerted for immediate foreign service (Vietnam).

FOR THE CHIEF OF STAFF:
MARK W. LOUMA
Major General
Deputy The Adjutant General

PART TWO

IX

(One)
Washington, D.C.
7 June 1969

Kildar Street in Alexandria, Virginia, is laid out like a snake through what was once a sixty-acre cornfield. On either side of the road, odd numbers to the right, even to the left, are what the developer called "town houses." Each town house consists of a living room (with dining area), an entrance foyer, a den, a half-bath, and a kitchen on the first floor, and three rooms (a master bedroom with private bath; two bedrooms with a shared bath) on the second. A pull-down ladder in the upstairs hall gives access to the attic. In many of the town houses, the attics have been finished, thus providing an extra room either for storage or as a bedroom or recreation room.

The town houses do not form a solid, monolithic wall. The front of every other town house is closer to the street than its immediate neighbors. This staggered arrangement is not only pleasing to the eye, but gives each house a view out the side that would not be possible otherwise. And fences or shrubbery that would obstruct the view up or down Kildar Street are prohibited. Fences or shrubbery in backyards or "patios," however, while not required, are encouraged.

The houses that are close to Kildar Street are seen to be more desirable than the others. They provide both a pleasant, unbroken view of lawn from their fronts, and the privacy of the patio to the rear.

Most desirable of all, it is generally conceded, are the town houses that are not only close to Kildar Street, but that are also at the point where undulation of the snake itself (imagine an "S" on its side) is at its apogee.

There is a much better view from such houses, and they also catch whatever breeze there might be on a hot summer Virginia afternoon or evening.

2301 Kildar Street not only extended closer to the street than its neighbors, but it was at the absolute apogee of the snake. It was owned and occupied by Sharon and Sanford T. Felter and their three children, Sanford, Jr., Craig, and Sarah.

Sharon Felter was both surprised and pleased, but also a little worried, to see Sandy's dirty-gray, battered Volkswagen putt-putting up Kildar Street at half past two in the afternoon. He should not be home at this time. She had done the laundry, and pressed several blouses for Sarah. And now, because she was baking, she had been sweating. She was a mess—or at least she felt that way. She didn't like Sandy to see her when she was like that.

She was kneading dough. The Eppes-Essen Delicatessen in the shopping center charged almost a dollar for a loaf of Jewish Rye bread. Highway robbery. She would have made her own bread if she had to knead it by hand (she knew how; she came from a family of bakers) rather than give them that kind of money. Sharon Felter had a machine to knead the bread, and Anna Felter got her fifty-pound bags of the special rye flour at wholesale whenever they went home to Jersey. Sharon made her own bread for about a quarter a loaf.

She even sold some of it to her neighbors. She didn't like to do that, but she didn't know how to say no, and she wasn't going to give it to them.

As she was washing her hands Sandy parked the Volkswagen

by the curb. Through the curtains she could see that he was carrying a briefcase, which meant that he was bringing work home from the office. She didn't like that, either. Sandy worked too hard. Sandy had worked too hard as long as she had known him, and she had known him all of her life.

He got to the door and was inside before she had finished drying her hands and taking the apron off.

"I'm in the kitchen, honey!" Sharon called.

"Stay there," he called. "I'm sweaty. I need a bath!" He smiled at her as he walked past the kitchen and started up the stairs.

An absolutely wicked thought popped into Sharon's head. The boys wouldn't be home until supper, and Sarah was doing something after school and had asked permission not to come home until half past five.

Sharon looked at the dough in the mixer. All she had to do was put a damp cloth on top of the bowl and let it rise on the windowsill instead of in the oven. It would take another thirty, forty minutes to rise that way; and that as all the time they would need.

She locked the front door and the side door, and hooked the hook on the sliding glass door off the living room. God spare me from sociable neighbors, she thought, and then she went up the stairs to her husband.

And now she knew that something was wrong.

Sandy had taken off his suit coat. The briefcase was on their bed. The harness—plastic-coated, multistrand steel cable, running around both shoulders and then down the sleeve of his coat—was still dangling from his sweat-soaked shirt. In the small of his back was a Colt .45 automatic pistol. It wasn't the regular .45 automatic that the Army issued. It had been cut down to make it smaller and more concealable. Instead of the usual seven, it held only five rounds, but it was a .45; and Sandy trusted the .45.

Most disturbing of all was what lay next to the briefcase on the bed. A clothing bag. Light blue. She'd bought it years ago in a sale at Montgomery Ward's. It had not been out of the closet for almost three years, because it held Sandy's class "A" winter and summer uniforms, and for almost three years Sandy hadn't had to wear his uniforms.

He looked at her and met her eyes and gave her a little smile.

"There's nothing to worry about," he said. "I'm just—"

The telephone rang. They both looked at it. Mounted unobtrusively on the base of the telephones in their bedroom and the den (telephones the children were forbidden to use) were small illuminated buttons. If one of these lit up, it was a call on the scrambled line. In the basement mounted against the rafters were two small, blank, steel boxes with scramblers. Pushing the button made the connection and activated the scrambler on the "regular" phones. The second scrambler in the basement was connected to the "other" telephones, one inside the bedside table, the other in a drawer of the desk in the den. They were connected to the White House switchboard, and they were permanently attached to the scrambler.

If the light didn't blink when the phone rang, then it was someone calling the number listed for *Felter, S.T. 2301 Kildar Alxdr*. The light was not blinking. What bothered Sharon was that she could see on Sandy's face that he had expected it to be blinking.

"Darn," Sharon said, and went to it and picked it up. "Hello?"

"Sharon? Sharon, is that you, honey? This is Roxy."

Roxy? It took Sharon a moment to connect the vaguely remembered voice and that funny name. *Roxy?* What in the world can she want?

"Hello, Roxy," Sharon said. "It's nice to hear your voice."

Sharon saw that the interest in Sandy's face was mixed with annoyance.

"Yours too," Roxy MacMillan said. "Listen, honey, the reason I called. I wanted to call before Sandy did something silly like renting a motel or something. You're going to stay with us. We've got room for you. And all the kids."

"Roxy, I don't know what you're talking about," Sharon said.

"You haven't seen the Mouse in the last couple of hours?" Roxy asked.

I really loathe her when she calls Sandy that, Sharon thought. It may be a sign of lasting endearment from old friends, tried and true, but I don't like anyone calling him that.

"I expect him any time, now," Sharon said.

"Well, if you don't know, then I better not tell you," Roxy said, half giggling. "You wait until he tells you, and then you tell him what I said. It's too good an opportunity to pass up, and I won't take no for an answer."

"I really don't know what to say, Roxy," Sharon said.

"Don't say anything," Roxy said. "Just tell the Mouse what I said, and that I'll never forgive him otherwise. He'll know what I mean."

"All right," Sharon said. "I'll tell him what you said."

"See you real soon, honey," Roxy MacMillan said. "Tootel-oo."

"Good-bye, Roxy. It was nice to hear your voice." Sharon put the handset into the cradle. "Roxy MacMillan," Sharon said to her husband. "I'm to tell you not to rent a motel or anything else silly."

"That's astonishing," Sandy said. "I just find that hard to believe. Unless Mac walked right out of the meeting and went to the nearest pay phone and called her, I can't believe it."

"Is there something you can tell me?" Sharon asked, forcing a smile on her face.

"Well, I have to go to Fort Bragg," Sandy said.

"Can I ask what He's going to do at Fort Bragg?" Sharon asked.

This *He* was the President of the United States, Richard Milhous Nixon. Sharon always thought of Him and what He did in capital letters. Sharon, who had known four Presidents, had not lost much of her awe for them. She had been most comfortable with Dwight Eisenhower, who had treated her as a junior officer's wife is treated by a commanding officer. When He had promoted Sandy to lieutenant colonel, He'd even had a little party for them, complete to artillery punch.

President Kennedy, may He rest in peace, may God look after the children, had been the friendliest, even though He never had gotten her name right and usually called her "Shirley."

She had always been more than a little afraid of Lyndon Baines Johnson, even though whenever she had been with Him, He had put His arms around her, called her "Honey," and otherwise acted as if He was her uncle. Just before He left office, He had sent Sandy's name to the Senate for Colonel.

Sandy had been pretty sure that when President Nixon took office, he could finally go back to the Army, because President Nixon liked to have His own people around him—political people—but he was wrong about that. Secretary of State Kissinger probably had something to do with it. In Sharon's hearing, he had once made a joke to the President about how he and Sandy were the Jewish Wing of the Holabird High Old Boy Network.

"Holabird High" was what people called the Army Counterintelligence Corps School at Camp Holabird in Baltimore. Secretary Kissinger had a staff sergeant in the CIC. Sandy had also started out in Intelligence in the CIC. And then, too, when He had been President Eisenhower's Vice President, President Nixon had known Sandy, and He remembered that. President Nixon was pretty cold, Sharon thought, but she liked Mrs. Nixon very much.

"He's not going," Sandy said. "I'm going alone. I'll be there a while, two, three weeks, maybe a month."

"In uniform?" Sharon asked, gesturing toward the clothing bag. Colonel Sanford T. Felter, Infantry, Detailed, General Staff Corps, rarely wore his uniform. Most people thought he was retired.

"Uh-huh," Sandy said. "Presuming I can still get in a uniform."

That was one of those remarks Sharon knew was just noise to fill an empty space. Sandy weighed within five pounds of what he'd weighed when he first put on a second lieutenant's uniform. His only noticeable physical change since then was that he was now quite bald.

She did not reply to the un-talk.

"I've been appointed liaison officer for a project down there," Sandy said.

That was more un-talk. Unlike the remark about the uniform still fitting, this un-talk was meant to explain without explaining. "Liaison officer" and "project" could have a thousand different meanings. And again she didn't reply.

"There's no reason you couldn't go down there," Sandy said. "None at all. I think it would be fun for you."

"How could I do that?"

He smiled at her. "You will find boxlike objects with handles in the attic," he said. "You open them, you put extra clothes in them, and then you carry them onto an airplane."

"And the children?"

"Oy vay, a Yiddishe mama yet!" He was smiling at her, a surprisingly warm, happy smile.

"What about them?" she asked, as sternly as she could.

"I can see no reason why a seventeen-year-old girl cannot be adequately chaperoned by two healthy old-enough-to-vote brothers," he said. "It would be good for them, and it would be good for you. Get you out of the house."

"It would cost a fortune," she said.

"You're going," he said. "You make the arrangements, and you come down tomorrow."

"I can't come tomorrow," she said. "Don't be silly. I have things to do."

"Suit yourself," he said. "Just remember that while you're here up to your ears in laundry and bread dough, I will be in Fort Bragg in my paratrooper suit. And you know how irresistible I am in my paratrooper suit."

"You really want me to go, Sandy?" she asked.

"Yeah. It will be good for you. Old Home Week. Bob Bellmon's the XVIII Airborne Corps commander. You can see Barbara."

"What would I do all the time?" she asked. "If she's the general's wife, she'll be too busy to entertain me."

"And Craig will be there," Sandy said, ignoring the objection.

Craig W. Lowell was Sandy Felter's best and oldest friend.
They had been in Greece together as young lieutenants. Felter
had saved Lowell's life in Greece, and Lowell had repaid the
favor years later by snatching Sandy from the Bay of Pigs when
the invasion went sour.

Sharon thought only she understood their friendship. Everyone else was baffled by it, for the two were opposites in just
about everything. But they had literally put their lives up for
the other—not once, but often. When Sandy's airplane had
been reported shot down at Dien Bien Phu, Sharon had had to
comfort Craig Lowell while he wept like a child.

Sharon loved Craig Lowell because she knew he loved her
husband. There were times when she didn't *like* Craig, but that
was because he was more like a brother than a friend. Brothers
are often annoying, but you don't stop loving them.

Lowell had gone to Vietnam with the First Cavalry Division,
and surprising almost nobody, had returned with a colonel's
eagle. It was also no surprise that there was a cloud of whispered
stories that he had called a general officer a "despicable glory-
hunting sonofabitch" and dared him to court-martial him.

He hadn't been court-martialed, but he had just about kissed
off his chances to become a general. He was now deputy president of the Army Aviation Board at Fort Rucker.

Felter saw that Sharon's eyes lit up on hearing that Lowell
was going to be at Bragg. He had known they would. And he
saw too that she wanted desperately to ask what was going on.
But, she knew the rule: "No questions. If I can tell you, I will."
And she was going to abide by it.

"All right," she said, "I'll call your bluff."

"Have I got a shirt to go with an OG uniform?" he asked.

"There's two or three in the drawer," she said. "In cello-
phane."

"That'll do it," he said. "Just enough to see me through the
first day. I can go the the PX and pick up what I need."

"When are you going?" she asked.

"I'm on the four oh five Eastern flight from National," he
said. "Changing in Atlanta." He looked at his watch. "I better
get moving."

He shrugged out of the stainless steel cable harness, took the revolver from his waistband, removed his trousers, hanging them neatly on a hanger; and then in his shirt, underwear, and socks, walked into the bathroom.

Sharon set the briefcase beside the bed and slid the clothing bag off the end onto the floor. She pulled the bedcover to the bottom and folded it neatly. Then she took off her clothes, and when she heard the sound of the shower, joined her husband in his bath.

(Two)

OPERATIONAL IMMEDIATE
TOP SECRET PAREN QUINCY SLASH FOX PAREN
6 JUN 69 1722 ZULU

FROM THE JOINT CHIEFS OF STAFF
TO COMMANDING GENERALS
    FORT BRAGG NC
    FORT RUCKER ALA
    POPE AF BASE NC
    JOHN F KENNEDY CENTER FOR SPECIAL WARFARE FORT BRAGG
    NC
    HURLBERT FIELD FLA

INFO COPIES
    CIA MCLEAN VA
    DIA WASH DC

DIRECTION OF THE PRESIDENT: INITIATE PHASE ONE OPERATION MONTE CRISTO. OFFICER COURIER EN ROUTE HOME BASE.

                FOR THE CHAIRMAN, JOINT CHIEFS OF STAFF
                WINSLOW, MAJ GEN, USMC

(Three)

Many of Sharon Felter's neighbors knew that Sandy worked in the White House. That sort of secret was hard to keep along Kildar Street, where practically everybody worked for the federal government. And some worked for the CIA in McLean and were likely to see Sandy's Volkswagen from time to time parked in Area "C" there. So it made no sense denying that Sandy worked in the White House and had a CIA "connection."

Those neighbors who had been in the house and seen Karl Marx's *Das Kapital* in German and Russian on the bookshelves had been able to put two and two together and conclude that Sandy was some kind of linguist, maybe the guy who was in charge of the Russian- and Chinese-language interpreters. This belief had been subtly encouraged. Sandy let it be known that he was a philologist by training. Once the mystery was solved, no further questions were asked. Everyone knew not to ask too many questions.

Colonel Sanford T. Felter, in fact, had been, under Dwight D. Eisenhower, John F. Kennedy, Lyndon B. Johnson, and now Richard Milhous Nixon, a "Special Presidential Assistant."

The notice of his appointment was typed on a small sheet of paper under the simple heading THE WHITE HOUSE and signed by the President. This notice resided in the personal safes of the Directors of the CIA, DIA, and FBI, the State Department's Deputy Secretary for Intelligence and Security, the Attorney General, the Chief of Naval Intelligence, and the Army and Air Force Deputy Chiefs of Staff for Intelligence. Its text was brief:

> Colonel Sanford T. Felter, GSC, USA, is announced as the President's personal liaison officer to the Intelligence Community with Rank of Counselor to the President. No public announcement of this appointment will be made. In the execution of his duties, Colonel Felter will be presumed to have the Need to Know.

Sharon *really* wanted to go to Bragg, maybe because that would take her away from Sandy's high-powered and secret world. And take Sandy, too, for a time back into the world she felt he *really* belonged in—the Army. And she wanted to go because Fort Bragg was their first post together after they were married. Although she hadn't wanted to admit it, she had known then that Sandy was never going to be a lawyer or a doctor or a college professor. Sandy, all five feet four and 128 pounds of him, wanted to be a soldier.

His mother and father, and her mother and father—and to tell the truth, Sharon herself—thought he was crazy. When Sandy had won a competitive examination for an appointment to West Point, they had agreed among themselves that that was a good thing because not only would it provide him with a free quality education, but it would keep him out of the war. He was in the class of 1946; the war would surely be over by then.

But Sandy had come across an obscure regulation that provided for the direct commissioning of linguists. Sandy spoke fluent Russian, Polish, and German, because the Felters and the Lavinskys spoke their native tongues at home; and he spoke French because he studied it and he soaked up languages like a blotter.

So, instead of staying at West Point where he could finish his education and be safe, Cadet Corporal Sanford T. Felter had been discharged from the Corps of Cadets for the purpose of accepting a commission as second lieutenant, Infantry (Detail: Military Intelligence [Linguist]). Which Sharon and both sets of parents thought was an act that was stark raving bonkers. Sharon heard later that he was sworn in at the Breakfast Formation. The Military Academy Band had played "Army Blue" (*"We say farewell to Kay-det gray* [crash of cymbals] *And don the Army blue* [crash of cymbals]") and then "Dixie" (*"In Dixieland, I'll take my stand* [crash of cymbals] *To live and die in Dixie* [crash of cymbals]") as the Corps of Cadets marched off to ham and eggs.

He was on a plane two days later for Europe, where he was put in charge of interrogation of Germans taken prisoner by

Major General Peterson K. Waterford's "Hell's Circus" Armored Division as it raced across Germany in the closing days of the war.

He was also in Task Force Parker, which had raced into eastern Germany to rescue General Waterford's son-in-law, Lieutenant Colonel Bob Bellmon, from the "protective custody" of the Russian Army, who "liberated" him from a German POW camp.

She didn't find out about that until much later.

What she expected when Sandy Felter came home with his ribbons and his first lieutenant's silver bar and his Combat Infantry Badge was that *now* (for God's sake) he would get out of the Army, continue his education, and maybe they could get married.

What happened was that he insisted on marriage right away. And not by their own rabbi (although Sandy politely invited him to the ceremony) but by the Jewish chaplain at West Point. Still, it was a nice ceremony. Outside the chapel, Sandy's classmates—still cadets—formed a line and held swords over Sandy and Sharon as they came out of the chapel. Then the cadet colonel gave them both Class of 1946 rings. He didn't know if he was entitled to by regulation, he said, but the class had taken a vote and wanted that, even if Sandy hadn't actually graduated with his class.

After that he'd gone off and left her at home so he could go to parachute school at Fort Benning. That took three weeks. And then he went to Fort Bragg for Ranger training, and he called her up and told her to come down.

Sharon rode to Bragg on the train—through Baltimore and Washington and finally to Fayetteville, North Carolina—where the first thing she saw was a sign on the water fountain in the station that said WHITE ONLY.

Their first home had been half of the second floor of what had been a barrack at Fort Bragg. Sharon remembered it clearly, and wondered if that old barrack was still there. Maybe some young lieutenant and his wife were starting out together as she and Sandy had started out. It might be fun to look. Sharon

realized she was glad Roxy MacMillan had called. She wanted
to go back to Bragg.

They rode from Alexandria to Washington National Airport
in the Dodge station wagon. Sharon really hated Sandy's Volkswagen, and it seemed to hate her. It never failed him; but every
time she got near it, pieces fell off. Or the engine died on some
superhighway.

When Sandy saw that she had turned out of the ARRIVING
PASSENGER lane into the SHORT-TERM PARKING lane, he looked
at her with annoyance on his face.

"I'll put you on the plane," Sharon said.

What she really had to do was go to the bathroom. She
decided that she had to do that even though she knew that
Sandy didn't like to have her waiting around airport terminals,
particularly when he was carrying something.

He didn't argue with her, though.

"I'll meet you in the Admiral's lounge," he said, when she
stopped the car and he was pulling his suitcase and the Montgomery Ward clothing bag out of the back seat.

She had been with him at the airport before when he had a
case fastened to his body with a plastic-coated steel cable and
a pistol stuck in the small of his back. She knew the drill. He
would go to the nearest departing gate, catch the eye of the
security officer, and show his identification. Sandy had a badge
and a plastic card identifying him as a Deputy U.S. Marshal.
These insured the cooperation of the security people, and kept
them from asking the wrong kinds of questions.

When Sandy went through Passenger Checkout for his flight,
the security officer would be there to pass him through the
metal detector without comment.

Sandy had been made a member of the Admiral's Club
because he flew so much. It *was* a lot nicer than waiting with
the crowd. There was a special lounge with plush furnishings
and stewardesses serving drinks. There was also a telephone
you could use for local calls free. He thought it was funny,
being named an admiral, and he'd framed the certificate the

airline sent him and hung it on the wall.

She parked the Dodge, and went into the Washington National terminal. The heat was something awful, and she was glad for the blast of cold air that struck her when the glass doors slid open.

She walked quickly to the Admiral's Club on the second floor of the terminal and entered through a door marked only with a numeral. She had a card but she didn't need it. "I'm meeting my husband," she said to the girl at the door. The girl smiled and let her pass, and Sandy rose to meet her.

The nicest thing about the Admiral's Club was the ladies' room, which was not only spotless, but even provided a four-stool vanity where you could brush up.

Sharon was at the vanity when the door to the ladies' room opened with such a bang that Sharon actually jumped with fright. It sounded like someone was trying to break in.

But it turned out to be two women, one of them sick. Sharon quickly closed her purse and stood up, while they made directly for one of the stalls. The sick one dropped her purse, and the contents scattered on the floor. As Sharon knelt to pick up the stuff from the purse, the sound of vomiting came from the booth.

When she picked up the woman's leather wallet, she noticed in the plastic window a green plastic card, and—without trying to be nosy—saw that it identified the bearer as the dependent wife of somebody who was a LTCOL USAF. Sharon had a similar card, which said she was a dependent wife of a COL USA. While the sound of vomiting continued, the other woman left the booth and came to Sharon. She looked like a very nice person, Sharon decided, as she offered her the purse.

"My friend is sick," the woman said, with a polite shrug.

"Is there anything I can do?" Sharon asked, but the woman shook her head.

"I'm an Army wife," Sharon said. The implication was clear. *We are a sorority, and one of our sisters needs help.*

"She's drunk," the woman said. "Her husband is a POW in 'Nam." That explained that.

"I'm so sorry," Sharon said.

"She insisted on putting me on the plane," the woman said. "And she just sat there in the bar and made an ass of herself, and now this."

"I'm sorry for her," Sharon said. But drinking wasn't the answer. Sharon had never understood women drinking; oh, a glass of wine, and maybe even once in a while, a martini or something. But not getting sick drunk. Women lost their femininity when they drank too much. "That must be awful."

"Maybe she's got the right idea," the woman said. "God knows, it might make things a lot easier."

"Yours, too?" Sharon asked, but she had known the answer even before the woman nodded.

After the sound of vomiting stopped, and the woman returned to the cubicle to help her friend, Sharon followed her. They got the woman on her feet, helped her to the stools in front of the vanity, and washed off the stained front of her dress with moistened Kleenex.

"I'm shorry," the woman said. "I'm truly shorry."

"Oh, damn you, Karen," the woman said. "Now I'm going to miss my plane."

"Catch your plane," Karen said, gesturing grandly. "I'm perfectly all right."

"I'm just seeing my husband off," Sharon said. "I can take care of her. Or I can try."

"I've got two kids at home," the woman said. "The oldest sixteen. If I miss this plane, I won't be able to get home until tomorrow."

"Let's get some coffee in her," Sharon said. "And an Alka-Seltzer."

"I'm sho shorry," the woman said, and started to sniffle. Then she saw Sharon. "Who the hell are you?"

"Just another officer's lady," Sharon said, with a little smile.

"Goddamn right," the woman said.

"I can't leave her like this," the woman said.

"Your children are more important," Sharon said, firmly. "And I can take care of her."

"Goddamn it," the woman said.

"I'll see the stewardess and get some coffee and Alka-Seltzer," Sharon said, and started for the door, but it opened before she got there and the hostess came inside.

"Mrs. Sand?" she asked.

"Yes," Sharon said. Sandy never used his own name in public places.

"Your husband's worried," she said, her eyes running professionally over the drunken woman before the vanity. "The Atlanta flight has just been announced."

"That's mine," the woman said.

"And you're taking it," Sharon insisted, taking the woman's arm and pushing her toward the door. "I'll be back in a moment to take care of her," Sharon said to the hostess.

Sandy was standing outside the door, holding his briefcase. If you did not look close, you would not see the stainless steel cable coming out of his shirt cuff and connecting to the briefcase.

"Are you all right?" Sandy asked.

"I'm just fine," Sharon said. "There's an officer's wife in there who's sick to her stomach. This is her friend, and she's on your plane to Atlanta, so I said I'd stay with her friend."

"Your wife is very kind," the woman said.

"I have to go, Sharon," Sandy said.

"I know," she said, and leaned on him, and kissed him. "Go on."

"I'll see you tomorrow," Sandy said.

"Or the day after," Sharon said. "Now go, the both of you."

"I don't know how to thank you," the woman said, and impulsively kissed Sharon on the cheek.

"You'd do the same for me," Sharon said.

"My name is Dorothy Sims," the woman said.

"My name is Sharon," Sharon said. She did not give her last name. She didn't think Sandy would want her to.

"We'd better get going, Mrs. Sims," Sandy Felter said. "Your luggage all checked through?"

"Through to Fayetteville," Dorothy Sims said.

"Well, then, I'll have the pleasure of your company all the way," Sandy Felter said, and they headed from the Admiral's lounge toward gate 13.

(Four)
Headquarters, XVIII Airborne Corps & Fort Bragg
Fort Bragg, North Carolina
1430 Hours, 7 June 1969

Headquarters, Fort Bragg and XVIII Airborne Corps occupied a three-story red brick building, which before World War II had been the post hospital. It was on a semicircular drive off the oak-shaded main street of main post, a pre–War II area of three-story brick barricks, parade ground, officer and NCO quarters, and chapel and post theater that looks far more like the campus of a small North Carolina college than an institution dedicated to the god of war.

The office of the commanding general, Fort Bragg, and the XVIII Airborne Corps is on the second floor of the old hospital building, in what had been a hospital ward, complete with sundeck at the end. From the windows of the sundeck, the commanding general could see both the barracks to the right and the parade ground, and beyond the parade ground the row of three-story, brick houses that made up Colonel's Row.

Lieutenant General Robert F. Bellmon, who commanded Fort Bragg and the XVIII Airborne Corps—but not the John F. Kennedy Center for Special Warfare, although JFK was on his post—waited somewhat impatiently for Major General Paul Hanrahan, the JFK CG, whom he had just summoned to his office by the nearly irresistible means of sending his aide-de-camp to fetch him in a helicopter.

In the interests of security (the fewer copies around, the less the chance of loss or compromise) JFK and Bragg/XVIII A/ BC had been furnished with just one copy of a document called OPERATION MONTE CRISTO. This was classified TOP SECRET QUINCY/FOX, which meant that personnel who wished access to the material must possess two additional security clearances,

QUINCY and FOX, beyond TOP SECRET.

This did not mean that they had been adjudged more loyal, trustworthy, or free of psychological quirks than those with a mere TOP SECRET clearance. It simply meant that they had been judged worthy to be brought in on WAR PLANS generally (QUINCY) and on this operation particularly (FOX).

Until ten minutes ago the copy furnished Bragg/XVIII A/BC and JFK had reposed in the Classified Documents Room of the old hospital, three floors below ground level. The two-inch-thick document, sealed with tape—which could not be removed without tearing into a heavy manila envelope—now reposed on General Bellmon's desk. The envelope had a cover sheet taped to it made of light cardboard with TOP SECRET printed in large red letters at each end. Neatly lettered with a Speedball pen in the middle of the TOP SECRET cover sheet was MONTE CRISTO.

General Bellmon heard the fluckata-fluckata of approaching rotor blades. He glanced out the window and saw an LOH-6 zipping across the parade ground toward his building. The LOH-6 made a straight-in approach to a circle in which a large H had been whitewashed, then flared and settled to the ground. Ducking under the flashing low rotor blades, one hand holding his green beret on his head, Major General Paul T. Hanrahan ran toward the old hospital.

Lieutenant General Bellmon (three stars, one more than Hanrahan's major general's two) walked to his desk and pushed a button.

"Coffee, black, mugs, the moment General Hanrahan walks in here," he ordered.

Hanrahan was a wiry Irishman, deeply tanned. He wore what were known as jungle ripstops and jungle boots. Jungle ripstops were of open-weave nylon, woven in a way that prevented rips. The jacket, which had four bellows pockets, the top ones angled, was tailored very much like the WWII paratrooper's tunic, except that the old jump jacket had been made of heavy gabardine. The sleeves of Hanrahan's jungle ripstops were folded in two two-inch folds above his elbows. The jungle boots had leather toes and heel pieces, but the rest was something like nylon netting so water could escape. There was a sheet of hardened steel between the cleated sole and the insole—for punji sticks—and there were eyelets for drainage on both sides of the arch.

General Bellmon thought that jungle ripstops (which came both in plain OD and camouflage material) were among the brighter ideas of the Quartermaster Corps. And so he had a half dozen sets. He was wearing, however, standard GI fatigues. It had been decided by some sonofabitch that the summer work uniform within Third Army would be standard fatigues. They were hot, bulky, and caused prickly heat, but budgetary considerations precluded the issue of the more comfortable ripstops to all troops.

Hanrahan and his Green Berets wore ripstops and jungle boots. Though they were attached to Fort Bragg for rations and quarters, they took their orders directly from the Deputy Chief of Staff for Operations. Red Hanrahan had in effect told the CG, Third United States Army (who had issued the fatigues order) to go fuck himself. Green Berets would wear what Red Hanrahan thought they should wear. He could get away with it.

General Bellmon could have worn ripstops, too. General officers (so the hallowed legend went) were permitted to wear any uniform they chose. But Bellmon wore fatigues and jump boots and suffered prickly heat because the troops had to wear fatigues and suffer prickly heat. Bellmon had also made it plain that none of his officers had better be caught in ripstops.

Red Hanrahan appeared at the door, came to attention, and threw a snappy salute.

Bellmon returned it with a casual wave of his hand.

"I hope I didn't take you from something important, Red," he said.

"No, sir."

"Sit down," General Bellmon said, waving Hanrahan onto a leather couch. A balding staff sergeant appeared with a tray on which sat two cups of steaming coffee and two Coca-Colas.

He set it on the coffee table before the couch and left the room, closing the door after him. Bellmon went to the couch and sat down beside Hanrahan.

"If I have a choice," Hanrahan said, with an Irish lilt, "I'll have both."

He picked up the Coke and drank about half of it. "Hotter than hell. I'm dehydrated."

"Are you aware of the Monte Cristo TWX?" General Bellmon asked.

"Execute Phase One, sir," Hanrahan said. "They got word to me."

It was OPERATIONAL IMMEDIATE, the highest military priority. Yet Hanrahan wasn't the slightest bit excited. That meant he obviously knew all about it. Or wanted to give the impression he did.

Bellmon stood up and walked to his desk to get the thick, sealed envelope. He took a black GI ballpoint pen from the pocket of his fatigue blouse, ripped loose the TOP SECRET cover sheet, and turned it over. He wrote on it the date, the time, and BELLMON, LTGEN. Then he handed the pen to Hanrahan, who wrote HANRAHAN, MAJGEN.

Then Bellmon tore open the envelope.

Inside were six smaller envelopes, each with a TOP SECRET cover sheet. The one on top had MONTE CRISTO on it. Bellmon tore that loose and they both repeated the business of writing date, time, and signature on the back. Then Bellmon tore the envelope open.

Inside was a thin sheaf of papers, held together with a metal clip. The words TOP SECRET were printed in inch-high red letters on the top and bottom of each page. The first page said:

OPERATION MONTE CRISTO

PHASE ONE

1. Phase One of OPERATION MONTE CRISTO will be executed when directed by the Chief of Staff, U.S. Army, or higher authority.

2. SYNOPSIS OF THE OPERATION:

A. It is contemplated that an operation will be mounted requiring coordinated effort by the U.S. Army, Air Force, and Navy in Southeast Asia. Coordination of this contemplated operation with Headquarters, Military Assistance Command-Vietnam, and/or any of its subordinate commands will be effected by, and only by, the Joint Chiefs of Staff. Any communication between the personnel of Operation Monte Cristo and Headquarters, Military Assistance Command-Vietnam, and/or any of its subordinate commands, is expressly forbidden.

B. The operation envisions a heliborne assault by Army and/or Air Force rotary-wing aircraft operating from a U.S. Navy aircraft carrier upon a Prisoner of War camp near Hanoi, North Vietnam, to liberate officer and enlisted personnel of U.S. Military Forces held by the North Vietnamese.

3. ACTION REQUIRED AT THIS TIME:

A. Establish a headquarters (Code Name: HOME BASE) at Fort Bragg, N.C., or on such military reservations as may be under the command of CG, Ft Bragg/ XVIII A/BC.

B. CG, Ft Bragg/XVIII A/BC will be prepared to receive the Commanding Officer (Code Name: OUT-FIELDER) who will hand-carry his authority with him. He will then render any assistance as OUTFIELDER may require from available assets, priority AAA-1. This document constitutes Direct Depot Requisitioning Authority for OUTFIELDER.

C. Other addressees will immediately dispatch to HOME BASE one officer in the Grade of Colonel to effect immediate liaison with OUTFIELDER. These officers have been selected and advised of their roles in MONTE CRISTO and will make themselves known to addressees. Paragraph C is intended solely to insure that in the event of death, accident, or other exigency of the service involving selected officers that a suitable replacement will be made immediately available.

D. No other action is required for Phase One, and
no action not specified herein should be initiated by addressees. Liaison, formal or informal, with persons or
headquarters not on list of addressees, specifically including any headquarters or agency of the U.S. Navy,
is expressly forbidden.
BY DIRECTION OF THE COMMANDER IN CHIEF:
James F. Keller
Rear Admiral, USN
Secretary, JCS.

There were six more pages in the PHASE ONE folder. The
other five were blank.

"I guess you've seen this, Red?" General Bellmon asked,
handing it to him.

"Yes, sir," Hanrahan said. He looked at Bellmon, smiled,
and added, "I wrote it, Bob."

"I thought you probably had, when I saw what it was,"
Bellmon replied. "Who's Outfielder?"

"One of ours, I guess."

"You guess?"

"All Mac said when he called is that he thought I'd like the
ball game."

"Mac *called?*" Bellmon asked, crisply incredulous.

"Mac is my guy in this," Hanrahan said. "He called from
Washington. From a pay phone in a Colonel Sanders Fried
Chicken. He said that if it wasn't raining, he'd like to play
baseball, and that he had an outfield I wouldn't believe."

"Jesus Christ, Red! This *is* Top Secret."

"Top Secret Quincy/Fox," Hanrahan agreed. "But I don't
think my phone is tapped—I *know* my phone isn't tapped. And
I don't think they've got a tap on every pay phone in every
Colonel Sanders."

"What did he mean about 'you wouldn't believe' his outfield?"

"I said, 'Is that so?' and he said, 'You'll like it but you
won't believe it.' I don't know what that means, except that it
wasn't bad news."

"Is he talking about you?"

"I wish he was, but I don't think so," Hanrahan said. "At least it looks like our ball game. No Air Force, no Marines."

"Most of the people in the Hanoi Hilton are Air Force," Bellmon said. "Or Navy."

"But we are the guys with the rifles who take and hold that small important piece of real estate," Hanrahan said.

"What do you need from me?" Bellmon asked.

"Right now, nothing, sir," Hanrahan said. "Presuming I have your permission to use McCall for Home Base."

"Sure," Bellmon said. "I expected that."

"I think McCall would attract less attention," Hanrahan said. "We do all kinds of strange things out there."

"Which of my officers is going to make himself known to me?" Bellmon asked. "Can you tell me?"

"I guess Mac is representing both of us, General," General Hanrahan said, carefully.

"And is Outfielder going to go to you or me?"

"I'm sure he'll come to you, sir," Hanrahan said.

"Then all we can do is wait until he shows up?"

"I would think so, sir."

"And there's nothing I can do for you?"

"I would be grateful if the general could see his way clear to loaning me that LOH for a ride back out to McCall," Hanrahan said, drolly.

"Help yourself, Red."

You feisty little Irish bastard, you know a whole lot you're not telling me. Half because you shouldn't, and half because you like to rub it in my face that I'm too old to do anything but run a desk.

(Five)

As they approached gate 13 at Washington National Airport, Mrs. Dorothy Sims realized that she was about to have another embarrassment to go with her drunken friend. She was traveling first class. People on orders under the rank of general traveled tourist. Since this nice little man beside her had a briefcase chained to his wrist, that made him, more than likely, a warrant officer courier. Warrant officer couriers traveled tourist.

"I wonder if I might see your ticket," the nice little man said. She opened her purse and got it and gave it to him.

"It's first class, I'm afraid," Dorothy said. "I just—"

"I'm glad it is," he said. "I was going to see if . . . What I mean is, I'm up in front, too."

"I travel a lot about the guys, the POWS," Dorothy said. "I just can't take a lot of travel in tourist."

"Be glad you can afford it," Sandy Felter said.

He steered her past the line of people waiting to have their carry-on luggage examined. A crew-cut man in a business suit, who had been standing near the wall, took three steps toward them.

"This lady's with me," Felter said. The crew-cut man made a small signal to the uniformed guards. Sandy Felter propelled her through the metal detecting arch, not slowing. She sensed that he knew they were not going to be stopped to explain what made the light flash red.

They boarded the plane. He gave her the window seat and then put his briefcase on his lap. He can't get rid of that, Dorothy thought. It must be a major nuisance.

The stewardess came to them as soon as the plane had leveled off.

"I'll have a Scotch please," Dorothy said. "Dewars, if you have it."

She was surprised when the nice man said he would have the same. He was obviously on duty, and he looked like the type who would not drink on duty. She was not surprised when he took a long time before taking his first tiny sip.

"I'm very grateful to your wife," Dorothy said. "I just couldn't miss this airplane."

"I'm sure Sharon was happy to be of service."

"Still, I'm grateful," she said, and for a moment she took hold of his hand. Then curiosity took her. "Your wife said she was an Army wife."

"A very good one," he said. "My name is Felter. Colonel Sanford Felter."

He meant "Colonel," Dorothy sensed, *bird* colonel. Full bird, not lieutenant colonel, although the customs of the service permitted lieutenant colonels to be addressed as "Colonel."

"Tom, my husband, is a lieutenant colonel. Air Force."

He smiled an acknowledgement.

"You said something about POWs?" he asked.

"Tom was shot down two years ago," she said.

"I'm sorry."

"Tom was flying C-131s out of Pope when he got his orders," she said. "They put him in A-20s when he went to 'Nam."

"And you stayed at Pope?" Felter asked. Pope Air Force Base, adjoining Fort Bragg, provided air transport to the 82nd Airborne Division.

"We were living off post," she said. "I just stayed."

He nodded understanding.

"You're stationed in Washington," she said. "I guessed that because your wife saw you off."

"A little TDY at Bragg," he said, and lifted the briefcase. "I'm in Operations Analysis."

Not knowing why she wanted to do it, she took her wallet from her purse, flipped it open, and showed him the picture of Tom—the last picture of Tom—standing beside his bird in a flight suit, with a pistol strapped to his side. She also had pictures of Tom, Jr. and Sue-Ann.

"You have lovely children," he said, and took out his own wallet (from which, she saw, judging by its looseness, he had recently removed a lot of cards and whatever) and showed her his three children and his wife.

She had another two drinks before they began the letdown to Atlanta. She told him that her kids were going to meet the plane in Fayetteville—Tom Jr. having recently (on his sixteenth birthday) gotten his driver's license. He told her that his oldest was at George Washington, and had just been accepted for the graduate school in foreign service. Neither of his sons wanted to follow their father into the service.

They would have "The Atlanta Standard," he told her: a two hours' wait and a mile's walk before they could reach

Piedmont 108 to Fayetteville. He had a pleasant, shy, but droll sense of humor.

When they walked into the Atlanta terminal, the public address system was asking passengers on Piedmont Flight 108 to come to the Piedmont counter in the main concourse.

She sensed that they were about to get bad news.

And even before it became obvious, she also sensed that the large, handsome, mustachioed Army colonel who got to his feet from one of the benches in the main concourse was looking for Colonel Felter.

"God doesn't love you, Mouse," he said. "Piedmont 108 has been scratched."

Colonel Felter appeared to be digesting that bit of information, as he made the introduction.

"Mrs. Sims, this is Colonel Lowell."

"How do you do?" Lowell said. He examined her a good deal more closely than she liked to be examined. I hope, she thought, that you find my parts satisfactorily arranged, Colonel. And I hope you don't think you've caught Colonel Felter and me doing something we shouldn't. And when he continued to examine her with growing approval, she thought: Why don't you take out *your* wallet, Colonel, and show me the picture of *your* wife and kiddies?

"I wonder why they didn't tell us in Washington?" Felter asked.

"They love to strand people in Atlanta," Colonel Lowell said. "I've got a U-8, Mouse. Let's get your luggage."

Colonel Lowell, she noticed, was wearing a Combat Infantry Badge, parachutist's wings, and a pair of the starred wings of an Army Senior Aviator. Tom used to say that meant Army Aviators could tell the difference between an altimeter and a propeller. Tom didn't think much of Army Aviators. No one in the Air Force did. All three of the metal devices were unauthorized, miniature versions of the issue qualification badges. That was kind of phony, Dorothy thought. People who wore miniatures were trying to make their qualifications seem unimportant. What they were saying was "Look what a modest, highly accomplished person I am." She realized she didn't like Colonel Lowell at all.

But he was a pilot, and a U-8 was obviously an airplane, and Colonel Felter was obviously not going to be stranded in Atlanta. She wondered what she was going to do.

"We'll have to do something for Mrs. Sims," Colonel Felter said. "She has to get to Fayetteville." Lowell didn't say anything, but Felter must have seen something on his face, for he added, "Colonel Sims is down in 'Nam, Craig."

His eyes lit up. *Does this arrogant bastard see an opportunity in that? To give me that which I am denied by the fortunes of war?*

"Mrs. Sims is obviously a friend," Colonel Lowell said. "And that being the case, she can come with us."

"Can you do that?" Felter asked, obviously surprised at the offer.

"Sure," Lowell said.

"I'll get our luggage," Colonel Felter said.

Colonel Lowell suddenly pursed his lips, and made a shrill, loud whistle. A skycap, who did not at all like being whistled at, came over. Colonel Lowell pulled a thick wad of money from his trousers pocket and peeled off a five dollar bill. Dorothy disliked people who carried around large sums of money (*look how rich I am!*). She also disliked people who whistled at waiters, skycaps, and other service types.

"There's a U-8," Colonel Lowell said to the skycap, "a Beechcraft King Aire at Southern gate 34. Would you fetch the luggage and put it on it?" He turned to Felter. "I haven't had a thing to eat since Washington. So why don't we get Mrs. Sims to a telephone so she can contact the kiddies?"

He looked at his watch. Dorothy was not surprised to see that he wore a three-thousand-dollar Rolex. *He was the type. While his wife wore a Timex and searched the commissary meat counter for cheap hamburger, he wore a three-thousand-dollar watch and custom-made uniforms. And two-hundred-dollar nonregulation shoes. I am supposed to throw myself in his arms, weak with adoration.*

"Thirty minutes to eat, fifteen minutes to get off the ground, an hour ten in the air. Call it two hours. Have yourselves met in two hours, Mrs. Sims," Colonel Lowell said, somewhat grandly.

She smiled thanks, but did not trust herself to speak.

Their luggage was aboard the airplane when they walked up to it. It was a larger airplane than she expected, with twin engines that she recognized as turboprops. The fuselage glistened, and inside it smelled new. And there were leather-trimmed seats and carpeting. A VIP transport.

"You can ride up in front with me if you like, Mrs. Sims," Colonel Lowell offered.

She was about to refuse when Colonel Felter encouraged her. "Why don't you?"

Why not indeed? Dorothy thought. As long as she had been married to Tom, he had taken her flying only twice. Both times were in a tiny single-engined Cessna not much more than an automobile with wings. It had been the kind of airplane her father would never have flown in. In fact Dorothy had never been in the cockpit of what she thought of as a real airplane, not even of one of her father's company airplanes. Her father regarded airplane pilots (including the one she was married to) as sort of flying chauffeurs. Deciding to take advantage of what might turn out to be her only opportunity, she followed him into the cockpit. He unbuttoned his tunic, took it off, and hung it on a hook.

"Fasten the door," he ordered. Dorothy pulled it closed. *Does he really think we are now going to be alone?*

He was already in his seat when he saw that she had misunderstood his orders. He left his seat, squeezed past her, and fastened the door open with a hook. She hated him for what she knew he was thinking: *Dumb broad.*

She took the right-hand seat and closed the seat belt. There were still some dangling straps. He looked down at her.

"The two coming over your shoulders snap into the buckle," he said, while passing over to her a small headset with one earplug only. She slipped it over her head. He threw a switch, and the instrument panel began to glow, displaying a baffling array of gauges, indicators, and levers.

He put on a light plastic headset with a tiny microphone on a boom and spoke into it.

"Atlanta Departure Control, Army One Three Seven, at Southern 34. Request taxi and takeoff. IFR Direct Fayetteville on leaving Atlanta Departure Control."

While waiting for the reply, Colonel Lowell fussed with gauges and switches. The airplane trembled as he started the right engine. She could see the propeller spinning silver immediately beside her. If it comes off, she thought, it will slice right through where I sit. That was a childish thought, and it embarrassed her. He started the left engine.

If the left propeller comes off, it will strike him. With a little bit of luck, right in the crotch.

The earphone spoke: "Army One Three Seven is cleared via Taxiway Three, Right, to the threshold of Runway Two Eight Left. You are number four to take off. Report on threshold."

"Three Right, Two Eight Left. Army One Three Seven leaving Southern 34."

The engine on her side changed pitch; and the airplane turned sharply and then began to move down a taxiway illuminated by blue lights. She saw a sign: THREE RIGHT. It's just like a highway, she thought. But it wasn't nearly as safe-feeling. There was something ominous out here.

Ahead, a brilliant white light flashed on and off from the tail of a huge jet transport. She hadn't been aware that they mixed little airplanes with big ones. Though this one was bigger than she had expected, it was a gnat compared to the jet in front of them.

"One Three Seven Number Two on the threshold of Two Eight Left," he said, and the plane lurched to a stop fifty feet or so from the tail of the jet in front of it.

"Atlanta Departure Control clears Army One Three Seven as number two for takeoff on Two Eight Left, behind the Delta 707. Beware of jet turbulence. Maintain two eight zero degrees. Climb to five thousand feet. Report at altitude.

"One Three Seven understands number two behind the Delta

on Two Eight Left. Maintaining two-eighty. Report at five thousand."

The jet ahead of them began to move.

"Delta One Eleven rolling," came over the earphones, and the huge passenger jet in front of them turned onto the runway. There was a sudden blinding light as he turned his landing lights on, and then she saw the insignia and the long, long line of lighted windows moving past and away, faster and faster into the night. Suddenly the nose came up, and it left the ground.

Colonel Lowell was now looking at his wristwatch, she saw. He pushed the button that made the timer start. Dorothy was surprised that the watch actually had some practical purpose. She had been quite sure it was solely for show.

She had no idea what he was timing.

His voice came over her earphone: "Army One Three Seven rolling."

The plane began to move. Still gathering speed, it made a right turn onto the runway between lines of white lights.

There were black scars of burned rubber from a thousand landings on the concrete; and she could see, just faintly, the lights of the Delta jet.

The rumbling noise increased, and the airspeed indicator suddenly jumped to life, indicating sixty knots, and then began to climb. At ninety knots, the nose lifted, and they were airborne. Colonel Lowell's hands were busy throwing switches, adjusting controls. There was the rumbling hydraulics, and she knew the wheels were now folding into the fuselage.

The line of runway lights disappeared beneath them. To her left were the lights of Atlanta, and below were streetlights. And then, suddenly, all she could see out the window was a gray, impenetrable haze.

A minute or two later they broke through that; and below them was a blanket of cotton, faintly lit by moonlight.

"Atlanta Departure Control, Army One Three Seven at five thousand."

"Roger, One Three Seven. Turn to zero four five, climb to and maintain ten thousand. Report over Athens omni. I am turning you over to Greenville, one twenty three point seven at this time."

"One Three Seven understand zero four five, ten thousand. Report over Athens, one two three decimal seven. Thank you, Atlanta."

They were almost level now, although Dorothy could feel in her belly that they were still climbing. Colonel Felter, free now of jacket and that briefcase, came into the cabin and handed Dorothy a plastic cup of steaming hot coffee.

"It's black, I'm afraid," he said. "But beggars can't be choosers."

"Thank you," she said. "Thank you for everything."

"I thought you'd like it," Colonel Felter said. "Craig took Sharon for her first ride in a cockpit, and she was thrilled."

He went back and returned with a cup of coffee for Colonel Lowell. The airplane was apparently flying itself, for he held the coffee in one hand while he lit a long, thick, nearly black cigar with the other.

OK, she admitted. I'm impressed. I understand why pilots like flying. This is like being God, far above the rest of the world. Maybe, she thought, if Tom had tried to share more of such things with me, our marriage would have gone differently.

As they neared Fayetteville, Colonel Felter asked: "Where had you planned to park this thing, Craig?"

"Anywhere you say, boss man," Lowell answered.

"I was thinking it might be a good idea to leave it in Fayetteville overnight," Felter said.

"You want me to drop you at Pope?" Lowell asked.

"Yes, please. And I'll arrange for a car to pick you up at Fayetteville."

"OK."

"If you're going to the post," Dorothy heard herself say, "I insist you let me drive you."

"You don't have to do that," Lowell said.

"You know what trouble it is to get a staff car when you want one," she said. "And it really wouldn't be far out of my way, really."

"OK, I accept," he said. "Where are we sleeping, Mouse?"

"With MacMillan," Felter said. "At least tonight. We can arrange something else tomorrow."

"Colonel MacMillan? Mac MacMillan?" Dorothy asked.

"Yes."

"Roxy and I are friends," Dorothy said.

"I would never have guessed *that,*" Lowell said, dryly. And then he reached for the microphone.

"Pope Air Force Base, this is Army One Three Seven, ten minutes from your station."

"This is Pope. Go ahead One Three Seven."

"One Three Seven has a Code Six aboard who will require ground transportation, no honors. Request approach and landing instructions."

"Pope Clears Army One Three Seven as number one on Runway One Six. Report on final."

"Why did you do that?" Felter asked.

"You're a colonel now, Felter," Colonel Lowell said. "Try to remember that. Colonels are not supposed to stand by the side of the road with their thumbs out. Bad for the image of the rest of us."

Felter shook his head and went back into the cabin.

They were met by a Follow Me pickup truck, which led them to Base Operations transient parking. Lowell shut the airplane down, then walked down the aisle and opened the door. Dorothy followed him.

An Air Force lieutenant colonel wearing an AOD* brassard was standing outside. He saluted Lowell.

"You're the Code Six, sir?"

"No, the Colonel will be along in a moment," Lowell said. The AOD recognized Dorothy.

"Tony," she said, "this is Colonel Lowell. When Piedmont went on strike, he was good enough to bring me with him and Colonel Felter."

Felter appeared at the door clutching his briefcase and dragging the blue clothing bag behind him.

---

*Aerodrome *O*fficer of the *D*ay.

"I have your car, sir," the AOD said.

"Thank you," Felter said. "And there's one more piece of luggage inside."

The AOD gestured to the driver of the staff car, who went to fetch the bag.

"Do you need a ride home, Dorothy?" the AOD asked.

"She doesn't need a ride home because she's not here," Lowell said. "Right, Colonel?"

"Right, sir," the AOD said. He smiled at Lowell, but Dorothy did not like the look he gave her.

"Why don't you get back in?" Lowell said. "We'll be leaving right away, Colonel. Thank you for your help."

X

(One)
Fort Bragg, North Carolina
7 June 1969

The Air Policeman at the gate of Pope Air Force Base did not salute as the Air Force blue Plymouth staff car rode past. He was, furthermore, slovenly, and Colonel Sanford Felter thought again that all of the services seemed more slovenly these days than they had been. Was that true? Or was he already becoming a crotchety chickenshit old man?

They were immediately in Fort Bragg—or as he thought of it, on the Bragg Reservation. It had been a long time since he had been at Bragg. But when the driver turned off Pope Avenue onto the main post at the post theater, everything seemed very much as he remembered it from his very first visit to Bragg, more than twenty years before.

The only lights on in the old hospital were at the main entrance, where there was also a large, neatly painted sign. HEADQUARTERS was painted in block letters above an enormous carved-wood pair of jump wings. Below the wings was FORT BRAGG, N.C. & XVIII AIRBORNE CORPS.

The Air Force driver helped him carry his luggage up the steps. He was long gone down the tree-shaded road before a

211

staff sergeant appeared in response to the ringing of the highly shined brass doorbell.

He unlocked the door and opened it about three inches.

"Yes, sir?" The sergeant was obviously not only fresh from his cot but confused to see a civilian seeking entrance at this hour.

"I'm Colonel Felter, Sergeant," Felter said, holding up his AGC card. "Would you please get the field grade OD for me?"

"Yes, sir," he said. The fact that Felter was a colonel quickly woke him up. "Can I give you a hand with your bags, sir?"

"Just set it inside the door, please," Felter said. "I don't think I'll be staying."

There was light coming from a doorway twenty feet down the corridor. Felter walked toward it. A captain, also obviously just risen from his cot, was tucking his shirt in his trousers.

"Be with you in a moment," he said.

The sergeant came hurriedly down the hall.

"Sir, this is Colonel Felter," he said. "He wants to see the FOD."

"Yes, sir," the officer of the day said, anxious to please. He went into an inner office, where Sandy knew the FOD would be asleep with his telephone disconnected.

He appeared in a moment, a young but already balding lieutenant colonel of the 82nd Airborne.

"Sir, I'm the FOD. Can I help you?"

Felter showed him his AGC card. "I've got something for the classified document vault. Would you please round up a classified documents officer?"

"Sir, they don't come in until 0700," the lieutenant colonel said. "I'll be glad to sign for whatever you have, sir."

"Please get a CDO," Felter said. He was polite but also cold and impatient.

"Yes, sir," the FOD said, then asked the OD for the SOP, which contained emergency nighttime numbers.

"I'd like a telephone book, please," Felter said. "I have a call to make."

The sergeant gave him the Fort Bragg directory, which was

the size of the book a city of forty thousand people would have. There were that many soldiers and their dependents at Fort Bragg, which made Bragg North Carolina's third largest city. Felter went down the *Mac*'s until he found MACMILLAN, R G COL JFKCENSW, then dialed the number.

Roxy answered the phone.

"Hello, Roxy, this is Sandy Felter."

"I heard that Piedmont went on strike," she said. "You stuck in Atlanta?"

"No, I'm here. On the post. At Post Headquarters. Is Mac there?"

"Mac!" she shouted, so loud Felter took the phone from his ear.

"Sir," the FOD said, "I don't seem to be able to get a CDO."

"Mouse, you little sonofabitch, how are you?" Mac came on the line. "More important, where are you?"

"I'm at XVIII Airborne Corps, looking for a CDO. They don't seem to be able to find one."

"You've got it with you?"

"Yes, I do."

"Is the field grade OD there? Let me speak at him."

"Colonel MacMillan, Colonel," Sandy said, handed the telephone to the FOD, and stood with his face averted while the lieutenant colonel had his ass eaten for not having a Classified Documents Officer on instant call. The FOD deserved it, but it still made Sandy uncomfortable. The FOD finally handed the telephone back to him. This time there was respect, even fear, on his face.

"Colonel MacMillan would like to speak to you again, sir."

"I'll be right over to pick you up," MacMillan said. "I don't want either to put a uniform on or to show up in my Hawaiian shorts, so wait for me on the curb."

"Thank you, Mac," Felter said, and broke the connection.

Mac's car arrived within minutes. He opened the door so the light would show Felter who it was, then closed it when Felter waved. Mac would understand that he hadn't been able yet to get rid of the briefcase.

Three minutes after Mac arrived, a stocky major of the Signal Corps arrived, obviously harried.

The FOD nodded at Felter.

"I'm the CDO, sir. Have you got something for me?"

"I'm Colonel Felter," Felter said. He set the briefcase on the OD's desk and pulled his shirt and jacket sleeve up so that he could work the combination lock on the stainless steel chain. "I transfer to you herewith one sealed and locked briefcase, which I tell you contains certain documents classified Top Secret Quincy/Fox. Will you examine the seals, please, and then give me a receipt?"

The FOD was impressed. He hadn't noticed the cables on the briefcase until Felter started to get free of them. The major examined the seals—four of them, one on each side—where they would be broken were there any attempt to open the briefcase.

"Seals are intact, sir," he said. "Sir, I have been instructed to inform the commanding general when this came into my possession."

"General Bellmon, you mean?" Felter asked.

"Yes, sir."

"At this hour of the night?"

"Whenever I got my hands on it, sir."

"Well, then, I guess we had better call him," Felter said. The FOD was already dialing the number of Quarters One.

"Ma'am," Felter heard him say, "this is the field grade duty officer at XVIII Corps. May I speak to the general, please, ma'am?"

"I'll take it, Colonel," Felter said, and took the telephone from the somewhat reluctant FOD.

"Bellmon."

"Good evening, sir," Felter said. "I understand you left word to be notified when certain documents arrived."

"Who's this?"

"Sandy Felter, sir."

"How the hell are you?" There was warmth in his voice.

"Oh, I'm still pretty much out of things, General. In outfield, so to speak. As always."

"Goddamn, Sandy, I'm delighted . . . to hear your voice."

"It's nice to hear yours, sir," Felter said. "I look forward to seeing you soon, sir."

Bellmon misinterpreted that to mean now.

"You want to come over here?"

"Mac's outside, sir. I'm going to spend the night with him."

"Then I'll see you first thing in the morning," Bellmon said. "I'll be damned."

"It's a small world, isn't it, sir?"

"Good night, Mouse," General Bellmon said. "I'll see you in the morning."

"Good night, General, sorry to disturb you at this hour."

"It's been an unexpected pleasure, Colonel. An unexpected pleasure," Bellmon said. He was still chuckling when he hung up the telephone.

"Will that be all, Colonel?" the CDO asked.

"Yes, I think so," Felter said. "No, wait a minute." He took off his jacket, and shrugged out of the stainless steel harness. Then he took the pistol from the small of his back and chained it to the briefcase with the stainless steel.

There was no sense in getting Roxy all upset. He could have marched in there with an SS-11 wire-guided missile over his shoulder, and Roxy wouldn't bat an eyelash. A cut-down .45, however, was something else. A cut-down .45 was ominous. There was no sense worrying Roxy—or worse, making her curious.

"Thank you, gentlemen," Felter said to the FOD, the OD, the CDO, and the charge of quarters. "I'm sorry to have disturbed your sleep."

Then he picked up his suitcase and the blue clothing bag from Montgomery Ward and walked out to MacMillan's shining Cadillac Fleetwood Brougham.

(Two)
Quarters No. 21
Colonel's Row
Fort Bragg, North Carolina

Roxy MacMillan came out of the kitchen bursting out of a filmy dressing gown. Roxy was big and large-boned (but she was not fat). She hugged Sandy Felter to her bosom and demanded—by way of greeting—"Where the hell is Sharon?"

"She's coming tomorrow or the day after," Sandy said.

"She'd better," Roxy said, then put her arm around his shoulder and led him into the kitchen. "If you guys think you're all getting together and we ladies are not you've got another think coming."

Oh, good God! How much has fat-mouthed MacMillan told her?

"You guys are not going to horse around at McCall trying to reclaim your lost youth," Roxy went on, but then changed the subject before she finished her thought. "How the hell did you get here, anyway, with the airline on strike?"

"I was rescued by a good Samaritan named Lowell," Sandy said. Roxy pushed him into a kitchen chair and shoved a plate of cheese cubes on toothpicks at him. "He had a plane and flew us from Atlanta."

"Well, where's he?" Roxy demanded, popping a cube of cheese in her mouth. "You're not going to tell me he's off and hunting already? That bastard. He's going to get himself shot. If not by some angry husband, then by me."

"Craig's not really that bad, Roxy," Felter said, smiling.

"I've known the Duke since Christ was a corporal . . . since the Duke *was* a *PFC*, as a matter of fact," Roxy said, laughing. "And I know he's *really* that bad; and *you* know he's really that bad."

"He took the airplane into Fayetteville," Felter said. "We brought a woman—"

"See? See?" Roxy cried, laughing. "My God!" There was a hint of admiration.

"A friend of yours, she said," Felter explained. "And of Sharon's. She came down with me from Washington, and got stuck in Atlanta."

"I hope you warned her, then," Roxy said. "Who is she?"

"Air Force wife named Sims," Felter said. "A very nice woman, I thought."

"Her husband's down in 'Nam," Roxy said, suddenly solemn. "I think even the Duke would draw the line there. I hope she told him."

(Three)

Colonel Lowell was landing the U-8 at Fayetteville Municipal Airport. He taxied across the field to the Business Aviation terminal. From there a carryall took them back to the passenger terminal, where Tommy and Sue-Ann Sims were waiting for their mother.

"This is Colonel Lowell," Dorothy introduced him. "He was kind enough to fly me here from Atlanta when the airline went on strike."

Tommy shook Lowell's hand, but it was clear that Tommy didn't like him. Because he sensed in him the same things I do? she wondered. That this is not a nice man?

She got in the back of the car with Sue-Ann, and Tommy drove them out to the post.

"Colonel Lowell will be staying with the MacMillans, Tommy," Dorothy told him. "Can you find it?"

Tommy nodded his head.

Pleading fatigue, Dorothy refused Roxy's invitation to come in for at least one drink. She thanked Colonel Lowell for his courtesy. Then she got in the front seat beside her son and had him drive her home to her manless house.

She had a hard time getting to sleep.

(Four)
Quarters No. 21
Colonel's Row
Fort Bragg, North Carolina
8 June 1969

"Jesus Christ!" Colonel Rudolph G. MacMillan said to Colonel Craig W. Lowell as Colonel Sanford T. Felter walked into the MacMillan kitchen. "Look at him, will you?"

Colonel Felter was wearing a class "A" tropical worsted

uniform, tunic and necktie, and all his ribbons; his CIB; his parachutist's wings; his RANGER tab; his General Staff Corps lapel insignia; and his Department of Defense medallion. It was an impressive collection of ribbons. The senior decoration was America's second highest, the Distinguished Service Cross. The foreign decorations included Korea's Tae Guk and France's Légion d'Honneur in the grade of Chevalier. There were many others.

Mac MacMillan, a stocky, ruddy-faced Scot, was wearing camouflage ripstops and jungle boots. Craig Lowell was wearing an apparently quite new tropical worsted shirt and trousers. He was sipping his second cup of Roxy's rich, black coffee.

"I'm awed," Craig Lowell said.

"I'm tempted to salute it," MacMillan said.

"I think he looks fine," Roxy said. "A lot better than you do in your hunter's suit."

"I guess I overslept," Sandy said, sitting down at the table.

"To what do we owe the honor?" MacMillan pursued.

"First impressions, and all that probably," Lowell answered for him. "He wants to dazzle the people who don't know what a ferocious warrior he really is."

"He'll dazzle them all right," Mac said. "He'll send them screaming from the room. Anybody wearing all that crap is the kind of guy who'll get you blown away if you give him half a chance."

"You guys leave him alone," Roxy said. "He never gets to wear his uniform. Why shouldn't he wear all his stuff if he wants to?"

They believe they have the right to make fun of me, Felter told himself, because they are my friends. And because they have as many medals as I do. Although he rarely did it, Mac MacMillan was entitled to wear the inch-long, white-starred blue oblong piece of cloth that signified the Medal of Honor. In addition to his own DSC.

And Lowell was right about his purpose in wearing them. He did indeed want to dazzle people who didn't know him. He didn't want any muttering—or even any unspoken thoughts—that the orders he was about to start issuing came from some Washington Chairborne Warrior who didn't know which end was up.

"You just ignore them, Mouse," Roxy said. "To hell with them. What do you take for breakfast?"

"A piece of toast, a cup of coffee," Felter said.

"Not in my house. How do you want your eggs?"

"I don't want to be any bother."

"Then ham and eggs," Roxy said.

"Just a couple of eggs, Roxy, please. Scrambled."

"Coming right up," Roxy said, and turned to the stove.

"Have you got a place over there," Felter said to MacMillan, "that can be quickly swept?"

"I thought we were going to meet at XVIII Corps," MacMillan said. "But sure, Mouse."

"Check on it, please, Mac," Felter said. "Can you lay on a car?"

"In this heat I use mine," MacMillan said. "It's less trouble anyway. I had less trouble getting a staff car when I was a lieutenant than I do now."

"I was hoping you'd make the offer," Lowell said. "I *need* air-conditioning."

"Mac, I wanted the car," Roxy protested.

"You've got the Ford."

"That damned thing is falling apart," Roxy said, laying eggs before Felter.

"Thank you."

"You can have the Caddie later," MacMillan said.

"How am I supposed to pick up Sharon? In the Ford?"

"When is Sharon coming?" Felter asked.

"You tell me."

"You can have the Caddie to pick up Sharon," MacMillan said. "When she comes."

Lowell was searching through his wallet. He came out with an American Express credit card and held it up to Roxy.

"Tell you what, Roxy," he said. "You call up Hertz and have them send a Cadillac, if they have one. If they don't, get the biggest car they have."

"You know what they charge to deliver a rent-a-car?" Roxy

asked, but she took the credit card.

"No," Lowell said.

"Forgive me, I forgot, Mr. Rockefeller," Roxy said.

"I should have rented one last night," Lowell said. "But Mrs. Sims wanted to do something for me."

"I hope you don't mean that the way it sounded," Roxy said, sharply.

"Oh, for Christ's sake, Roxy," Mac said.

"I've known lover boy since he wore short pants," Roxy said. "I can tell him what I think."

"I never wore short pants," Lowell said.

"She's nice, Craig," Roxy said. "Really nice."

"And her husband is down in 'Nam," Lowell said. "You made your point, Roxy."

"Jesus, Roxy," MacMillan said.

The odd truth was, Lowell thought, that Mac had probably gotten more strange poontang in the last couple of years than he had. Maybe he was getting old. Or maybe 'Nam had done something to him. Whatever the reason, he hadn't done any hunting at all. And he had even turned down offers.

The truth probably was that there was something to that old soldier's tale that a man got X many pieces of ass per lifetime, and that he had run through his allocation while very young. He'd done a lot of plain and fancy screwing after Ilse had been killed, and then again after he had been left at the altar by Cynthia Thomas. Now it had to be something very special—without any complications whatever—before he'd have a go at it.

Maybe that was it; maybe his relative celibacy was a function of age and increased wisdom. He no longer jumped women where there was a chance of trouble, and he hadn't met any women lately who met that carefree criterion. If that was the case, this Mrs. Sims was as safe as she could be. Only a fool who was also a three-star sonofabitch would play around with a POW's wife.

"I'm sorry, Duke," Roxy said. "But I know what that woman's going through. It's even worse for her than it was for Mac and me. When Mac was a prisoner in Germany, he got to send a postcard once a month; and I could send packages. He never got them, but I could send them. It's not like those poor bastards in Vietnam. I don't know how she stands it."

"I'll make those calls," MacMillan said, ending the conversation.

(Five)
Headquarters
John F. Kennedy Center for Special Warfare
Fort Bragg, North Carolina
0830 Hours, June 1969

The U.S. Army Center for Special Warfare, originally a well-weathered collection of World War II "temporary" frame barracks and office buildings, had received a massive infusion of funds under President John F. Kennedy. Kennedy believed that Special Forces—small teams of highly trained, highly motivated junior officers and senior noncoms—would be very effective in fighting the brushfire wars that he knew the United States could not help but be involved in.

It was generally believed that Kennedy had a powerful personal involvement with the young, unconventional warriors who wore green berets. Kennedy's own wartime service had been as captain of a PT boat. And PT boats did at sea pretty much what Green Berets were supposed to do on land.

The Green Berets wore their cap "by Direction of the President." There were powerful forces within the Army who did not like the Green Berets, period, and were offended by their "foreign type" headgear. As Commander in Chief, Kennedy had countermanded an order proscribing their wear.

Later Green Berets had carried their Commander in Chief to his grave at Arlington, and the U.S. Army Center for Special Warfare was soon after that named for him.

The JFK Center was a collection of modern buildings, connected by concrete walkways crossing wide expanses of neatly cropped grass. The Headquarters building—one storied and rambling—shows the influence of Frank Lloyd Wright. Some of the exterior walls are tinted glass, and much of the masonry construction is of exposed aggregate.

Deep inside the Headquarters Building is Conference Room II. In the conference room is a huge oak table surrounded by comfortable upholstered chairs. It is equipped for rear-screen projection. And at the drop of a button, microphones descend automatically from the ceiling so that the words spoken by each conference participant can be faithfully recorded.

Major General Paul Hanrahan, Commanding General, the John F. Kennedy Center for Special Warfare, hands on his hips, in ripstops and jungle boots, stood at the beginning of the corridor leading to the only entrance to Conference Room II.

A table had been set up, occupied by a sergeant major. Around his waist was a web belt and a leather-holstered .45 pistol. Two sergeants, both approaching middle age, leaned on the wall behind General Hanrahan. Each was armed with an Uzi 9-mm machine pistol, hanging on a web strap from his shoulders.

There was also a neatly lettered sign reading: ABSOLUTELY NO ADMISSION. CLASSIFIED CONFERENCE IN SESSION. The classified documents officer from the night before, a .45 in a holster around his waist, sat on a chrome-and-plastic seat. He had Felter's briefcase and the cut-down Colt .45 automatic on his lap.

Colonels Felter, MacMillan, and Lowell came down the corridor and stopped when they saw Hanrahan and the guards just inside the corridor.

"Morning, sir!" MacMillan boomed.

"Good morning, gentlemen," General Hanrahan said. "I had this set up. I thought you'd want it. How are you, Mouse?"

"Good to see you, General," Felter said, shaking his hand. He then turned to the CDO and took from him his attaché case, checking to see the seals were intact.

"Major," Felter said, "this'll be going back in the vault. I'm afraid you'll have to stick around awhile."

"I'm at your service, Colonel."

"Sergeant," General Hanrahan said. "I will personally vouch for these officers. It has been my unfortunate fate to know Colonels Felter and Lowell for many years. And of course, we all know Colonel MacMillan. How do you want to check out the Air Force, Mouse?"

"I'll identify them. I've got some ID in here." He tapped the briefcase. "For everybody but General Bellmon. You've had the room swept?"

"The room and the building, the room ten minutes ago."

"Here comes the Air Force," MacMillan said, *sotto voce*.

Accompanied by an armed Green Beret sergeant, two Air Force Officers came down the corridor. One was in tropical worsted and the other was in the camouflage ripstops and Aussie (brim fastened to the crown on one side) hat of the Air Commandos.

"You find a place to park your horse?" Colonel MacMillan inquired courteously.

"Go to hell, Mac," the Air Commando colonel said, and then he noticed General Hanrahan. "Good morning, General."

"That's everybody, except for General Bellmon," Felter said. "We might as well get started. No access, Sergeant, for anybody except General Bellmon."

"Yes, sir."

"You're going to start without him?" Hanrahan asked. Before Felter could reply, Lieutenant General Robert Bellmon, trailed by an aide, came down the corridor.

"The general's aide, sir?" the sergeant major asked.

Felter shook his head no.

Introductions were performed inside. General Bellmon knew the Air Force colonel from Pope, but he had not met the Air Commando. He knew everybody else. He and MacMillan had been prisoners of the Germans together in World War II. And Felter had been instrumental, as a first lieutenant, in freeing him from "Russian liberation." He had known Craig Lowell since Lowell was a second lieutenant. And Lowell's father-in-law, Generalleutnant Graf Peter-Paul von Greiffenberg even longer. Von Greiffenberg had been Bellmon's and MacMillan's jailer near Stettin, Poland, during War II.

Despite the connections, Bellmon didn't really like Duke Lowell. There were things about him (he was a superb officer, smart as a whip, make no mistake, *but)* that were just not right—starting with his well-earned (after his wife had been so tragically killed in an auto accident) reputation for fucking anything in a skirt.

"How are you, Craig?" General Bellmon politely inquired.

"Good morning, General."

Sandy Felter was something else. The Mouse was one of General Bellmon's favorite people.

"We don't often have the opportunity to see you in a uniform, Colonel Felter," he said. "I'm impressed. How the hell are you, Sandy?"

"It's good to see you, sir," Felter said.

"Let's get this show on the road," General Bellmon said. He put his hand on Felter's shoulders, led him down the corridor to Conference Room II, and installed him in a seat beside the head of the table. One of Hanrahan's sergeants closed the door.

"Be seated, gentlemen," General Bellmon said.

All eyes were on Sandy Felter. He worked the combination of the cable harness first. Then he took a small, golden penknife from his pocket and slit the seals. He unlocked the briefcase, took out an envelope, and handed it along with the penknife to Bellmon. Bellmon slit the envelope open, took out a single sheet of paper, read it quickly, and then again, aloud.

"Attention to orders, gentlemen," he read. " 'The White House. Washington. 7 June 1969. Operation Monte Cristo is approved. Colonel Sanford T. Felter, General Staff Corps, U.S. Army, is named action officer under my personal direction.' It is signed, Richard M. Nixon, Commander in Chief."

General Bellmon passed the letter to the Air Commando colonel, who had taken the seat to his immediate right. Then he stood up, and gestured for Sandy Felter to swap seats with him.

"The chair at the head of the table is yours, Sandy," he said.

"Thank you, sir," Felter said, and went to take it. "The reason advanced to me for giving me the responsibility for this operation," Felter said, "was that I was in the best position to run this operation non-parochially. I'm sure I will have all your cooperation."

"Sandy," the Air Commando colonel said, "what happened, did the Navy take their ball and go home?" He half expected a laugh for a reply.

"Right about this time, I would guess," Felter replied seriously, "a Marine battalion at Turtle Neck, Virginia, is beginning training to conduct a hit-and-run amphibious operation on North Vietnam. It will provide valuable training, I am sure, and it will also serve, it is hoped, as a diversion. I think I should tell you, gentlemen, that I recommended the Marines for the job."

Hanrahan and Bellmon gave him surprised and angry looks.

"The final decision—which was made by the President, after he heard all the arguments—was aerial, rotary-wing, assault, utilizing Special Forces only," Felter said.

"Only?" the Air Commando colonel asked.

"Only. The ground element will be Special Forces."

"And am I supposed to go home and start running some cockamamie phony training program?" the Air Commando colonel said.

"You're supposed to sit here, Colonel," Colonel Felter said, with a steel, an ice, a fury in his voice that made everyone uncomfortable, "and do what I order you to do."

There was a long pause that grew longer as the others became aware of it.

Finally, flush-faced, the Air Commando colonel realized what was required of him.

He stood up and came to attention.

"Colonel Felter, sir," he said. "I apologize. No excuse, sir."

Felter examined papers before him for another thirty seconds, an eternity. He wondered if his own furious outburst had been intentional—as he would like to think: a "leadership technique" designed to make it clear who was in charge—or whether it was really something more out of control that reflected his own uneasiness.

As he looked around the room, he thought of something he

hoped would not occur to the others. Despite the dazzling display of decorations on his breast, he had never personally commanded more than a handful of men, never a unit as large as a platoon, much less a company.

Bellmon, at twenty-five, had been a major commanding a tank battalion in North Africa when he was captured. He had had a regiment in the last days of the Korean War, and he had been promoted to Lieutenant General after command of a division in Vietnam. He was now commanding the two-division (plus supporting troops) XVIII Airborne Corps.

MacMillan had been platoon sergeant of the Pathfinder Platoon of the 508th Parachute Infantry on four of the regiment's jumps with the 82nd Airborne Division in War II. When the platoon leader had been killed on the fifth jump, the ill-fated jump across the Rhine, he'd assumed command and won both a second lieutenant's bar and the Medal of Honor. MacMillan had also recently returned from Vietnam, where he had commanded the First Special Forces Group—all the Green Berets in Vietnam.

Lowell, as a badly wounded eighteen-year-old second lieutenant, had taken over command of a company of Greek mountain infantry when their officers had been killed, and he'd done so well the King of the Hellenes had given him the five-inch-across gold medal of the Order of St. George and St. Andrew. As a twenty-four-year-old captain in Korea, he had led a battalion-strength tank task force with enough skill and valor to earn him a major's leaf and his first DSC. When the Army finally got around to giving Lowell another command, it had been of an aviation battalion in Vietnam. He had done that so well that he'd been given his second DSC, God only knew how many air medals, his colonel's silver eagle, and command of an aviation group—roughly equivalent to a regiment.

Felter, when picking the Air Forces to be involved in MONTE CRISTO, had used as one of his own criteria command experience. The two Air Force types sitting at the table had commanded sections, squadrons, groups, and in the case of the Air Commando, a fighter wing.

While there was nothing in his combat experience that he had cause to be in any way bashful about, a dispassionate assessment of that record would still show that his exploits had nothing to do with the exercise of his command. He could just as easily have been a lieutenant or a sergeant, for what he had done in military action, he had done just about alone. He had been with only three Korean Marines when he'd won his DSC on the east coast of North Korea. In the incident at Dien Bien Phu, which got both him and MacMillan named to the Legion of Honor, it had been him, Mac, and a sergeant. His last decoration for valor had been no different. He had been awarded (but of course was not wearing) the CIA's Medal of Merit for "distinguished service in Cuba." He had gone into Cuba with one other man. There had been no command involved.

And now he was going to have to take charge of several hundred people—from two services—in an operation whose success or failure would have powerful consequences.

Finally, smiling, Felter stood up and handed an envelope to the Air Commando colonel, who was still at attention.

"Here you go, Tex," he said, his voice once again soft and warm. "That's the numbers of people and the weight of the equipment. I'll want your first estimate of what we're going to need as soon as you can get it back to me. This afternoon if you can."

"Yes, sir," the Air Commando colonel said.

"Mac MacMillan will handle the ground element," Felter went on. "You, George, [this addressed to the colonel from Pope Air Force Base] will handle long-range air transport, and then when we get that far along, liaison with the Navy. Duke Lowell will work with Tex on the rotary-wing aircraft problem and generally serve as my deputy."

"Yes, sir."

"General Hanrahan's people are already at work erecting a mock-up at Camp McCall," Felter went on. "It is hoped that no one will pay more attention to it than they do to the other mock-up villages around Bragg and McCall. While our primary mission is being formed, we will conduct a simultaneous training evaluation program, classified Secret. I hope that when the curious break that security classification, their curiosity will be satisfied."

"You're letting it out, Sandy?" General Bellmon asked.

"No. I figure that will take care of itself," Felter said. He had forgotten to say "sir," but if Bellmon noticed, he did not take offense. "Secret, these days, is what Confidential used to be. Operational details will be limited to personnel in this room. There will be no exceptions. Is that clear?"

There were nods, murmurs of "Yes, sir."

"One more thing," Felter said. "I'm going to have your orders changed to Temporary Duty in excess of 180 days. That will permit your dependents to join you. I want your dependents to join you, gentlemen. I want them to go through the motions, and the only way I can assure that they do is to order you herewith not to confide in your wives that the move is diversionary in nature. So far as they are concerned, you have been transferred to Bragg, period."

"They also serve, who pack and move," the Air Commando colonel said.

Though it was just slightly artificial, Felter joined in the chuckling. Still, the Air Commando colonel picked up on it as an olive branch.

"Sandy," he asked. "You said something about a training evaluation? Can you tell us what kind of training we're evaluating?"

"Why, Tex," Felter said, jokingly. "I thought you'd know. Inter-service cooperation: 'Can the Air Corps ever find happiness with the Army?'"

This time the laughter was genuine. But no one in the room would for a long time forget the tone of voice Felter had used on Tex when the dumb shit made that sour-ass remark. The only one in the room it didn't surprise was Duke Lowell. He and the Mouse went back a long time. He had heard the ice in the Mouse's voice before.

(Six)
Headquarters, XVIII Airborne Corps & Fort Bragg
Fort Bragg, North Carolina
9 June 1970

"Office of the Corps commander, Captain Hollis, aide-de-camp, speaking, sir." It was the prescribed military manner of answering the telephone.

"Let me speak to him, please," the caller said. "This is Colonel Lowell." That was not the expected manner of inquiry.

"The general is in conference, sir. May I help you?"

"Yes," Lowell said. There was arrogance, not blatant but undeniable, in Lowell's voice. "Slip a note to him, will you? Telling him I'm on the line?"

"I'm not sure I can do that, sir. May I ask the general to call you back?"

"Give him the note, Captain, please," Lowell said. This was delivered in a firm that-is-an-order-which-you-will-obey tone of voice.

"Yes, sir."

Fuck you, Colonel.

Captain Hollis wrote "Col. Lowell insists on speaking to you on line 3" on a notepad, ripped it off, and entered the general's office without knocking. General Bellmon looked at him in annoyance, which suited Captain Hollis just fine. If he was annoyed now, wait till he saw the note. Colonels do not insist on talking to generals.

Bellmon glanced at the note, excused himself to the others at the conference table, and reached for the telephone on his desk. Captain Hollis quickly left the office and picked up his extension in time to hear ". . . can I do for you?"

"Sir, I wondered if the general could fit a little skeet into his schedule today?"

There was a moment's hesitation.

"What time did you have in mind, Lowell?" General Bellmon replied, surprising Captain Hollis no small degree.

"I've taken the liberty, General, to reserve a field at three."

"OK, Craig, fifteen hundred," General Bellmon said.

"Thank you, sir," Colonel Lowell said. "I'll look forward to it."

I'll be goddamned. Captain Hollis shrugged, then he picked up the telephone and called Quarters Number One and told the general's orderly to have the general's shotgun and ammo box loaded into the general's personal automobile. The general did not like to use his shining staff car for trips to recreational facilities.

At 1450, the general's driver reported to Captain Hollis that the general had driven himself to the skeet range. Captain Hollis told him to stay loose; he didn't know what the general's plans were for the balance of the day.

General Bellmon found Colonel Lowell waiting for him at the Fort Bragg Trap and Skeet Club, a facility of the Fort Bragg Rod and Gun Club. Lowell was sitting on the open tailgate of a Ford station wagon, hatless, wearing a shooting vest over his tropical worsted open-necked shirt and trousers.

He got up when Bellmon pulled in beside him.

"Sorry to disrupt your day, General," Lowell said.

"To tell you the truth, Craig," Bellmon said, shaking his hand as if he hadn't seen him for a long time, "it was a welcome interruption."

He pulled a leather-covered case from the floor of the back seat and laid it on the tailgate of Lowell's station wagon. He took from it the stock and action of a Browning over-and-under shotgun.

"What are we shooting?"

"Does the general feel confident with a 28-bore?" Colonel Lowell asked, obviously a challenge.

"Against the present competition, the general feels very confident with a 28-bore," the general said, and selected the 28-gauge set of barrels from the four sets of barrels in the case. "I'll have to get some shells, though."

Lowell reached into the station wagon and came up with a box of Winchester Western AA shotshells. He handed it to Bellmon. He took another box and dumped the shells into the pocket of his shooting vest. Then he took his shotgun from a case.

"What is that, a Holland and Holland?" General Bellmon asked. Lowell handed him the shotgun.

"An *Augshofer*," he said. "He makes the best, I think, live-pigeons guns. He really didn't want to make this one, but when I finally talked him into it, it was worth all the trouble. Would you like to shoot it?"

"May I? I don't think I've ever seen one before."

"That's it," Lowell said.

General Bellmon was very seriously tempted to ask him what he had paid for the shotgun. Three thousand? Five thousand? More? Hand-made shotguns by Austrian gunmakers were the most expensive. Very probably more.

"Nice piece," he said, throwing the gun to his shoulder. "And it fits."

"I went through that business at the Holland and Holland shooting school in London. You know, the gray-haired expert and the try-gun with all the adjustments. And I found out my measurements, as measured by the greatest experts, are exactly those of an off-the-shelf Winchester 101."

"Nice piece," Bellmon repeated. He handed Lowell his Browning, and they walked to the skeet field, both of them stuffing rubber earplugs into their ears as they walked. The NCO in charge waited for them there. He saluted.

"Afternoon, General," he said. "We're all ready for you."

"Hello, Sergeant DeMarco," Bellmon said, offering his hand. "You've met Colonel Lowell?"

"I've been admiring the colonel's gun, General," DeMarco said.

"So have I," General Bellmon said, and held it up. "You'll notice who's going to be shooting it."

The sergeant chuckled. "I'll be pulling for you, sir," he said.

Bellmon and Lowell walked to Station One. Lowell waved the general onto the paint-marked shooting place. General Bellmon broke the shotgun and dropped shells into the chambers.

"Let's see one," he said, and the target-throwing machine sent a clay pigeon flying first out of the high house above Bellmon's shoulder, and then from the low house across the field. He nodded. "Everything going smoothly, Duke?" he asked, and then called, "Pull!"

A clay pigeon flew out of the house above him. The shotgun fired, and the pigeon disappeared in a puff of gray-black debris.

"Mark!" Bellmon called, and another pigeon flew out, this time from the low house. He broke that one quite close to him.

He opened the shotgun and the fired shell casings flew out of the chambers.

"Very nice," Lowell said, as Bellmon reloaded.

"Everything going along all right, Duke?" Bellmon asked.

"Your vehicle inspection station seems unable to handle a rental car, but aside from that, there have been no major problems.".

Bellmon looked at him. "Is there a problem with your car?"

"I told the provost marshal that I had your personal permission to have a rental car furnished with a sticker," Lowell said. "I don't really think he'll check with you."

"We don't have many people able to afford rental cars indefinitely," Bellmon said. He called, "Pull," and two clay pigeons were simultaneously thrown from the houses. He broke both of them, opened the action, ejected the shells.

"Very nice," he said, admiring the gun. "Points beautifully."

Lowell moved onto the shooting station.

"Can you arrange a series of unscheduled battalion-sized airlifts in the division?" Lowell said. "Say from here to Hurlbert*? And from here to Yuma Test Station? And Fort Hood?"

"I can give you the people, Duke," General Bellmon said. "But I don't have the funding for the Air Force."

"The Air Force has just found some funds," Lowell said. "That won't be a problem."

"OK," Bellmon said. "Consider it done. Tell me when."

Lowell reached in his back trousers pocket and handed Bellmon a folded sheet of paper.

---

*Hurlbert Field, on the Gulf of Mexico on the Florida Panhandle, was the home of the USAF Air Commando Wing.

"Those are the dates the Mouse would like," he said. Without looking at it, Bellmon put it in his trousers pocket.

"The Air Force will use C-5As for the first couple of trips," Lowell said. "Then there will be some mechanical difficulty, requiring the C5-As to be grounded here for maintenance and inspection. One of them will be made available to MacMillan's Berets for on-site loading familiarization."

He called for his bird, broke it. Then he called for the low house and missed.

"Damn," he said, and reloaded and called for it again and broke it.

"You're going to use C5As?" Bellmon asked.

"Tex Williams says we can make it nonstop to Okinawa," Lowell said. "And he also says the Jolly Green Giants can make it from Okinawa to the carrier off 'Nam without any problem."

"It looks like you're putting all your eggs in one basket."

"We'll have a fifty percent redundancy in Green Giants," Lowell said. "Pull!"

He broke his doubles, and then walked to Station Two.

"And a two hundred percent redundancy in C5As," Lowell said. "We'll take off together, either from here or from Hurlbert. An empty one will precede us, they're about ninety knots an hour faster empty. And a third will follow. You can only put so many Jolly Greens on a carrier."

"When are you going to tell the Navy?"

"The Mouse is going to go two days early. Tex has laid on a two-seater jet for him. One last check of Intelligence in Saigon, and then he's going to have the Chief of Naval Operations lay it on the task force commander at sea, as an Operational Immediate, with no details. He will personally deliver those."

"I hope the Navy doesn't decide to take their ball and go home," Bellmon said. "They're not going to like being just about shut out of this."

"Fuck 'em," Lowell said. "The Marines are still fighting World War II."

Bellmon stepped into the shooting position and called for his doubles. He broke all four.

"Anything else?" Bellmon asked.

"Have you got a set of very nice bachelor officer quarters suitable for a full colonel?"

Bellmon looked at him, his right eyebrow arched.

Lowell pretended to cringe. He held up his hand, in mock self-protection.

"What the Mouse wants is some very angry bird, loudly complaining that he has been turned out of his quarters by a goddamned aviator, here for six months, on some cockamamie paper-pushing operation."

"Done," Bellmon said. "I know just the guy." He chuckled. "The Mouse covers every base, doesn't he?"

"While we are discussing the Mouse, sir. Colonel Felter's compliments, sir," Lowell said, dryly. "The colonel asked me to inform the general that he would be most appreciative if the general and Mrs. Bellmon could find time in their busy, busy schedule to attend Mrs. Rudolph G. MacMillan's cocktail soirée tomorrow. Five-thirtyish."

"Oh, I think Mrs. Bellmon will be able to squeeze it in," Bellmon said, grinning. His wife and MacMillan's were old and close friends. And they were both very fond of Sharon and Sandy Felter. It would have taken a war to keep Barbara Bellmon from being with old friends.

Lowell moved to the shooting position and broke all four of his birds.

"There's a VIP suite, two quarters with the walls knocked out between them in the BOQ on Smokebomb Hill," General Bellmon said.

"Oh, jolly," Lowell said. "With the corridors full of drunken platoon leaders and the shrill laughter of their girlfriends. How will I ever get my sleep?"

"Some of the company grade officers are now in skirts, Duke. Consider that."

"That's damned near incestuous," Lowell said. "I do draw a line somewhere, despite my reputation."

"I'm very glad to hear that," General Bellmon said. They walked to Station Three.

"How's Peter?" General Bellmon asked.

As a very young officer, still bandaged from his wounds in Greece, Craig Lowell had married Ilse von Greiffenberg. Peter-Paul Lowell had been born in the Station Hospital, Fort Knox, Kentucky, five months later. Three years after that, his missing and presumed dead grandfather, Colonel Graf Peter-Paul von Greiffenberg, had been released from Soviet captivity in Siberia.

Von Greiffenberg—who had attended the French Cavalry School at Samur with Barbara Bellmon's father, when both Major General Porky Waterford and (ultimately) Lieutenant General Graf von Greiffenberg were captains—had, as a wounded colonel, commanded the POW camp where Major Bellmon and Technical Sergeant Mac MacMillan were imprisoned.

When Lowell had been ordered to Korea, his wife and child went to live with her father, by then a major general and Chief of Intelligence for the *Bundeswehr*. The day before Task Force Lowell, moving north from Pusan, had linked up with the American forces that had landed at Inchon; the day before Lowell had been awarded a battlefield promotion to major and the Distinguished Service Cross; Ilse von Greiffenberg Lowell, while driving from the Giessen Quartermaster Depot PX to her father's home, had been struck and instantly killed by a car driven by a drunken major of the Quartermaster Corps.

The boy, who was unharmed, had been thereafter raised by Graf von Greiffenberg and members of his family.

"Very well, I understand," Lowell said, bitterness showing in his voice. "I take *Stern*. He is one of their brighter reporters."

"Do you see him often?"

"I don't see him at all," Lowell said coldly, matter-of-factly.

There was nothing General Bellmon could think of to reply to that, so he stepped into shooting position and called for his birds.

(Seven)
Fayetteville, North Carolina
10 June 1970

"Colonel Sims's quarters," the boy said when he answered the telephone.

It wasn't Colonel Sims's quarters. It was a civilian house in Fayetteville, rented by Mrs. Sims while Colonel Sims was in a POW camp in North Vietnam. Dependents are entitled to reside in government quarters only when the sponsor is present for duty. TDY to the Hanoi Hilton doesn't count. But Colonel Sims's son and namesake answered the phone by saying "Colonel Sims's quarters" because that was about the only way he could hang on to his father.

"Tommy, this is Roxy MacMillan. Is your mother there?"

"Yes, ma'am," Tommy said. "I'll call her."

"Hello, Roxy," Dorothy Sims said.

"I need a favor, Dorothy," Roxy said.

"Name it."

"I need an extra lady for a little party," Roxy said. Dorothy didn't immediately reply, so Roxy plunged on. "I have two bachelors, one temporary, and the other confirmed."

"Roxy—" Dorothy Sims started to protest.

"One of them is Tex Williams. I don't know him, but he's in this training evaluation project with Mac, and Mac wants to make him feel welcome. And he knows you and Tom."

"I'm not in a party mood," Dorothy said.

"I know that," Roxy said. "But it will do you good to get out of the house. Tom would want you to, you know that."

"I don't think so, Roxy. Thank you just the same."

"The other bachelor is Duke Lowell," Roxy said. "If you don't let him catch you in a corner, he's a lot of fun. And I need you, Dorothy. Your friend Sharon Felter's coming, too. She'll be in on the four o'clock Piedmont from Atlanta. They'll be staying with us until Sandy can get quarters."

I am being silly, Dorothy Sims suddenly realized. *Or a masochist. I would like to get out of the house. I am sick of it, I am sick of other POW wives. Tex Williams is an old* friend, and there is absolutely no reason I should not go, unless it is to maintain this facade of patient, suffering, saintly wife.

"Come on, Dorothy. Come on out this afternoon, and we'll have a couple of belts while I'm getting ready," Roxy said.

"I'm not sure if a couple of belts is a good idea," Dorothy said. "I seem to be taking a couple of belts far more often than is good for me."

"Well, then, do it with friends," Roxy said, and there was compassion in her voice. "The only man you'll have to worry about here is Duke Lowell, and I will sit on him."

"Is he really that bad?"

"Don't misunderstand me," Roxy said. "I love the Duke like a brother. And I've known him since Christ was a corporal. I have just found it wise to warn people about him. He has a certain something that seems to make women uncross their legs. I'm not sure if it's his blue eyes and mustache, or his money."

"That's a dangerous combination," Dorothy laughed.

"Forewarned is forearmed," Roxy said.

"If you're sure I wouldn't make everybody uncomfortable."

"Listen, honey," Roxy said. "The Bellmons are going to be here. Barbara and I know what you're going through. Both of ours were in a POW camp, too, you know."

"All right," Dorothy Sims said. "When do you want me to come?"

"Get dressed now and come," Roxy said. "That way you don't have time to change your mind."

Dorothy chuckled. "Can I bring anything?"

"Just your body, dear," Roxy said, and laughed, and hung up.

Dorothy told Tommy what she was going to do, and gave him three dollars to take his bike to the Winn-Dixie to get the superdeluxe pizza for supper.

And then she went upstairs and took a shower. She was not surprised when the telephone rang the moment she was soaking wet. When else would it ring?

"I'm glad I caught you," Roxy said. "I was just thinking,

you know Sharon, and it would save me a trip to town if you could pick her up."

"Oh, I'd be happy to," Dorothy said, and looked at the clock on the chest of drawers to see what time it was. Roxy had said something about four o'clock. It was quarter after three. "I've got time, I'll pick her up and bring her out."

"You're a darling," Roxy said.

Dorothy hung up thoughtfully. Somehow, the idea had been formed that she and Sharon were old friends, when actually she hardly knew her. Well, that wasn't important. It could be straightened out.

She looked at the clock again, and this time she saw her reflection in the mirror. She didn't normally like to see herself naked. She was thirty-nine. The smooth-bellied nymph of yesterday was gone. But I don't look bad, she thought. I'm still desirable.

And that's wasted, too. Oh, you bastard, why did you get shot down! If you had gotten through your tour, you'd have been home eighteen months ago, and we would have been divorced six months later. If you hadn't got yourself shot down, I would be free of you, and I could flirt with this dangerous Lowell character.

God, *that's* a dangerous line of thought! Stop that right *now!*

Averting her eyes, she walked quickly back into the bathroom and finished her shower.

XI

(One)
Fayetteville, North Carolina
1705 Hours, 10 June 1969

The Fayetteville Airport terminal was circular and glassy, a small-town airport turned busy-busy by the war-generated travel to and from Fort Bragg. The days of troop trains were over. Now the troops traveled by commercial air. But they still looked scared and they made Dorothy sad. Even the Green Berets, who seemed genuinely pleased to be leaving Fort Bragg to exchange make-believe war for the real thing, made her sad. The Fayetteville Airport terminal reminded Dorothy of one of those new, splendiferous funeral homes, patterned on Tara in *Gone with the Wind*.

And when the plan bringing Sharon Felter to Fayetteville arrived, she felt even worse. The first items out of the cargo compartment were two flag-draped caskets.

Was Tom going to finally come home that way? Please God, no. Not for the children's sake. Give them back their father.

She saw that Sharon was not alone. There was a teenaged girl with her. A tall (much taller than Sharon) awkward gangling girl with a mouthful of silver braces, looking sad and sullen.

"Sharon?" Dorothy called.

"Well, hello," Sharon said, after a moment's pause while she recalled just whom she was talking to. "How nice to see you again."

"I'm here to meet you," Dorothy said.

Sharon Felter looked a little confused.

"Roxy MacMillan asked me to," Dorothy said.

"You're a friend of Roxy's?" Sharon replied. She was pleased.

"Yes, and Roxy has somehow gotten the idea that you and I are dear old friends," Dorothy said.

"Dear new friends," Sharon said. "Sarah, this is Mrs. Sims. Dorothy, this is my daughter."

"Hello, Sarah," Dorothy said.

Sarah managed a faint smile.

"Sarah is not happy to be in Fort Bragg," Sharon said. "Could you tell?"

"No!"

"Mother!"

The mothers of daughters exchanged smiles. They walked to the Baggage Claim area.

"I really don't know what's going on," Sharon said as she heaved her suitcase from the carousel, grunting a little. "Sandy was planning to be here only a couple of weeks, and then he called and told me to come prepared to stay for some time."

Dorothy smiled. She didn't know what to say. But then she thought of something:

"It looks like a gathering of old friends," she said.

"Sandy told me Craig Lowell is here," Sharon said. "We've known Craig for a long time. Is that who you mean?"

"Roxy has warned me about him," Dorothy said.

"Roxy gets carried away," Sharon said, loyally. "As I'm sure you know."

They got in the car and drove out to Fort Bragg.

Sharon seemed pleased when Roxy enveloped her in a bear hug. Ruth seemed to resent it.

"Sandy and Duke are off somewhere in Duke's airplane," Roxy said. "But they promised to be back at six-thirty."

(Two)

It was quarter to seven before they appeared in a dust-covered Ford station wagon. Colonel Felter was in a class "A" tropical worsted uniform. Lowell was in a well-worn flight suit, a grayish tan coverall, grease- and sweat-stained.

They disappeared immediately upstairs, and Dorothy could hear the sound of a shower running.

General and Mrs. Bellmon arrived, introducing themselves to Dorothy as Bob and Barbara. The general was in civilian sports clothes and helped himself to the gin and vermouth, wordlessly offering a glass to Dorothy. She accepted with a nod of her head.

It was icy cold and she liked it.

Colonel Felter appeared first, in a cotton knit shirt and wash pants.

"You got that message, Sandy?" Bellmon asked, shaking his hand.

"Lowell and I flew up and got it," Felter said. He declined a martini and fished a bottle of wine from the beer cooler. He made himself a spritzer, adding ice and soda to the white wine.

Lowell appeared, also in civilian clothes. The metamorphosis was complete. He didn't look like an officer in civvies. He looked like a model in an advertisement in *Town & Country* for fifty-year-old brandy. He had a cord jacket on and crisply pressed gray slacks, loafers with tassels, and even an ascot knotted around his neck. And the aviator's wristwatch was gone, replaced by a dime-thin gold watch on an alligator band. No wonder they called him the Duke. She remembered that Roxie had said something about his having money.

Dorothy hadn't thought anything about it then. "Money" to Roxy, as to most service wives, almost always meant that a parent had died and left an unexpected multi-thousand-dollar windfall—enough to pay off the car, or the house, or to send the kids to college without strain. It wasn't "money" as Dorothy's father thought of money, or as she was again letting herself think of money. To her father "money" meant wealth. She was suddenly *sure* that "wealthy" was the word to apply to Colonel Craig Lowell.

"Hello, again, Mrs. Sims," he said, smiling distantly, impersonally, at her. "It's nice to see you again."

"Please call me Dorothy," she said. "That's a lovely watch."

He gave her a strange look.

"It was a Christmas present," he said.

"It's lovely," she repeated and put out her hand. It *was* a Patek Philippe. Three thousand dollars.

"She must be a very good friend," she said.

He gave her a strange look.

"My mother's husband gave it to me," he said.

She wondered why that bit of information pleased her so much. Because meeting someone else who was wealthy in these surroundings was like meeting another American in Vladivostok?

She smiled at him. Colonel Lowell looked at her strangely, with what could have been contempt in his eyes.

What do I do now, say, "It's OK, Colonel, my father is the Carolina Tobacco Company"?

When he disappeared and came back with a bottle of Ambassador Twelve-Year-Old Scotch whiskey she knew was his own bottle, she was a little jealous. He didn't care if his friends knew he was rich, while she had spent her married life pretending that her own wealth didn't exist. His way obviously worked better than hers did.

"I had to write Mother twice this week, Craig," Barbara Bellmon said, smiling with clearly genuine warmth. "Once to tell her that no, I hadn't the faintest idea what had happened to you, and then to tell her that you now have dropped out of the sky looking as dapper as ever."

"Please give her my fondest regards," Lowell said, and Dorothy sensed that his words weren't just ritual courtesy. Lowell clearly genuinely liked Barbara Bellmon's mother. "She's still in Carmel?"

"Playing golf and raising roses," Barbara said.

"I was just thinking," Lowell said, "looking at Mac's stove..." He inclined his head toward the cut-in-half fifty-five-gallon drum set up in the rear of Mac's quarters, "that that is probably the very same stove on which General Waterford burned perfectly good meat into carbon for Mrs. Waterford and me at Mac and Roxy's place in Bad Nauheim."

"No, it's not, Duke," Roxy said. "It's the same kind of barbecue, but it's a new one. I just can't talk him into getting something decent."

"You should never have married a paratrooper," Lowell said. "They don't know decent."

"Oh, go to hell, Duke," Roxy said, fondly.

"I gather you served with Mrs. Bellmon's father, Colonel?" Dorothy asked.

"Yes, ma'am," he said, and smiled at her. His "ma'am" sounded quite as phony to her ears as her own "I gather, Colonel." Was he mocking her?

"I began as Mrs. Waterford's golf pro," he went on. "And then, after I had done so splendidly at that, I was promoted to Master of the Royal Horse."

Barbara Bellmon laughed.

"I have no idea what you're talking about," Dorothy said.

"The Duke," Roxy said, "was a PFC, the golf pro at the Constabulary golf course." Dorothy wasn't sure she was hearing correctly. It was difficult to imagine this tall—what?— *aristocrat* as an enlisted man.

"I was perfectly happy," Colonel Lowell said, "teaching the ladies how to swat the ball. And then MacMillan, who was then—believe it or not—a lean, lithe, flat-bellied paratrooper captain, put his two cents in."

"Mac was Daddy's aide, Dorothy," Barbara Bellmon explained, "after he and Bob came home from the POW camp." Dorothy understood that comment had been injected in the story for her benefit. "And Daddy was a polo player."

"And he told me to round up the best polo players in the Constabulary," MacMillan said.

"One of whom was PFC Lowell?" Dorothy asked.

"Uh-huh," MacMillan said. "What the general did not say was that he wanted commissioned polo players. Not lousy PFCs."

"I was perfectly happy as a PFC," Lowell said.

"But you were a polo player?" Dorothy asked.

"Madame," he said. "I must object to the past tense."

"You still play?"

"When I can find the time," he said. "And some generous soul with a large string."

"My brother plays a little," Dorothy said. "Ted Persons?"

"Sure," he said, immediately. "I played with him several times last year in"—there was the slightest hesitation— "...California."

He did not want to say, she realized, "Palm Springs."

He was now looking at her with the first interest he had shown.

"And then we found out that the Frogs don't let their enlisted men play polo," Mac went on, impatient at their exchange. "At least not with their officers."

"So what did they do," Dorothy asked. "Send you to OCS?"

"The Duke wouldn't have lasted ten minutes in OCS," Mac said. "And I knew it. Besides, there wasn't time."

"So what happened?" Dorothy asked.

"All of a sudden," Colonel Lowell said, "my talents, which had previously been hidden—literally—in the manure pile in the stable, were suddenly recognized. I became an instant officer and gentleman."

"How?" Dorothy asked.

"Yon bald, fat man," Lowell said, pointing with his cigar at MacMillan, "had me directly commissioned as a second lieutenant in the Finance Corps."

"Just like that?" Dorothy asked.

"General Waterford told me he wanted a commissioned polo player," MacMillan said. "I got him a commissioned polo player."

"And then," Dorothy said, looking first at Lowell, then averting her eyes, "you liked it, and stayed?"

"Oh, no," Lowell said. "Shortly after I was commissioned, they sent me to Greece, where people shot at me. That really wasn't what I had in mind to do with the rest of my life."

"That's where I met him," Colonel Felter entered the story. "I had just nearly killed myself getting through the Ranger School here. If you were the honor graduate, you could pick your assignment. I wasn't the honor graduate, and I picked Greece. And I met the Duke on the plane from Frankfurt."

"And the first thing I asked him," Lowell said, "was 'What have you done wrong, to get yourself shanghaied to Greece?'"

"What happened to the polo?" Dorothy asked.

"When Daddy finally got to play the French," Barbara Bellmon said, her voice sounding just a little strange, "he had a heart attack on the field. He died on his pony."

"Which left the Army," Lowell said quickly, "faced with the problem of what to do with an absolutely unqualified-to-do-anything second john. So they sent me to Greece, in the prayerful hope I would get blown away."

"Greece?" Dorothy asked. "What was going on in Greece?"

"Believe it or not," General Bellmon said, "these two worked for Paul Hanrahan." He indicated Lowell and Felter. "The way Paul tells the story, he asked for experienced combat officers of the highest possible quality, and they sent him a midget and a moron."

"Bob!" Barbara Bellmon snapped. "Jesus Christ!"

"No offense, Mouse," General Bellmon said. "I hasten to add that they both came back bona fide heros. The Duke did a John Wayne scene on a mountaintop, and the Mouse pulled the Duke's feet out of the fire."

"You'll notice, Mrs. Sims," Colonel Lowell said, "that the general has offered no apology to me for describing me as a midget."

"Well, since we're telling stories," Barbara Bellmon said, "why don't you tell Dorothy how you met the Duke?"

"I'm sure we're boring Dorothy," General Bellmon said.

"Not at all," Dorothy said.

"It would embarrass the Duke," the general said.

"It will embarrass you," Barbara Bellmon said. "Tell it!"

"How could I possibly be more embarrassed, after what the general has been calling me?" Lowell asked, innocently.

"We were at Knox," Barbara Bellmon said. "Bob was on the staff. One of the personnel problems was a lieutenant in the student officer company. He had everybody on the post above the grade of major sore at him."

"What did you do to the post commander, Colonel?" Dorothy asked Lowell.

"How do you know she's talking about me?" Lowell asked.

"The general was very proud of his Packard convertible," Barbara Bellmon went on. "And he was also sort of a bigot."

"That's not fair, Babs," General Bellmon said.

"It's the truth," Barbara insisted. "And you know it is. So what happened is that one day, the general saw a Packard convertible, like his, same color and everything, except that this one was a sedan, and a larger model—"

"It was a 280," Lowell corrected her. "Not a sedan. But it was the classier one. It's still in a garage on the island, by the way. I gave it to my mother's husband."

"... classier," Barbara Bellmon picked up the story, "than the general's pride and joy. Two second lieutenants were in it. One of them was white. He was driving. The other one was black. He was in the back seat, grandly returning all the crisp salutes from people who thought that there was only one bright yellow Packard convertible on the post, the post commander's."

"It looked as if they were mocking him," Bellmon said.

"So the general found out who owned the car," Barbara Bellmon continued, "and asked around about him. When he found out that the source of his commission was questionable, he put the wheels in motion to have him kicked out of the Army. The wheel he set in motion was Bob. He was then a lieutenant colonel."

"Do you have to go on with this?" General Bellmon asked.

"So Bob spent long hours collecting dispositions about this officer's bad attitude, and proving conclusively that he shouldn't have been commissioned in the first place. And just when he had everything ready to bring the Duke before a Board of Officers, the Army sent him one more piece of paper for his file."

"Which was?" Dorothy asked.

"On the recommendation of the Secretary of State, the Congress had just authorized the acceptance by a serving officer of a decoration from a foreign potentate. Bob had a thick file of depositions saying 'subject officer clearly fails to demonstrate the characteristics required of an officer,' you know what I mean, and here comes this medal from the King of Greece himself, saying the Duke's performance in Greece made John Wayne look like a pansy."

"So I couldn't get him thrown out of the Army, worse luck," General Bellmon said. "And here he is."

"The really humiliating thing for Bob was to find out that the black guy, the one who rode around in the back seat with the Duke playing chauffeur, was not only a fine officer, but the son of an officer who was not only an old friend of both our families, but the man who had commanded the task force that rescued Bob from the Russians."

"Phil Parker," Lowell said. He looked at Dorothy Sims. "They've got him in a POW camp in 'Nam, too."

He has nice eyes, Dorothy thought. And he's not the fool he might have been as a young man. I was wrong, she decided. He is a nice man. The look in his eyes told her that despite the warning she had been given by Roxy, there was no way Duke Lowell would make a pass at her. Pity, she thought, a little ashamed.

"And it gets worse," Barbara said. "Over Bob's violent objections, we had the Duke for dinner with the Felters. The Duke and his wife. And thirty minutes after she was in the house, it comes out that her father and my father were old friends, and that Ilse's father had commanded the POW camp where Bob and Mac were locked up."

"Where's your wife tonight, Colonel?" Dorothy heard herself asking.

"She was killed a long time ago in a car crash," Lowell said, evenly.

God forgive me, I was glad to hear that! Dorothy thought.

"Did I understand you to say Colonel Lowell's wife's father

commanded their POW camp?" she asked.

"Then Colonel—now Lieutenant General—Count von Greiffenberg," Bellmon said.

"One of the good Krauts," MacMillan said.

He's rich and he's unattached. And I am thrilled with that idea. What the hell is the matter with me?

Tex Williams arrived with Colonel Meany, who was stationed at Pope, and whose presence surprised Dorothy. Tex was dressed Texan, even to cowboy boots and a Stetson. Not a cowboy hat. A hat Dorothy thought of as a Lyndon Johnson. They apologized for being late.

They took drinks from MacMillan, who was tending bar now, and then Colonel Meany led Felter to the far end of the lawn to speak in confidence. As they were talking, there was a sound of aircraft engines, an unfamiliar jet roar, and as Dorothy watched, Colonel Meany pointed toward the sky, and Dorothy turned to look where he pointed.

The sound was from an enormous airplane, a C-5A, and as Dorothy watched it drop through the skies toward Pope's runways, she remembered just how huge they were. The C-5A could carry three Greyhound buses inside its cavernous fuselage, with lots of room left over.

C-5As were uncommon, even at Pope, and Dorothy was surprised when two more appeared in the failing light. She wondered what the connection was between Colonel Meany, Sandy Felter, and the C-5As.

She felt Craig Lowell's eyes on her.

And felt her face flush.

The party broke up early. At home in bed she dreamed about him: She was naked in his bed when the door opened and Tom came in. Tom looked at her with contempt, so she pulled the sheet up tightly over her face and prodded Lowell with her fingers to wake him up. But for a long time, he just lay there. Finally he opened his eyes, got out of bed, and walked past Tom. Dorothy was afraid that Tom would hit him, but he didn't. When he was past Tom, he turned and beckoned for her to come with him. And she did follow him. She dropped the bedsheet and walked past Tom and the pain and loathing in his eyes.

Dorothy was sweating when she woke up. The bedroom was stuffy. She kicked the clammy sheet off her legs, got out of bed, walked to the curtain and opened it, and then slid open the glass door to the tiny patio outside the bedroom.

It was cooler outside than it was in the house, and there was the smell of spring in the air. She crossed her arms over her chest. Noticing again the strange jet roar, she looked up into the sky. A C-5A was climbing out of Pope. One of those she had seen earlier, she concluded. She watched it disappear, and then saw that the other two she had seen earlier were also leaving. Shivering lightly, she went back into her bedroom.

(Three)
Fayetteville, North Carolina
1145 Hours, 11 June 1969

Dorothy Sims got up when the alarm went off, made the kids breakfast, and sent them off to school; and then, hating herself for it, she watched a soap opera. The picture was crystal clear, so clear that she could see where the makeup on the actor's face left off at his hairline. Duke Lowell looked like an actor—but without the makeup. Of course, his tan hadn't come out of a tube.

She suddenly got up and called the beauty parlor, and they had a vacancy. So she drove the four blocks to the shopping center and had a rinse, set, and facial, all of which made her feel good enough to consider buying herself a dress. She went into Haverty's Department Store.

And there Lowell was in the Lawn & Garden Department. After a moment, she realized there was no way he could have known she would be there too. She walked over to him. He was in crisply pressed tropical worsteds, bent over a charcoal stove.

"Good afternoon, Colonel," she said.

He straightened and looked at her, surprised and pleased.

"You've done something to your hair," he said. "It's different."

"Thank you for noticing," she said. "I just came from the beauty parlor."

"I'm delighted to see you," he said.

"Are you really? Why?" she replied.

"I'm sure you know more about these things than I do." He gestured toward the charcoal stove; and she recalled his remark the night before about Mac's charcoal stove, the cut-in-half fifty-five-gallon drum.

She looked at the stove more closely. It was enormous, of heavy cast-iron construction, with two adjustable firebeds and racks and all the options.

"You seem to have found the best one right off," Dorothy said, after glancing at the others. The saleswoman, she imagined, had obviously decided that a colonel should be shown the most expensive model first.

"Good," he said, clearly not eager to linger over a decision. "I'll take it," he said to the saleswoman.

The saleswoman got out her book and Lowell gave her the MacMillans' name and quarters number at Fort Bragg.

"Have you got some kind of card I can put in it?" he asked.

"I'll see if I can find one," the saleswoman said. "With the tax, that comes to $369.65." She seemed slightly afraid that the price would ruin the sale.

Lowell reached into his trousers pocket, spread a wad of bills with his thumb, shook his head, and then took out his wallet. From it he withdrew four one-hundred-dollar bills. He casually handed them over.

"Thank you very much," the saleswoman said.

"That's quite a gift," Dorothy said.

"Mac and his wife have been very good to me for a long time," he said. "I owe them that and more."

There was nothing else for them to say, and they both knew it, but she didn't want to leave.

"I haven't had my lunch," he said. "As a matter of fact, I haven't had my breakfast, either. I wonder if you'd care to have a little lunch with me?"

I should now say that I've had my lunch, thank you just the same, and go buy a dress.

"There's a little place right next door," Dorothy Sims said. "Mario's. If you like Italian."

"Anything but spaghetti," he said, and smiled at her in a way that made her tremble.

The saleswoman returned with his change and a gift card in an envelope.

Dorothy watched what he wrote: "I should have sent this in Bad Nauheim. Thank You. CWL."

He took her arm and then let go of it as if it burned.

Once they stepped inside Mario's, it took a long moment for her eyes to adjust to the blackness. She thought that when she left, she would be blinded again by the sunlight.

They were shown to a small table.

"You're a martini drinker, aren't you?" he asked when the waiter appeared. So he had noticed at least that much. And he had noticed her hair, too. She didn't want a martini, really, but she said nothing.

"A martini for the lady, please, and what kind of Scotch can I get?"

They had Johnny Walker Black. "Soda, in a large glass," he instructed, and then opened the menu.

"Why didn't you go to the PX?" she asked.

"I beg your pardon?"

"To buy the stove?"

"I suppose I should have," he said. "But I think they probably wouldn't have had a stove like that. There's some sort of rule about price, I think. Anyway, I was here, and the impulse occurred simultaneously with the opportunity."

"What *are* you doing here?" she asked.

"I've taken an apartment right around the corner," he said. "With a lovely view of the shopping center parking lot."

"I thought I heard them say you had been given the VIP suite in the Smokebomb Hill BOQ."

"That doesn't mean I have to sleep there," he said. "I'm too old for beer brawls in BOQs. And besides, a colonel cramps lieutenants' styles."

He ordered shrimp scampi. And she took veal scallopini. Since the waiter said that would take a few extra minutes, he asked if Madame would like another cocktail.

She smiled and nodded. And immediately regretted it.

Lowell looked at her; she averted her eyes.

"This may not have been one of my better ideas," he said.

"I beg your pardon?"

"I have a certain reputation," he said. "The facts are not as colorful as the reputation, but it's the reputation I'm concerned about."

"Roxy warned me about you," she said. "If that's what you mean. You're not going to make a pass at me in here, are you, Colonel?"

"No, of course I'm not," Lowell said. "But you're liable to be seen with me. That would be enough, I'm afraid."

"I don't think anyone could see us in here," she said. "I'm on the verge of asking for a flashlight."

The second martini arrived and she sipped at it, aware that she could already feel the warmth from the first one sinking into her body.

"I'm a little disappointed," she said, recklessly.

"How's that?" he said, taking a swallow from his drink.

"Your certainty when you said, 'No, of course I'm not.'"

"No offense intended," he said, with a smile. "But despite popular rumor, I don't make passes at ladies. And you are a lady."

"Don't be too sure," she heard herself say, dropping her eyes. She had no idea what she was feeling.

After a long moment, he said: "Why did you say that?"

"I don't know," she said, faintly. "Please, pretend I didn't."

"A martini in the middle of the day," he said. "Completely forgotten."

"You sound relieved," she heard herself say.

"I'm not a saint," he said. "Disappointed and relieved. Both."

"Thank you," she said. "Women dislike being rejected."

"No offer was made," he said. "So there can be no rejection." She didn't reply, and after a moment, he added, "You have enough trouble without getting involved with me."

The food was delivered. There was a split of white wine. Although she hadn't asked for one, the waiter gave her a glass. But she nodded her head when he raised the bottle and poured.

"I like your friend Sharon," she said.

"I frequently consider running Felter over with a truck so I could marry the widow," he said.

"I'm half afraid you mean that," she said.

"I do, I do," he said. "That's one hell of a woman."

"I know," she agreed. "I've seen her in action."

His eyebrows raised in question, and she told him how she had met Sharon in the airport.

"You were in Washington about the POWs?" Lowell asked.

"I'm in charge of legislative liaison," she said.

"Which means what?"

"That I can afford to spend a lot of time and money traveling," she said.

"You made a point last night of letting me know you're comfortable," he said. "Why did you need to do that? And why again now?"

She felt her face flush.

She decided the truth was the best answer.

"After I had to learn if that Patek Philippe was real, I guess I wanted to make sure you knew..." She stopped. She didn't know what else to say.

"You're not the gold-digger type," Lowell said. "I just thought you were nosy."

"I was," she said.

"I'm flattered," he said.

She didn't want to reply to that.

"Before I was married, I worked for our senator," she said. "He finds it harder to say politician things to me than he would to somebody else."

"As a general rule of thumb, I can't stand politicians," he said. "What did you do?"

"I'm a lawyer," she said. "Tax law."

"Really?" he asked. He was genuinely surprised. "Tax lawyers are my favorite people. If they're good. Are you good?"

"I don't know," she said. "I was swept off my feet by a flier. What would you like to know about raising children and the PTA?"

"Well, from what Roxy said, you're really the brains behind the POW wives."

"You want to talk law?" she asked. "That whole war is illegal. The things the government is doing—or really not doing—about the POWs are generally illegal."

She saw that she was making him uncomfortable.

"Did Roxy tell you that I am the difficult female who took the Defense Department to court and kept them from declaring a lot of the POWs legally dead?"

"I didn't know it was you," he said. "But I heard about that. One of my best friends is over there. His wife told me about that."

"I am practically persona non grata with the DOD," she said.

He started to say something, but stopped.

"You were about to say?" she said.

"It might sound cold," he said. "But, whether DOD likes you or not, you're at least in a position to feel you're doing something to help your husband. My friend's wife tells me the worst part is not being able to do a damned thing to help him."

"I have an ulterior motive," she said.

He looked at her curiously, and she wondered why she had started this. It would be too easy to blame it on the martinis.

"I want to get my husband back so I can divorce him," she said.

His eyebrows went up.

"That shocks you," she challenged.

"You can't divorce him while he's gone?"

"No," she said. "For a number of reasons."

"There's a lot of guys over there," he said. "Statistically, a certain number are bound to be sonofabitches."

"You're granting me the benefit of the doubt," she said.

"Roxy likes you, Sharon likes you. That's a pretty good recommendation."

"He's not a sonofabitch," she said. "I just don't like him. I never should have married him. My money came between us. Can you understand that?"

"Sure," Lowell said. "It has been said that the rich should be kept in enclosures, so they won't offend the poor people."

"You don't seem to trouble to hide yours."

"I was with friends last night," he said.

"I was jealous," she said.

"That's silly," he said.

There was a moment's silence, and then Dorothy blurted, "I was gathering my courage to write him to tell him I wanted a divorce when he got shot down."

"Somebody else come along?" Lowell asked. "Somebody comfortable?"

"Not until I met you," she blurted.

"Jesus!" Lowell said.

"I can't imagine why I said that," she said, flushing.

He tried to make a joke of it: "I have this Dutch uncle aura," he said. "All the girls tell me their darkest secrets."

It was time to change the subject.

"Why didn't you ever get married again?" she asked.

"Now it's my turn to confess all?"

"I'm sorry, I shouldn't have asked that."

"I came close once," Lowell said. "Somebody else comfortable. My cousin Craig was ecstatic."

"What happened?"

"You're looking at a man who was left at the altar. There are not very many of us."

"Really at the altar? Just before the wedding?"

"Instead of coming to the wedding, she sent the letter," he said.

"What did it say?"

"She didn't like the Army, and I am a solider," he said. "She was right."

"How did you take it?" Dorothy asked.

"I cried a lot, but I didn't do anything really foolish."

"I can't imagine why I started this whole thing," she said.

"The martinis," Lowell said.

"No," she said.

He stopped, a forkful of shrimp halfway to his mouth, and looked at her. Their eyes met. She fought the temptation to look away.

"You said something before," she said, softly, "about the impulse occurring simultaneously with the opportunity."

"Yes, I did," he replied.

"My husband has been gone two and a half years," she said.

He felt his heart jump. He wondered where the warning flags were. This was trouble if he ever saw it, and he had seen a lot of it. Jesus Christ, all he had to was get caught screwing a POW's wife!

He had walked away from a dozen situations like this. Now that he was older and wiser, it was easy. He'd become skilled at it. Most often, he could refuse the offer with tact and kindness, and in the morning congratulate himself on his wisdom.

But he didn't want to walk away from this. And he wondered why.

Then he understood.

"I don't think this has anything to do with how long your husband has been gone," he said. "Don't cheapen yourself that way."

"What else could it be?" she asked, faintly. "Or are you trying to turn me down with kindness?"

"I know what we're getting into," he said. "And I know what it's likely to cost. I want to be sure you do."

"I knew what I was liable to get into when I walked up to you in the store," she said, averting her eyes once more.

It was all so much easier now that it was in the open. She looked at him again.

"Do you really want any more to eat?"

He pulled his money from his pocket, laid a couple of bills on the table, and led her out of the restaurant.

She did not let herself think as he walked her across the shopping center parking lot and then through an opening in the hurricane fence that separated it from the apartment complex.

The door to an apartment on the third floor was open, and

a man from the telephone company was sitting on the floor of the living room screwing something into a socket.

"The door was open," he said. "So I figured you'd left it open for me."

"Yes, I did," Lowell said.

"You've got two lines, Colonel," the installer said. "Two instruments. One in here and one in the bedroom. Both of them are unlisted. I'm supposed to tell you that you have to understand the operator will not give out the numbers, not even in an emergency."

"Yes, I understand."

The telephone installer nodded and went back to work. Dorothy looked around the apartment. He had filled it with really ugly furniture, the kind displayed in stores advertising WE FINANCE ANYBODY. There were two bedrooms, a kitchenette, and a "dining bar"—a divider with two cheap plastic-upholstered wooden stools in front of it. The bathroom had a swan engraved on the sliding door to the shower. A dozen assorted towels (still in their plastic wrapping) lay on the Formica "vanity" top in the bathroom beside a six-pack of toilet paper.

In the "master" bedroom, suitcases, a golf bag, a gun case, and sheets and pillow cases (also still in their plastic wrapping) were all dropped on top of the bed. He had clearly only moved in a few minutes before he'd walked over to Haverty's to buy the charcoal grill.

Dorothy corrected herself. He had gone to Haverty's to buy something for the apartment. The charcoal grill had been a combination of impulse and opportunity. She wondered what he had really been after.

She walked back out into the living room: Sears, Roebuck television set with rabbit ears, two armchairs, and a couch. Plastic, woodgrained veneer, and more plastic.

It was horrible.

On the kitchen counters: a wooden box full of whiskey bottles and two other boxes, one containing a twenty-four piece assortment of "household drinking glasses" and the other an electric drip coffeepot and two pounds of coffee. A bag, when she opened it, contained four china mugs.

She opened the refrigerator: two bottles of champagne on their sides.

Had he been expecting somebody else? Could he have been expecting her? How many others were going to come here? *Am I like all of them?*

She ripped open the assortment of glasses and rinsed out two that were the most suitable for champagne. The champagne, when she touched it, was still warm. She opened the freezer compartment, took out some ice cubes, put them in the glasses, and then opened one of the champagne bottles. The price tag from the State Liquor Store was still on it. He didn't use the cheaper Fort Bragg Class VI to buy his booze. He went to the civilian store and paid $8.50 a bottle for Moët.

She unwound the wire, popped the cork, filled the glasses, and went to find him.

"Home, sweet home," she said.

"Thank you," he said, and tapped her glass.

The telephone installer crawled to his feet. "That'll do her," he said. "The line in use lights up that button."

"Thank you very much," Colonel Lowell said.

"What do you think?" he asked, turning to her after the other man was gone.

"It's ghastly," she said.

"Yes, isn't it?" Lowell said, with a wide smile. Then the smile tightened a little. "If you haven't changed your mind, I suppose we had better draw the curtains."

He crossed over to the sliding glass door in the living area and pulled the curtain shut over what was in fact a really splendid view of the shopping center parking lot.

Dorothy went into the bedroom and set his luggage and the other stuff that he had tossed on the mattress onto the floor. Then she ripped the sheets out of the plastic wrapping and made the bed.

He leaned on the doorjamb.

"This isn't what you could call really terribly romantic, is it?"

She straightened the top sheet and stood up.

"Does that mean you've lost your appetite?"

"I thought perhaps you might have," he said. "*I've* been looking down your dress."

She flushed.

"I don't think you're going to be a casual roll in the hay for me," he said.

She met his eyes.

"And that may not be good for either of us, is that what you're saying?" Dorothy replied.

"I don't have very much to lose," he said. "You do."

"Only my virtue and my good name." She laughed.

Unsteadily, she walked over to him, sorry that the champagne in her glass was gone.

"Would you believe it if I told you you make my heart beat unsteadily?" he asked. He took her hand and placed it flat on his chest so she could feel his heart beating. Then she moved her hand away and rested her head where the hand had been. She felt his hand move to her back, felt him take in his breath. His fingers found the zipper on her dress. He pulled it down and then she felt him fumbling with her brassiere catch. When it came. loose, he slipped the straps and the dress over her shoulders. She shrugged her shoulders to help everything fall off. Timidly, but certainly, her hand moved to him, and she felt his stiffness against the back of it. She then turned her hand around and cupped him.

"Oh, Craig," she cried out softly. "Do please come inside me!"

He picked her up and carried her to the bed. As he stood over her and unbuttoned his shirt, she worked her half-slip and panties down off her hips, kicked them away, raised one leg, and looked at him.

He lay down beside her, bending to kiss her nipple. Shameless now, she reached down and grabbed him. He moved between her legs. She guided him into her.

Afterward—after their climax and a long, tender, quiet embrace—he sat up and looked down at her.

"I don't know what you feel," he said, not quite matter-of-factly, "but I feel extraordinary."

"I do, too," she said softly.

He looked at her but said nothing.

"I hate to run away from a moment like this," he said, "but I have to play soldier this afternoon."

"Really?" she said, and laughed. "I thought colonels always quit for the day at noon."

Not this one," he said. Lifting himself up, he went into the shower. She didn't want to get up, so she just pulled the sheet over herself and smiled. After he finished his shower, Craig came out and took clean boxer shorts and a T-shirt from one of his suitcases. When he pulled them on, his back to her, she saw faint scars on his back. One of them looked like a flesh zipper. After that he tore open a brown-paper package on the dresser and took out ripstops. There were also a green beret and a pair of jungle boots in the package.

"I didn't know you were a Green Beret," she said.

He laughed. "Technically," he said. "Legally. Once I served with foreign troops. That's half the on-the-job equivalency. And then Hanrahan and MacMillan conspired against me several years ago and had me thrown out of an airplane. That was the other half of the on-the-job equivalency. I'm not a *real* snake-eater, but would you believe I'm going to slide down a rope from a helicopter this afternoon?"

"I don't believe it," she said. "You're not the type."

"I know," he said with a chuckle. He was apparently serious, however, for he put on the ripstops, and pulled the trouser tops around the new jungle boots. Then he put on the green beret and looked at himself in the mirror.

"John Wayne," he said, "eat your heart out!"

She laughed. "What's this all about?"

"I guess MacMillan doesn't want me to look out of place," he said.

"The infantry thing," she said, meaning the Combat Infantry Badge he wore. It had two stars on it, meaning the third award. "Is that real?"

"Two of them are," he said. "The third one's kind of questionable."

"Tell me," she said.

"Oh, when some of Mac's people were down in the jungle, I went after them, and I went down, too. It was two weeks before they finally got us out; and Mac, who then had First Special Forces Group, heard about it, and said that since I was senior guy there, I was in command, which meant I qualified for it again."

"What was a colonel doing flying a mission like that in the first place?"

"The colonel had the mistaken notion he was a better flier through the soup than turned out to be the case. I flew into the trees."

"What are you doing down here, anyway?"

"It's *up* here from Rucker, where I'm stationed," he said. "We conducted some troop tests."

"You're a little old to be sliding down a rope from a helicopter," she said.

"Right now I feel like I'm twenty-one," he said. He looked at her again. "Nineteen. Eighteen."

She smiled, but said nothing.

He turned to the dresser, and when he turned around, he was snapping his expensive gold-cased Rolex chronometer around his wrist.

"Dorothy," he said, not looking at her. "This place comes with two sets of keys. My sole virtue is that I never lose keys. The second set of keys is on that counter in the kitchen. Either way. Whatever you think is best for you."

And then he walked out of the bedroom. The boots made creaking noises on the linoleum. She heard the door shut.

Dorothy got up and took a shower, and then cleaned up after him. He had thrown his towel into a corner of the bath, and his underwear and tropical worsteds were casually tossed onto the miniature plastic-covered armchair in the bedroom.

Dressed, she examined herself in the mirror.

She liked what she saw.

After she straightened the bed, she walked into the living room. The keys were where he said they would be. She looked down at them for a moment, then picked them up and put them in her purse. Then she went to the telephone and wrote down both numbers.

(Four)
Camp McCall, North Carolina
1415 Hours, 11 June 1969

Colonel Rudolph G. MacMillan and Colonel Craig W. Lowell, red-faced and puffing slightly from the six-story climb up rough wooden stairs, emerged at the top of the rappelling tower. Colonel Sanford Felter and two Green Beret noncoms, a big, flat-nosed master sergeant and a younger kid who wore the stripes of a staff sergeant, came to attention and saluted crisply.

"Afternoon," Lowell said, returning the salutes.

"It's been a long time since I've seen you looking like a soldier," Felter said.

"So this is how the other half lives," Lowell replied.

The rappelling tower was a wooden structure—heavy planks bolted to huge telephone poles—rising more than sixty feet above the sandy ground. There were large coils of darkish brown nylon rope on the flat, plank roof. The top of the tower was forty feet square, and it smelled faintly of creosote.

Lowell saw, over the trees, the mock-up of the POW camp. He walked closer to the edge, and stared at the mock-up, careful not to look over the side of the tower.

"I don't see anybody working," he said to Felter, who walked over with the master sergeant.

"They finished just before noon," Felter said. "We're running a little ahead of schedule."

"We'll lose that," Lowell said. He turned to the master sergeant. "OK, Sergeant. Somewhat reluctantly, I place myself in your hands."

"Yes, sir," the sergeant said. "I'm sure the colonel remembers most of the way it's done."

"Sergeant," Lowell said. "I'm afraid I'm traveling under false colors."

"Sir?"

"All of this is new to me. The only time I've ever seen this sort of thing is in the movies."

"Yes, sir," the master sergeant said. There was a faint but unmistakable change in his attitude. Lowell knew that he had been judged by the green beret, the ripstops, and the parachutist's badge sewn below his CIB and above his master aviator's wings on the ripstop tunic.

"I am a Green Beret," Lowell said, "solely because of a very loose interpretation of the rules by General Hanrahan and this fat colonel. I have made one—one only—parachute jump. When his fat colonel had me thrown out of an airplane."

"Oh shit, Duke," MacMillan said. "But since he brought it up, Sergeant, he's qualified. He got that third CIB from First Group, and the one jump he made was a HALO from thirty-two thousand feet."

"I know who the colonel is, sir," the sergeant said. "Mr. Wojinski told me about him."

"Nevertheless, Sergeant," Lowell insisted, "I want you to keep what I said in mind when we do what you have in mind for me to do."

Lowell saw the coils of rope were no longer where they had been. They now trailed over the sheer edge of the building. He walked across and looked over the edge.

"Oh, good God!" he said. "A man could break his ass here!"

The master sergeant chuckled again. Lowell sensed that he was back in the sergeant's esteem.

"OK, Sergeant," Lowell said. "Bearing in mind that I'm old and fragile, let's get on with it."

"Yes, sir," the master sergeant said, crisply. "If you'll just watch, Colonel, Sergeant Quinn will rig Colonel MacMillan. Is that all right, Colonel?"

MacMillan nodded. The staff sergeant wrapped a short length of the nylon rope around MacMillan's back and legs, making a seat harness, which he fastened with a D ring.

"The rate of descent is controlled by friction," the master

sergeant explained. "You can stop yourself at will. There is a stretch factor in the line, however, which you will learn by experience. In other words be careful as you approach the ground."

"You have never been careful before, Sergeant," Lowell said. "Believe me."

MacMillan waddled to the edge of the tower; and looking somewhat bored, he picked up the rope that hung over the edge, wrapped it around his waist, snapped it into the D ring, adjusted it so that it was taut, and then leaned backward over the side.

"Watch carefully, Duke," he said. "I'm not going to climb those damned stairs again."

The master sergeant handed Mac a leather work glove, and he put it on his right hand. Then he simply jumped backward off the six-story rappelling tower. Fifteen feet down, he bounced against the side, and then pushed himself away again.

"Jesus Christ!" Lowell said. Looking over the edge made him dizzy.

"It's not as bad as it looks, Colonel," the master sergeant said. "Just don't look down at first if it makes you dizzy."

"And let the ground come up as a surprise?" he asked.

"You'll sense when you're close to the ground," the master sergeant said. "Would you like to watch it again?"

"Absolutely," Lowell said. He nodded at Felter. "If he doesn't go, I don't go."

Felter, grinning, allowed himself to be roped into a harness, and then went over the edge with as much ease as MacMillan had.

"It's not hard, Colonel," the master sergeant said.

"Colonels Felter and MacMillan are well known for their insanity," Lowell said. Then: "OK, let's do it."

The staff sergeant roped him in the harness, while the master sergeant wrapped himself.

"I'll go down with you, Colonel," he said. "If you want to stop yourself, just do it. No problem."

"As the bishop said to the nun," Lowell said.

He made the rope taut, put on a leather-palmed glove, and forced himself to stand, backward, on the edge of the platform. He looked down at the rope and the harness. The way it fit around his midsection, it bunched the ripstops into what looked like an oversized camouflage jockstrap.

He remembered the touch of Dorothy Sims's hand. She had indeed made him feel young enough to be doing something like this. What the hell! He pushed himself into space, and almost immediately applied friction. He fell about three feet.

"You can give it a little more, Colonel," the master sergeant said. He let loose, pushed himself away from the wall, and let himself fall as far as he dared. There was an elastic sensation, as if he were at the end of an enormous rubber band.

"You've got the idea, Colonel," the master sergeant said.

"It's as easy as falling off a six-story building," Lowell said. He was now pleased with himself. Four bounds later—too soon—he sensed that he was getting close to the ground. When he looked down, he saw it was five feet below him.

He had just been set to push himself off again for a long swoop. If he had done that, he would have crashed heavily into the ground.

Felter and MacMillan watched him, smiling, as he opened the D ring and got loose of the rope.

"Now that wasn't as bad as you thought it would be, was it, son?" MacMillan said, mockingly solicitous.

"I think I'll do it again," Lowell said. "If I can make it up the stairs."

He climbed the stairs with his mind full of Dorothy Sims. Logic told him that it had been her long abstinence rather than anything he had done . . . but there was no denying that having a woman thrashing beneath him in glorious passion did wonderful things for his ego. That had been one hell of a piece of ass.

Or was she just an oversexed lady who latched onto visiting officers? She was, he supposed, about thirty-five. Women were supposed to be at their sexual peak in those years. What was she supposed to do, with her husband gone, use a banana?

In fact, he believed what she said about getting a divorce. When Tom came home.

If Tom came home.

If they were successful.

According to Sandy's list, Lieutenant Colonel Thomas B. Sims, USAF, was in the Hanoi Hilton.

Hang tight, Colonel. The Green Berets are on the way, after a brief pause for station identification, during which I am diddling your loving wife.

Welcome home, darling. You will be hearing from my lawyers.

The staff sergeant was waiting for him on the top of the rappelling tower. Lowell was pleased to see that the master sergeant was huffing and puffing as much as he was when he came through the stairwell.

He went down the rope four more times, until he felt very confident. The last two trips were from the skid of a Huey, which had been mounted to the tower on four by eights so that it was five feet away from the wall of the tower. You could still stop yourself whenever you wanted to, but there was no wall to plant your feet against and stop the oscillation. You swung back and forth like a rock tied to the end of a string.

Whether by coincidence, or more likely by intent, a Huey— an HU-1D—appeared. It fluttered near the mock-up while Lowell was catching his breath after the fourth trip up the stairs.

When he slid to the ground the final time, still wearing the rope harness and D ring, they walked over to the Huey. The pilot, who was sitting on the floor of the cargo compartment, stood up when he saw them coming. He saluted.

"Nice to see you again, Colonel Lowell," he said, putting out his hand. "I heard you were in on this."

Lowell looked at Felter, who nodded, a signal the pilot had been cleared for Operation Monte Cristo.

"I'm glad you are," Lowell said. "It's nice to see you, too."

"The way this works, Colonel," the pilot said, "is that I will hover somewhere around one hundred feet over the roof— you know how hard that is to do—to keep your oscillation down. You will not be given the word to go down the rope until we're in the best hover I can manage. Once you get the word from the crew chief, get out as quick as you can. There will be some movement of the aircraft from the imbalance. Once you start to oscillate, the only way you can stop it is to start down the rope again in the middle of the swing. You understand, sir?"

"All things considered, I'd rather be driving," Lowell said.

The pilot smiled at him, and went on. "Get out of the harness immediately. There will be another change of center of gravity the moment you touch down and the rope goes slack. Unless you get free of the rope right away, you're liable to be dragged off the roof."

"You're just a fountain of pleasant information, aren't you?" Lowell said.

"We'll be a little light, with just the five of us," MacMillan said. "Did you bring ballast?"

"Yes, sir," the pilot said. "Everybody's in there. A thousand pounds of sand, and all the field equipment."

For the first time, Lowell looked closely inside the fuselage. There was a pile of field equipment, web belts and ammo pouches, even weapons. And strapped to the nylon-and-aluminum seats were bags, each stenciled BALLAST 50 POUNDS.

The crew chief stood at the door holding out a set of web equipment. Lowell reached for it. It was suspenders, a web belt with a .45 in a holster, several magazine pouches for the M-16 rifle, and even two concussion grenades taped to the suspenders. He strapped the suspenders on. It had been a very long time since he had worn web equipment. This was brand-new stuff, nylon. He wondered idly if nylon was such a good idea. Nylon burns. He didn't think the old stuff—what was it, cotton?—would burn.

The crew chief handed him an M-16 rifle. Loosening the strap, he put it across his shoulders. He was the last one finished dressing. The others didn't tease him about it or offer to help. They just waited. There's one guy in every squad, Lowell thought, who is always last.

He stepped inside the Huey. He had a lot of time in Hueys, but very little time in the back seat of one. The crew chief indicated where he was to sit, between two of the seats stacked with fifty pounds of ballast.

The turbine began to whine, and the rotor blades slowly began to revolve. He looked up and saw the crew chief touch his mike button, apparently telling the pilot they were ready any time he was.

The pitch of the turbine and the rotor changed, and Lowell felt the chopper grow light on the skids. The pilot picked it two feet off the ground, lowered the nose, and made a running takeoff in the direction of the mock-up, keeping low across the ground until he had the speed he wanted, then pulling up on the cyclic, jerking the bird into the air.

They passed over the mock-up at fifty feet. Lowell wished he were closer to the door so that he could get a better look at it, but then reminded himself he would in a couple of minutes be on it, where he could take a really close-up look at it.

The Huey banked, maybe half a mile from the mock-up, at five hundred feet now, and out the open door Lowell could see that the area was ringed with concertina: barbed wire in three-foot coils. Not the old barbed wire but the new stuff, flat ribbons of razor-sharp steel. He thought he saw a guard post, but he wasn't sure. They were certainly there, because Sandy Felter certainly would have sealed off the entire area like a drum.

The Huey leveled off and slowed down.

The crew chief, in an olive drab flying helmet that concealed most of his head, made a "get-up" signal with his hands. They were making a slow, flat descent back to the mock-up. Apparently on orders from the pilot, the crew chief threw a coil of rope out each door, outside the skid so the rope could not interfere with the VHF antenna mounted on the bottom of the fuselage.

MacMillan and the staff sergeant hooked the rope to their D rings and stood facing inward, holding themselves in place with a hand placed flat against the top of the door opening, looking over their shoulders.

The Huey's engine pitch changed. The most difficult maneuver of a helicopter is a hover outside ground effect. This was what the pilot was now attempting. Lowell could sense the minute changes he was making with the cyclic and with the stick. He could not, for the life of him, remember the pilot's name, but he remembered he was a good one.

And then all of a sudden, simultaneously, MacMillan and the staff sergeant launched themselves into the air, jumping backward over the skid. Lowell thought he could detect a slight upward (as their weight left the helicopter) and then downward (as they brought their weight back by stopping their descent movement), but he wasn't sure.

He stepped closer to the door and saw the staff sergeant first, and then MacMillan, land on the flat roof of the mock-up. Immediately, they unstrapped their rifles and moved to the edges of the roof, MacMillan training his rifle on the courtyard, and the sergeant pointing his at the ground outside.

Felter nudged him, pointed to the rope. Lowell picked it up, put it in the D ring, and stood in the door, wondering how hard he was going to have to jump to get over the skid.

The crew chief, now standing in the center of the passenger compartment, legs spread, one hand flat on the roof, looked to see that Lowell and the master sergeant were ready to go. He held his balled fist in front of him and then extended the thumb upward. Then he made a sudden up-ending motion. The thumb was now pointed down.

"Shit!" Lowell said, aloud, and pushed himself backward out of the helicopter. The skid passed in front of his nose, and he saw that some of the OD paint had flaked off, exposing the reddish primer paint beneath. Then he applied friction, and his descent ended in an elastic jerk. He started to swing from side to side under the helicopter, and at the same time began to spin around on the rope.

He saw that the master sergeant was far beneath him. Lowell let loose and felt himself dropping. When he stopped the slide, he was oscillating worse than ever. He remembered that he had been told to start his descents only when he was in the middle of the oscillations. He hadn't done that. He would the next time.

He let go, and the next thing he knew, he had crashed into the roof. Damn it! His leg and knee hurt. *Stupid!*

He remembered to unsnap the rope from the D ring. MacMillan looked over to see if he needed help.

He forced a smile and gave a little wave, then looked up to watch Sandy come sliding down the line as if he had been doing it all his life.

This whole fucking thing is a facade, Lowell thought as he painfully flexed his knee. I'm not going to be sliding down a goddamned rope, and Sandy isn't even going to be there. Sandy will be on the aircraft carrier drinking coffee. Sandy was too much walking-around information to risk having him captured. Commanders are too valuable to risk sliding down ropes.

He was surprised MacMillan hadn't figured out yet that he was not going to get the actual command, time in grade or no time in grade. There was a sop to his ego on the final operations order. He was to be "commander of ground troops."

But the Commander of Air Landing, Consolidation, and Air Evacuation—in other words, the whole show once they took off from the carrier—was Colonel Craig W. Lowell.

Sandy unhooked himself and ran over with concern on his face.

For me? No way. For the operation?

"You OK? You landed with a bang."

"I'm all right. I just need a little practice is all. This is hardly my line of work."

Lowell forced himself to his feet. It hurt like hell, but nothing seemed to be broken.

He noticed that the Huey was on the ground. The pilot must have made one hell of a skillful autorotation. Lowell made a note to make sure that the landing plan was changed. The Huey was right in front of the main door to the building. There would certainly be guards there, even if most of them were trying to see what the hell had happened in the courtyard.

"What are you thinking?" Sandy asked.

"We shouldn't land Number Three right in front of the door," Lowell said. Sandy picked up on it immediately. His nod showed understanding; and you could take it to the bank that the plan would be corrected. Sandy was a master of detail.

"You all right, Colonel?" the master sergeant asked.

"Nothing that a stiff drink won't fix," Lowell said. "And some Sloane's Liniment."

"The drink I can arrange," the master sergeant said. He handed Lowell his canteen. It was full of bourbon.

He got Sloane's Liniment in the drug store in the shopping center. He also bought epsom salts and an Ace bandage. Jesus Christ, he hoped that nothing was broken or badly sprained. He really wanted to make this operation.

He had just filled the bathtub with hot water when the telephone rang.

He hobbled over to it. It had to be either Felter or Bellmon. He had given the number that was ringing only to them. MacMillan and Hanrahan and the others had the second number.

"Hello," he said.

"Hello, yourself," Dorothy Sims said.

"Oh," he said, astonishingly glad to hear her voice. "How are you?"

"How are *you?*" she countered.

"Would you believe I sprained my knee?"

"I was about to go out to the drug store," she said. "Is there anything I could get for you?"

"Nothing you can buy in a drug store," he said.

"All right," she said. "I'd be happy to. But I can't stay but just a minute. I have to pick up Tommy after Scouts."

Somebody, Lowell deduced, could hear her talking.

She hung up without saying anything else.

He hobbled back into the bath and lowered himself into the steaming epsom-salted water. In a few minutes, he heard the key in the door, and then the door slamming against the intruder chain. Damn, he'd forgotten about that.

He heaved himself out of the tub and hobbled, dripping, to the door, with a towel wrapped around his middle.

She saw him favoring the leg.

"You really did hurt it, didn't you?" she asked. "Let me have a look at it."

He got on the bed, propping his back against the plastic-covered headboard.

She probed the leg knowledgeably, made him flex it.

"It's going to swell," she said. "I should have gone to the drug store and gotten you an Ace bandage. What did you do to it, anyway?"

"I fell off a rope," he said. "There's an Ace bandage in the bathroom."

"Have you got some kind of liniment?"

"A bottle of Sloane's," he said.

She went back into the bathroom and returned with the liniment and the bandage. She rubbed the liniment in, and then wrapped the knee with the bandage.

"If it's badly swollen in the morning, you'd better see a doctor," she said.

"How much time did you say you had?" he asked.

"I was afraid you'd never ask," she said. With her eyes meeting his, she stood up and pulled her sweater off over her head.

XII

Headquarters, JFK Center for Special Warfare
Fort Bragg, North Carolina
1440 Hours, 21 June 1969

The conference table was stacked high with paper, and four desks with IBM typewriters had been set up. They were manned by muscular young Green Berets who looked as if they would be far happier throwing the typewriters around like basketballs.

"May I have your attention, gentlemen?" Colonel Craig Lowell called out.

The others at the conference table—the senior of whom was General Hanrahan—looked up from the stacks of paper with a mixture of annoyance and curiosity.

"I have a military profundity to utter," Lowell announced solemnly. "Napoleon was wrong. Armies don't travel on their stomachs. They slide along on paper."

It was a bad joke in any circumstances. It was not appreciated now.

"Jesus Christ, Duke!" General Hanrahan said, impatiently.

"I little stir crazy, Craig?" Sandy Felter said.

"An understatement," Lowell said. "I have been here seven long, long hours."

273

"Jesus," General Hanrahan said. "Has it been that long?"

"You will recall, General, I'm sure," Lowell said, "from the foggy recesses of fond memory, that we fought a whole goddamned Greek division with less paper than this."

"We weren't moving three-quarters of the way around the world in secret," Hanrahan said. He took off his glasses—shaped and colored like aviator's glasses—and rubbed the bridge of his nose.

"Do I hear a motion to adjourn?" Lowell asked.

"Why don't we knock off?" General Hanrahan said, "Hanrahan's Law holds that the more you look at figures, the more they lie."

"I don't know about the rest of you," Lowell said, "but I'm finished. I only say that because the general says we can have the weekend off. Otherwise, Colonel Felter, I'm sure, would find something to keep me busy."

"You've got plans for the weekend?" Sandy Felter asked.

"All work and no play, and so on," Lowell said.

"The troops have been at it hot and heavy, General," MacMillan said. So they had, Lowell realized. He had just about forgotten about the troops. But they had been rehearsing all week. Despite their reputation for being able to fight anywhere any time, they had not been trained in large-strength helicopter assaults. In other words, while they were highly skilled at rappelling down from a helicopter, and in being extracted from beneath a jungle canopy more or less the same way, they had not been trained (as ordinary troops were) to make a heli-landing from a fleet of helicopters. So they had been practicing that all week, and they had also been practicing loading and unloading "the basic load" into Chinooks* and Jolly Green Giants.**

On Friday of next week, the troops would make their first practice assault on the mock-up. Once that happened, they

---

*Chinook: U.S. Army Boeing-Vertol CH-47 helicopters capable of carrying either forty-four passengers or, for example, a 155-mm cannon, its crew, and a basic load of ammunition, on a mission radius of 120 miles.
**Jolly Green Giant: USAF Sikorsky HH-53C transport helicopters, equipped with two jettisonable 450-gallon auxiliary fuel tanks and normally used for long-range rescue of downed aircraft crews.

would be locked up. After the practice assault, the risk that they would have a couple of drinks and talk about what they were doing was too great.

Some of the troops were of course already privy to many of the details of the "high-risk-factor" mission for which they had volunteered. Since most of the Berets were not only very bright, but very experienced, they would have figured it out for themselves. So it had been Felter's decision (opposed by MacMillan and General Bellmon, supported by Lowell) to tell the ones who would actually assault the Hanoi Hilton. Lowell's support as well as MacMillan's and Bellmon's objections had been pissing in the wind. Sandy Felter was the action officer, and it was his decision to make.

If it were my decision to make, Lowell thought, watching Felter, I would knock off for the weekend. Working through weekends caused interest. Interest caused speculation, and not a hell of a lot of speculation would be required before some bright young Green Beret trooper put everything together and concluded that what they were going to do with their helicopters and five full colonels running around in ripstops playing John Wayne was go grab the guys in the Hanoi Hilton and bring them home.

"Yes, sir," Sandy Felter said, "I think you're right. I think we ought to knock off right now, this minute, right where we are, and pick up again at oh six hundred Monday morning."

"Sergeant Major!" Hanrahan said.

"Sir?" the sergeant major replied.

"Seal the place. Nobody gets in but you and the senior officers," Hanrahan said.

"Consider it sealed, sir. Sir?"

"You've got something?"

"I thought Colonel Mac was going to mention it, sir," the sergeant major said.

"Yeah, Jesus Christ," MacMillan said. "I guess I'm a little foggy, too. General, what about TOWs*?"

---

*TOW: *T*actical, *O*ptical *W*ire–guided rocket, a shoulder-fired missile with the impact power of a 155-mm artillery shell, intended to be used against tanks.

"What about them?" Hanrahan asked, confused.

"There's twenty of them on the post," MacMillan said.

"And that's supposed to be Secret," Hanrahan said. "Or is it Top Secret?"

"Top Secret, sir," MacMillan said.

"And you found out about them, huh?"

"Some of the troops have been watching the tests, sir," MacMillan said. "And they have asked me—"

"Some of the troops have been watching the tests? And apparently counting the stock?" Hanrahan asked. He seemed more resigned than disturbed. Certainly not surprised.

"They ran it as an infiltration problem, sir," MacMillan said, uneasily.

"And they figure what the hell, let's get some?" Hanrahan said. "No way, Mac."

"What's your reasoning, Mac?" Felter asked, quietly.

"The first thing the bad guys are going to do, once they know we're there, is send T-34s from Nnon Pac," MacMillan said. "There are eighteen of them there, sixteen apparently operable."

"How did your guys find that out?" Hanrahan asked.

"They don't know it," MacMillan said. "Sir, I didn't say—"

"Go on, Mac," Felter interrupted him.

"Mouse, they just figured it out. Shit, I could figure it out. What's the best way to deal with a prisoner situation? With tanks. The only way to deal with tanks is with other tanks. Against tanks, there's not a hell of a lot you can do, and a T-34 is a sonofabitch to knock out with a rocket launcher. If the bad guys sent a column of tanks to the Hilton, and one of them got blown off the road, they would stop and reconsider their position, that's for sure. It would buy us some time."

"The way to deal with those tanks," Tex Williams said, "is to take them out with a bombing raid the night before."

"We've decided against that," Felter said. "For one thing, we can't count on results. If they aren't taken out, all we're going to do is draw attention to the area. And if they are taken out, we've still drawn attention to the area. Why those tanks, and not T-34s elsewhere? Christ, Tex! You don't give up, do you?"

The icy tone was back in Felter's voice. And the profanity. The Mouse has a hard-on, Lowell thought, smiling.

"The current plan is to take out the roads," Felter said, thinking aloud. "There are three roads. One demolition team cannot support another, the distances are too great. We are proceeding on the assumption that the demolitions teams will be successful. That is a shaky assumption. On the other hand, we would be risking the premature disclosure of our TOW development status. That would make a number of people very uncomfortable. I don't even like to think about having a TOW fall into Russian hands."

There was a long pause.

"We could rig them with a quarter pound of C-4*," MacMillan said.

"If we are to believe the initial test reports," Felter went on, still thinking aloud, his voice very much like the voice of a computer in a science fiction movie, "the TOW has a seventy-five percent kill rate at two hundred yards or less. Let's cut that in half. A thirty-seven decimal five kill rate at two hundred yards. In the hands of a skilled operator. How hard are they to use? Unknown. The figures come out this way. Three TOWs on each road would give us a one decimal one two five kill rate. One hundred twelve decimal five. Cut *that* in half. Fifty-six decimal five.

"We have previously calculated the odds of tank reinforcement at eighty decimal zero. Four chances out of five. We have calculated successful demolition of the roads at sixty-six decimal six. Two out of three. What that boils down to is that they will *probably* send tank reinforcement, and that we have presently only two chances out of three of stopping them via road demolition.

"The question is thus whether it is best to insure the success

*C-4: Plastic explosive

of the mission against tank reinforcement at the cost of prematurely disclosing a Top Secret weapon."

"You better pass that one upstairs, Sandy," General Hanrahan said. "If you're seriously considering this."

That was the reaction to be expected of a general officer in Hanrahan's position, Felter thought. When you believe a decision is too important for you to make yourself, ask the next higher echelon of command. It was normally a reasonable practice. But it wasn't going to work here. The President had meant it when he used the phrase "Under my personal direction." The command of Monte Cristo was his, delegated to Felter. Felter knew if he asked for a decision whether or not to use the TOWs, he would have to ask the President. And that meant he would first have to explain to the President (and probably as well to Kissinger and Colonel Al Haig, Kissinger's Chief of Staff) what a TOW was, and why he thought it should be used, and what the ramifications of its capture by the North Vietnamese might be.

And one of two things would most likely happen. Al Haig (who had more or less tactfully suggested that he had more command experience than Felter, and Q.E.D. should have been given Monte Cristo) was liable to say, "Why don't we run it past the Joint Chiefs?"

Or, more likely, the President—probably annoyed at being bothered with what he considered a minor operational detail—would say "Do what you think is best, Felter."

"Upstairs to whom, General?" Felter asked softly.

Hanrahan's eyebrows rose, but he didn't reply.

Felter sat for a moment, shoulders hunched, and with his fingers rigidly extended, he slapped his hands together.

"General," he said, finally, "would you please get in touch with General Bellmon? Tell him it has come to your attention that the security of the TOW testing program has been compromised. And tell him that until the matter is resolved, testing will be suspended, and that he will place the stock of TOWs under your protection."

"I don't think I have the authority to do that, Sandy," Hanrahan said. "They don't even belong to him. They belong to the Airborne Board."

"Not any more they don't," Felter said. "They belong to Monte Cristo. We will fire ten of them over the weekend. We will take ten with us. See to it that the project officer, who presumably knows how these things work, comes with them, and see to it that he is informed that if it ever comes out that he has opened his mouth to anyone about anything he sees, or suspects, or *thinks*, he can expect to spend the rest of his career in his permanent rank counting snowflakes in Alaska."

"Yes, sir," General Hanrahan said. He knew that for all practical purposes it was the President of the United States who was giving that order.

Felter looked at Lowell.

"You want to keep an eye on this, Craig?" he asked.

"I think that General Hanrahan would be the best one to do that," Lowell said. "I don't want to draw attention to Monte Cristo through me."

"And you also want to play this weekend, right?" Felter said.

"Guilty," Lowell said.

"I'll take it over, Sandy," MacMillan volunteered, glowering at Lowell.

"That would draw attention to us through you," Lowell said. "Let Hanrahan do it. There's a hundred reasons he would be legitimately interested in them."

"The Duke's right, sir," Felter said to Hanrahan. "Sorry to take your weekend."

"Hell, I don't mind," General Hanrahan said. "I haven't even seen one of them."

Felter leaned forward and pulled a red dialless telephone to him. He picked it up. "Please engage your scrambler," he said. He paused. "This is Outfielder. Let me speak to the secretary of the general staff." There was another pause. "This is Outfielder," he said again. He ran his finger down a line of words and numbers before him in a folder, and then glanced at his watch. The signal operating instructions had a code for each hour of the day. He said: "Victoria three three nine. Confirm."

"Wisconsin four two seven," the Secretary of the General Staff of the U.S. Army replied.

"I want a teletype message sent to the President of the Airborne Board, Fort Bragg," Felter said. "I want it sent *Priority,* and I want it backdated, but I want it hand-carried and dispatched immediately. The message—classified Top Secret—is 'TOW compromised. You will cooperate fully with General Hanrahan. More follows. End message.' Send it out over the Chairman's personal signature. Will you read that back, please?" There was a pause. "Thank you very much," Felter said. He dropped the red handset back in its cradle.

He smiled shyly around the table.

"I was really a little worried about those damned roads," he said. "Thank you, Mac. Thank *you,* Sergeant Major."

"From what I hear, Colonel," the sergeant major said, "you can send out a PFC with one of those things and he'll bring you back a tank."

"They are not to be used unless the demolitions team fails," Felter said. "I'll leave it up to you, Sergeant Major, to make that point with the demolitions people. There may be a time when he can use them against Russian armor, but I devoutly hope this is not it. You understand me?"

"Yes, sir," the sergeant major said.

"We are not going where we are going to bring back tanks," Felter said.

"Is that it, Sandy?" Lowell asked.

"I presume you're leaving the area," Felter said. "Check in every three hours, please Duke."

"Including three A.M.?" Lowell said, getting to his feet.

"Including three A.M., Duke," Felter said.

(Two)
Winston-Salem, North Carolina
21 June 1969

Dorothy Sims sat at the counter of the coffee shop, an

untouched cup of coffee cold in front of her, an unread magazine under a package of cigarettes, a makeup kit and a small overnight bag on the polished aggregate floor beside her.

She was marveling at her previously unsuspected ability to lie with skill and artistry. First she told her mother that the kids were just dying to come "home" to see Grandma and Pawpaw. Absolutely untrue. The kids wanted to stay in Fayetteville and enjoy their vacation. She then told the kids that Grandma and Pawpaw wanted to see them (which was true) and that they should remember that they would themselves be that old one day, which was a cheap shot if there ever was one.

She next told her mother and her father that she really must go to a protest meeting in Washington, clearly implying that it was her wifely duty to Tom. That was the same story she gave Roxy MacMillan, though in fact, she wasn't going anywhere near Washington.

The trouble was that now Craig Lowell had not showed up. Where the hell was he?

She had called the apartment twice, but there had been no answer.

And the terminal was practically deserted, which meant that no plane was scheduled soon to arrive or depart.

She forced herself to slowly sip the lukewarm coffee until it was gone, which took two more cigarettes. She asked the cold-faced bored impatient waitress in a beehive hairdo for the bill. Then she put the magazine under her arm, picked up the makeup case and the overnight bag, and walked out of the nearly empty restaurant into the nearly empty terminal.

There weren't even people working the ticket counters! Just a girl at the Hertz desk and a distracted security officer leaning on a wall.

The glass doors from outside opened, and she looked and saw a man in a cotton windbreaker coming through. He seemed to be looking for her.

"Mrs. Sims?" he asked.

"Yes," she said.

"I'm from Lewis Aviation, ma'am," he said. "Your charter

just called in. He's ten minutes out. He asked me to fetch you."

"Thank you very much," she said.

"Here, let me have your bag. I've got a truck outside."

She gave it to him and walked on light feet—light-headed—after him. She should have known that Craig would have thought of something like a charter.

The man in the windbreaker put her bag in the back of a pickup, and then slammed the door once she'd got in.

"You're Mrs. Sims, aren't you?" the man said, as he drove away from the passenger terminal. "I mean, you were Dorothy Persons, weren't you?"

"Yes, I was," she said. "Or I am. Do I know you?"

"I used to work for your dad's company," he said. "Before I went to work for Lewis. I'm still a backup pilot for them. I've seen you around."

"I think I've seen you, too."

Dear God, don't let him bump into my father out here, and tell him that "it was nice to see Mrs. Sims, when the charter came and picked her up."

"That's probably him now," the man said, gesturing out the windshield. It was dark, but still bright enough to see a light twin airplane making its landing. Where did he get that plane? She'd expected him to show up in the Army plane he'd flown her in from Atlanta.

The plane was now down and taxiing toward the commercial aviation facility.

An attendant in a white suit went out to guide it to a parking stop, then ran to a fuel truck and drove that to the airplane. She was driven directly to the airplane.

Craig was standing beside the plane—what looked to be a brand-new Cessna 310, a sleek, fast, twin-engine aircraft—watching the attendant open the fuel filler plate. He turned.

"Mrs. Sims?" Craig Lowell asked, his eyes smiling. She nodded. "I'm sorry to be late."

"It's perfectly all right."

"We'll be ready to go in just a moment," he said. "We'll make up the lost time."

"There's nothing to be concerned about," she said.

It didn't take much gas. Craig put her bags on the floor of the back seat of the plane. He signed the credit slip for the gasoline, put the credit card back in his pocket.

"Where would you like to ride?" he asked. "Up front? Or in the back?"

"In front," she said. "If I won't be in your way."

"Not at all, ma'am," he said. "I like company. But I'll have to get in first. Be careful of your head."

He climbed onto the wing, and then got inside the plane, crawling into the left-hand pilot's seat. She climbed in, and the man from Lewis Aviation closed the door after her.

He checked to see the door was closed, and that she had fastened her belt.

And then he started the engines, waved good-bye to the man from Lewis Aviation, and started taxiing toward the runway.

"Winston-Salem ground control, Cessna Four Niner, taxi to the active," he said into a hand-held microphone.

"Cessna Four Niner is cleared to the threshold of Runway Two Eight," a speaker said in her ear. "Contact Departure Control on one two one point nine."

He fiddled with the radios.

"Winston-Salem Departure Control, Cessna Four Niner, request takeoff from Two Eight, visual to Atlanta, Fulton County."

He braked the airplane to a stop, raced the engines, checked dials.

"Cessna Four Niner, you are cleared for takeoff from Runway Two Eight. The winds are negligible. There is no traffic. The time is five past the hour. The altimeter is two niner niner eight."

He looked at her. She looked back at him.

"Hello, my darling," he said, and leaned over and kissed her.

"Hello yourself," she said. She could taste cigar on his tongue.

"Winston-Salem," he said. "Four Niner rolling. Thank you."

The plane gathered speed quickly and lifted off into the sky. She fished in her purse for her cigarettes and took one out. She looked around for a lighter. There it was, right under a little illuminated sign saying LIGHTER.

"What did you do, rent this?" she asked, as she pulled the tray outward.

"No, this is mine," he said. "I just got it, as a matter of fact. I used to have an Aero Commander. This is a lot faster, and I really didn't need all that room. I had it brought up from Alabama."

"It's a nice plane," she said. "Now will you kiss me again!"

He leaned over and kissed her again, and she kissed him hungrily.

He went back on the radio, asking something called Atlanta Area Control for an IFR flight plan.

"We have a decision to make," he said to her. "We can either go into Fulton County, which is miles from Atlanta, and where there isn't much chance of anyone seeing us together, or we can go into Atlanta itself, where, if we're seen together, we can look innocent. If we're seen at Fulton County, we will have a hard time looking innocent."

"You obviously have more experience in this sort of thing than I do," Dorothy said.

"But you have more to lose," he said, not taking offense.

"Let's go into Atlanta," she said. "And take our chances."

He parked the plane at the Southern Airways portion of the terminal, beside several comparatively huge commercial airliners.

"You don't see many little airplanes here," she said.

"And they don't like this one, either," he said. "It is a courtesy discourteously offered."

She smiled, hoping for a better explanation, but he offered none.

He locked the airplane door, gave the keys to a Southern attendant, and then they caught a taxi to the Hyatt Regency Hotel. At the end of their elevator ride outside the building was a suite furnished in what she thought of as North Carolina

Louis XIV. Compared to Craig's apartment, it was the height of elegance.

They were no sooner in the door than a waiter appeared with a cart, on which were hors d'oeuvres, whiskey, and a bottle of champagne. He had apparently taken some pains with the arrangements. She was touched. And then he sprawled into a chair and picked up the telephone, and dialed a number.

"Sign that thing, will you?" he said, gesturing at her.

What am I going to sign? she wondered, taking the bill from the waiter.

She signed "Mrs. Craig Lowell," looked at the key and wrote "2406," and then "Add 15% tip."

"Thank you, Mrs. *Lowell*," the waiter said, and left them alone.

What the hell, Dorothy thought.

"Colonel Lowell, Sergeant Major," he said to the telephone. "I'm in 2406 of the Hyatt Regency in Atlanta. You got anything for me?" There was a pause. "Yes, thank you," he said, and chuckled. "I intended to have a good time."

He dropped the phone in its cradle and motioned to her. She went and sat in his lap.

"What was that all about?" she asked.

"Do you really care?" he asked.

She kissed him, and after a moment she felt his hand on her leg, sliding up it under her slip.

(Three)
Point Clear, Alabama
26 June 1969

When Colonel Craig Lowell saw the pilot crawl out of the Hughes LOH-6 and walk toward Base Ops at Hurlbert Field on the Gulf Coast west of Eglin Air Force Base, he was genuinely surprised, furious, and a little sick. He knew the captain. The captain was just back from his third 'Nam tour. He still had the 'Nam look.

He was a tall, good-looking young officer, tanned and lean.

There was an anticipatory smile on his face. And he walked with a jaunty step. He was good at what he did, and he knew it. And right now he was specially pleased with himself. He thought he was being really clever—and that he would be welcomed with open arms because of that.

Lowell had called the Aviation Board and asked them to send him a chopper. He had expected the pilot to be one of the warrant officers, or a young lieutenant. Not a captain, and certainly not *this* captain.

The captain pushed open the door to Base Ops and threw Lowell a snappy salute.

"Colonel Lowell," he said. "How nice to see you again, Colonel. I have your aircraft, sir."

Because the Air Force was watching, Lowell returned the salute.

"May I observe, sir, that the colonel looks a little beat?"

"I have been in the Army nearly as long as you are old," Lowell said. "I am entitled to look beat."

"That's right, isn't it?" the captain said, doing the arithmetic.

"Let's go, Captain," Lowell said.

"Yes, sir," the captain said, and held open the door for Lowell to pass before him.

They walked back to the Hughes LOH-6, a small, single-rotor helicopter. On the day it had been certified for flight by the FAA the LOH-6 had set fourteen world records. It was, among other things, the fastest helicopter flying.

Lowell got in the copilot's seat and fastened his shoulder harness. The captain climbed in the other side, strapped himself in, and reached for the master switch.

Lowell put out his hand and stopped him.

"What the *hell* are you doing here, Geoff?" he asked.

Captain Geoffrey Craig looked at Colonel Craig Lowell. His smile was not quite as self-satisfied as it had been a few moments earlier, but he was still smiling.

"Inasmuch as that remark was not preceded by 'How's Ursula and the kids?' I presume that's a Colonel Lowell, as opposed to Cousin Craig, interrogatory?"

"You bet your sweet ass it is," Lowell said.

"Ursula and the boys are doing very nicely, thank you for asking," Geoff said.

"Answer the goddamn question," Lowell said, sharply.

"I was available when the mission came in," Geoff said. "When I heard it was you, I took it."

"That's all?"

Geoff looked at him and hesitated a moment before replying.

"I thought maybe there would be a chance for a little chat," he said.

"That's what I was afraid of," Lowell said. "Let's get it in the air, Geoff."

"You want to drive?" Geoff asked.

"No. You drive," Lowell said. He had been flying all day, and while the Chinook had a complete electro-hydraulic control system and was allegedly capable of reducing pilot effort to the minimum, it was still a heavy sonofabitch to fly, especially if you were one year shy of a quarter century's service.

"I've got an hour thirty's fuel aboard," Geoff said. "Is that going to be enough."

"You have a credit card?"

"Yeah. But I filed local, and you're not supposed to charge gas if you file local."

Despite everything else, Lowell was touched. Geoff had decided that his cousin had requested an "unofficial" (unauthorized) ride. So instead of having it down on paper, he had filed a local flight plan ("test" or "proficiency") within the Fort Rucker immediate area.

"When you go back, say you got the wrong word," Lowell said. "I'm authorized."

"Sorry, Craig," Geoff said. He smiled mischievously at Lowell. "I thought maybe it was a pussy mission."

"Why would you think that?" Lowell asked.

"No particular reason," Geoff said.

"I wish it was," Lowell said, thinking that sounded more credible than a fervent denial. "No, it's authorized. Call the board and tell them I said it was authorized."

"Christ, and here I had visions of New Orleans," the captain said.

"You're out of luck," Lowell said.

Geoff cranked it up.

"You say we're authorized? You want me to file?"

"Just buzz west along the beach," Lowell said.

"You care if I lay a little rank on them?"

"If you've got it, flaunt it," Lowell said.

"Hurlbert, Army Chopper Two One," Geoff said to his microphone. "In front of your Base Ops. Taxi and takeoff, VFR nap of the earth. I have a Code Six aboard."

Hurlbert came right back: "Hurlbert clears Army Helicopter Two One for immediate takeoff from the parking area. There is a C-131 inbound, five miles out. The winds are negligible, the time is four-five past the hour, and the altimeter is two niner eight. Have a nice flight, Colonel, and hurry back to Hurlbert."

"Two One, light on the skids," Geoff said. The Hughes climbed smoothly to about fifty feet, with no more feeling of motion than in a good elevator. After swooping over the other parked aircraft, the main highway, and the beach, it turned west. Jesus, Lowell thought, he flies this thing as if it's part of him. Well, he's had a lot of practice, and it's a lot easier when they're not shooting at you.

"Bill Franklin sends regards," Geoff said.

"Yeah, I thought maybe he would," Lowell said. "How is he?"

"About as well as any man who learns on his return from 'Nam that his wife apparently went right from the maternity ward to some other fucker's bed," Geoff said bitterly. "And the bitch is trying to take him for everything he owns."

"Is there anything we can do?" Lowell asked.

"He spends a lot of time at our house," Geoff said.

"Thank you, Geoff," Lowell said.

"What the hell, he's my friend, too. He was my CO, you remember."

"Poor sonofabitch," Lowell said.

"Ah, what the hell," Geoff said. There was no point in

talking about it. "What's going on in Mobile?"

"We're going to a field on this side of the bay," Lowell said. "A place called Fairhope."

"Steer a minute and let me look at the chart," Geoff said. Lowell took the controls.

"I've got it," Lowell said, and added, "all you have to do is follow the beach. It's off the airways."

Geoff found Fairhope Municipal Airport on his Jeppeson chart.

"Very interesting," he said. "Right there in the middle of nowhere. Fifty-eight hundred feet, lighted runways, twenty-four-hour radio. Avgas and JP-4. Now what do you suppose a dinky little town like that is doing with an airport like that?"

"There's a hotel there. A lot of business jets," Lowell said. The question confirmed his suspicions that Geoff's arrival in the Hughes was not entirely because he wanted to be nice to his cousin.

"I got it," Geoff said, taking the controls back. "And you don't care if someone knows you're landing there. So it's really not a pussy flight."

"If you learn to keep your mouth shut," Lowell said, "and don't fly into any mountains, and eventually make colonel, you will learn that captains very seldom question where colonels go. That is known as 'Rank Hath its Privileges.'"

"Yes, sir, I'll remember that, sir," Geoff said. "Colonel, sir, am I going to be very surprised to see maybe a dozen Chinooks parked at Fairhope Municipal Airport?"

Goddamn it to hell! He does know! The only question is how much.

"I would be very much surprised if there was anything there painted olive drab," Lowell said, as calmly as he could.

"The most astonishing thing has happened lately, Colonel," Geoff said, "while the Colonel has been taking the sun with the Air Force at Hurlbert."

"Is that so?"

"Major Franklin and I were discussing it just before I flew down here, as a matter of fact."

Major Franklin (then Sergeant) and Colonel Lowell (then

Captain) had met when Lowell had been an assistant military attaché in Algiers, watching the French use of Piasecki H-21s against Algerian guerrillas. Lowell had arranged for him to get into the Warrant Officer Candidate (Flight Training) Program. When he'd gone to get Sandy Felter off the beach at the Bay of Pigs fiasco, Bill Franklin had been his copilot. When they somehow managed to pull that off, Kennedy had promoted him from warrant officer to lieutenant on the same order Lowell had been made lieutenant colonel. Major Franklin had commanded a company of Huey-Cobras under Lowell in Vietnam.

His interest in whatever Colonel Lowell was up to was understandable, Colonel Lowell thought, but right now it was the worst fucking thing that could happen.

"Go on, Geoff," Lowell said.

"There's about a dozen Chinooks missing," Geoff said, more than a little smugly. (Listen to what I found out, clever fellow that I am.) "Four from Rucker, four from Benning, and two each from as far away as Riley and Bliss."

Lowell didn't reply. He had to hear him out.

"And each of these machines, by another interesting, strange coincidence, happens to be crewed by some very experienced Chinook pilots. Not just one very experienced Chinook pilot and some kid along to learn from his betters, but *two* very experienced Chinook pilots. Some of them are even almost as experienced as I am."

He looked over at Lowell.

"One of the pilots, whose name I happen not to be able to recall, talks a lot to his wife. And his wife said that all she knew was that he had gone to Bragg for three weeks or so. But the next day, Bill Franklin just happened to be at Bragg, and when he asked about this guy, Bragg swore they didn't know anything about Chinooks."

"Isn't that interesting?" Lowell said. "Do you suppose they have been swallowed up in the Bermuda Triangle?"

"And then when I was zipping merrily along on my way to Hurlbert Field just now, you'll never guess what I saw flying down the middle of the Eglin Reservation."

"Eglin is a restricted zone," Lowell said. "What were you doing flying across a restricted zone?"

"I guess I was lost," Geoff said. "But I was so low, I would be very surprised if they picked me up on their radar. I was telling you what I saw, Colonel, sir. I saw a dozen Chinooks zipping in from the ocean about six inches off the waves."

"That's enough, Geoff," Lowell said. "I mean it, stop right there."

"And do you know what I thought when I saw those Chinooks?" Geoff went on.

I can't stop him, Lowell realized.

"I mean, since they didn't have any gunship support or anything? I mean, it was an assault, but it wasn't a combat assault with gunships and colored smoke and some jackass sitting up at thirty-five hundred feet in a command-and-control Huey playing with his toys."

"I have flown a command-and-control bird myself on several occasions," Lowell said. "I never felt like a jackass playing with toys."

"You wouldn't believe what they've got over there now, Colonel," Geoff said, unwilling to back down here, either. "Graduates of some VIP flight courses who literally don't know their ass from a hole in the ground."

"What kind of an assault did you think they were practicing?"

"Like I said, Major Franklin was over at Bragg one day last week. And he thought that he would pay his respects to his former commanding officer, who he knew was at Bragg, because the President of the Army Aviation Board himself told him he was at Bragg. At Bragg, he met a guy who told him his ol' buddy was out at Camp McCall, which didn't surprise him, since his ol' buddy and former commanding officer was in tight with the snake-eaters, and had even been seen, on occasion, wearing a green beret hisself."

"Franklin went to Camp McCall?"

"Yeah. He wanted a little time in one of these, so he flew some paper-pusher over there in one. He was empty going back and in no big rush, so he figured, what the hell, I'll drop in and say 'Howdy' to the Duke. The major tells me that when he put down at McCall, a bunch of very angry Berets came running up and pointed guns at him and otherwise pissed their pants."

"Is that so?"

"But that isn't what he found over there that was *really* interesting," Geoff said. "What he found absolutely fascinating, would you believe it, was that there's a mock-up of the POW camp at Dak Tae out there."

"I'm sure he was mistaken."

"Come on, Craig. Franklin flew a dozen Mohawk photo-recons of Dak Tae. The last time two months ago."

"I'm telling you, Geoff," Lowell said. "Franklin's mistaken."

"We want in," Geoff said. "That's what I wanted to talk to you about."

"In what?"

"I'm a good Chinook pilot, and you know I am. Franklin was a test pilot on the sonofabitch; he's got about a thousand hours in it. And we're still even current in 'Nam. If you're going to get those guys, and don't tell me that you're not, we want to go."

"How many people have you and Franklin discussed this James Bond fantasy with?" Lowell asked.

"Nobody," Geoff said. "Christ!"

The implication was clear. They knew when to keep their mouths shut.

"Think over that answer, and then tell me again," Lowell said.

Sensing how serious Lowell was, Geoff took a moment to think it over.

"Nobody," he said. "Absolutely nobody."

"You're absolutely sure?" Lowell asked. "If for some reason you and Franklin suddenly vanished from Rucker tonight, Geoff, who would get curious? I mean, aside from people concerned with where you were? Would somebody start coming up with theories about where you would likely be?"

"No, sir," Geoff said, believing he had won; that he and Franklin would be going along.

"I want you to listen to me very carefully, Geoff," he said. "I am speaking as an officer. This is an order."

"Yes, sir?"

"You are to consider yourself under arrest. When you drop me off, you are to return to Fort Rucker and make contact with Major Franklin. You are to inform Major Franklin that on my authority, he is under arrest. You are permitted to tell your wife that you have been placed on TDY to Fort Bragg, North Carolina, and will be out of touch for several weeks, and that she is not to tell anyone of your location. Then you and Major Franklin will fly to Camp McCall in this aircraft—I remind you that you are under arrest—and report to a Lieutenant Colonel Seaman, he's the security officer. You will inform Seaman that I have ordered you to relay him the instructions that your arrest is to be immediately reported to Colonel Felter. Do you completely understand me?"

The blood drained from Captain Geoff Craig's face.

"I never dreamed you'd turn us in," Geoff said.

"Geoff, if necessary," Lowell said, "I'd have you shot. You two are just too fucking smart for your own good. I don't think I have to tell you that you're not to get clever with Felter. You'll tell him exactly what you told me, and anything else he wants to know."

"Then what happens to us?"

"You'll probably be taken to a place that's been set up on McCall and put on ice for the next three weeks or a month. You won't be alone, but so far, there's only one other officer who got nosy."

"So you are going," Geoff said.

"I want you to give Colonel Felter the name of your friend who talks too much," Lowell said. "We have to find out how much damage he's done."

"And what happens to him? He gets court-martialed?"

"What do you think should happen to somebody who opens

his fat mouth when the lives of a couple hundred people are concerned? A slap on the wrist?"

"He didn't do anything I haven't done," Geoff said.

"If Felter tries to court-martial you and/or Franklin later, I'll testify for you, testify that I *ordered* you to speculate, make wild guesses. That's presuming you don't play smart-ass to Felter."

"Why don't you just take us along?"

"It's too late for that," Lowell said. "For which answer, I deserve to be court-martialed. I would be grateful if you left that out of your conversation with Felter."

"Craig, if I've fucked things up for you, I'm really sorry."

"Geoff, I am perfectly capable, as my career has proved, of fucking things up for myself with no outside help."

Ten minutes later, the Hughes dropped Lowell at Fairhope Municipal Airport. Geoff unloaded Lowell's luggage. The airport operator called the Grand Hotel, who sent a station wagon for Lowell. When it came, Geoff offered Lowell his hand and wished him good luck.

"I'm sorry, Geoff, I really am," Lowell said.

"What would happen if I just flew back to Rucker, and denied I ever had seen you?"

"You wouldn't do that, Geoff. For better or worse, you're a soldier."

"Yeah," Geoff said. "Ain't that the truth? Do not pass Go. Do not collect two hundred dollars. Go directly to jail." Then he came to attention and threw Lowell a crisp salute. Lowell returned it, as crisply.

Captain Geoffrey Craig said, "God, I'd give my left nut to be there when the bugler blows the fucking charge."

Then he climbed into the Hughes and pulled the door closed and put on his shoulder harness.

(Four)

A black, gray-haired bellman met the Grand Hotel station wagon at the entrance to the hotel and took Lowell's luggage from the back seat.

"Nice to see you again, sir," he said, to Lowell.

"It's been some time."

"I expect it's Colonel by now, isn't it?" the bellman said. Well, Lowell thought, I'll be damned. He really does remember me.

"If it wasn't," he said, "you would have really blown your tip."

The bellman smiled back. "And the next time, I expect it'll be *General*," he said.

"You wouldn't want to hold your breath and wait for that," Lowell said. He followed the bellman into the wide, long lobby of the luxury resort hotel and walked up to the desk.

"My name is Lowell," he said. "My wife is already here, but you'd better give me a key."

"You're in 216-220, Colonel," the desk clerk, a good-looking young woman, said, handing him the key. "Nice to have you back with us."

She wasn't old enough to remember me, Lowell decided. So they must check a card file or something. I hope the card file doesn't record that the last time Lowell, C W was here, his wife had red hair.

Suite 216 had windows opening on Mobile Bay. There was a bottle of Chivas Regal, a bucket of ice cubes, and a quart bottle of soda on the dresser in the bedroom. Taped to the mirror of the dresser was a note on hotel stationery: "I'm in the pool. 1550."

He gave the bellman five dollars and told him he couldn't think of a thing he needed. He locked the door after him and checked his watch. She had gone to the pool at ten minutes to four. It was now a quarter to five. What he should do, he thought, was go down to the lobby and use the telephone in the pay station. But Dorothy wasn't likely to come back in the next couple of minutes.

He sat down on the bed, took a thin notebook from his pocket, got the hotel operator on the line, and, subtracting two from each number he had written down, gave her Sandy Felter's number at Hulbert Field.

"Sandy," Lowell said. "I'm sending you two officers, Major

Bill Franklin and Captain Geoff Craig. They have been playing guessing games."

There was a moment's hesitation.

"Have they been good at it?"

"They are both very clever people," Lowell said.

"All right, Craig, I'll handle it," Felter said. "Where are you?" he asked.

"In 216, the Grand Hotel, Point Clear, Alabama," Lowell said. "The number is 928-9201."

"You're alone?"

"At the moment," Lowell said, a tone of belligerence in his voice.

"Tell me more about Franklin and Geoff," Felter said.

"Franklin was at Bragg last week and stopped off at McCall to see me."

"McCall has been closed to transient traffic."

"It wasn't the first time that Franklin has been with me somewhere we weren't supposed to be," Lowell said.

Chew on that a little, Sandy. Remember that Franklin was in the cockpit of the Catalina when we picked your wet, bedraggled, and about-to-be captured ass off of the beach at the Bay of Pigs.

"I'm surprised he wasn't asked to stay at McCall," Felter said.

Lowell felt like a fool for not wondering before why Franklin hadn't been grabbed and sent off to the detention facility at McCall. Anyone who had been there had to be presumed to have seen the mock-up at Dak Tae. That was one of the causes established for detention.

The chances were good that the officer of the guard had been plucked out of the jungle by Bill Franklin. One would be naturally reluctant to cause trouble for someone who had hovered over the jungle canopy to pluck one out of the jungle. Helicopters on insertion and withdrawal missions were sitting ducks for 'Cong ground fire. They were called "high pucker factor" missions, making reference to the sphincter muscles. Bill Franklin and Geoff Craig had both made so many high pucker factor missions that the First Special Forces Group had somehow seen to it that they had been awarded the Expert Combat Infantry Badge.

"He has a lot of friends," Lowell said. "Including me."

"I've already taken your point, Craig," Felter said, coldly.

"Good. I'm glad you have," Lowell said, as coldly. "Sometimes you're a little dense about things like that."

"Is there anything else you feel you should tell me?" Felter asked.

"On the way to pick me up," Lowell said, "Geoff saw some interesting sea gulls on the beach."

"Good God!" Felter said.

"And he knows a sea gull that talks like a parrot," Lowell said. "And as I say, he's a very good, very bright officer."

"And they're on their way here?"

"Not the parrot," Lowell said. "Bill and Geoff. I don't have the parrot's name."

"I'll get it," Felter said.

"Sandy, let's take them with us. They're both good Chinook pilots, and they both just came back."

"That's out of the question," Felter said. "You know that."

"Sandy, I don't want you to fuck either one of them up," Lowell said.

Felter ignored him. "When are you coming back from suite 216 in the Grand Hotel?"

"Now that I've lost my ride, and don't want to ask for another one, I thought about going back direct."

"I think it would be best if you arranged to come back here," Felter said. "After I talk to those two, I will probably want to talk to you."

"Yes, sir," Lowell said, sarcastically. "You know where to reach me, sir."

"If you're going to be gone from there for more than an hour or so, check in, will you please?" Felter said. "Thank you for calling, Craig." He hung up.

Lowell went in the other room and took out of his suitcase a pair of swimming trunks and a cotton polo shirt. He decided he would not shower. He was going to jump in the pool anyway. He was just about to step into the trunks when the telephone rang in the second bedroom. Naked, holding the trunks in his hand, he went to answer it. Probably Dorothy, he thought, checking to see if he had shown up.

"Hello?"

"The nearest airstrip to where you are is Fairhope Municipal Airport. I'll have an L-23 there to pick you up at 1630 tomorrow. Is there any reason why you can't arrange to be ready?"

"No, sir. I will be there, sir."

"Spare me the sarcasm, Craig," Felter said. "Act your age." The line went dead.

He pulled his trunks and the polo shirt on, then slipped his feet into rubber sandals. There was an exit at the end of the corridor; the Grand Hotel was the sort of place where one did not traipse through a lobby in one's swimming attire.

The enormous, fan-shaped pool was three hundred yards from the main hotel building and separated from it by a cluster of cottages. He had tried to get a cottage; but on short notice, none had been available.

He stopped at the gate to the pool and looked around. He saw Dorothy on the far side on a plastic-web chaise longue. He felt sure that she was sitting there so she could watch the entrance and that she had seen him, but she didn't wave.

He pulled the polo shirt off his head and slipped out of the sandals. He was about to dive in when a waitress walked by.

"Would you bring two vodka tonics over next to the diving board?" he said. If Dorothy didn't want one, he would drink both.

Then he dived in the pool and swam across. When he reached the far side and hoisted himself up the ladder beside the diving board, he was tired and puffing. Dorothy removed her sunglasses and looked up as she shook water off. He bent over and kissed her on the lips. She didn't pull away, but neither was she burning with passion. He pulled a chaise longue up beside her.

"I'm sorry, I couldn't get away," he said. "Any sooner, I mean."

"I was getting a little worried," she said.

"Wild horses, and such as that, couldn't have kept me away," he said.

"I saw the LOH," she said, making a loose gesture toward the sky, using the military acronym for *L*ight *O*bservation *H*elicopter. "I figured that must be you."

"Uh-huh," he said. He saw the waitress coming their way with two plastic cups on a plastic tray. "Here come duh booze. And do I need it."

"I've had a couple waiting for you," she said.

I am being sniped at, he realized. A wifely-type complaint. Oddly enough, I don't mind at all.

"Mea culpa, mea culpa, mea maxima culpa," he said.

"You didn't say 'noon,'" she said, but she smiled.

The waitress delivered the drinks. He signed the tab.

"If you're going to drink that," he said, "I think I'd better order another one right now."

"I'm going to drink it," she said. He nodded at the waitress.

"Bring two more, please," Dorothy said. That surprised him.

"Booze time, huh?"

She cocked her head and didn't reply. Then she raised her glass to him, and sipped from it.

"I was wondering when I saw the LOH," Dorothy said, "whether the Army treats all of its colonels that well, or whether you are a very senior colonel indeed."

He looked at her, trying to understand the reason for the question.

"And then I realized that you really couldn't use an F-105 to go away for a weekend."

Lieutenant Colonel Thomas Sims had been flying an F-105 when he was shot down. He didn't want to respond to that.

"Actually, I'm a very junior colonel," he said. "I was a major for sixteen years."

"You're kidding," she said. That much time in grade was very unusual. He had surprised her.

"And a lieutenant colonel eighteen months and three days," Lowell said. He smiled. "Colonels are selected on merit alone.

And I am obviously very meritorious."

"Why were you a major that long?" Dorothy asked. "Tom went from major to light colonel in five years and three months."

She was, he realized, compelled to bring her husband up.

He didn't want to talk about him.

"At the time, I thought I was pretty clever," he said. "I made captain in the National Guard, simply by joining up. And then I was in on the early stuff in Korea, where there was a lot of confusion, and you could get promoted by holding down a job."

"A battlefield promotion, you mean?" Dorothy asked.

"Yeah," he said. What the hell, a battlefield isn't anything to be ashamed of. And then he said, without really being aware he was going to say it, "I got my gold leaf and a TWX telling me my wife had been killed on the same day."

"Oh," she said, with an intake of breath.

"And then I had to wait for the other guys to catch up on me," he said. "And then wait until most of them were far, far ahead of me."

She chuckled understandingly.

"You never talk much about your son," Dorothy said. He leaned his head to look at her. "I've been sitting here thinking, really thinking. Asking questions."

"Peter is twenty-two, about to be twenty-three," Lowell said. "He's a journalist. Works for a German magazine called *Stern*. Sort of *Life* with more words."

"Do you see him often?"

"No. Not lately anyway. He's a man with a life of his own. I missed him by three hours in Da Nang about ten months ago."

"He's a war correspondent?"

"If you can call it that," Lowell said, and the bitterness slipped out. "He seems to think we're the bad guys and Ho Chi Minh is the rice-paddy Son of God."

"I'm sorry," she said. "I was thinking about my own kids waiting for you."

"Oh?" He didn't like the sound of that.

"They would not understand this," she said.

"Honey," Lowell said. And then he didn't know what else to say.

She reached over and took his hand.

"That wasn't an accusation," she said. "Just a statement of fact."

"If things were different," he said, "and there was a nice juicy scandal for everybody to talk about, would they understand that better?"

"I don't know."

"You're not the first married woman in history to fall out of love with her husband. Or to fall in love with another man, you know," Lowell said. "Presuming, of course, that you are in love with me?"

"It looks that way," she said. "I was so mad at you when you were late that it must be love." She squeezed his hand.

The waitress delivered the second round of vodka tonics, and smiled at the couple holding hands. When she had gone, Dorothy added, "And jealous, too."

"What have you got to be jealous about?" he asked, sitting up on the chaise longue and handing her her drink.

"When I checked in here, the desk clerk said, 'It's nice to have you with us again, Mrs. Lowell.' You have obviously been here before, Colonel."

"They're programmed to do that," he said. "They must have a card file or something. But yes, long, long before you, I have been here before."

"Whoever she was, and don't tell me," Dorothy said, "I hate her."

"Good."

"Why didn't you marry her? Was she married too?"

"No. But the thought of marriage never entered my head."

"And now?"

"Oh, yes," Lowell said.

"Which, under the circumstances, is not going to be easy to resolve, is it?"

"We'll work it out."

"I feel like the original bitch-slut right now," Dorothy said.

"Sitting here like this"—she gestured around the pool at the other guests, and at the general atmosphere of luxury and wealth—"with my kids stashed with my parents and Tom where he is."

"I don't feel that way," Lowell said. "So help me, I don't feel guilty at all."

Dorothy finished her drink. She stood up and tucked her hair into a white rubber bathing cap. The motion stretched the one-piece suit against her body; Lowell was very much aware of her mound of Venus. She smiled down at him.

"Something funny?" he asked. The last thing he wanted to do was horse around in the water. He was tired. She leaned over him.

"When I caught Tom playing around on me one time," she whispered, "he said something funny. He said 'a stiff prick has no conscience.'"

She stuck her tongue, very quickly, in his ear, and then turned and made a running dive into the pool.

He got awkwardly, stiffly, off the longue and dived in after her. She was far faster than he was, already toweling herself off when he reached the far side of the pool. He got out and she took his hand, and they walked hand in hand to suite 216.

(Five)

"Shit!" Lowell said, when the telephone rang.

They were lying satiated together. He had made a drink for himself before, and it had gone untasted until afterward. He had expected her to do the ritual female business in the john. Instead, she had simply slipped out of the bathing suit and stretched out on the bed with her legs and arms spread to receive him.

The glass now rested on his stomach, rising and falling with his breathing.

"Ssssh," she said. She took the drink from his stomach, while he rolled over on his side and picked up the telephone.

"Hello," he snapped.

"Mrs. Lowell, please," a deep masculine voice said.

"Who is this?" Lowell demanded, angrily.

"I'm Mrs. Lowell's charter pilot," the voice said, obviously taken aback.

"Oh, sure," Lowell said. "Just a second." He handed Dorothy the telephone. "It's the pilot."

She spoke briefly to the pilot, and then, holding the headset away from her ears, said, "What time do you have to go?"

"They're going to pick me up at half past four," Lowell said.

"Could you be ready to go at say half past four, quarter to five tomorrow afternoon?" Dorothy said. "Thank you very much. I hope you have a pleasant evening."

She handed the telephone back to Lowell, who hung it up.

"I'd completely forgotten about him," Lowell said. "Is he here in the hotel?"

"No. There's a motel a couple of miles down the road. I had to hire a car for him, though."

"Put it on the credit card," Lowell said.

"I did," she said. "I signed Mrs. Craig Lowell to it. I suppose whoever pays your bills is used to that?"

"I only pass out my credit card to women I'm in love with," he said. "My airplane, my credit card, and my toothbrush are sacred."

"I'm not sure I believe that," she said.

"Sometimes, in a pinch, I'm not so fussy about my tooth-brush," he said.

"I had another bitchy thought on the way down here," Dorothy said. "About the airplane, I mean."

"I don't understand that."

"I like it," she said. "To live like this. What I mean is that what I thought is that I'm entitled."

"I agree," he said.

"You don't understand what I'm saying," she said. "Rich women should not marry poor men."

"Oh," he said.

"The masculine ego gets involved. That's probably what

happened to Tom and me. I'm a bitch, underneath. I realize now that I resented living on his pay when I didn't have to. And he had to prove whatever it was he had to prove—that he didn't need me, I suppose—by playing around."

"The possibility exists that he's just a horny airplane driver," Lowell said. "I understand the Air Force has quite a reputation that way."

"I'm serious, damn you," she said.

"Sorry."

"I realize the whole damned fool thing of pinching pennies was a charade. My brother and I are going to get our parents' money, and the kids are going to get their own. It was going to come to a head soon, anyway."

"You've lost me," Lowell said.

"We're going to have two kids in college at once," she said. "And you have to send them to the best place they can get in. Try doing that on Air Force pay. And I've been spending a hell of a lot of money running around with the POW Wives. That money didn't come out of the check I get every month."

"Rich women should marry rich men," Lowell said. "Leave it at that."

"But it does make me a bitch to think like that, doesn't it?"

"It makes you a realist," Lowell said. "I have wondered, from time to time, whether some of my lady acquaintances would have been as willing to join me in the Budget Motel as they were to join me in the Regency Hyatt House."

"You bastard, you," she said. "There, too?"

"I only met you the day before yesterday, relatively speaking," Lowell said. "But, for what it's worth, since I came home from 'Nam and met you, I've been damned near as chaste as a monk."

"Why?" she asked. The announcement had pleased her.

"I don't know," he said. "But don't let it go to your head. I have not taken a vow of celibacy. I thought it was old age. But then I met you, and I'm suddenly as randy as a twenty-year-old."

"I'll take that as a compliment," she said.

"It was intended as one," he said.

"How would you feel about a vow of fidelity?" she asked.

"Oh, yeah," he said. "I have all those noble notions running through my head. Forsaking all others, et cetera."

"If I would cheat on Tom, what makes you think I wouldn't cheat on you?"

"I don't think you're cheating on Tom," Lowell said.

"You didn't exactly carry me out of the barroom on your shoulders and rape me," she said.

"Do you really need all this reassurance?" he asked.

"I guess I do," she said.

"OK," he said. "You wanted to get laid. Which is certainly not the first time that's happened to a POW wife. I've heard—"

"What have you heard?" she said, suddenly furious and hurt.

"I have a very good friend," he said. "A doctor. Who has sort of become an expert in dealing with POW wives. And their problems, sexual and otherwise."

"And this doctor can't wait to come and tell you that some poor, lonely, frightened POW wife has climbed into somebody's bed? Because she's easy prey to some bastard? Or because she needs to feel a man's arm around her? That's the most disgusting thing I've ever heard of. I really hope you had a good laugh."

"Oh, shut up," he said. "It's not that way at all."

"How is it, then?" she asked. She was so angry he felt her spittle on his face. "God, you make me sick!"

He wiped his face on the pillow.

"The doctor's husband is in Dak Tae with your husband," Lowell said. "Don't jump to the wrong fucking conclusion."

The flush in her face vanished.

"She needs somebody to talk to," Lowell said. "And I listen. OK?"

"How do you know where Tom is?" Dorothy asked. It was more of an accusation.

"I don't," he said, automatically.

"Yes, you do. You said 'Dak' something. You *know*, Craig."

"OK," he said. "I know. But leave it there, Dorothy."

"*'Leave it there?'* How is he? If you know where he is, you know something more, too. *How is he?* The government, god damn them, hasn't even confirmed he's alive. Just 'reported' to be alive."

"So far as I know, he's all right," Lowell said.

"And you're going to go after him, aren't you?" she said. "That's really a joke. My lover is going to rescue my husband, after which my husband will shoot my lover for playing around."

"You're hysterical," Lowell said.

"That's what this is all about!" she said. "All this Air Force-Army cooperation. What you're doing at Hurlbert."

"For Christ's sake, Dorothy," he said. "Shut up. I just turned in my cousin Craig, who is a young captain of whom I'm extraordinarily fond, and a major, who is one of my best friends, for making guesses about what's going on. I don't want to turn you in, but I will."

She looked at him, and saw how serious he was.

"I'm sorry," she said. "Subject closed, OK?"

XIII

(One)
The Grand Hotel
Point Clear, Alabama
27 June 1969

It started to thunder about midnight, a mass of cold air from somewhere in Canada colliding with a mass of warm wet air from the southern Atlantic in the Gulf. When Lowell saw the lightning out the plate glass windows in the Bird Cage Lounge in the Grand Hotel, he recalled the weather briefing he'd had that morning at Hurlbert Field.

A band in the Bird Cage Lounge played music from the forties and fifties, catering to the fiftyish and older clientele of the Grand Hotel. There were several couples who were younger, but who were obviously newlyweds, experiencing luxury on their honeymoon that they probably wouldn't be able to afford again until they were in *their* fifties.

He looked at one kid, who was staring with awe in his eyes at the girl in his arms, this creature who not only had just promised to love him and honor him and cherish him until death did them part, but who had, as obviously, just given him what he knew was the best piece of ass any man ever had in the evolution of the species.

Me too, kid, Lowell thought. The only difference between you and me is that society is shouting hurray at you, and I don't think it would be likely to smile knowingly at me if they knew the lady was legally mated to somebody else. And he thought of another difference: "Until death do you part" is nothing more for you than a quaint, touching, but very remote phrase—part of the ceremony. It's a little more real, a little more immediate threat to me.

Not that I can find fault with this little Vietnamese jaunt I'm about to take. The man who laid it out, the man who will lead it, is not only the recognized expert in operations of this type, but a warrior of considerable experience as well. Your humble servant, sir.

Whose considerable experience and recognized expertise have in the last two or three weeks—since a stray piece of tail turned into something quite extraordinary, not to mention wholly unexpected—have forced him to conclude that the way that the ol' ball sometimes bounces is for Lady Luck to snatch something away from you right after she has given you just enough of a taste to make you desperately, hungrily want more. Your life, for example.

Good old Sergeant Benedict, that methodical sonofabitch, kept a score during Tour Two on the colonel's birds. One hundred fifty-one fuselage punctures believed to be .50 caliber or larger. Three hundred fifty-one fuselage punctures believed to be .30 caliber. Six forced landings in hostile-held terrain. Two HU-1B gunships; one HU-1D (Command and Control); one Chinook, one gloriously aflame HU-1G Huey Cobra, and one lumbering Caribou that had fifty-eight total hours on the airframe when he laid the thermite grenade on the wing over the fuel tanks and blew it up.

Viewed objectively, that was tempting the actuarial statistics.

Fuck George Patton! *I* don't want to die with the last bullet fired in the last battle.

"What are you thinking about?" Dorothy asked, leaning forward and touching his hand.

"I was just thinking that George Patton was a damned fool," Lowell said. He turned his hand over and caught hers, then stood up and bowed. Dorothy made a mock curtsy, and came into his arms. The Jack Normand Trio was playing "I'm Gonna Buy a Paper Doll That I Can Call My Own."

"We're going to get rained on," he said, his lips against her cool ear.

"Ummmm," she said. "I like the sound of rain on the roof."

"I love you," he said.

"Ummm," she said. "I like the sound of that, too." And then she said, "Honey, you're holding me too tight. I can't breathe."

The rain started about half past one, a heavy drumming rain. They could hear the water cascading from the gutters onto the ground.

They slept together naked (she had come to bed in a nightgown; he had it off her in ten seconds) like honeymooners, and like honeymooners they began the following day with the act of love. But when that was over, it was still raining. After he had called the FAA weather station at the airport in Mobile and learned that they were in for more of the same, it no longer seemed like a charming romantic idea to have breakfast in bed. So they dressed and went downstairs and had an enormous breakfast in the huge dining room.

They lingered over their coffee, watching the rain drench the paths alongside the bay, watching the other guests watching the rain drench the paths.

"Let's get the hell out of here," Lowell said. "I'm getting depressed."

"I was afraid to say something," Dorothy said. "And I really should go fetch the kids."

They went back to the room and called the pilot he had hired to fly his Cessna 310. He would be at the airport in an hour. The pilot was obviously relieved not to have to sit around his motel room in the rain all day.

And then Lowell impulsively picked up the telephone and gave the hotel operator the number at Hurlbert. What he wanted to do was fly back with Dorothy; at the least, he could have Sandy send a plane for him now.

"Colonel Lowell for Colonel Felter," he said.

"Sorry, sir, the colonel's not here."

"Where is he?"

"I'm sorry, sir, I can't tell you that."

"This is Monte Cristo Five," Lowell said, frantically taking out the Signal Operating Code and making the mental transformation from the numbers written down to what they represented. "Fourteen seventeen zero one," he said. "Get me through to Monte Cristo Outfielder."

"Hold on, sir." There came the sound of metallic clicking, and electronic pings.

"Home Base," a voice finally said.

"Monte Cristo Five," Lowell said. "Fourteen. Seventeen. Zero. One. Verify."

The verification came back. The voice changed. It was now the voice of Lieutenant General Robert Bellmon. What the hell was he doing in the conference room at half past ten on Sunday morning?

"Go ahead, Five."

"Is Outfielder available?"

"Negative. What is your location?"

"I'm still here," Lowell said. "But I wanted to cancel my airplane ticket. I am proceeding directly to Home Base. ETA about three hours thirty."

"Outfielder expects you to be at Site Four at seventeen hundred," Bellmon said.

"I'm proceeding directly to Home Base, please advise Outfielder," Lowell said.

"Acknowledged," Bellmon said. Bellmon wasn't in command. He couldn't order him to go to Hurlbert.

Lowell dropped the telephone in its cradle, and looked up at Dorothy and smiled at her.

"I'll ride up with you," he said. "You can drop me at Fayetteville."

She smiled faintly, and then said, "I wished you'd asked

me," she said. "The pilot will see you."

His reply wasn't directly to her. He was thinking aloud.

"If I really have to be at Hurlbert at five, they can take me down in a jet."

Lowell rode to Fayetteville in the right seat working the radios. He was worried about the weather. It was turning worse, and the last thing he wanted was to have to abort the flight.

It was raining when they reached Fayetteville. He got soaked getting his luggage out of the nose. He walked inside the office of the Business Aviation hangar and watched the Cessna take off. Dorothy was going to her parents' to pick up her kids.

He asked if he could get a cab, and they called one for him; but before the cab got there, he saw MacMillan's Cadillac splashing down the narrow macadam road from the main terminal. When it stopped in front of the building, MacMillan jumped out and ran into the building.

"How'd you know I was coming?" MacMillan asked.

"I didn't," Lowell said, and canceled the taxicab. He turned to MacMillan. "How did *you* know *I* was coming?"

"I knew. We knew."

"Here, I mean."

"We figured you would have to file Instruments," MacMillan said. "We just asked Regional Control for a report."

"And now I have to go back to Florida? Is that why you're here?"

"No, that's not why I'm here," MacMillan said, and Lowell sensed that he was pissed about something.

In the car, headed toward Bragg, they did not turn off where they should have to go to Lowell's apartment.

"You missed the turn," Lowell said.

"Bellmon wants to see you," MacMillan said.

"What about?"

"He'll tell you," MacMillan said, coldly.

"If you didn't want to meet me, you could have sent a car and a driver," Lowell said.

"I wanted to meet you," MacMillan said.

"Hadn't I better put on my uniform?" Lowell asked.

"You're all right the way you are," MacMillan said, coldly.

"What's going on, Mac?" Lowell asked.

"Do me a favor, Lowell," MacMillan said. "Just shut up."

He has found out that I'm going to run this show, and he's pissed. Well, he was going to have to find out eventually.

MacMillan drove them to the JFK Special Warfare Center Headquarters Building.

There were three Berets at the entrance to the corridor leading to Conference Room II, a master sergeant and two sergeants first class, each with an Uzi 9-mm submachine gun hanging on a strap from their shoulders.

"Excuse me, Colonel," the master sergeant said. "But I'll have to see your ID card."

The master sergeant, who knew Lowell, examined the card, and then nodded "OK." Lowell followed MacMillan down the corridor to the conference room.

Lieutenant General Robert F. Bellmon and Major General Paul Hanrahan were at the conference table, Bellmon in a class "A" uniform and Hanrahan in his ripstops.

"Anything interesting happening?" Lowell asked cheerfully.

"Where is Mrs. Sims?" Bellmon asked.

"He was alone at the airport, General," MacMillan said. "I thought I saw his plane taking off again."

Bellmon looked at Lowell. Lowell said nothing. He was surprised that they had been found out. It didn't matter how. But it was clear that everyone was furious.

"Where is Mrs. Sims, Craig?" Bellmon asked, icily. When it was obvious Lowell wasn't going to reply, Bellmon's face tightened with anger.

"I asked you a question, Colonel," he said. "Where is Mrs. Sims?"

"With all respect, General," Lowell said, carefully, "I can't see where that's any business of yours."

"You're in no position to be insolent, Colonel," Bellmon said, in a cold fury. Bellmon seemed to be having trouble controlling his temper. He gestured at the four enlisted men in the room.

"You guys get a cup of coffee or something," he said. "I'll handle the phones. I'll send for you when I need you."

General Bellmon waited until the enlisted men had gone, closing the door behind them, leaving the two general officers, Rudy MacMillan, and Lowell alone.

"Now, Lowell," Bellmon said. "Where is Mrs. Sims?"

"I must again respectfully decline to answer the question," Lowell said. "My personal life is my own business."

"The hell it is!" Hanrahan snapped. "We're about to abort this operation because of your 'personal life.' Now stop fucking around, Craig!"

"Abort the operation? What the hell are you talking about?"

"Colonel Lowell," Bellmon said. "Mrs. Bellmon and I were entertained at dinner last night at the Club on Pope Air Force Base. While Mrs. Bellmon was in the ladies' room, she overheard a conversation between two Air Force officers' wives not known to her. They were commenting that Mrs. Sims was really in the middle, with her boyfriend about to try to get her husband out of a POW camp."

Lowell didn't say anything for a moment. Bellmon, and Hanrahan too, were really enraged. Bellmon was being very formal, "Colonel" and "Mrs. Bellmon." They were among his oldest, closest friends. He knew they would be unhappy when they learned—as they inevitably would—about Dorothy, but he had not expected this cold rage.

Choosing each word carefully, Lowell said, "General, I can assure you that she didn't hear anything from Mrs. Sims."

"Where is she, God damn it? You're not qualified to make that judgment," Bellmon snapped.

"Has Monte Cristo been aborted?" Lowell asked.

"Where is she?"

That answered the question. If Monte Cristo had been aborted, they wouldn't care where she was.

"With her parents, sir, in Winston-Salem," Lowell said. He moved his eyes to the clock. "That's about a hundred miles. She should just be getting there."

"Get on the telephone," Bellmon said. "And get her back

down here right away. I don't care what you tell her, just get her back down here."

Bellmon used a telephone across the conference table. "You understand that we'll have to talk to her."

"I don't know the number," Lowell said. "And I don't know her maiden name."

Hanrahan reached across the conference table and pulled the telephone back to him. He consulted a directory, and started to dial a number.

"That's the outside line, General," MacMillan said.

"Goddamn," Hanrahan said, then reached for another telephone and dialed a number. "This is General Hanrahan, Captain," he said. "I need the next of kin of an Air Force dependent wife, Mrs. Thomas Sims. Her husband is Lieutenant Colonel. Her first name is Dorothy. I don't have a serial number. I'll stay on the line."

"When you get her—" Bellmon said, and then interrupted himself. "I presume Mac was right, she's traveling in your airplane?" Lowell nodded. "Tell her you'll meet her in Fayetteville. Tell her to leave her children where they are."

"I'm not sure she'll do that, General," Lowell replied.

"Why not? She was willing to cache them to spend the weekend with you. You're obviously very persuasive, Lowell. Talk her into it."

Lowell was about to say, "I resent the implication of that, General." But he stopped himself in time.

Hanrahan wrote something with a red nylon-tipped pen on a sheet of lined paper and slid the pad and the outside-line telephone across the table to Lowell. Lowell dialed the number.

"Persons' residence," a deep, sonorous—probably black— male voice answered.

"Mrs. Thomas Sims, please," Lowell said. "Colonel Lowell is calling."

There was a small squeal, feedback, toward the end of his sentence. Bellmon had thrown a switch to amplify both ends of the conversation over loudspeakers.

"Hold the mouthpiece close in front of your mouth," Bellmon said.

Another male voice, assured, came on the line.

"Colonel," he said. "This is Hartley Persons, I'm Mrs. Sims's father. Has this telephone call to do with Colonel Sims?"

"No, sir," Lowell said. "It does not."

"I see," Dorothy's father said. "Well, she's just this moment walked in the door. She's upstairs changing. I'll see if she can come to the phone."

When Dorothy came on the line it was obvious that her father was listening.

"This is Mrs. Sims," Dorothy said. "What can I do for you, Colonel?"

"Can your father hear what I'm saying?" Lowell asked.

"Yes, as a matter of fact, Colonel," the male voice said, "I can."

"What do you *want?*" Dorothy asked.

"I want you to come back to Fayetteville right away," Lowell said. "It's very important that you do. I'll explain when you get here."

"Your plane is already gone," Dorothy said. "It's raining cats and dogs, and I'm going to come home in the morning. On my dad's plane."

"That'll be too late," Lowell said.

"Oh, my God, are you going tonight?" Dorothy said.

"Well," Bellmon said, bitterly, quietly. "Guess who else is in on our little secret?"

"Dorothy," Lowell said. "I can't explain on the telephone. But it's very important that I see you tonight."

"It seems to me, Colonel," Dorothy's father said, "that if you are asking my daughter to travel in this rain, you owe her at least some sort of explanation."

"I'll explain on the way to the airport, Dad," Dorothy said. "Can I use your plane?"

"Who is this man, Dorothy?"

"Is there a number where you can be reached?" Dorothy asked. Lowell looked at Bellmon, and pointed to the telephone he was using. Bellmon nodded, and Lowell gave her that number.

"Something is the matter, isn't it?" Dorothy asked.

"The jig is up," Lowell said. "Brace yourself for that."

She paused, and then said, "I'll call when I know something."

The line went dead. Bellmon made a movement with his hand. The telephone loudspeakers popped. He had shut them off.

"How much does your lady friend know?" Bellmon asked.

"That we're going," Lowell said. "Nothing else."

"You told her that, did you?"

"No, sir. She put that together herself."

"Your hands are completely clean, in other words?" Bellmon asked, icily sarcastic.

"No, sir," Lowell said. "One thing slipped out of me. She knows I know her husband is in Dak Tae."

"Was that part of your comfort-the-poor-POW-wife routine?" Bellmon asked.

"Was that a rhetorical question, sir, or do you really want to know?"

"Don't you dare talk to me in that tone of voice, Colonel Lowell!" Bellmon snapped.

"*Why* did you tell her you knew where her husband is confined? God damn it, Craig. That's Top Secret, and you know damned well it is," Hanrahan said, angrily.

"No excuse, sir."

"Let's hear the circumstances," Hanrahan said.

"Yes, sir," Lowell said. "I was talking to her about Phil Parker's wife. As 'Dr. Parker.' She somehow got the idea that Dr. Parker was a man and violating POW wives' confidences. I am ashamed to say, in my defense of Toni Parker, I said that 'her husband is in Dak Tae with yours.'"

"Oh, for Christ's sake," Hanrahan said, disgustedly.

"Having admitted that I was wrong, however," Lowell said, "I fail to see the reason for the hysteria. At least, so far as Mrs. Sims is concerned. Those women Barbara heard talking in the can at the Pope O Club scare the hell out of me."

"Colonel!" Bellmon raged. "Don't you ever again dare refer to my wife by her first name!"

"I can't believe you're serious," Lowell said.

"I am perfectly serious," Bellmon fumed. "I cannot tell her about your despicable conduct, Lowell, obviously, but I can certainly see to it that you never speak her name again."

"For Christ's sake, Bob," Lowell said. "Listen to yourself! Before you start making moral judgments, ask me what's going on between me and Dorothy Sims."

"I know all I need to know," Bellmon snapped.

"I don't think so," Lowell said. "For one thing, she had already made up her mind to divorce him before I came along. For another, I intend to marry her."

"The facts are, Colonel," Bellmon said, "that in addition to blatantly violating the security of an important operation, you have been committing open and notorious adultery with the wife of a brother officer, who just happens to be in a POW camp. I can think of nothing more contemptible. Be advised that it is my intention to bring charges against you."

Lowell looked at him, shook his head, and laughed.

"You know what you can do with your charges, Bob," he said. "Stick them right up there with your moral purity."

Bellmon, moving so quickly that his blow landed before anybody could think of stopping him, reached across the table and struck Lowell with his fist. Not expecting the blow, Lowell fell to the floor, dragging his chair with him.

Bellmon came charging around the end of the table, his fists balled, obviously ready to throw another punch.

"For God's sake, General!" General Hanrahan said, stepping in his path. "Control yourself."

Bellmon looked at him as if he were speaking a foreign language. And then his face changed and took on a look of horror, as if he had just realized what he had done.

"I have been a soldier thirty-one years," General Bellmon said, very softly, very distantly, with unnatural calm. "That is the first time I have ever completely lost control of myself. I offer you my shamed apologies, Colonel. I offer you all my shamed apologies."

"Don't be an ass, Bob," Lowell said from the floor, examining the blood he had wiped from the corner of his mouth.

"Don't you say one more goddamned word, Lowell!" Hanrahan said loudly, almost a shout, pointing his finger at Lowell. "You just sit down in your goddamned chair and don't say one goddamned word!"

Lowell turned the chair upright and sat down in it.

"What I meant to say, sir," Lowell said, "is that General Bellmon owes me no apology."

"You're goddamned right he doesn't, you sonofabitch!" MacMillan said. "If you weren't always fucking anything you can talk into a horizontal position, none of this would have happened! You knew her husband was a POW, damn you!"

Lowell lost his own temper, but he was not a shouter by nature.

"What about your enlisted women, Mac?" he asked, his voice almost conversational. "When you have them in the sack, do you ask them if any of their husbands are in a POW camp?"

From the stricken look on MacMillan's face both Hanrahan and Bellmon saw that Lowell had struck home, that MacMillan had indeed violated the unwritten code that officers do not have sexual congress with enlisted women. It was, in fact, more of a violation of the officers' code than Lowell's having an affair with an officer's wife. Even with a POW officer's wife.

MacMillan looked as if he were going to say something, but didn't.

MacMillan realizes, Bellmon thought, *that Lowell knows. And no matter what he said, he would only dig himself in deeper.*

"That's enough from both of you," General Bellmon said.

"The problem we have before us," Hanrahan said, "is whether or not we have compromised our mission."

"If it were up to me," General Bellmon said, "I would have already scratched this operation."

"I have to say this again," Lowell said. "I'm worried about what Barbara overheard in the Pope Officers' Club."

"Yes," General Bellmon agreed. He did not remonstrate with Lowell for calling Mrs. Bellmon by her Christian name.

Hanrahan went to the door and opened it.

"Sergeant Major," he ordered. "Get the commanding officer of the CIC detachment on the phone, and tell him to get over here."

Bellmon looked at him curiously.

"I'm going to ask him what his people have heard," Hanrahan explained.

(Two)

Dorothy Sims telephoned thirty minutes later. She was at the Winston-Salem airport, waiting for the pilots of her father's Lear jet. She had the children with her. They had insisted on leaving, and there wasn't anything she could do about that.

"That poses a problem," Bellmon said. "If this thing is still going to be Go, what do we do about her kids? *If* she is willing to voluntarily enter the detention facility?"

"I'll meet her," MacMillan said. "I'll take Roxy with me. Roxy can keep the kids at our house."

"OK," Bellmon said. He did not look directly at MacMillan. He had not looked at him since Lowell had—obviously with conviction—accused him of sleeping with enlisted women. Something an officer just didn't do.

"I'll send Patricia in with her," Hanrahan said. "That way there will be another civilian car." He reached for one of the on-post telephones and told his wife that she was going to have to help baby-sit the Sims kids—she knew why—and that Roxy MacMillan would be calling with the details.

He pushed the telephone to MacMillan, who called Roxy and told her essentially the same thing, except that she was to pick him up right away at the Center. When he hung up, he looked at General Bellmon, who nodded, and then he left the room.

When the door was closed behind him, Lowell said, "About Mrs. Sims." Both Bellmon and Hanrahan looked at him. "She's no slut. She's an officer's wife—"

"I don't think I want to hear any of this," Hanrahan interrupted him.

"I'm not interested in any justification you might offer," Bellmon said.

"She's an officer's wife, like Roxy," Lowell pursued. "And Patricia Hanrahan and Barbara."

"Not exactly, Colonel," Bellmon said, growing angry again. "Not exactly. The similarity between your Mrs. Sims and Roxy and Barbara ends with the fact that they all are POW wives."

"Get off your self-righteous horses and *listen* to me," Lowell said.

"How dare you?" Bellmon snapped.

"What's your point, Lowell?" Hanrahan said, impatiently.

"What . . . what . . ." Lowell said, stumbling, and then going on, "has come to pass between Mrs. Sims and myself does not alter the fact. She is an officer's wife, and she has not been running off at the mouth about this operation any more than Roxy and Barbara have. Don't you think Mrs. Hanrahan knows what's going on around here? Don't you *know* that Barbara Bellmon knows everything about this operation but the date?"

"Barbara," Bellmon said, and corrected himself, "Mrs. Bellmon has nothing but the vaguest suspicion what's planned," he said.

"That's why she picked up on the ladies' room gossip, right?" Lowell said. "If she thought it was just gossip, do you think she would have told you?"

Bellmon thought that over a moment.

"You've made your point," he grudgingly admitted.

"Not completely," Lowell said. "I don't think we have been compromised. I don't want Monte Cristo aborted because of some notion you have that because Dorothy Sims doesn't measure up to your notion of what a POW wife should be that she's been running around shooting off her mouth."

General Hanrahan shrugged, but didn't say anything.

The telephone rang. Bellmon answered it.

"Yes, he's here," he said. There was a pause. "OK," he said, and hung up. "That was Outfielder," he said. "He said to keep you here. You can tell him how much you feel we can rely on your Mrs. Sims not having blown this operation. The decision whether or not to abort is his."

"It's not going to be that easy," Lowell said. "The Mouse has one major character flaw."

"Which is?"

"He doesn't believe what Patton had to say about not taking counsel of your fears," Lowell said. "You start talking 'compromised, compromised,' you're going to make the abort decision for him," Lowell said.

"And I should encourage Felter to go?" Bellmon said. "And risk the lives of two hundred thirty-eight officers and men? Not to mention the international military and political implications if Monte Cristo gets wiped out on landing?"

"I've never been accused of being a fool," Lowell said. Bellmon snorted. "All right. In a tactical situation," Lowell said, qualifying his statement. "I can see no reason not to go."

"You don't have a hell of a lot to lose, Lowell," Bellmon said, more calmly. "And you wouldn't be going alone."

"I have more to lose than I ever have before," Lowell said. "I really want to come back from this operation." Bellmon looked at him. "But that isn't the point," Lowell went on. "The point is that if we abort Monte Cristo, we will very likely never get another chance. And it *will* be aborted unless we—unless *you,* General—give Felter a little backbone."

"You're not accusing Felter of cowardice, are you?"

"I'm accusing Sandy of being very very cautious by nature," Lowell said. "I'm not accusing him of anything else."

"And what happens if we go, and the entire North Vietnamese army is waiting for us?"

"We've considered that," Lowell said. "We even have the letters from the President to the next of kin all typed up and ready for his signature. Eisenhower had a speech ready, too, in case the invasion of France failed."

Bellmon looked at him.

"I've got to take a leak," Bellmon said and walked out of Conference Room II.

When they were alone, Hanrahan said, "I hope you realize that no matter what happens, Duke, you're through."

"I have that feeling," Lowell said. "I've had it before."

"If you came out of this with the Congressional, they'd hand it to you at your retirement parade. You finally went too far. Was this piece of ass worth it?"

"Would you believe it's not a piece of ass, Paul?" Lowell replied.

"I might," Hanrahan said. "Bellmon won't. And it doesn't matter one way or the other, so far as you're concerned."

Colonel Sanford T. Felter and Mrs. Dorothy Sims arrived at the Headquarters Building of the John F. Kennedy Center for Special Warfare within minutes of each other.

Mrs. Sims came first.

The telephone rang, and General Bellmon, who had been sitting with his feet up on another swivel chair, reached over and punched the button that put the call on the loudspeakers.

"Go," he said.

"Mac, General," MacMillan's voice said. "I've got Mrs. Sims with me."

"Bring her in," Bellmon said.

"I thought maybe you hadn't had the chance to cover the maps," Mac said.

"Bring her in," Bellmon repeated. Hanrahan and Lowell stood up and started to slide the covers over the map boards.

"Leave them," Bellmon said. "Let her see how close we came to getting her husband back."

Dorothy was wearing a light sweater with the sleeves pushed halfway to her elbows and a pleated skirt. There was a strand of pearls around her neck.

The three men stood up when the door opened. Dorothy looked around the room, at Lowell and then at General Bellmon.

"Thank you for coming, Mrs. Sims," Bellmon said. "Won't you sit down? Would you like a cup of coffee?"

She walked around the table and slipped into the chair beside Lowell.

"I would like some coffee," Dorothy said. "Please."

Bellmon gestured for Mac to get her a cup of coffee.

"I deeply regret any embarrassment you may have been caused," Bellmon said. "I can only ask you to believe that your presence here is of great importance."

Before Dorothy could reply, Felter, in a class "A" uniform, came into the room. He looked at Lowell and shook his head. Then he went to the head of the table and sat down.

"This room is the Operations Center for a mission which we believe may have been compromised by your relationship with Colonel Lowell," Felter began. "Do you understand what I mean by 'compromised'?" He didn't wait for an answer. "It means that the opposing forces might have prior knowledge of our operation, which would of course cause us to call it off."

"I understand," Dorothy said. "What is it you want from me?"

"I want you to discuss your association with Colonel Lowell in some detail," he said. "The first thing we have to know is how much he has told you about what's going on here. Then we have to uncover any possible occasion you might have had where you might have passed on what you have learned to third parties."

"I'm not a fool, Colonel," Dorothy said. "At least about something like this. I've said nothing about this operation to anybody."

"Excuse me," Felter said. "But we have to satisfy ourselves about that."

Dorothy shifted in her chair, and reached for Lowell's hand.

"All right," she said. "Ask away."

Ten minutes into Felter's interrogation, the phone rang. Bellmon answered it, said, "Send him in," and a moment later a pudgy man in civilian clothing entered.

"Reporting as ordered, sir," he said to Bellmon, but did not salute.

"This is Colonel Alworth," Bellmon said. "He runs the CIC detachment on the post. You know Colonel Felter and General Hanrahan, I believe, Colonel, and Colonel MacMillan. This is Colonel Lowell, and this is Mrs. Sims."

"I know Mrs. Sims, General," Alworth said. "And I know who Colonel Lowell is."

He might know Dorothy, Lowell thought, but he didn't say hello to her. The clear implication was that he knew what Colonel Lowell and Mrs. Sims had been doing, and, if anything, was much more morally outraged by it than were Generals Bellmon and Hanrahan. Lowell felt Dorothy squeeze his hand.

Lowell was surprised, however, at how much Alworth knew about what he and Dorothy had done.

"Have you had people watching me, Colonel?" Lowell asked, finally, angrily.

Alworth looked at Bellmon, who nodded.

"Yes, we have," he said, matter-of-factly.

"Well, I can only hope we led you a merry chase," Lowell said.

"You're in no position to be difficult, Craig," Felter snapped.

"I don't like people peeking in my bedroom window," Lowell said. "Whether or not they're supposed to be soldiers."

"I approved the surveillance, Craig," Felter said. "When Colonel Alworth suggested it. Obviously, it was necessary."

"I should have left you on the beach, you little bastard!" Lowell fumed.

"Craig!" Dorothy said. "Darling. Shut up."

Ten minutes later, the telephone rang again. After a moment Bellmon answered it and handed it to Felter. Whatever it was, it displeased Felter very much.

"Colonel Lowell is being ordered to Camp McCall," Felter said, when he hung up. "We have established a small camp there, Mrs. Sims. A detention facility. We would be grateful if you would agree to go there until such time as the need for all this secrecy is past. We cannot, of course, order you to go there."

"But you're implying, aren't you," Dorothy asked, "that if I don't go, that would be an argument for canceling this mission?"

Felter nodded.

"How long would I be there?" Dorothy asked.

"I can't tell you that," Felter said. "For obvious reasons."

"I was just curious," Dorothy said. "Thinking about my children. Of course I'll go."

(Three)
Camp McCall, North Carolina
28 June 1969

There was a sign: ROAD CLOSED. RESTRICTED AREA. NO ADMISSION.

Four miles down the slippery clay dirt road, they came around a bend and to a barricade of concertina wire placed across the road.

The sergeant behind the wheel got out and walked to the barrier. As he started to pull the barrier out of the way, three Berets, two of them armed with Uzi submachine guns, the third with a Remington 12-gauge riot gun, slipped silently out of the woods. The one with the Remington, a captain, walked close enough to make sure he was looking at Felter before saluting.

"Captain Donahue will be along with another woman in a while," Felter said. "Don't let them in until you check with me. If they get here before we leave."

"Yes, sir." He spotted Lowell in the back seat. "And who's the civilian you've got back there?" he asked, jokingly, making reference to Lowell's civilian clothes.

No one responded, and the captain, realizing he had said something wrong, backed away from the carryall. He made a wholly unnecessary wave of his hand, passing them through the barrier.

The detention facility was in the middle of a recently bush-hogged open area. Lowell saw the remnants of chimneys and concrete block barracks footings. This had been, he realized, a War II regimental barracks area. There was a quarter century's overgrowth, but it was still recognizable. On what had been the regimental parade ground, now surrounded by a double line of razor concertina, half a dozen Quonset huts had been set up. Two six-by-six vans were parked side by side. Kitchen vehicles. There were soldiers in cooks' whites making supper.

Until very recently, there had been twenty-seven people here, twenty-four enlisted men, two officers, and the nurse. Now there were many more. A jeep, which had been parked in the shade of one of the young trees that had grown up where the old barracks had been, came rolling over to them. It held three Green Berets, all armed with M-16A3s, the short-barreled, pistol-gripped version of the M-16A2 5.56-mm standard shoulder weapon.

There was a gate in the concertina on the other side of the trucks, and the jeep led them up to it. As they got out of the carryall, a Beret opened the gate.

I will need a change of clothing, Lowell thought, and a toilet kit. But then he remembered that when he had made plans for this place, he'd thought of that too. The detainees would be provided with clean fatigue clothing, toilet articles, everything they would need for reasonable comfort. He had even included sanitary napkins, on the off chance that some of the detainees would be women.

It had not occurred to him that he would be among those provided with "comforts."

The sergeant on his left got out of the carryall, and then when Lowell got out, he stepped back in. He would not be needed anymore. Felter made a motion with his hand for Lowell to follow him. Lowell caught up with him. He had decided to beg, though it probably wouldn't do any good, he was willing to go down on his knees, if that's what it would take.

"Sandy, for Christ's sake, don't do this to me."

"Do what to you?" Felter asked.

"Detain me here," Lowell said.

"You deserve it, Craig—" Felter said.

"I am just unable to see how I've caused so much harm to this operation," Lowell interrupted.

They were at the door of the Quonset. Felter motioned Lowell to enter.

Major Bill Franklin and Captain Geoffrey Craig were inside, Franklin on a bunk, Craig on a chair.

"I'll be back in a minute," Felter said, and closed the door after Lowell.

"Are you really going to keep us here?" Franklin asked.

"The question is," Lowell said, "'is Felter really going to keep us here?'"

"What does that mean?" Franklin asked. He was a tall, thin, intelligent-looking light brown man.

"I'm in here with you, is what it means," Lowell said. "I expect that Felter went to see about a cot for me."

"What did you do?" Geoff Craig said.

"The consensus is that I have compromised the mission," Lowell said.

"Oh, shit," Franklin said in disbelief. "How?"

"A lady was involved," Lowell said.

"Oh, shit," Franklin repeated. He was an old friend, and not surprised that a lady was involved. There was resignation on his face.

Captain Geoffrey Craig looked at his cousin, saw the look on his face, and decided there was nothing he could say to make things better.

"Ever the Boy Scout," Geoff said, jovially, "I have come prepared." He slipped his hand under the neatly made up bed's blanket hood and came out with a bottle of Scotch.

"Why not?" Lowell said. Franklin came up with a stack of plastic cups. There was water, so they had a warm scotch and water. They were working on their second when Felter returned.

"Would you come with me, please, Craig?" he said. "Bring Captain Craig with you, if you like. And you can come, too, Bill, if you like."

"Where are we going?" Lowell asked.

Felter didn't answer him, but led them into another Quonset Hut. He stopped before a door, and smiled at Lowell.

"I'll be interested to see how you suggest we handle this, Craig," he said. He pushed the door open and waved Lowell in ahead of him.

The room held a civilian, a young man with long blond hair and a bushy blond beard, lying on a cot reading a newspaper. He sat up, swung his feet off the cot, and smiled at Lowell and Felter.

"Well, well," he said, in German. "If it isn't my papa and my uncle Sandy."

"They caught him trying to get in here," Sandy said. "He had a camera and a tape recorder."

"When?" Lowell asked.

"About six o'clock yesterday afternoon," Felter said. "Right after I talked with you about Geoff and Bill."

"I haven't had the pleasure of meeting these gentlemen," Peter-Paul von Greiffenberg Lowell said, switching to an English that—while fluent and vernacular—had an unmistakable British-sounding accent.

"This sarcastic punk is your cousin, Geoff," Lowell said.

"So you're Cousin Geoff?" Peter-Paul said. "The famous warrior? I've heard all about you. According to my grandfather, you are everything I should be and am not."

"I know who you are, too," Geoff said, coldly.

"Sorry to get you all the way down here from wherever you were, Papa and dear Cousin," Peter-Paul Lowell said. "But I hadn't really planned to get caught."

He slipped his feet into sandals and stood up.

"But now that you are here, Uncle Sandy, I presume that you will make that unpleasant major give me back my cameras and my tape recorder so that I can go?"

"You're not going anywhere," Lowell said.

"Oh, come on, Papa!" Peter-Paul said. "You've got no right to hold me, and you know you don't."

"We souped the film," Sandy reported. "He had pictures of the mock-up, and of—"

"You souped my film?" Peter-Paul asked, incredulously, furiously. "Christ, it's probably ruined."

"You just shut up a minute, son," Lowell said. "Just shut up. You don't know what you're into."

"I've got a pretty good idea, Papa," Peter-Paul said.

"I said shut up!" Lowell said, angrily.

"And of," Felter went on, "the Jolly Green Giant dress rehearsal."

"That means he's been here four or five days," Lowell replied. "Five."

"Six, actually," Peter-Paul said.

"Which leaves us with the question of where the rest of his film and tapes are," Felter said.

"Where are they, son?" Lowell asked.

"No way, Papa," Peter-Paul said, "am I going to let you have that film."

"I don't suppose it would do much good to appeal to either your decency or your patriotism, would it?" Lowell asked.

"I'm afraid not," Peter-Paul said. "That doesn't surprise you, does it?"

"No," Lowell said. "I subscribe to *Stern* just to see what left-wing, anti-American crap you're writing."

"'Ye shall know the truth, and the truth shall make you free,'" Peter-Paul quoted sarcastically. "Now look, I've really had about enough of this. I'm willing—to keep you from being embarrassed—to overlook your thugs grabbing me the way they did. But now I want to go."

"I suppose you have figured out what we're doing," Sandy Felter said, his voice kind and gentle.

"Yeah, I think so," Peter-Paul said. "And as I told your major, I'm willing to put a delay on the story until after you guys try it."

"I don't understand that," Lowell said.

"I put a delay—a hold order—on the story until this operation of yours is over," Peter-Paul Lowell said.

"That, for obvious reasons, won't work," Lowell said. "What if your story isn't held?"

"And what if I go to a pay phone and call the German Embassy to tell them I've just been arrested by the U.S. Army because I am about to put a piece in *Stern* with tacit approval of the German Embassy. Can you imagine how quick you'll have the big brass down on your neck? *Herr Sekretar* Kissinger himself would probably jump on you."

"If that story got out prematurely," Lowell said, "the lives of several hundred brave men would be placed in jeopardy. Not to mention what would happen to seventy-four men who have already been locked up for up to six years."

"If you hadn't been over there in that illegal and immoral war, they obviously wouldn't be in a POW camp," Peter-Paul said.

"What we have to know is where the other film and tape is," Felter said to Lowell. "Otherwise it's no go."

"If we don't go, there goes your story," Lowell said. "Have you thought about that?"

"'*Stern* reporter's exclusive story stops U.S. widening of war,'" Peter-Paul quoted. "Yes, I've thought about it."

"Your father is going to be in that operation," Sandy said. "Your father. Have you considered that?"

"As I understand it," Peter-Paul said, "it's entirely a volunteer operation. Willing, would-be heroes only. He doesn't have to go unless he wants to."

"I want to go, and they won't let me," Geoff said.

Felter gave him a dirty look but chose not to say anything. Peter-Paul met Geoff's eyes and shrugged. *So what?*

"What I'm saying," Felter said, gently, as if trying to explain an obscure point in a complicated argument, "is that he's liable to be injured, perhaps killed, if the other side has prior information of this mission."

"In that case, Papa," Peter-Paul said, "I would suggest you don't go, and that you be grateful, Cousin Hero, that they won't let you."

"Give me three minutes with this sonofabitch," Franklin said levelly. "I'll get your film for you, Colonel Felter."

"Major, tell me," Peter-Paul said. "Are you what they call an 'Uncle Tom'?"

There came a knock at the door.

"Perimeter Guard on the horn for you, Colonel Felter," a male voice called.

Felter looked between them, and then walked out of the Quonset Hut.

Lowell looked at his son.

"Peter," he said. "I have to know where your film and tape is."

"I'm sorry," Peter said. "I don't trust you."

"I give you my word of honor as an officer and a gentleman," Lowell said, "as your father, that I will not destroy it, and that I will return it to you intact. But I have to know where it is."

"It's already on the way to Germany," Peter said.

Lowell looked at his son for fifteen seconds, not blinking his eyes.

"You want my word of honor?" Peter-Paul said. "OK. You have it. The tapes and the film are already on their way to Germany. On my word of honor."

No, they're not, Lowell decided. He would not risk having the film ruined by exposure to routine antibomb X-rays of airmail.

"The word of honor of a young man who would give up his citizenship to avoid getting drafted isn't worth very much to me, I'm afraid," Lowell said.

"I'm half-German," Peter said. "That was my right. I'm more German than American. I was raised there, you will remember."

"I'm going to ask you one more time, son," Lowell said.

"And then what?" Peter-Paul replied, defiantly.

Craig Lowell grabbed his son by his shirtfront. He had his right hand drawn back over his left shoulder, prepared to slap Peter-Paul's face with the back of his hand, when Felter came back in the room. Lowell glanced at Felter, then let Peter-Paul go.

"That's not going to do it," Felter said, matter-of-factly. "On the other hand, we have to get this film. Or abort."

Lowell met Felter's eyes.

"Sodium Pentothal," Lowell said.

"You wouldn't dare!" Peter-Paul said.

"Sometimes it doesn't work," Felter said. "And there is a six-hour recovery period. We don't have six hours, Craig."

Lowell didn't answer.

"Peter," Sandy Felter said. "I need that film."

Peter-Paul Lowell just looked at him.

"Colonel Felter," Geoff Craig said. "Are you willing to bargain?"

Felter looked at him curiously.

"What have we got to bargain with?"

"We don't have anything," Geoff said. "You have the authority to authorize me to go along. I'll get that film from him, and I get to go along."

"*We* get the film," Franklin said, "and *we* get to go along."

"We don't need you," Felter said. "The pilots are all specially trained for this."

"I'll go as a grunt," Geoff said. "I want to go, Colonel. A friend of mine is in Dak Tae. A master sergeant named Petrofski."

"How do you know that?" Felter snapped. "From your cousin?"

"He didn't tell me, I swear," Geoff said. "But I won't tell you who did."

"I have more time in Chinooks than anybody else I know," Franklin said. "Please don't tell me I need any more training."

There was a knock at the door. Felter turned and went to the door and opened it. Three stocky Green Berets, one of them an enormous black warrant officer, came into the Quonset.

Lowell tried hard not to let his distress show on his face. He knew what the Berets were for. Felter intended to get the film from Peter-Paul.

"For Christ's sake, Sandy," the father said. "Let Geoff and Bill have a shot at it before you turn him over to these guys."

"Presuming, of course, sir," Geoff said, "that we have a deal."

Felter considered his options for a moment.

"Mr. Jefferson," he said to the enormous black warrant officer, "would you take Colonel Lowell, please, to his quarters, and handcuff him to a cot?"

"What the hell?" Lowell asked, angrily.

"I don't want you interfering," Felter said. "Either Geoff gets the film from Peter-Paul, or Mr. Jefferson will."

"What are you going to do?" Peter-Paul said. "Beat me?"
There was just a suggestion of fear behind the bravado.

"You want to come with us, Colonel, please?" Mr. Jefferson said.

He walked toward Lowell, with the other two behind him.

"There's nothing you can do, Colonel," Mr. Jefferson said, reading Lowell's mind. "There's three of us."

Lowell allowed himself to be led out of the room.

XIV

"Now that we're alone, Cousin Peter-Paul," Captain Geoffrey Craig said to Peter-Paul von Greiffenberg Lowell, "I hope that we can settle this little difference between us like gentlemen."

"I don't suppose it matters to you," Peter-Paul said. "But has it occurred to you that your friends can't afford to get thrown out of the Army?"

"With reason," Geoff said. "And I think the first thing I should tell you is that I am extraordinarily fond of your father. Among other things, he once got me out of the stockade. I was in the stockade because I was then what you are, a wise-ass who couldn't really tell his ass from a hole in the ground."

Peter-Paul ignored him.

Geoff slapped him with the back of his hand, hard enough to make his eyes water.

"Do I have your attention?" Geoff asked.

"You sonofabitch!" Peter-Paul said.

"I would have hit you a lot harder," Bill Franklin said.

"The next thing I think we should discuss is who are the

335

good guys in this world, and who are the bad guys."

"You're the good guys, of course," Peter-Paul said.

"Relatively speaking," Geoff said. "I don't paint myself as a saint, the proof of which I devoutly hope is not going to be necessary, but relative to the other side, I *am* one of the good guys."

"So you're one of the good guys, so what?"

Geoff slapped him again, this time drawing a little blood at the corners of his mouth.

"That's going to cost you, when I eventually get out of here," he said.

Geoff slapped him again.

"The next time I want to hear you say something is when you are prepared to tell me where we can find your film," Geoff said. "Is that clear?"

Peter-Paul glowered at him, but said nothing. This was all a bluff, he decided. They would slap him around a little and deny that they had. It would be their word against his, and they would probably get away with it. That realization made him furious.

"We were talking about the good guys and the bad guys," Geoff said. "I suppose you know that I'm married to a German girl. But you probably don't know much about her, so I'll tell you just a little bit. She was born and raised in East Germany. The People's Democratic Republic, they call it. Which is about as accurate as calling you a decent human being. My wife has a brother, who used to be an officer, a lieutenant of engineers, in the East German Army."

Peter-Paul forgot Geoff's admonition to keep quiet until he was prepared to tell him where the film was.

"It may come as a surprise to you, cousin," he said. "But I am really monumentally disinterested in your German wife."

Geoff hit him so hard he fell off his chair.

"That wasn't telling me where the film is," he said. "Get back in your chair, I'm not through talking to you."

"Fuck you!" Peter-Paul blurted.

He did not get off the floor. Geoff walked over to him and kicked him in the ribs.

"I told you to get back to the chair," he said.

"You sonofabitch," Peter-Paul said, as he decided the best thing to do was get back in the chair. He had been wrong that they would go no further than slapping him around. But certainly they would go no further than kicking him. Still there was no sense getting kicked for no good reason.

"'For yea, tho' I walk through the valley of the shadow of death,'" Geoff quoted, liltingly. "'I will fear no evil, for I am the meanest sonofabitch in the valley.'"

Despite what had just happened, Peter-Paul could not resist a smile.

"Except, perhaps, that big black sonofabitch who was just in here," Geoff went on. "Major, would you be good enough to ask him to step back in here."

Peter-Paul was a little frightened by that.

"You wanted to see me, Captain?" Mr. Jefferson asked.

"This little interview is not going as well as I hoped it would," Geoff said. "I'm very much afraid that an aerial reconnaissance may be necessary. Would you be good enough to lay that on, please? Major Franklin has kindly consented to fly the aircraft."

Peter-Paul couldn't quite figure that out. Did Geoffrey Craig actually intend to go looking for the film from the air?

"You check that with Colonel Felter, Captain?" Jefferson asked.

"Trust me, Mr. Jefferson," Geoff said. "And would you send in the other two gentlemen, to protect me from this walking turd while you and the major are off setting things up?"

Then Geoff looked at Franklin.

"I volunteered you for that," he said, "didn't I? You don't have to fly it."

"'In for a penny, in for a dime,'" Major Franklin quoted dryly, and walked out of the room. The two Green Berets came in.

"I was just explaining to this turd why I dislike Communists," Geoff said. "I was telling Peter-Paul about my brother-in-law."

"Yes, sir," they said, in chorus.

"My brother-in-law, in order to hold his head up as a man, felt it was necessary to sever his connection with the East German Army. He was then engaged in laying mines at the Wall in Berlin, which we all know was built to keep all the West Germans from breaking into East Germany to avail themselves of the benefits of socialism.

"He had to come over the wall by literally crashing through it. He also had with him my wife-to-be. She fucking near got shot. Fortunately, they missed. She and Karl-Heinz—my brother-in-law's name, Peter Hyphen Paul, is Karl Hyphen Heinz Wagner, which is apparently yet another odd Kraut custom. Anyway, the first thing that happened when Karl-Heinz got to America was that he enlisted in the Green Berets. Which is where I met him, and through him the lady who was to be my wife—and the mother of my sons. We have two sons, Porter, after my father, and Craig, after *your* father. He will probably call himself C. Lowell Craig, because Craig L. Craig sounds a little funny.

"But I digress. I was telling you about Karl Hyphen Heinz and the Green Berets. It was his great ambition to become a Green Beret officer, and I daresay he was a bit miffed when I made it before he did. But he finally made it, and he went to Vietnam to murder babies and shoot innocent people and do the other things we Green Berets do. He was inspecting, one afternoon, one of a number of medical clinics he had set up . . . to turn innocent Vietnamese children into drug addicts, as I'm sure you're aware. Anyway, while he was there one afternoon, the forces of liberation and good decided that the best way to keep the Americans from turning all those innocent Vietnamese children into drug addicts was to blow up the clinic.

"They did so, Peter-Paul. They killed about thirty children and some mothers and a couple of Berets. But Karl Hyphen Heinz wasn't so lucky. He didn't take the full force of the explosive. All he got was a piece of shrapnel through his spinal cord.

"He is currently retired from military service, living in a place near Ursula and me in Alabama. I don't go to see him often, because every time I do he asks me, as one officer and a gentleman to another, to get him a pistol. He doesn't like being a paraplegic.

"All of this makes my wife very unhappy. I suppose it boils down to that, Anybody that makes my wife unhappy is a bad guy. There is just one more thing I think you should know about me. There is a guy in Dak Tae, a guy named Petrofski, who saved my ass on more than one occasion. I would very much like to get him out of Dak Tae. They are very unkind to people in Dak Tae. Now the point I'm trying to make to you, Peter Hyphen Paul, is that making this operation is personally important to me. I intend that it will go forth. If I have to kill you to see that it does, I will kill you. Do I make my point? You may now speak."

"You were doing pretty good until you got to the end. I almost believed that business about your brother-in-law," Peter-Paul said.

"Lieutenant Wagner's your brother-in-law, Captain?" one of the Green Berets asked. "'Dutch' Wagner?"

"Yes."

"Very clever, Sergeant," Peter-Paul said.

"One more time, Cousin Peter Hyphen Paul, where is that fucking film?"

"One more time, go fuck yourself."

"Well," Geoff said to the Green Berets, "it can't be said he wasn't given every possible opportunity to do right. Aerial reconnaissance is going to be necessary. Would you help me wrap the package please?"

"Yes, sir," the Berets said, almost in unison.

They walked toward Peter-Paul.

"Just what the hell do you think you're doing?" Peter-Paul asked.

Then he suddenly felt himself flying backward off the chair. He landed on his back. Before he could even sit up, the larger of the two Green Berets was sitting on his chest, pinning Peter-Paul's arms over his head to the floor. Peter-Paul flailed his legs around, but after a moment the other Green Beret and

Geoff Craig caught them and pressed them to the floor. He felt something being wrapped tightly around his ankles.

When Peter-Paul's legs had been taped together and immobilized, Geoff moved up to his head. He had a roll of something in his hand. In a moment, Peter-Paul recognized it as medical adhesive tape, except that it was overprinted in a camouflage pattern. Geoff ripped off a two-foot-long strip of the inch-wide tape. And then with a practiced gesture—holding Peter-Paul's head immobile by grabbing a fistful of hair above his forehead—wrapped it around the back of his head and then over his mouth.

Without moving, he ripped open two foil-wrapped field dressings, set them down, and ripped off a longer piece of the surgical tape. Peter-Paul struggled, but with one Green Beret sitting on his legs and the other sitting on his chest, he was effectively immobilized.

His head was pulled by the hair off the floor again. Tape was looped around the back of his head. Geoff shifted his grip and pinned his head to the floor. With his free hand, he picked up one of the field dressings, held it over Peter-Paul's left eye, then fastened it in place with the tape. Then he covered the right eye with a field dressing and taped that in place.

"You better get his knees, Captain," Peter-Paul heard one of the Berets say.

There was a rosy haze over his eyes, instead of the blackness he expected. But he couldn't see anything. Someone, probably the Green Beret who had taped his legs, was now working on his knees. He felt them being lifted, felt something being shoved under them, felt them being drawn together, heard the ripping noise adhesive tape makes when pulled from its roll. He tried to spread his knees, but they were locked together.

A hand grabbed his hair again, and pulled him into a sitting position. He kicked his legs, hoping at least to connect with someone, but they just flailed uselessly. He realized that each of his wrists was now held by two hands.

He felt something being put onto his shoulders, a belt of some kind, and then something tucked between his legs. With his knees taped together, it was hard to get whatever it was between his legs.

"Captain," a voice Peter-Paul recognized as belonging to the enormous warrant officer asked. "What if you kill him?"

There was no answer.

Peter-Paul decided these people had the art of psychological terror down pretty good. If he didn't have the experience to know that there was only so far they dared go, he might be a little frightened himself.

He felt straps coming together. Buckles, snaps. They had put him in some kind of harness.

He was pushed to the floor again and roughly rolled on one side. He heard the sound of tape being ripped from a roll again, and then felt the pressure of tape at his elbows and around his chest. His arms were being taped to his sides. He was rolled over and over as the tape was wound around him.

"If you kill him, Captain," the warrant officer's voice said, "you're going to have to worry about what to do with the body."

Cousin Geoff could apparently think of no clever answer to that, for he made no comment.

Peter-Paul was on his back again. And then he was being dragged across the floor, a hand on each shoulder. He heard the sound of a door opening, and then, immediately, he felt himself being picked up and thrown like a bag of potatoes. He landed painfully on his shoulder.

"Take it easy, Captain," one of the Berets said.

There was the sound of a truck door closing, and in a moment the floor under him shook. He was in some kind of a truck. He was in an *ambulance*. He remembered seeing ambulances when they'd brought him in here.

Doors, up front, closed. The truck engine started, and with a heavy whine of gears, moved off. He tried to move his mouth to loosen the tape. He pulled some skin on his lip loose, but the tape stayed in place.

They rode for fifteen minutes slowly over rough, dirt roads, and then stopped. He heard the door open, and there was a brighter light on the gauze over his eyes. Hands were laid on his feet, and he was pulled out of the truck. A hand on the harness pulled him into a sitting position, and then he felt hands under him, lifting him.

Someone's warm breath was on him, and there was grunting. He was dumped onto the ground, then pushed flat on his back. Someone touched his shoulders, and there was a clicking sound.

Then he heard the ambulance doors shut, and the engine start.

After a minute or two, the pounding of his heart stopped, and he forced himself to breathe regularly. He could hear nothing, not even the sound of breathing. Just the wind blowing in trees.

What the hell were they doing to him?

He got control of his emotions. What they were doing was scaring him. Well, they'd done a good job. But it wasn't going to work. There was no way they could do anything more than threaten him. He was a German citizen, a journalist, and they couldn't hurt him.

And when they were through with their little games, they would pay. It would be a diplomatic incident. He would have them all court-martialed, see them all in jail, see Sandy Felter kicked out of the Army in disgrace. They couldn't cover up something like this.

He heard footsteps approaching. They were going to ask him if he had enough.

He was sure of it when the tape was ripped from his mouth. There was a sharp pain on his lips, more skin pulled off, and he tasted warm, salty blood. They'd pay for that, too.

"You bastards!" he said.

Fingernails scraped at the tape holding the field dressing over his eyes, loosened the end. It was jerked off. His eyes hurt at the sudden light. He heard the footsteps going away and twisted his head to look. His eyes focused on the back of a man in a green beret walking away from him. Where the hell was he going?

He twisted his head back. He was in the middle of a field somewhere. There were two thirty-foot-tall poles stuck in the ground, guyed with nylon cord. At first, he thought they were antennae, but then he was sure they weren't. There was a rope stretched between the poles, which curved loosely to the ground and finally snaked over to him. He twisted around and saw that it came directly to him.

What the hell was that?

And then he heard, then saw, the Bell Huey making an approach to the field. Its nose was up, and something was hanging ten feet down underneath it—a hook, or something like a hook.

The helicopter appeared to be heading straight for him. But it didn't seem to be slowing down.

It was low, no more than fifty feet off the ground, and then it dropped even lower. His neck painful from straining to look, he saw the hook approaching the rope stretching between the poles. He saw the hook catch the rope and drag it off the poles. He saw the rope straighten.

He screamed as the rope snapped taut and he was snatched suddenly into the air, spinning and twisting violently as the helicopter rose. Something slashed viciously at his face, and he knew his cheek was cut. He spun around again, and saw that he had been dragged through the tops of the pine trees on the edge of the field.

He screamed again in fear and rage.

The helicopter picked up speed; and the force of the wind against him became painful. He was growing dizzy. Without warning, he threw up. The wind blew the vomitus over his face, up his nostrils, into his eyes. He vomited again, spasmodically.

He was still spinning, but not as far as before. He became aware that they were climbing, and while there was still wind lashing at him, he no longer had a sense of speed.

He became aware of a jerking motion, as if he were on the end of a stretched rubber band. The belly of the Huey appeared over him, and he could see that the rope that held him was connected to a winch mounted above the cabin door.

A foot came down and pushed his body, so that it would

pass between the skids of the helicopter and the fuselage. When
he was even with the door, he was pulled inside.

Geoff Craig, Mr. Jefferson, and the Green Berets who had
taped him were in the cabin, all wearing safety harnesses.

As Mr. Jefferson and another Green Beret held him erect,
Geoff Craig stood next to him, supporting himself with a hand
on the cabin roof.

"Have you got anything to say to me, cousin?" Geoff asked.

"Fuck you," Peter-Paul said. He tried to spit in Craig's face,
but could find no saliva.

Geoff shrugged. "Throw him out," he ordered.

Peter-Paul was pushed to the door of the helicopter and
shoved out. Again he was tumbling through the air. He screamed
again, the sound lost in the roar of the wind. He fell thirty feet,
then was suddenly snapped up short. The harness between his
legs jerked painfully tight against his scrotum. He screamed
again and tried to pull his legs up.

They flew him that way for a couple of minutes. He became
sure he was about to lose consciousness from the spinning.
Then he was hauled back into the helicopter. Mr. Jefferson and
another Beret held him erect.

"We could keep this aerial reconnaissance up, Peter-Paul,"
Geoff said, "until you either tell me what I want to know, or
you bleed to death through the ears and asshole. But I'm tired
of it. Last, last, chance. You either tell me where the film is,
or we terminate you."

"You can't kill me," Peter-Paul said. "How would you explain my death?"

"No sweat," Geoff said. "You and your father were watching
our training. There was a tragic accident."

"You think my father wouldn't turn you all in?" Peter-Paul
said.

"I don't know if he will or not," Geoff said. "If he did,
who would believe him?"

"You've done your little thing, and it's failed," Peter-Paul
said. "I'm not going to give the film."

"Take the harness off," Geoff ordered. "Cut him free. Throw
him out."

Mr. Jefferson pulled a Fairbairn* knife from a scabbard strapped to his leather-and-nylon jungle boots. He cut Peter-Paul's arms loose first, slicing the tape where it crossed between his elbows and his stomach, then ripped it off. A hand grasped his wrist, directed it to the upper part of the door. He would have expected his blood to have been cut off, his hands and arms to be asleep. But they weren't. These bastards knew exactly what they were doing. His hands and arms felt perfectly natural. His fingers closed on the doorframe.

Fingers and hands disconnected the harness straps, and it was pulled off him, the buckles dragged roughly past his scrotum. Then Jefferson knelt and cut and tore loose the tape binding his ankles together, throwing the discarded tape out the door.

And finally, he cut loose the tape from around his knees.

Peter-Paul spread his feet to give himself a better stance, and then spread them again.

The huge black warrant officer had moved out of his sight. Peter-Paul was standing in the open door of the helicopter. He could see the pine stands below. Something caused him to snap his head around. What he saw horrified him. Jefferson was getting a grip with both hands on an overhead structural member of the cabin.

What he was going to do was kick Peter-Paul out the door with both feet.

Peter lost control of his sphincter muscles. There was a spasm in his anus.

"The film's in a locker in the men's shower at the Pinehurst," Peter screamed. "In the clubhouse of the golf course."

Geoff Craig picked up a crew chief's headset and spoke into it.

Peter closed his eyes, and then opened them quickly when he felt dizzy.

A moment later, he felt hands around his waist and saw that he was being strapped into a safety harness.

*A ten-inch, think-bladed stiletto, designed by a World War II English Commando named Fairbairn.

He looked into the eyes of the huge black warrant officer.

"Most people," the warrant officer said, "would have given up sooner."

There was admiration in his voice.

(Two)

The door to the Quonset hut opened two inches, then—as whoever it was remembered there were women inside—it stopped, and there was a knock.

"Come in," the captain who had identified herself to Dorothy Sims as Phyllis Donahue called.

Colonel Craig Lowell stepped into the room.

"Are you all right?" he asked.

"Yes," Dorothy replied.

"I'm sorry about this," he said.

"It's all right," she said. "Your face looks terrible."

"My son is next door," he said.

Her face asked questions, but she said nothing.

"I don't know what those bastards did to him," Lowell said. "But when they finished, they sedated him. After a while, would you tell him I'm sorry?"

"You're going?" Dorothy asked.

"Tell him," Lowell said, "that there was no other way."

"You are going," she said, and now it was a statement of fact.

"They'll see you have whatever you need," he said.

"Colonel," Captain Phyllis Donahue said, "I don't think you're supposed to be in here."

Craig Lowell looked at her, and then turned around and walked out of the Quonset hut.

Dorothy went to the door, and started to pull it open. Captain Donahue leaned her back against it, her palms pressing on it.

"Please, Mrs. Sims," she said, gently but with determination. Dorothy looked out the narrow crack and saw Craig walk to a GI station wagon. Colonel Felter was in the front seat. There were two men, a young captain and a tall skinny black major, in the back. Craig got in the back seat, and a large Green Beret with a submachine gun hanging from a canvas strap around his shoulder got in beside him.

She let go of the doorknob. Captain Donahue's pressure against it made it slam closed.

(Three)

It was dark when the carryall brought Felter, Lowell, Franklin, and Craig to the Special Warfare Center Headquarters Building. The door was locked, and it took a moment for the guard to open it. MacMillan, who had apparently been waiting for them in the lobby, walked up to them.

"I've got to take a leak," Sandy Felter announced. "You get all the officers and key noncoms in the conference room. I'll be there in a minute."

"What about these two?" Mac asked, nodding at Geoff and Bill Franklin.

"Them too, Mac," Felter said. He went down a corridor in the opposite direction, while Lowell—still trailed by a master sergeant with an Uzi—walked to Conference Room II. Mac opened the locked door.

"Colonel Felter wants the brass and the key noncoms," MacMillan said to General Hanrahan. "He has an announcement to make."

"How's your face?" Hanrahan asked Lowell. Lowell put his hand to it. It was tender. He remembered banging it against the desk when Bellmon had gone for him.

"I'll survive," he said.

MacMillan picked up a telephone, dialed a number, and spoke briefly into it. Perhaps thirty-five people in all, most of them in ripstops, quickly began to file into the conference room. They tried not to look at Lowell's bruised face, but it was hard not to. The rumors had already started to make their rounds.

Felter squeezed his way through the crowd.

"Let me have your attention," he said, when he was standing beside General Bellmon at the table. "I'm sorry you have all had to wait around all day. It couldn't be helped. There have been some problems, all now resolved. And I have an announcement to make."

That brought a hushed silence, marred by one cigarette hack.

"You may consider Phase Three of Operation Monte Cristo completed," Felter said. "As of. . ." He looked at the clock, read it. "Nineteen-thirty-six hours, we are in Phase Four. We're going. From this point onward, the tactical commander is in charge."

Bellmon was surprised that they were going. He looked at MacMillan to see what Mac was up to. But it wasn't MacMillan who spoke, it was Lowell.

"I have been appointed tactical commander, gentlemen," he said. "The buses will be at the barracks at twenty-one-hundred for the troops. By twenty-thirty, I want the C5As loaded. After the loads are checked, I want the loadmaster to report that fact to me. If there's anyone drunk, take his ammo away and bring him along. He can sober up en route. It'll be a long flight."

(Four)

The C5As took off one after the other to the north. They made slow, sweeping turns to the left, and quite by coincidence flew over Camp McCall.

Dorothy Sims saw them silhouetted against the moon-bright sky. She ground out her cigarette under her shoe and walked to the Quonset hut next to hers. Captain Donahue trailed behind her.

"He's asleep, lady," the Green Beret on guard said.

"It's all right, Sergeant," Captain Donahue said.

Dorothy Sims walked past him to the cot and shook Peter-Paul Lowell's shoulder gently. When he didn't wake, she shook him much harder. There were bandages all over his face and neck. His lower lip was scabbed and badly swollen.

He opened his eyes finally and looked at her.

"You hear that noise? The airplane engines?" Dorothy asked.

He listened and nodded his head.

"I think that's your father," she said. "And your cousin Geoff. I'm not sure, but I think it is, and I thought you should hear it."

He nodded, and they listened together until the sound of the engines had so faded that the only sound was the steady roar of the diesel generator.

"Who are you?" Peter-Paul asked.

"We'll be here a while still," Dorothy said. "There will be time to tell you." She put her hand out and touched his face, and then she walked out of the Quonset hut.

XV

(One)
The Gulf of Tonkin
1 July 1969

COMNASFSEA had his flag aboard the USS *Forrestal*. When the Marine orderly—crisp in starched khakis, a white cover on his cap, his shoes and the holster of his .45 Colt glistening—appeared at the entrance of the admiral's cabin, the Commander, Naval Air Support Forces, Southeast Asia, was sitting on a green leather couch with his feet on a coffee table watching the Pittsburgh Steelers play the Green Bay Packers on the *Forrestal*'s closed-circuit TV. The film of the game had been flown aboard four hours before. It would be shown three times. The admiral, having nothing better to do for the moment, was watching it on the first run.

His aide-de-camp got up and went to the Marine, his hand extended for the message in the Marine's hand.

"Sir, it's an *Eyes Only* for the admiral," the Marine said.

The aide turned to look at the admiral. The admiral had heard. He beckoned for the Marine orderly to come in. The Marine walked to the admiral, with the clipboard extended so the admiral could sign the receipt. After he signed it and took the message form, the Marine stood at attention in case there would be a reply. The admiral unfolded and read the sheet of paper.

OPERATIONAL IMMEDIATE
FROM COMMANDER IN CHIEF PACIFIC
TO COMNASFSEA

FOLLOWING TOP SECRET EYES ONLY FOR COMNASFSEA FROM
CHAIRMAN JOINTCHIEFS: DIRECTION OF THE PRESIDENT: YOU WILL
PREPARE TO RECEIVE ACTION OFFICER OPERATION MONTE CRISTO
WHO WILL IDENTIFY HIMSELF TO YOU. HE IS ACTING WITH AU-
THORITY OF THE PRESIDENT, AND HIS MISSION SUPERCEDES ALL
OTHER OPERATIONAL PRIORITIES. ON RECEIPT OF THIS MESSAGE,
NO REPEAT NO PERSONNEL AND NO REPEAT NO PERSONAL MAIL
TO BE OFFLOADED FROM YOUR TASK FORCE. NO FURTHER CLAR-
IFICATION WILL BE FURNISHED.

                    DE MOYE ADMIRAL
                    CINCPAC

COMNASFSEA folded the message in half, and then again. He tucked it in the breast pocket of his khaki short-sleeved shirt.

"Son," he said to the Marine orderly, "would you ask the captain to come see me, please?"

"Admiral," the aide-de-camp said. "I believe we're recovering aircraft." The captain, like the admiral, was a naval aviator and hated to leave the bridge when aircraft were being recovered. Some of them came back with holes in them.

"You'd better ask the steward to get us some coffee," the admiral said. "And turn off the TV."

The admiral's sea cabin and the admiral's bridge were one deck below the bridge of the *Forrestal*. All the captain had to do was go down one ladder. He went down it quickly. Though he was reluctant to leave his bridge, he told himself that the admiral had something on his mind beside the Steelers-Packers game.

"Admiral?" he asked, walking through the door.

"First things first, Tony," the admiral said. "Nobody goes ashore, from this moment. And hold the mail. You'd better put a lid on any messages ship-to-shore and ship-to-ship. Clear them through me," the admiral said.

The captain picked up the telephone and spoke to the bridge, relaying the admiral's orders. And then he looked at the admiral.

"Are you scheduled to receive any visitors?" the admiral asked.

The captain thought a moment before replying.

"I got a message from COMNALOMACV about three hours ago, ordering me to have a Grumman at Da Nang to pick up two passengers from DOD, Admiral," the captain said.

"Did they?" the admiral asked. COMNALOMACV was Commander, Naval Liaison Office, Military Assistance Command, Vietnam, the senior naval officer present at what was universally known as the Pentagon, East.

"I sent a Grumman, sir," the captain said.

"Top off the tin cans, Tony," the admiral said. "And as soon as the people from the Department of Defense are aboard, bring them up here. Two, you said?"

"Yes, sir."

"And the minute they're aboard, delay launching aircraft," the admiral said.

"Yes, sir," the captain said. He waited for an explanation. He got none.

After he had gone, the admiral sat back down on his couch and turned the Steelers-Packers game back on the TV. When it was over, he got up and climbed the ladder to the *Forrestal*'s bridge.

"The admiral is on the bridge," a Marine guard at the door sang out. The captain was surprised. The admiral rarely came to his bridge, thereby scrupulously avoiding any suggestion that he was in any way taking part in the operation of the *Forrestal*. The captain, who had been sitting in a high, leather-upholstered stool welded to the port side of the bridge, slid off his perch and walked to the admiral.

"We're about to recover the Da Nang Grumman, Admiral," he said.

"Very well," the admiral said. He walked to the port side of the bridge, from which it was possible to look aft down the flight deck. The captain followed him.

"Won't you sit down, sir?"

"I'll stand, thank you, Tony," the admiral said. "I could use some coffee."

"Coffee for the admiral!" the Marine guard sang out. A white-jacketed steward appeared almost immediately with a tray holding a silver pot, two cups and saucers, silver cream and sugar vessels, and spoons, all on a crisp white cloth.

"All vessels have better than three-quarters fuel, Admiral," the captain said.

"How far out is the Grumman?" the admiral asked.

"About five minutes, Admiral," the captain answered.

"You better get him off the catapult," the admiral said, pointing down to a jet fighter being maneuvered into place over the steam catapult. The catapult would literally throw the fighter into the air.

"You want the flight deck cleared, sir?" the captain asked.

"No. I just want to knock off launching for a while," the admiral said. The captain picked up the telephone and issued the necessary orders.

Two minutes later, a lieutenant commander, earphones and a microphone clamped to his head, asked: "Permission to recover the Grumman, sir?"

"Recover the Grumman," the captain said. The admiral looked out through the thick glass. The Grumman transport, a twin-prop-jet transport aircraft designed to operate from the deck of aircraft carriers, was making its approach.

"Sir," the lieutenant commander said, "the Grumman reports two Code Six aboard."

"Inform the officer of the flight deck," the captain ordered.

"Only Code Six?" the admiral said. Code Six indicated officers in the grade of Naval captain, or Marine, Army, and Air Force colonel. No one replied.

The Grumman came in, a little long, and touched down. The hook caught the second arresting cable, and the Grumman lurched to a stop. Crewmen in hearing protectors and varicolored shirts ran to the aircraft. They disconnected the hook from the cable. With practiced skill a tractor quickly backed up to the nose-wheel and hooked up, while crewmen opened the hatch in the Grumman. As the officer of the flight deck trotted to the side of the plane, two army officers in jungle fatigues climbed out of the plane. Both wore green berets. The wind caught the green beret of the taller of the two officers, tore it from his head, and sailed it down the flight deck. There were chuckles and laughter from the captain and the admiral.

"Ask those officers to join me in my cabin," the admiral said, turning from the window. "See if you can recover his hat for him." Then he walked toward the ladder to his cabin. He stopped. "Tony, I'll probably send for you," he said, and then he left the bridge.

The captain looked out the window again and saw a sailor run out to the flight deck officer apparently with the message to bring the army officer's green beret to the admiral's cabin. The flight deck officer gestured to one of the sailors, who reached inside the Grumman and came out with two sets of web harness.

The admiral rose to his feet as the two officers entered his cabin. The first thing he thought was that they were not very military looking. They both needed shaves, and their uniforms were mussed. The little one had a .45 in a shoulder holster. The big one had what was unmistakably the butt of a German Luger sticking out of a nonstandard holster on his web belt. A brass plaque had been welded to the GI buckle. It read GOTT MIT UNS. Both had the eagle of a colonel, embroidered in black, on their collar points, and both, incongruously, carried attaché cases. The admiral saw the cases were attached to stainless steel cords running up their sleeves.

"Welcome aboard the *Forrestal*, gentlemen," the admiral said.

They both saluted, somewhat discomfiting the admiral. The Naval service does not render the hand salute indoors.

"Thank you very much, Admiral," the little one said. "My name is Felter. This is Colonel Lowell."

Without being invited to do so, Felter sat down on the couch, laid the attaché case on the coffee table, and worked its combination lock. He took out a sealed envelope and handed it to the admiral.

"My orders, Admiral," he said.

The admiral tore it open. There was a single sheet of paper inside, crisp white paper on which was imprinted THE WHITE HOUSE, WASHINGTON. The admiral read it.

"I'm at your orders, sir," he said. "May I suggest that I send for the captain?"

"I think that would be a good idea, sir," Felter said.

"Admiral," the taller one said. "Do you suppose I could have some of that coffee?"

"By all means, Colonel. Forgive me," the admiral said. He picked up the silver pot and poured the coffee himself.

A Marine guard appeared with the lost green beret. On his heels came the captain. The admiral first handed the captain the original message (the one he had folded and put in his pocket) and then the letter bearing the signature of the President of the United States.

"May I inquire, Colonel," the captain asked, "the nature of Operation Monte Cristo?"

"We're going to go get the guys out of the Hanoi Hilton, Captain," Craig Lowell said.

"I heard that was going to be a Marine landing," the admiral said.

"Let's hope," Felter said, "that Hanoi thinks the same thing."

(Two)

Fifty minutes after the Grumman was jerked to a stop on the deck of the *Forrestal*, two Army Vertol Chinook helicopters appeared off her stern no more than three hundred feet off the sea. Flying no further than one hundred feet apart, they approached the flight deck cautiously, creeping over the trailing edge. Their airspeed indicators showed thirty-five knots. But since the *Forrestal* was headed into a ten-knot wind while she made twenty knots, the helicopters were actually making five knots relative to her landing deck.

Almost at the same time, they flared and touched down. Immediately, crewmen rushed to them, and a half dozen Marines in khakis ran out from a hatch in the superstructure and formed a curved rank at the rear doors of the machines. The scream of the rotor brake could be heard over the dying whine of the engines.

A line of soldiers—all identically attired in jungle fatigues and green berets—came smoothly but not hastily down the lowered rear doors of the large, twin-rotored Chinooks. In the lowered position the doors formed ramps. The Marines guided the soldiers toward a hatch in the *Forrestal*'s superstructure.

Before the last Green Beret's were out of the Chinooks, a crew chief, kicking his toe into spring-loaded step covers, climbed on top of each machine, went to rotor heads, applied a wrench, and caused the blade to fold back against the top of the fuselage. Then he turned the rotor head so as to reach the other blades.

A cluster of twenty sailors pushed each helicopter forward to the elevator, while the crew chiefs carefully made their way back on top of the fuselage to fold the rear rotor blades.

By the time both helicopters were on the elevator, two more Chinooks were landing.

The process was repeated four times. After the eight Chinooks had reached the hangar deck, a ninth helicopter appeared, an Air Force Sikorsky, the one known as the Jolly Green Giant. When she touched down, the ground handling crew pushed her immediately behind the superstructure, and lashed her to the deck.

Inside the superstructure, the Green Berets descended into the bowels of the *Forrestal*—down an escalator, then stairwells and through passageways until they reached an area bearing a legend: CHIEF PETTY OFFICERS' QUARTERS—EMERGENCY TRANSIT ONLY.

There was some confusion here and some crowding. The word had been passed to all chief petty officers billeted there to immediately report to their quarters. The master at arms, the senior chief petty officer aboard, was there to inform a generally outraged Chief Petty Officer Corps that they were to

go to their staterooms, get a fresh uniform and a change of
linen, and report to the Petty Officers' Mess, where their over-
night billeting would be arranged. The Green Berets would be
quartered in their billets.

"Because the fucking captain says so, Chief. Any other
question?"

An Army full bull colonel was waiting for the Berets in the
chiefs' quarters. He was now dressed in Navy officer's khakis,
but he was still wearing the green beret.

He had the same message for all of them.

"There's a supply room at the end of this hall. Draw a set
of Navy fatigues and underwear. Then change into it. Take
your dirty clothes back to the storeroom. The Navy's going to
wash everything. As soon as that's done and you've had a
shower, we'll get you something to eat."

The chiefs and the Green Berets examined one another as
if looking at creatures from an alien stellar system.

"Where'd you guys come from?"

"The good fairy brought us."

"Jesus, will you look at this? They've got fucking *television*."

"I see you men have all been issued live ammunition."

"Only the ones we're sure are on our side, Chief."

"Where the fuck is our gear?"

"On the C-5As. If you don't get killed, they'll get it for
you."

"When do we eat?"

"What the hell are you guys up to? How long are you going
to be here?"

"We came to quell your mutiny."

"What mutiny?"

"You mean you don't have a mutiny? Shit, another wild
goose chase."

Eventually, the chiefs were all ushered out of their quarters
and the passageways were crowded with muscular men—very
few of whom were out of their twenties—in various stages of
undress. The exhaust fans could not dispel all the steam from

fifty shower heads running at once; the compartment became misty.

They found the Chief Petty Officers' Mess.

"Jesus, I'm in the wrong service. Do you believe this chow?"

The menu was tomato juice, chicken noodle soup, steak to order, french-fried potatoes, stewed tomatoes, string beans, and cherry cobbler.

The milk was reconstituted.

"Hey, Colonel, what are you doing down here in steerage with the peasants?"

"Colonel Felter said I wasn't allowed to eat with the Naval gentlemen."

"How's it going, Colonel?"

"Right on the dot so far."

"Something will go wrong."

(Three)

The helicopters crossed over the coast in a double V formation, two V's of three Chinooks. The Jolly Green Giant brought up the rear. But as they passed the coast, it picked up speed until it was flying immediately beneath the first of the Chinook V's.

The pilot of the first Chinook, at a nod from Colonel Lowell, pressed his microphone switch three times. He didn't speak, but the activated transmitter caused a pop in the earphones of every pilot and copilot. The V formations immediately changed shape. The Chinook in front pulled ahead, and the Chinook just behind it closed on its tail. The remaining six Chinooks formed a diagonal line, one immediately behind and slightly above the other. The Jolly Green Giant picked up speed and took up a position behind the two Chinooks in the lead.

They were no more than 150 feet off the ground now, flying over rice paddies and thatch-roofed villages but below a line of hills (and thus below any known radar sites).

The prison compound appeared ahead around a curve. It was possible to see barbed wire suspended from concrete poles, and two guardhouses. Inside the compound was a six-sided building.

Colonel Lowell touched the microphone switch hanging from the headset microphone assembly on his head.

"Fire," he said.

From four-foot-by-three-foot windows on each side of the lead Chinooks, what looked to be four ribbons of fire reached out to the ground. Each came from a six-barrel, electrically driven version of the Gatling gun. From each gun 168-grain tracer bullets—one hundred of them per second, six thousand rounds per minute—streaked to the ground at three thousand feet per second.

First the radio shack and then the two guard towers disappeared. They were literally disintegrated by thousands of bullets.

The Jolly Green Giant flared over the building, came to a midair hover, and then crashed straight down.

"He's down, Colonel," the Chinook pilot, Major William B. Franklin, reported matter-of-factly.

"Get us over the building, Bill," Lowell ordered.

The Chinook made a sharp 180-degree turn and flew back over the building, hovering thirty feet over the roof of the building in the center of the compound. Nylon ropes snaked out the back of the Chinook. Then Chief Warrant Officer Stefan Wojinski hooked his D ring to the other rope and jumped after him.

They both landed heavily, lost their balance, and fell to their knees. Lowell's "Green Beret" version of the M-16 (the M-16A3 had a shorter barrel and a folding stock, and was designed for use as a hand-held machine pistol rather than as a shoulder weapon) fell from his hands.

A North Vietnamese soldier, his Frank Buck–style pith helmet cockeyed on his head, suddenly appeared and sprayed the roof with his AK-47.

Lowell dived for the rooftop, bile in his mouth, reaching for the Luger at his side. The M-16A3 was out of reach. And if the NKA had taken Ski out with his first burst—which seemed likely—and unless he could get the Luger in action—

which seemed unlikely—he was going to get it right here.

There was a single shot, sounding somewhat like a muffled shotgun, and a 70-mm grenade crossed the roof, struck the North Vietnamese soldier in the chest, then exploded.

The NKA soldier, his torso an ugly, bloody mess, fell backward onto the roof.

"Shit!" Wojinkski said, angrily. "That sonofabitch wasn't supposed to be there."

He broke his grenade launcher, and the fired 70-mm case flew out. He reloaded.

Wojinski looked down at Lowell.

"You all right, Duke?" he asked, concern in his voice.

"I'm all right," Lowell said. "Thanks, Ski."

"You better pick up your weapon," Wojinski said, matter-of-factly.

Lowell found the M-16A3, fired a short burst to see that it was still working, and then stood up. The remaining Chinooks were coming in to land. He walked to the inner side of the roof and looked down into the courtyard and saw Colonel Tex Williams climbing out of the Green Giant.

So far, so good.

(Four)

According to the intelligence they had—which was admittedly sketchy at best—the command post of the Dak Tae prison compound was a frame building in the center of the six-sided building's courtyard. It housed whatever administrative offices were required. The office of the commanding officer was supposedly on the second floor, and guard rooms and what were called "classrooms" were on the first.

Although the prison (formerly a mental institution) was itself only two stories high, it had been built by the French, and was taller than the interior building, which had been built later by the Vietnamese. Moreover, the interior building was flat-roofed. It had thus been possible for the Vietnamese to stretch a canvas awning from the rain gutter line of the exterior prison over the administrative building in the center. It was not sure whether this was to provide concealment, or shade. The answer was probably both.

The problem had been how to get rid of the damn thing. Gatling guns could have torn it to pieces in less than a minute. But it was dangerously close to the masonry cells of the prisoners, whose windows opened onto the courtyard. The bullets consequently would have ricocheted around the courtyard until they entered the open, barred windows of the cells. Once inside, they would have ricocheted around the cell walls.

Lowell, who was familiar with the effects of high-speed projecta ricocheting around the interior of a tank, had flatly ruled out the use of the Gatling guns. Putting mortar shells or even a two-hundred-pound aerial bomb through the canvas suited him no better.

The solution finally reached was to drop a helicopter onto the canvas. From a height of twenty feet, a helicopter of sufficient weight would break right through the canvas, the support structure (if there was any), and the roof of any frame building below these.

The available rotary-wing aircraft had been individually considered, and all but one was rejected: The Bell Huey was too small. The Chinook, which had dual rotors, was rejected because of its rotor sweep; it would not fit well into the available space. The Sikorsky Sky-Crane had at first seemed a likely choice. It would be unnecessary to expand the machine if a weight—carried as a sling load—could be dropped through the canvas. But the final choice had been the Sikorsky Jolly Green Giant. It could be loaded internally to a greater weight than the Sky-Crane could drop. Its mass was immediately beneath the single rotor head, and the rotor sweep fit neatly into the available space.

Two Jolly Greens were requisitioned. One had been expended during the dress rehearsal. The second expenditure had been accomplished just now.

As the two Chinooks with the Gatling guns circled back to drop people by rope onto the roof of the prison proper, two more Chinooks came in behind them, and hovered two feet off the ground on both sides of the entrance to the prison building.

Captain Geoffrey Craig, with a Remington Model 870 12-bore shotgun in his hands, was first out the rear door.

He ran for the prison entrance with thirty Green Berets jumping out and running after him.

As soon as the men were out, the Chinooks took off and moved several hundred yards away, behind a copse of trees.

Geoff Craig knew that one of two things was going to happen at the entrance. Either the doors would be locked—in which case three Special Forces men were each equipped with an adhesive-backed satchel charge and five-second fuse. Any of these would be sufficient to blow the double doors inward.

Or else Vietnamese troops inside would rush out to do battle.

To take care of that contingency, there were two Berets with M-70 grenade launchers and two more with 7.65-mm machine guns, 120-round belts of ammunition draped around their shoulders.

It didn't happen that way of course.

The left of the double doors opened, and half a dozen North Vietnamese soldiers rushed out. Then somebody inside concluded that discretion was the best part of valor, and hurriedly closed the door.

Geoff fired the shotgun as fast as he could at the soldiers outside. The shotgun was loaded with XX shotshells, each shell containing twelve lead pellets about the size and weight of the bullet in a .32 ACP pistol bullet.

The hair at the base of his neck curled as the Green Berets fired around him, the hissing crack of 5.56-mm M-16 rounds; the sharper, deeper crack of 7.62 NATO rounds; and the sort of a whistling thump of the 70-mm grenade throwers.

The North Vietnamese went down quickly, but not before they had taken out three Green Berets.

Geoff dug in the pockets of his ripstop camouflage nylons for more shells. At the same time he glanced at the downed Berets. Experience told him they were dead. Then his eye caught a fired shotshell on the ground to his left. The way it had landed he could read "DEER & BEAR LOAD" in gold letters. As he loaded the last shotshell, he looked at the building, and then up at the roofline.

Craig Lowell, carrying a cut-down M-16 barrel up in the crook of his elbow, was looking down at them.

Geoff returned his attention to what was going on in front of him.

In very much the same position a quail hunter assumes when his dogs have gone on a point, two of the Berets carrying grenade launchers walked up to him, put the stocks to their shoulders, and carefully aimed the launchers at the doors. There was a muted, shotgun-like noise, and a half moment later, the sound of the 70-mm grenades going off.

The left door fell inward.

There followed sustained bursts from two M-60 machine guns, to sweep the corridor beyond. The Berets reloaded the grenade launchers as they walked, unhurriedly, to the door. Then they fired another round into the corridor.

Geoff hoped that Tex Williams would not be in the line of fire. When the Berets with machine guns trotted to the door, and peeked inside, Geoff ran after them.

The corridor inside held fifteen dead North Vietnamese. Growing puddles of blood were on the stone floor. At the far end of the corridor was another set of double doors opening onto the interior courtyard.

Though they had been blown off their hinges by the 70-mm grenades, they were not down. And then one of the doors moved.

The machine-gunners raised their weapon muzzles.

"Hold fire!" Geoff shouted.

When they looked at him curiously, he explained, "It may be Colonel Williams."

They nodded, but one of them put his machine-gun to his shoulder like a rifle and trained it on the door.

It was Williams. He had a cut on his face, and the right side of his gray flight suit was torn open, but otherwise he seemed all right. He ran down the corridor to join them. In his hand he held a small Smith & Wesson .38 Special revolver (standard Air Force issue for flight crews).

"There's a couple of men down outside," Geoff said. "If you want a weapon."

Williams went after it.

There was no excess firing—which had been about the last
point Craig Lowell had touched on in his briefing on the carrier:
"I'm not asking for noble heroics," he had said. "But keep in
mind what a fucking shame it would be for one of those poor
bastards to be taken down by an American bullet."

It had apparently got to the men.

"The Torches"—Berets carrying satchel charges in their
hands, and a bagful of thermite grenades in back packs—-came
through the corridor and began to distribute the thermite grenades around on the ruins of the frame building and under the
Jolly Green (which had come to rest slightly nose down).

After "preparing the Jolly for demolition," the Berets split
themselves into two teams and started down the side corridors.
The team on the left encountered the North Vietnamese who
had retreated into the building, and there was a sudden vicious
exchange of gunfire and the crump of the grenade launchers.

Aside from this they met little resistance. Not very much
had been expected. The weaponry immediately available to the
Vietnamese had been the machine guns in the towers destroyed
by the Gatling guns and the small arms of the guards in the
headquarters building into which Tex had crashed the Jolly
Green Giant.

What resistance they expected to encounter was going to
arrive in about five minutes from the guards' barracks (again
French built) several hundred yards from the prison compound
itself.

The idea had been debated—and rejected—of having Gatling
gun–armed Chinooks assault the barracks. Since the Gatlings
were not very effective against stone buildings, the Vietnamese
attempting to reinforce the prison would be met on the ground
by Force II, the 115 officers and men under Colonel Mac-
Millan, who were now still airborne.

Those four Chinooks would land on open areas convenient
to the prison compound. Since these landing areas looked entirely too inviting, it had to be presumed they were either mined
with conventional mines (the kind that would detonate under
weight) or with emplaced mines (which could be detonated on

command from—it was hoped—the headquarters destroyed by Tex's Jolly Green).

Lowell was disappointed when the destruction of the guard towers and the radio shack had not resulted in a second explosion of the mines that were likely placed in the landing fields.

When the firing inside the prison died down, Geoff left the corridor and went outside to see how the mine-clearing operation was proceeding.

He saw that teams of Berets had fanned out around the landing zones. When they were on opposite sides, two hundred yards from each other on the roughly square landing zones, there came other shotgun-like sounds. The United States Coast Guard Supply Depot at Cape May, New Jersey, had not long ago had its stock of eleven line-throwing devices completely depleted in a sudden, and unexplained, priority requisition.

White line snaked through the air from one side of the landing field to the other. Green Berets caught it in the air, or fished it out of small trees. Then, very carefully, they began to pull the line toward them.

To the lines were now attached—every twelve feet—three-pound blocks of Composition C-3, over which had carefully been taped a sandbag. These would direct the force of any explosion downward, into the ground.

The ropes were pulled in very slowly and carefully, until the field was criss-crossed with explosive charges.

Two Berets hooked up detonation devices. Each was capable of detonating the entire system of charges. But there were a pair of both detonators and operators in case one was taken out. If both were taken out, two more Berets would place and blow C-3 charges and short fuses. This would blow the rest—it was devoutly hoped—by a physical phenomenon known as "sympathetic detonation."

"Fire in the hole!" a voice shouted.

A moment later, there was an awesome roar. And a moment after that the shock wave nearly knocked Lowell and others off the roof. But there was no secondary explosion. The Coast Guard's reluctant contribution to Operation Monte Cristo and the elaborate plans for redundancy had proved unnecessary.

Lowell took his miniaturized ground-to-air transmitter from his pocket. But it was unnecessary to talk to the Chinook crews. They had seen the explosion, and were already making an approach to the landing site.

He waited until he saw MacMillan leap from the first Chinook. Once Mac was on the ground, defense of the prison was his responsibility.

"Ok, Ski," Lowell said. "Let's go downstairs."

Wojinski took a folding grappling hook that had been strapped to his leg and smashed the terra cotta roof beam away. He next unfolded the grappling hook, sank two of its points into a now exposed wooden beam and tugged it with all his weight. Then he threw the line down into the courtyard. He waited now for Lowell.

"Shit," he said, as Lowell took the line in his hand. "All that fucking around with the line-throwers for nothing."

Lowell pushed himself from the roof and started down the line. Six feet down the side of the building, he found himself looking through rusty one-inch bars into the hollow, blank eyes of a cadaverous unshaven white man.

He had already dropped another six feet—out of sight— before he finally understood that he had been looking at one of the men they had come to get. The dull-eyed skeleton behind the bars was a commissioned officer of the Armed Forces of the United States of America.

One of the captains in Force I was waiting for him, holding his M-16A3 loosely in his hand.

"Mac's down," Lowell said.

"Can't find any keys, Craig," Geoffrey Craig replied.

"Oh, shit!"

Since Intelligence had reported the steel doors of the masonry cells were locked with padlocks (one at the bottom and one at the top), it had been hoped that keys would be locally available.

"No turnkeys?" Lowell asked.

"Two," Geoff answered. "Both had keys that opened a lock on the little doors they fed them through. But nothing that opens the padlocks on the doors."

"You put the torches to work?" Lowell asked.

"Yes, sir," Geoff said. He nodded toward the passageway through the building. A cloud of dense white smoke was curling out of it, close to the ground. As Lowell watched, a Beret came stumbling out of a side corridor, coughing and rubbing his eyes.

"Goddamn," Lowell said. "We didn't think about the damned smoke."

Geoff looked at him, but said nothing.

"There's nothing that can be done, I suppose," Lowell said. "But go ahead and do what you're doing."

"If we torched the Jolly Green now," Geoff suggested, "the heat might draw some of the smoke upward."

"And it might not," Lowell said. He went to the sergeant, who was leaning against the stone walls, coughing, and helped himself to a half dozen of the previously prepared thermite charges.

They were small, foil-wrapped packages, which were ignited with a twenty-second pull-fuse; and they would literally melt the hinges from the cell doors.

Lowell took a deep breath, and then ran into the side corridor. Ten feet inside, his eyes began to tear; and twenty feet inside, he couldn't see his hand in front of his face. He moved to the side, found the wall with his hand, and moved down it.

The balls of his fingers were suddenly burned. He had come to a door to which the thermite charges had already been applied. He decided against trying to pull the door down (it would be better to wait until the smoke cleared) and moved farther down the corridor. The third door down had not been torched. He pulled the plastic protector from the adhesive that backed the charge and put it in place, immediately pulling the fuse cord. It began to hiss. Then he dropped to his knees and put the second charge in place and ignited that.

Then he grew dizzy. He was suddenly terrified, soaked with sweat. He didn't want to die of asphyxiation.

On his hands and knees, he crawled as rapidly as he could to the central passageway. Then he got to his feet, coughing heavily, and staggered out the front of the prison.

Someone handed him a canteen. He took a deep swallow. It wasn't water, it was whiskey.

"You sonofabitch!" he spluttered.

"Colonel, you want water, I got water," the Green Beret said, deeply embarrassed, and handed him another canteen. "I thought you needed a drink."

Lowell spat up some of the water, and then took a drink of the whiskey. That seemed to straighten him out. He smiled at the Beret. "Thank you," he said.

A very small skeletal man, with hair cropped very close to his head and a week's growth of beard on his shrunken, haggard cheeks, shuffled four steps toward Lowell.

And then his hand rose haltingly in a salute.

"Malloy," he said, "Lieutenant Commander, USN, sir."

"The program is to get these people immediately on the choppers," Lowell said, angrily.

"That's what I was doing when you staggered out here," the Green Beret said.

Lieutenant Commander Malloy of the United States Navy stood there in the gray pajamas he was wearing, his hand still raised in salute.

Lowell returned the salute, and took his arm.

"Come with me, Commander," he said. "We're going to take you home."

He started to lead him out to the Chinooks, but after a few shuffling steps, gave it up. He scooped Lieutenant Commander Malloy up in his arms, carried him out to the nearest Chinook and up the ramp, and sat him on the floor.

Then he ran forward in the cabin and stuck his head up into the cockpit.

"Back this thing around so you can blow your rotors into the building," he said.

The pilot looked at him uncomprehendingly.

"The place is full of smoke," Lowell said. "I want you to blow it out."

"Got it," the pilot said.

Lowell went through the fuselage. Lieutenant Commander Malloy had gotten himself off the floor and was sitting on the nylon seats that run along the fuselage walls.

"Do you know a Major Parker?" Lowell asked.

Malloy didn't seem to comprehend what he was being asked.

"Parker. A great big black guy."

"He's dead," Commander Malloy said, tonelessly.

"You're sure?"

Malloy nodded his head in confirmation.

The Chinook had been bumping over the ground, and then it stopped. The pitch of the engine changed, and Lowell ran down the ramp again. There was a steady, heavy pressure of air from the blades. He didn't know how much good it would do, but it couldn't hurt.

He heard explosions and looked up in alarm at the roof. It took him a moment to realize that the Berets, without orders, were solving the problem of the thermite smoke in their own way. They had tried blowing enormous holes in the roof. But not very much smoke rose from these, so Lowell decided that wasn't going to work, either. Then there were other explosions, and sections of the stone wall (from already empty cells) were blown outward.

The smoke, which had settled close to the floor, now began to flow out and dissipate.

He looked around for Geoff, but didn't at first find him. He found Tex Williams first. Williams was crying. He was leading another of the walking skeletons toward the Chinooks.

The skeleton was saying, "Is that you, Tex? Is that really you?" over and over and over.

Then he found somebody else staggering out of the passageway. Another walking cadaver—six feet three and no more than a hundred pounds. The cadaver made it outside and then leaned against the wall. Lowell ran to him, afraid he was about to pass out.

The cadaver looked at him out of sunken, bloodshot eyes. He had the shredded remnants of a green beret on his head.

"You sure took your fucking sweet time to get here, rich boy," Major Philip Sheridan Parker IV said.

Lowell wrapped his arms around him, partly because he

was so glad to see him, and partly because he knew he couldn't talk for the moment.

Finally, he broke the embrace, and, his voice stiff and artificial, said, "Come on, Phil, I'll put you on the Chinook."

"Nevertheless, under the circumstances," Major Parker IV said, his own voice breaking, "you may consider yourself pardoned."

On the way to the Chinook, he found Geoff and Geoff's radio man.

"I'll take care of the major," Geoff said. "Mac's on the horn."

Lowell passed Parker into Geoff's arms and motioned for the radio handset.

"Mac, this is Duke," he said.

"How's it going?"

"Oh, we're holding all right," Mac replied. "But I hear some tanks, I think."

"Great!" Lowell said. Even with the TOW, Mac could not hold against tanks. All he had was small arms.

"How's it going over there?"

"No problem," Lowell said.

"Oh, shit, they are tanks," Mac said, and the carrier went dead. A moment later, over the roar of the helicopter engines, there came a heavy, dull noise. A tank's fuel cells blowing. Lowell knew the sound.

Geoff came back from the Chinook.

"We're in trouble," Lowell said.

"We've got thirty-nine out, Colonel," Geoff said. "Nineteen to go."

"Forty-one," Lowell corrected him. Two more prisoners, one thrown over a Green Beret's shoulders in the fireman's carry and the other cradled like a baby in the arms of CWO Jefferson, were on their way from the prison building to the waiting choppers.

The radio operator pushed Lowell's arm with the handset.

"Go ahead," Lowell said, taking it.

"I just had three blown away," Mac reported, laconically.

"They're shooting canister, Duke." Canister is an artillery round loaded with thousands of steel balls—an enormous shotgun shell that is very effective against exposed troops.

"Can you get the bodies?"

"Parts of them," Mac replied.

"We've got seventeen to go," Lowell said. "You can start pulling back in a couple of minutes, but wait for the word."

"Yeah," Mac said, and the carrier went off the air again.

Two prisoners went crazy. Both crouched in corners and fought off ferociously all attempts by the Berets to lead them out until Mr. Jefferson finally got them to come along. It took brute force to do it.

"All we can find are loaded, sir," Geoff said. "I can't find Petrofski."

"I would hate to leave anybody here," Lowell said. "Are we sure?"

"Yes, sir."

Lowell motioned for the radio handset.

"Let's go home, Mac," he said.

"Something's wrong with Colonel Mac," a fresh voice said.

"Who's this?" Lowell snapped. "What's wrong with him?"

"Sergeant Knowlton, sir. I dunno. He all of a sudden started spitting blood from the mouth—"

"Withdraw, Sergeant. Bring your dead and wounded with you," Lowell ordered.

"Yes, sir."

"Make sure you bring the TOWs. Or blow them up."

"They're already blown, Colonel," the sergeant replied.

Lowell turned to Geoff.

"Torch the Jolly Green," Lowell ordered. He ran toward the cluster of Chinooks. They all seemed intact, their rotors turning. He climbed up the side of the nearest one and stuck his head in the copilot's window.

"Contact Gander Leader," he said. "Tell him to execute Angry Gander."

The copilot already had the frequency dialed in. He pushed his mike button.

Of all birds, the female goose—or gander—is the fiercest

in protecting its young.

The first Navy fighter bomber of Gander Flight screamed in at 550 knots to lay napalm, 20-mm cannon fire, and 4.5-inch rockets on the North Vietnamese forces attempting to move toward the Dak Tae prison compound. Then a short, squat Green Beret who didn't look like he was large enough for his burden, ran up to Lowell's Chinook and dumped Colonel Rudolph G. MacMillan, quite obviously dead, on the cabin floor.

"I don't know what happened, Colonel," the Green Beret said. "He wasn't shot or nothing."

"What did happen?" Lowell asked.

"Well, we had two TOWs left, and Colonel Mac went out after a tank."

"*He* went out after a tank?"

"Yes, sir. And he got it," the sergeant said. "And then he came running back and said there was another tank and picked up the other TOW. And he said, 'Oh, shit' and there was blood in his mouth, so I figured he caught a round. Then he fell down and I looked for the wound and there wasn't any."

Patton, Lowell remembered, *expressed regret that he had not been killed with the last round fired in the last battle. Mac was too damned old to be running around taking out T-34 tanks with TOWs. But maybe a heart attack, or an embolism, or a stroke, or whatever had killed him was the next best thing to the last round in the last battle. This would have been Mac's last battle, as it will be mine.*

"Get aboard, son," Lowell said. He pushed his throat microphone. "Take off when loaded," he ordered. "I've got Colonel MacMillan and..." He leaned forward and wiped away the blood that had run down from Mac's gaping mouth and covered the Beret's name tag. "Sergeant Frost with me."

"You say you got Frost?" a voice inquired.

"I say again, Frost and MacMillan," Lowell said.

"Six light on the skids," the voice replied. He had been waiting for Frost and MacMillan. Now he could get the hell out of here.

"One, light on the skids," another voice said, much louder.

The Chinook in which Lowell rode jumped almost straight into the air and headed over the prison building for the coast. As he flew over the prison he saw the skeleton of the torched Jolly Green settle into the inferno that raged beneath it.

He looked at his watch. They had been on the ground thirty-seven minutes. The program had called for forty-five.

(Five)

The message from the Chairman of the Joint Chiefs of Staff (in response to Colonel Felter's message that OPERATION MONTE CRISTO had been successfully concluded) read as follows:

OPERATIONAL IMMEDIATE
THE JOINT CHIEFS WASH DC
TO COMNASFSEA
FOLLOWING EYES ONLY FOR COMNASFSEA AND OUTFIELDER.

DIRECTION OF THE PRESIDENT. FOR REASONS OF NATIONAL SE-
CURITY ALL REPEAT ALL DETAILS OF OPERATION MONTE CRISTO
REMAIN CLASSIFIED. NOTIFICATION OF NEXT OF KIN OF KILLED
AND WOUNDED IN ACTION AND OF RETURNED PRISONERS OF WAR
WILL BE ACCOMPLISHED BY THE OFFICE OF THE JOINT CHIEFS.
COMNASFSEA IS APPOINTED OFFICER IN CHARGE RETURNED POWS,
REMAINS OF KIA AND WIA. FURTHER INSTRUCTIONS WILL BE IS-
SUED. ARMY AND AIR FORCE PERSONNEL OF OPERATION MONTE
CRISTO WILL RETURN TO HOME BASE AS PLANNED. WELL DONE.

DELAHANTY
ADMIRAL CINCPAC

Epilogue

Despite the orders to the contrary, all the Special Forces, wounded, as well as the bodies of the seven dead Green Berets, including that of Colonel Rudolph C. MacMillan, returned to Fort Bragg on the C5A aircraft that had carried them to the Far East. Colonel C. W. Lowell assumed responsibility for the action.

Lieutenant Colonel Thomas Sims, USAF, whom Colonel Lowell never saw at Dak Tae or on the *Forrestal* was reunited with his wife several weeks later, after a period of hospitalization and physical evaluation. He shortly afterward sued for, and was granted, a divorce on grounds of open and notorious adultery. As was the usual custom in such cases, he was awarded the custody of his children. He retired from the military service in 1980 as a Major General and Deputy Commander of the Air War College.

Colonel Rudolph G. MacMillan was buried, with full military honors, in Mauch Chunk, Pennsylvania. In 1976, after President Carter made good his campaign promise to pardon draft evaders and deserters, Mrs. MacMillan mailed President Carter Colonel MacMillan's decorations, including his Medal of Honor and the Distinguished Service Medal he had been posthumously awarded for his service in OPERATION MONTE

CRISTO. She received the package back several weeks later, together with a form letter stating that the President could not accept a gift of military decorations no matter what the motives of the donor.

Lieutenant General Robert Bellmon died of cancer in 1976 in retirement in Carmel, California. Mrs. Barbara Waterford Bellmon was elected to the United States House of Representatives as a Republican in 1978, and reelected in 1980, 1982, and 1984.

Major General Paul Hanrahan retired in 1974. He is now Associate Professor of Romance Languages at Utica State Junior College, Utica, New York.

The remains of Master Sergeant Pietr Petrofski were returned to American control in 1976, in the next-to-the-last transfer of "previously unlocated remains."

Examination of the remains by the Pathology Department of the Walter Reed U.S. Army Medical Center, Washington, suggested—but could not conclusively prove due to the advanced state of decomposition of the remains—that Sergeant Petrofski had died of injuries sustained shortly before his death. Other tests indicated that that had occurred in 1969, five years after he was captured, and approximately two months before OPERATION MONTE CRISTO freed other prisoners from Dak Tae.

Colonel Philip Sheridan Parker IV was retired in 1981. He had been a Professor of Military Science at Norwich University at the time of his retirement, and on his retirement was named Petrofski Professor of Military History at that institution. The Petrofski Chair resulted from an anonymous grant in 1981 of sufficient funds to establish it in perpetuity.

Dr. Antoinette Parker is Martin Haley Professor of Pathology at the Harvard Medical School. She and her husband live on a farm almost exactly equidistant between Norwich, Vermont, and Cambridge, Massachusetts.

Colonel William B. Franklin was retired in 1982. He now owns and operates Inter-Island Airways in Jamaica.

Lieutenant General William R. Roberts, who had commanded the 1st Cavalry Division (Airmobile) in Vietnam, retired shortly after relinquishing command of the XVIII Airborne Corps. On his retirement, he was the last member of his USMA ('40) Class, Army or Air Force, on flying status. He then became Vice President of the Bell Helicopter company, but subsequently retired from that, too, and is now a consultant. When last heard from, he was on his way to Arabia, where he had been commissioned to evaluate rotary-wing aircraft for the Royal Saudi Arabian Government.

General E. Z. Black became Executive Vice President of the U.S. Steel Corporation. Following retirement from that position, he divides his time between Honolulu, Hawaii, and Dublin, New Hampshire.

Lieutenant General Sanford T. Felter retired in 1979. His last post was as Director, the Defense Intelligence Agency. He is now employed as a consultant to Arthur D. Little & Company in Cambridge, Massachusetts.

Chief Warrant Officer Stefan Wojinski is proprietor of Wojinski Cadillac-Oldsmobile in Wilkes-Barre, Pennsylvania.

After Peter-Paul von Greiffenberg Lowell renounced his American citizenship, in a decision that affirmed his right to German nationality, the Supreme Court of the Federal Republic of Germany granted permission for him to drop the surname "Lowell." He remained estranged from his father and grandfather until 1979, when a reconciliation between the three was arranged by Mrs. Geoffrey Craig at Schloss Greiffenberg during the last illness of his grandfather. The eighth Graf von Greiffenberg is Managing Director, *De Hessisches Nachtrichten*, and sits on the Board of Directors of Craig, Powell, Kenyon and Dawes (Germany) G.m.b.H. The Graf and Grafin have three children, the youngest of whom is Craig Lowell, Baron von Kolbe, now three.

Colonel Craig W. Lowell was retired immediately upon returning from OPERATION MONTE CRISTO. Colonel and Mrs. Lowell, the former Dorothy Persons Sims, maintain their legal residence at Broadlawns, Glen Cove, Long Island, but spend much of their time traveling. In 1982, while playing polo in Palm Springs, Lowell suffered a compound fracture of his right leg, and was hospitalized for six months. In 1983, after he had successfully crash-landed at LaGuardia Field, New York, a Lear jet aircraft whose landing gear refused to extend, Lowell was fined $35,000 for six violations of Federal Aviation Administration regulations, including operating an aircraft after his pilot's license had been medically revoked. He was warned at the time that if he appeared in court again on similar charges he would be imprisoned. So far as is known, he has not flown— at least alone—since. In 1984, he won the International Live Pigeon Shoot in Madrid, Spain.

Colonel (Brigadier General Designate) Geoffrey Craig, who had commanded a regiment of parachutists in the Grenada rescue mission, was recently assigned as Chief, Special Operations Division, Office of the Deputy Chief of Staff for Operations, Headquarters, Department of the Army.

W.E.B. Griffin
Fairhope, Alabama
June 15, 1985

W.E.B. Griffin is the author of the bestselling Brotherhood of War, Corps, Badge of Honor, Men at War, Honor Bound, and Presidential Agent series. He has been invested into the orders of St. George of the U.S. Armor Association and St. Andrew of the U.S. Army Aviation Association; is a life member of the U.S. Special Operations Association; and is a member of Gaston-Lee Post 5660 of the Veterans of Foreign Wars, China Post #1 in Exile of the American Legion, and the Police Chiefs Association of Southeast Pennsylvania, South New Jersey, and Delaware. He has been named an honorary life member of the U.S. Army Otter & Caribou Association, the U.S. Army Special Forces Association, the U.S. Marine Corps Raider Association, and the USMC Combat Correspondents Association. Visit his website at www.webgriffin.com.